Natural Causes

Natural Causes

JAMES OSWALD

Harper Weekend

Natural Causes
Copyright © 2012 by James Oswald
All rights reserved

Published by Harper Weekend, an imprint of HarperCollins Publishers Ltd

Originally published in an electronic edition by Penguin Books: 2012

First published in Canada by HarperCollins Publishers Ltd in an electronic edition: 2013
First HarperCollins Publishers Ltd trade paperback edition: 2014
This Harper Weekend paperback edition: 2014

HarperCollins books may be purchased for educational, business, or sales promotional use through
our Special Markets Department.

HarperCollins Publishers Ltd
2 Bloor Street East, 20th Floor
Toronto, Ontario, Canada
M4W 1A8

www.harpercollins.ca

Library and Archives Canada Cataloguing in Publication information is available upon request.

ISBN 978-1-44342-604-6

Set in Garamond MT
Typeset by Jouve (UK), Milton Keynes

Printed and bound in the United States of America
RRD 9 8 7 6 5 4 3 2

To my parents, David and Juliet.
I wish you were here to share in this.

1

He shouldn't have stopped. It wasn't his case. He wasn't even on duty. But there was something about the blue flashing lights, the Scene of Crime van and uniforms setting up barriers that Detective Inspector Anthony McLean could never resist.

He'd grown up in this neighbourhood, this rich part of town with its detached houses surrounded by large walled gardens. Old money lived here, and old money knew how to protect its own. You were very unlikely to see a vagrant wandering these streets, never mind a serious crime, but now two patrol cars blocked the entrance to a substantial house and a uniformed officer was busy unwrapping blue and white tape. McLean fished out his warrant card as he approached.

'What's going on?'

'There's been a murder, sir. That's all anyone's told me.' The constable tied off the tape and started on another length. McLean looked up the sweeping gravel drive towards the house. A SOC van had backed halfway up, its doors wide; a line of uniforms inched their way across the lawn, eyes down in search of clues. It wouldn't hurt to have a look, see if there was anything he could do to help. He knew the area, after all. He ducked under the tape and made his way up the drive.

Past the battered white van, a sleek black Bentley glinted in the evening light. Alongside it, a rusty old Mondeo lowered the tone. McLean knew the car, knew its owner all too well. Detective

Chief Inspector Charles Duguid was not his favourite superior officer. If this was one of his investigations, then the deceased must have been important. That would explain the large number of uniforms drafted in, too.

'What the fuck are you doing here?'

McLean turned to the familiar voice. Duguid was considerably older than him, mid-fifties at least; his once-red hair now thin and greying, his face florid and lined. White paper overalls pulled down to his waist and tied in a knot beneath his sagging gut, he had about him the air of a man who's just nipped out for a fag.

'I was in the neighbourhood, saw the patrol cars in the lane.'

'And you thought you'd stick your nose in, eh? What're you doing here anyway?'

'I didn't mean to butt in to your investigation, sir. I just thought, well, since I grew up in the area, I might've been able to help.'

Duguid let out an audible sigh, his shoulders sagging theatrically.

'Oh well. You're here. Might as well make yourself useful. Go and talk to that pathologist friend of yours. See what wonderful insights he's come up with this time.'

McLean started towards the front door, but was stopped by Duguid's hand catching him tight around the arm.

'And make sure you report back to me when you're done. I don't want you sloping off before we've wrapped this up.'

The inside of the house was almost painfully bright after the soft city darkness descending outside. McLean entered a large hall through a smaller, but still substantial, porch. Inside, a chaos of SOC officers bustled about in white paper boilersuits, dusting for fingerprints, photographing everything. Before he could get more than a couple of steps, a harassed young woman handed him a rolled-up white bundle. He didn't recognise her; a new recruit to the team.

'You'll want to put these on if you're going in there, sir.' She motioned behind her with a quick jab of her thumb to an open door on the far side of the hallway. 'It's an awful mess. You'd no' want to ruin your suit.'

'Or contaminate any potential evidence.' McLean thanked her, pulling on the paper overalls and slipping the plastic covers over his shoes before heading for the door, keeping to the raised walk-way the SOC team had laid out across the polished wood floor. Voices muttered from inside, so he stepped in.

It was a gentleman's library, leather-bound books lining the walls in their dark mahogany shelves. An antique desk sat between two tall windows, its top clear save for a blotter and a mobile phone. Two high-backed leather armchairs were arranged either side of an ornate fireplace, facing the unlit fire. The one on the left was unoccupied, some items of clothing neatly folded and placed across the arm. McLean crossed the room and stepped around the other chair, his attention immediately drawn to the figure sitting in it, his nose wrinkling at the foul stench.

The man looked almost calm, his hands resting lightly on the arms of the chair, his feet slightly apart on the floor. His face was pale, eyes staring straight ahead with a glazed expression. Black blood spilled from his closed mouth, dribbling down his chin, and at first McLean thought he was wearing some kind of dark velvet coat. Then he saw the guts, blue-grey shiny coils slipping down onto the Persian rug on the floor. Not velvet, not a coat. Two white-clad figures crouched beside them, seemingly unwilling to trust their knees to the blood-soaked carpet.

'Christ on a stick.' McLean covered his mouth and nose against the iron tang of blood and the richer smell of human ordure. One

of the figures looked around and he recognised the city pathologist, Angus Cadwallader.

'Ah, Tony. Come to join the party have you?' He stood, handing something slippery to his assistant. 'Take that will you, Tracy.'

'Barnaby Smythe.' McLean stepped closer.

'I didn't realise you knew him,' Cadwallader said.

'Oh, yes. I knew him. Not well, I mean. I've never been in this
place before. But sweet Jesus, what happened to him?'

'Didn't Dagwood brief you?'

McLean looked around, expecting to see the chief inspector
close behind and wincing at the casual use of Duguid's nickname.
But apart from the assistant and the deceased, they were alone in
the room.

'He wasn't too pleased to see me, actually. Thinks I want to
steal his glory again.'

'And do you?'

'No. I was just off up to my gran's place. Noticed the cars . . .'
McLean saw the pathologist's smile and shut up.

'How is Esther, by the way? Any improvement?'

'Not really, no. I'll be seeing her later. If I don't get stuck here,
that is.'

'Well, I wonder what she'd have made of this mess.' Cadwallader waved a blood-smeared, gloved hand at the remains of what
had once been a man.

'I've no idea. Something gruesome I'm sure. You pathologists
are all alike. So tell me what happened, Angus.'

'As far as I can tell, he's not been tied down or restrained in any
way, which would suggest he was dead when this was done. But
there's too much blood for his heart not to have been beating when
he was first cut open, so he was most likely drugged. We'll know
when we get the toxicology report back. Actually most of the

4

blood's come from this.' He pointed to a loose red flap of skin cir-
cling the dead man's neck. 'And judging by the spray on the legs and
the side of the chair, that was done after his entrails were removed.
I'm guessing the killer did that to get them out of the way whilst he
poked about inside. Major internal organs all seem to be in place
except for a chunk of his spleen, which is missing.'

'There's something in his mouth, sir,' the assistant said, standing up with a creak of protest from her knees. Cadwallader
shouted for the photographer, then bent forward, forcing his fingers between the dead man's lips and prising his jaw apart. He
reached in and pulled a slimy, red, smooth mess out of it. McLean
felt the bile rise in his gorge and tried not to retch as the pathologist held the organ up to the light.

'Ah, there it is. Excellent.'

Night had fallen by the time McLean made it back out of the
house. It was never truly dark in the city; too many street lights
casting the thin haze of pollution with a hellish, orange glow. But
at least the stifling August heat had seeped away, leaving a fresh-
ness behind it that was a welcome relief from the foul stench
inside. His feet crunched on the gravel as he stared up at the sky,
hopelessly looking for stars, or any reason why someone would
tear out an old man's guts and feed him his own spleen.

'Well?' The tone was unmistakable, and came with a sour odour
of stale tobacco smoke. McLean turned to see Chief Inspector
Duguid. He'd ditched the overalls and was once more wearing his
trademark over-large suit. Even in the semi-darkness McLean
could see the shiny patches where the fabric had worn smooth
over the years.

'Most probable cause of death was massive blood loss, his
neck was cut from ear to ear. Angus . . . Dr Cadwallader reckons

time of death was somewhere in the late afternoon, early evening. Between four and seven. The victim wasn't restrained, so must have been drugged. We'll know more once the toxicology screening's done.'

'I know all that, McLean. I've got eyes. Tell me about Barnaby Smythe. Who'd cut him up like that?'

'I didn't really know Mr Smythe all that well, sir. He kept himself to himself. Today's the first time I've ever been in his house.'

'But you used to scrump apples from his garden when you were a boy, I suppose.'

McLean bit back the retort he wanted to give. He was used to Duguid's taunting, but he didn't see why he should have to put up with it when he was trying to help.

'So what do you know about the man?' Duguid asked.

'He was a merchant banker, but he must have retired by now. I read somewhere that he donated several million to the new wing of the National Museum.'

Duguid sighed, pinching the bridge of his nose. 'I was hoping for something a bit more useful than that. Don't you know anything about his social life? His friends and enemies?'

'Not really, sir. No. Like I said, he's retired, must be eighty at least. I don't mix much in those circles. My gran would have known him, but she's not exactly in a position to help. She had a stroke, you know.'

Duguid snorted unsympathetically. 'Then you're no bloody use to me, are you. Go on, get out of here. Go back to your rich friends and enjoy your evening off.' He turned away and stalked towards a group of uniforms huddling together smoking. McLean was happy to let him go, then remembered the chief inspector's earlier warning about sloping off.

'Do you want me to prepare a report for you, sir?' he shouted at Duguid's back.

'No I bloody well don't.' Duguid turned on his heel, his face shadowed, eyes glinting in the reflected light of the street lamps. 'This is my investigation, McLean. Now fuck off out of my crime scene.'

2

The Western General Hospital smelled of illness; that mixture of disinfectant, warm air and leaked bodily fluids that clung to your clothes if you spent more than ten minutes in the place. The nurses at reception recognised him, smiling and nodding him through without a word. One of them was Barbara and the other Heather, but he was damned if he could remember who was who. They never seemed to be apart for long enough to work it out, and staring at the too-small badges on their chests was just embarrassing.

McLean walked as quietly as the squeaky linoleum floor would allow along the soulless corridors; past shuffling men in skimpy hospital smocks, clutching their wheeled intravenous drip stands with arthritic claws; busy nurses weaving their way from one crisis to another; pallid junior doctors looking like they were about to drop from exhaustion. It had all long since ceased to shock him, he'd been coming here that long.

The ward he was looking for was at a quiet end of the hospital, tucked away from the hustle and bustle. It was a nice room, with windows looking out over the Firth of Forth to Fife. It always struck him as a bit daft, really. This would be a better place to put people recovering from major operations or something. Instead it was home to those patients who couldn't care less about the view or the quiet. He wedged open the door with a fire extinguisher, so the distant hum of activity would follow him, then stepped into the semi-darkness.

She lay propped up on several pillows, her eyes closed as if she were sleeping. Wires flowed from her head to a bedside monitor, which ticked a slow, steady rhythm. A single tube dripped clear liquid into her wrinkled and liver-spotted arm and a slim white continuous pulse monitor was clamped onto one withered finger. McLean pulled up a chair and sat down, taking his gran's free hand and staring at her once-proud and lively face.

'I saw Angus earlier. He was asking after you.' He spoke softly, no longer sure she could hear him. Her hand was cool, room temperature. Apart from the mechanical rising and falling of her chest, his grandmother didn't move at all.

'How long have you been in here now? Eighteen months is it?' Her cheeks had shrunk away more since the last time he had visited her, and someone had cut her hair badly, making her skull look even more skeletal.

'I used to think you'd wake up eventually, and it would all be the same. But now I'm not sure. What is there for you to wake up to?'

She didn't answer; he hadn't heard her voice in over a year and a half. Not since she had phoned him that evening, saying she didn't feel well. He remembered the ambulance, the paramedics, locking up the empty house. But he couldn't remember her face when he had found her, unconscious in her armchair by the fire. The months had wasted her away, and he had watched her fade until all he knew was this shadow of the woman who had raised him since he was four.

'Who's done this. Honestly.' McLean looked around, startled by the noise. A nurse stood in the doorway, struggling to remove the fire extinguisher. She flustered in, looking around and then finally seeing him.

'Oh, Mr McLean. I'm so sorry. I didn't see you there.'

Soft Western Isles accent, her pale face topped with a bob of flame-red hair. She wore the uniform of a ward sister and McLean was sure he knew her name. Jane or Jenny or something. He thought he knew the names of almost all nurses in the hospital, either from work or his regular visits to this quiet little ward. But for the life of him, as she stood staring, he couldn't remember hers.

'It's OK,' he said, standing up. 'I was just going.' He turned back to the comatose figure, releasing her cold hand. 'I'll come see you again soon, Gran. I promise.'

'D'you know, you're the only person who comes here to visit regularly,' the nurse said. McLean looked around the ward, noting the other beds with their silent, motionless occupants. It was creepy, in a way. Queued up for the morgue. Waiting patiently for the Grim Reaper to get around to them.

'Don't they have family?' he asked, nodding his head in the direction of the other patients.

'Sure, but they don't visit. Oh they come at first. Sometimes every day for a week or two. Even a month. But over time the gaps get longer and longer. Mr Smith over there's not had a visitor since May. But you come here every week.'

'She doesn't have anyone else.'

'Well, still. It's not everyone would do what you do.'

McLean didn't know what to say. Yes, he came to visit whenever he could, but he never stayed long. Not like his gran, who was condemned to spend the rest of her days in this quiet hell.

'I have to go,' he said, making for the door. 'I'm sorry about the fire extinguisher.' He stooped, lifting it back onto its hook on the wall. 'And thank you.'

'For what?'

'For looking after her. I think she would have liked you.'

The taxi dropped him off at the end of the drive. McLean stood for a while in the evening coolness, watching the steam of the retreating exhaust dissipate into nothing. A lone cat strode confidently across the road not more than twenty yards away, then stopped suddenly as if realising it was being watched. Its sleek head moved from side to side, sharp eyes scanning the scene until it spotted him. Threat detected and assessed, it sat down in the middle of the road and began licking a paw.

He leant against the nearest in a line of trees that burst through the paving slabs like the end of civilisation, and watched. The street was quiet at the best of times, almost silent at this hour. Just the background quiet roar of the city to remind him that life went on. An animal shriek in the distance stopped the cat mid-lick. It peered at McLean to see whether he had made the noise, then trotted off, disappearing into a nearby walled garden with an effortless leap.

Turning back to the driveway, McLean faced the blank edifice of his grandmother's house, the dark windows as empty as the old lady's coma-shrunk face. Eyes shutter-closed against the never-dark night. Visiting the hospital was a duty he undertook willingly, but coming here felt more like a chore. The house he'd grown up in was long gone, the life of the place leached out of it as surely as it had been leached out of his grandmother until there was nothing left but bones of stone and memories gone sour. He half wished the cat would come back; any company right now would be welcome. But he knew it was really just a distraction. He'd come here to do a job; might as well get on with it.

A week's worth of junk mail littered the front hallway. McLean scooped it up and took it through to the library. Most of the furniture was covered in white sheets, adding to the other-worldliness of the house, but his grandmother's desk was still clear. He checked the phone for messages, deleting the telesales offerings without bothering to listen to them. Should probably switch the machine off, really, but you never knew if some old family friend might be trying to get in touch. The junk mail went into the bin, which he noticed would need emptying soon. There were two bills that he'd have to remember to forward on to the solicitors dealing with his grandmother's affairs. Just the walk-around and he could go home. Maybe even get some sleep.

McLean had never really been afraid of the dark. Perhaps it was because the monsters had come when he was four, taken his parents away from him. The worst had happened and he'd survived. After that, the darkness held no fear. And yet he found himself switching lights on so that he never had to cross a room in darkness. The house was large, far larger than one elderly lady needed. Most of the neighbouring houses had been turned into at least two apartments, but this one still held out, and with a substantial walled garden surrounding it. Christ alone knew what it was worth; one more thing he'd have to worry about in the fullness of time. Unless his grandmother had left everything to some cat charity. That wouldn't really surprise him; definitely her style.

He stopped, hand reaching up to flick off the light switch, and realised it was the first time he'd thought about the consequences of her being dead. The possibility of her dying. Sure, it had always been there, lurking at the back of his mind, but all the months he'd been visiting her in the hospital it had been with the thought that eventually there would be some improvement in her condition. Today, for whatever reason, he had finally accepted that wasn't going to happen. It was both sad and oddly relieving.

And then his eyes noticed where he was.

His grandmother's bedroom was not the largest in the house, but it was still probably bigger than McLean's entire Newington flat. He stepped into the room, running a hand over the bed still made up with the sheets she'd slept in the night before she'd had her stroke. He opened up wardrobes to reveal clothes she'd never wear again, then crossed the room to where a Japanese silk dressing gown had been thrown over the chair that stood in front of her dressing table. A hairbrush lying bristles up held strands of her hair; long white filaments that glinted in the harsh yellow-white glow of the lights reflected in an antique mirror. A few bottles of scent were arranged on a small silver tray to one side of it, a couple of ornately framed photographs to the other. This was his grandmother's most private space. He'd been in here before, sent to fetch something as a boy or nipping through to the bathroom to pinch a bar of soap, but he'd never lingered, never really taken much notice of the place. He felt slightly uneasy just being in here, and at the same time fascinated.

The dressing table was the focus of the room, much more so than the bed. This was where his grandmother prepared herself for the world outside, and McLean was pleased to see that one of the photographs was of him. He remembered the day it was taken, when he passed out of Tulliallan. That was probably the tidiest his uniform had ever been. Police Constable McLean, on the fast track sure, but still expected to pound the beat like any other copper.

The other photo showed his parents, taken at their wedding. Looking at the two pictures together, it was clear that he'd inherited most of his looks from his father. They must have been similar ages when the two photographs were taken, and apart from the difference in film quality, they could almost have been brothers. McLean stared at the image for a while. He barely knew these people, hardly ever thought about them anymore.

Other photographs were dotted about the room; some on the

walls, some in frames on the top of a wide, low chest of drawers that undoubtedly contained underwear. Some were pictures of his grandfather, the dour old gentleman whose portrait hung above the fireplace in the dining room downstairs, presiding over the head of the table. They charted his life, from young man through to old age in a series of black-and-white jumps. Other pictures were of his father, and then his mother too as she came into his life. There were a couple of McLean's grandmother too, as a strikingly beautiful young woman dressed in the most fashionable of 1930s clothes. The last of these showed her flanked by two smiling gentlemen, also dressed for the period, and in the background the familiar columns of the National Monument on Calton Hill. McLean stared at the photograph for long moments before he realised what was bothering him about it. On his grandmother's left was his grandfather, William McLean, quite obviously the same man who appeared in so many of the other pictures. But it was the man on her right, one arm around her waist and smiling at the camera as if the world were his oyster, who looked the spitting image of the photos of the newly married man and the fresh out of training college police constable.

3

'Just what exactly's gone missing, Mr Douglas?'

McLean tried to settle himself into the uncomfortable sofa; there were lumps in the cushions that felt like bricks. Giving up, he looked around the room as, beside him, Detective Sergeant Bob Laird, Grumpy Bob to all his friends, took down notes in a long, loopy scrawl.

It was a well-furnished room, the lumpen sofa notwithstanding. An Adam fireplace filled one wall, a collection of tasteful oil paintings covering the rest. Two more sofas formed a neat cordon around the hearth, though all that filled it in the sweltering summer heat was a neat arrangement of dried flowers. Mahogany dominated, the smell of polish competing with the faint odour of cat. Everything was old but valuable, even the man sitting opposite.

'Nothing was taken from here.' Eric Douglas touched his black-rimmed spectacles with a nervous finger, pushing them up to the bridge of his long nose. 'They went straight to the safe. Almost as if they knew exactly where it was.'

'Perhaps you could show us, sir.' McLean stood up before his legs went numb. He might gain useful information from seeing the safe, but even more he needed to move. Douglas led them through the house to a small study that looked like it had been hit by a tornado. A wide antique desk was piled with books, pulled from the oak shelves behind to reveal a safe door. It hung open on its hinges.

'This is pretty much how I found it.' Douglas stood in the doorway, as if not entering the room might make it revert to normal. McLean pushed past him and picked his way carefully behind the desk. Tell-tale grey-white dust on the shelves and around the frame of the one large window showed that the fingerprint specialist had already been and gone. She was still busy elsewhere in the house, dusting doorframes and windowsills. He fished in his jacket pocket for a pair of rubber gloves anyway, snapping them on before reaching for the small pile of papers still sitting on the floor of the safe.

'They took the jewellery, left the share certificates. They're worthless anyway. It's all electronic these days.'

'How'd they get in?' McLean replaced the papers and turned his attention to the window. It was painted solid, no obvious sign of having been opened in the past decade, let alone the last twenty-four hours.

'All the doors were locked when I got back from the funeral. And the alarm was still set. I've really no idea how anyone could have got in.'

'Funeral?'

'Mother.' A frown passed over Mr Douglas' face. 'She passed away last week.'

McLean silently cursed himself for not paying attention. Mr Douglas was dressed in a dark suit, with a white shirt and black tie. And the whole house felt empty; it had that indefinable air of a place where someone has recently died. He should have known of the bereavement before barging in and asking questions. He cast his mind back over the meeting so far, trying to remember if anything he had said might have been insensitive.

'I'm sorry to hear that, Mr Douglas. Tell me, was the funeral well-advertised?'

16

'I'm not sure what you mean. There was an announcement in the paper; time and place, that sort of. . . Oh.'

'There are evil people who'll take advantage of your grief, sir. The men who did this probably keep an eye on the papers. Can you show me the alarm?'

They left the study, crossing the hall once more. Mr Douglas opened a door tucked under the wide staircase, revealing a set of stone steps leading down to the basement. Just inside the door, a slim white control panel flickered green lights. McLean studied it for a while, noting down the name of the company who serviced it. Penstemmin Alarms, a well-respected firm, and a sophisticated system too.

'You know how to set this properly?'

'I'm not a fool, inspector. This house contains many valuable things. Some of the paintings are worth six-figure sums, but to me they are priceless. I set the alarm myself before making my way to Mortonhall.'

'I'm sorry, sir. I just need to be sure.' McLean slipped his notebook into his pocket. The SOC officer trudged down the main stairs. He caught the eye of the young technician but she just shook her head, crossed the hall and went out of the door.

'We'll not take any more of your time, but if you could supply us with a detailed description of the stolen items, that would be very helpful.'

'My insurance company has a full inventory, I'll have them send you a copy.'

Outside, McLean approached the SOC officer as she struggled out of her overalls and threw her equipment into the back of her car. She was the new girl he'd seen at the Smythe murder scene; quite striking with her pale skin and unruly mop of black hair.

Her eyes were lined with some kind of thick make-up; either that or she'd been on a serious bender.

'Find anything?'

'Not in the study, no. Place is as clean as a nun's mind. There's plenty prints around the rest of the house, but nothing unusual. Probably the owner's mostly. I'll need to get a set of reference prints.'

McLean swore. 'They cremated her this morning.'

'Well, there's not much we can do anyway. There's no sign of forced entry, no prints or other marks in the room with the safe.'

'Get me what you can, eh?' McLean nodded his thanks and watched as she drove off. He turned back to the anonymous pool car Grumpy Bob had signed out that morning when he'd been handed the case. His first proper case since being made up to inspector. It wasn't much, really; a burglary that would be damned hard to solve unless they got lucky. Why couldn't it just be some crackhead stealing the telly to pay for his next fix? Of course, something like that would have been left to a sergeant to investigate. Mr Douglas must have had some influence to get an inspector involved in such a minor crime, however new he was to the job.

'What d'you want to do next, sir?' Grumpy Bob looked across from the driver's seat as McLean climbed into the car.

'Back to the station. Let's make a start on putting these notes into some sort of order. See if there's anything similar in the unsolved pile.'

He settled himself into the passenger seat and watched the city flow by as they drove back through the busy streets. They'd only gone five minutes when Grumpy Bob's airwave set went off. McLean picked it up, fiddling with the unfamiliar buttons until he managed to answer the call.

'McLean.'

'Ah, inspector. I tried your mobile, but it doesn't seem to be switched on.' McLean recognised the voice of Pete, the duty sergeant. He pulled his phone out of his pocket, pressing the power button. It had been fully charged when he'd left home that morning, but now, just a few hours later, it was as dead as old Mrs Douglas.

'Sorry, Pete. Battery's gone. What can I do for you, anyway?'

'Got a case for you, if you're not too busy that is. The super said it would be right up your street.'

McLean groaned, wondering what petty misdemeanour he'd be given now.

'Go on, Pete. Give us the details.'

'Farquhar House, sir. Over in Sighthill. Some builder phoned, said they'd uncovered a dead body.'

4

McLean stared through the car window past light industrial units, factory outlets, shops and grimy warehouses to the towers hovering in the middle distance over a haze of grey-brown pollution. Sighthill was one of those parts of the city they didn't show in the tourist brochures, a suburban sprawl of social housing spilling out towards the bypass along the old Kilmarnock road, dominated by the imposing, brutalist bulk of Stevenson College.

'Do we know anything more about this, sir? You said a body'd been found.'

McLean still couldn't get used to Grumpy Bob calling him 'sir'. The detective sergeant was fifteen years his senior, and it wasn't that long since they'd been the same rank. But the moment McLean's promotion to inspector had come through, Grumpy Bob had stopped calling him Tony and switched to sir. Technically, he was correct to do so, but it still felt strange.

'I'm not sure of the details myself. Just a body found on a building site. Apparently the chief superintendent said something about it being just the right case for someone like me. Not sure she meant it as a compliment.'

Grumpy Bob said nothing for a while, steering the car down a bewildering maze of side streets lined with identical grey semi-detached houses. The occasional personal flourish – a different coloured door or modern roof lights – marked the few homes owned by someone other than the council. Finally they turned into a narrow lane, pebble-dashed walls blocking the view into tiny gardens on either side. At the end, incongruous amongst the sprawl of council housing, stood a once-grand set of gates, their ornate ironwork overgrown with ivy and hanging at a perilous angle from two cracked stone pillars. A sign on the left one read: 'another prestigious development from mcallister homes.'

The house beyond was in the Scots Baronial style, four storeys tall with high, narrow windows and a round tower jutting out of one corner. Scaffolding supported one wall, and the last of what had once been a large garden was now filled with builders' vans, skips, portacabins and other detritus of the trade. Two squad cars waited at the front doors, watched over by a lone PC. She managed a weary smile as McLean showed her his warrant card, then led them into the darkness of the front hall. It was cool after the outside heat, raising goose bumps on his skin and sending an involuntary shiver down his spine.

The PC noticed. 'Aye, it's like that in here. Creepy so it is.'

'Who found the body?'

'What? Oh.' The constable dug out her notebook. 'Mr McAllister phoned us himself. Seems his site foreman Mr Donald Murdo, from Bonnyrigg, was working late last night tidying up some stuff in the basement. Gave himself quite the shock when he . . . You know.'

'Last night?' McLean stopped so suddenly that Grumpy Bob almost walked into him. 'When was this called in?'

'About six.'

'And the body's still there?'

'Yeah, well, they're just finishing up now. They were a bit busy last night, and this wasn't considered high priority.'

'How can a dead body not be high priority?'

The constable gave him what could only be described as an old-fashioned look.

'The police surgeon declared death at seven-fifteen last night. We secured the crime scene and I've been here keeping an eye on it ever since. It's not my fault that half the SOC team were out on the piss last night, and quite frankly I think someone from CIB could've come out a bit sooner, too. There's far nicer places to spend the night.'

She stomped down the stairs towards the basement. McLean was so astonished at the outburst, he could do nothing but follow.

A scene of industrious determination greeted them as they reached the bottom of the steps. Thick cables slithered across the dusty floor towards several powerful arc lights; shiny aluminium boxes lay open, their contents piled around; a narrow strip of portable walkway had been set up down the middle of the main corridor, but no one was using it. Half a dozen SOC officers busied themselves with putting things away. Only one figure noticed their arrival.

'Tony. What have you done to piss off Jayne McIntyre so early on in your new career?'

McLean picked his way through the dust and equipment to the far end of the basement. Angus Cadwallader stood by a large hole hacked into the wall, light glaring out from powerful spot lamps beyond. The pathologist looked distinctly uneasy, not his usual chipper and irreverent self.

'Piss off?' McLean bent down to peer through the hole. 'What've you got for me this time, Angus?'

Beyond lay a large circular room, its wall smooth and white. Four lamps had been erected near the centre, all angled inwards and down, as if their subject were some up and coming star of the

22

stage. Spread-eagled, desiccated and brutalised, it was unlikely she would be taking any applause.

'Not a pretty sight, is she.' Cadwallader pulled a pair of latex gloves from his suit pocket and handed them to McLean. 'Shall we take a closer look.'

They stepped through the narrow opening hacked in the brickwork, and McLean instantly felt the temperature drop. The noise of the SOC team fell away as if he had closed a door on them. Looking back, he felt a sudden urge to retreat from the hidden room; not so much fear as a pressure in his head, forcing him away. Shrugging it off with no little difficulty, he turned his attention to the body.

She had been young. He wasn't sure how he knew, but something about the diminutive size spoke of a life cut short before it had really begun. Her hands stretched out wide in parody of crucifixion; black iron nails hammered through her palms, their heads bent over to stop her ripping them out. Time had dried her skin to leather, stretching her hands into claws, her face into a grimace of utter agony. She wore a simple, floral print cotton dress that had been pulled up over her breasts. McLean noticed in passing how dated it looked, but the detail was soon lost as he took in everything else.

Her stomach had been opened up, a neat cut from between her legs to between her breasts, the skin and muscle peeled back like a rotting flower. Ribs poked white through dark dry gristle, but nothing remained of her internal organs. Down further still, her legs were splayed wide apart, hips disjointed so her knees almost touched the floor. Her skin had tightened like biltong over dried muscle, each bone clearly visible right down to her slender feet, nailed like her hands to the floor.

'Jesus Christ. Who could do such a thing?' McLean rocked

back on his heels, looking up past the lights to the featureless walls all around. Then into the bright arc itself, as if staring at the glare would wash the image out of his mind.

'Perhaps a more pertinent question would be when it was done.' Cadwallader squatted down on the other side of the body, drew out an expensive fountain pen and used it to point at various parts of the girl's remains. 'As you can see, something has prevented decay from occurring, allowing a natural mummification to take place. The internal organs were removed, presumably disposed of elsewhere. I'll need to run some tests once I get her back to the mortuary, but I can't see her being killed anything less than fifty years ago.'

McLean stood up, shivering slightly in the cold. He wanted to look away, but his eyes kept being dragged down to the body at his feet. He could almost feel her agony and terror. She had been alive, at least when this ordeal had started. Of that he was sure.

'Better send a team in to move her,' he said. 'I'm not sure if the techies can get anything useful from the floor underneath, but it's worth a try.'

Cadwallader nodded and left the room, stepping around the brick rubble that had spilled in when the workman had knocked the first hole. Alone with the dead girl, McLean tried to imagine what the place must have looked like when she died. The walls were smooth white plaster; the ceiling a neat vault of white-painted brickwork, its apex directly above the dead body. In a chapel, he would have expected to find an altar directly opposite the bricked-up doorway, but there was no ornamentation in the room at all.

The arc lights cast strange shadows over the dark wooden floorboards, seeming almost to ripple as McLean stood, waiting for someone to come back in. He found the shapes hypnotic, curling glyphs at regular intervals around a wide circle, perhaps three feet in from the walls. Shaking his head to rid himself of the illusion, he stepped out of the central glare of the lights, then stopped dead. His own shadow had moved, gliding over the floor in four different shades. But the patterns on the floor had remained solid underneath it.

Stooping, he peered closer at the wooden boards. They were polished smooth and only slightly dusty, as if the room had been hermetically sealed until the wall was broken through. The light from the arc lamps was confusing, so he pulled a slender torch from his pocket and twisted it on, pointing it directly at the patterns on the floor. They were dark, almost indistinguishable from the wood. Ornate knots of lines, thickening and thinning as they intertwined to form a complicated whorl. The edge of a circle etched in the floor ran away in both directions. He followed it around anti-clockwise, noting five more intricate marks, all equidistant. The line between the first and the last had been neatly intersected by the falling brickwork of the walled-up doorway.

Digging out his notebook, McLean tried to make rough sketches of the signs, noting their relationship to the position of the dead girl. They lined up perfectly with her outstretched hands and feet, her head and the central point between her legs.

'You ready for the body to be moved, sir?'

He almost jumped out of his skin, spun around to see Grumpy Bob staring through the hole hacked in the wall.

'Where's the photographer? Can you get him back in here a minute.'

Bob turned away, shouted something McLean couldn't quite make out. Then a moment later a short man stuck his face into the room. McLean didn't recognise him; another new recruit to the SOC team.

'Hi there. You photo the body?'

'Aye.' Glasgow accent, slightly clipped and impatient. Fair enough, he didn't much want to be here either.

'Did you take any of the markings on the floor here?' He pointed to the nearest one, but the photographer's puzzled expression answered his question.

'Here, look.' He beckoned the man into the room and pointed to the floor with his torch. For a fleeting instant he saw something, but then it was gone.

'Cannae see a thing.' The young man squatted down to look. A heavy odour of soap rose off him, and McLean realised it was the first thing he had smelled since entering the room.

'Well, can you photograph the floor anyway? All the way around the body. About this far in from the wall. Close-up.'

The photographer nodded, glancing nervously at the silent figure in the centre of the room, then set about his task. The flash gun on his camera popped and whined between each recharge, little explosions of lightning spearing the room. McLean straightened up, focusing his attention on the wall now. Start from the body and work your way out. He felt the cold plaster through the thin protection of his latex gloves, then turned his hand around and rapped his knuckle on the surface. It sounded flat and solid, like stone. Moving round a bit, he rapped again. Still solid. Glancing over his shoulder, he moved around until he was in line with the dead girl's head. This time his knuckle produced a hollow clunk.

He knocked it again, and in the confused light of the flashgun and shadows thrown by the arc lamps, it looked like the wall bowed in under the pressure. Turning his hand once more, he pushed gently, feeling the wall give way under his fingers. Then with a crack of brittle bones, a panel about a foot wide and half as tall again split from the wall and fell to the floor. It had concealed a small alcove, and something glinted wetly from within.

McLean pulled out his torch again, twisted it on and directed the beam into the alcove. A slim silver ring lay on a folded piece of parchment, and behind it, preserved in a glass jar like a specimen in a biology classroom, was a human heart.

5

'Is this the best we can do?'

Grumpy Bob paced around the walls of the broom cupboard that was all they could muster for an incident room, complaining all the while. McLean stood silent in the middle. At least there was a window, though it looked out onto the backs of other parts of the building. Across from it, a whiteboard still bore the scribblings of a previous investigation, long-forgotten names circled and then crossed out. Whoever had written them had taken the marker pens away with him, along with the wiper. There were two small tables, one shoved under the window, the other sitting in the middle of the room, but all the chairs had long since departed.

'I quite like it.' McLean scuffed his shoe on the stained carpet tiles and leant against the single radiator. It was belting out heat even though outside the sun was baking the streets. He reached down to twist the thermostat to zero, but the flimsy plastic casing broke off in his hand. 'Might have to do something about the facilities, though.'

A knock at the door distracted them. McLean opened it to reveal a young man balancing a couple of boxes on one knee as he tried to reach for the door handle. He wore a brand new suit, and his shoes were polished to shiny mirrors. His freshly shaved face was a pink full moon, close-cropped pale ginger hair frizzing his scalp like a teenager's five o'clock shadow.

'Inspector McLean? Sir?'

McLean nodded, reaching out to take the top box before it spilled its contents all over the floor.

'Detective Constable MacBride,' the young man said. 'Chief Superintendent McIntyre sent me to help with your investigation, sir.'

'Which one?'

'Um . . . She didn't say. Just that you'd need another pair of hands.'

'Well, don't stand there in the door letting all this heat out.' McLean dumped the box down on the nearest of the two tables as MacBride came in. He put the other one beside it, then looked around the room.

'There's no chairs,' the constable said.

'Looks like Her Majesty's given us an eagle-eyed detective, sir,' Grumpy Bob said. 'There's nothing gets past this one.'

'Pay no attention to Sergeant Laird. He's just jealous because you're so much younger than him.'

'Err . . . Right.' MacBride hesitated.

'You have a first name, Detective Constable MacBride?'

'Um . . . Stuart, sir.'

'Well then, Stuart, welcome to the team. Both of us.'

The young lad looked from McLean to Grumpy Bob, then back again. His mouth hung slightly open.

'Well, don't just stand around looking like you've had your arse skelped. Get on out there and find us some chairs, laddie.' Grumpy Bob almost chased the constable out of the room, closing the door on his retreating form before laughing out loud.

'Go easy on him, Bob. It's not as if we're going to get much more help with either of these cases. And he's good. At least he should be. First in his year to make detective.'

McLean opened up one of the boxes, pulled out a thick pile of folders and laid them out on the table: unsolved burglaries, dating back over the previous five years. He sighed; the last thing he wanted to do was wade through endless reports on stolen goods that would never be recovered. He looked at his wrist and remembered that he'd forgotten to wind up his watch that morning. Sliding it off, he began turning the tiny brass knob.

'What time is it, Bob?'

'Half three. You know, they've got new-fangled modern watches with batteries now. They don't need to be wound up. You might consider getting one yourself.'

'It was my dad's.' McLean tightened the strap against his wrist, then checked his pocket for his mobile phone. It was there, but it was dead. 'Don't suppose you fancy a walk over to the city mortuary?'

Grumpy Bob shook his head. McLean knew how the old sergeant was with dead bodies.

'Never mind, then. You and young DC MacBride can make a start on these burglary reports. See if you can find any pattern that tens of dozens of other detectives have missed. Meantime I'm off to see a man about a mummified corpse.'

The afternoon air was thick and warm as he walked down the hill towards the Cowgate. Sweat stuck his shirt to his back, and McLean longed for a cool breeze. Normally you could rely on the wind to make life bearable, but for several days now the city had been becalmed. Down in the canyon of the street, shadowed by tall buildings on either side, the heat was stagnant and lifeless. It was a relief to push open the door to the city mortuary and enter the air-conditioned cool.

Angus Cadwallader was already prepped and waiting when McLean walked into the autopsy theatre. He gave the inspector an appraising look.

'Hot out there?'

McLean nodded. 'Like a furnace. You all set up?'

'What? Oh. Yes.' Cadwallader turned, then shouted for his assistant. 'Tracy, you ready?'

A short, round, cheerful young woman looked up from a cluttered counter on the far side of the room, pushed back her chair and stood. She wore green medical scrubs, and pulled on a pair of latex gloves as she walked over to the dissecting table. A white sheet covered it, mounded up in the middle over the dead body waiting to reveal its secrets.

'Right, better get on with it then.' Cadwallader reached into his pocket and pulled out a small jar. McLean recognised the preparation, a mixture of skin cream and camphor designed to blot out the smell of decay. The pathologist looked at it, then at McLean, sniffed, and put the jar back in his pocket.

'Don't suppose we'll be needing that today.'

McLean had witnessed too many autopsies over the course of his career. He wasn't comfortable with them, but neither did they sicken him in quite the way they used to. Of all the murder victims, hapless accidents and just plain unlucky people he had seen on this table, the mummified corpse of the young girl was perhaps the strangest. For starters, she had already been cut open, but Cadwallader still examined every inch of her slight frame, muttering observations into a microphone hanging from above. Finally, when he was satisfied her skin would yield no more clues as to her cause of death, he got to the part McLean hated most. The high-pitched whine of the bone-saw always set his teeth on edge, like fingernails scraped down a blackboard. It went on far too long, and ended with the horrible sound of the top of the skull being cracked off like a boiled egg.

'Interesting. The brain appears to have been removed. Here, Tony. Look.'

Steeling himself, McLean moved around. Seeing the dead girl's head opened up only made her look smaller, younger. The cavity inside her skull was dull, lined with dried blood and flecks of bone from the saw, but it was plainly empty.

'Could it have rotted?'

'Not really, no. Not given the state of everything else. I'd have expected it to have shrivelled up a bit, but it's been removed. Probably through the nose; that's how the ancient Egyptians used to do it.'

'Where is it then?'

'Well, we've these samples, but none of them looks like a brain to me.' Cadwallader pointed at a stainless-steel trolley upon which sat four specimen jars. McLean recognised the heart he'd seen the day before, but didn't want to hazard a guess as to the other organs. Two more jars stood in white plastic containers to prevent their desiccated contents leaking from large cracks that split the glass. All had been uncovered in hidden alcoves, arranged symmetrically around the dead girl's body. There had been other items in each of the alcoves too, yet another piece of the puzzle still needing to be put together.

'What about the broken ones?' McLean peered at some browny-grey sludge smeared on the inside of a jar. 'That could be brain, couldn't it?'

'It's difficult to tell, given the state of them. But I'd hazard a guess that was one of her kidneys and the other one a lung. I'll run some tests to be sure. Whatever it was, the jar's the wrong shape for it to have been her brain. You should know that, Tony. I've shown you enough. And besides, if it did come out through her nose, it would have been pretty well mushed up. No point sticking that in a preserving jar.'

32

'Good point. How long ago do you reckon she died?'

'That's a difficult one. The mummification shouldn't have happened at all; the city's too humid, even in a walled-up basement. She should have rotted away. Or at least been eaten by rats. But she's perfectly preserved, and I'll be damned if I can find any trace of the chemicals you'd need to do that. Tracy can run some more tests, and we'll send a sample off to be carbon dated; we might get lucky with that. Otherwise, judging by her dress, I'd say at least fifty, sixty years. Any better than that's up to you.'

McLean picked up the thin fabric that was laid out on the trolley along with the sample jars, holding it up to the light. Brown stains smeared the lower half, and the delicate lace around the neck and sleeves had frayed into gossamer strips trailing in the air. It was a skimpy thing, a cocktail dress rather than something a young woman might wear every day. The faded floral pattern looked cheap; he turned it around and saw a couple of neatly hand-sewn patches around the hem. No manufacturer's label. It was the dress of a poor girl trying to impress. But as he looked back at her twisted, desecrated body he was all too aware that he knew nothing else about her at all.

6

The front door of the tenement was unlocked again, wedged half open with a bit of broken paving slab. McLean thought about shutting it properly, but decided against it. The last thing he wanted was to be woken by the students from the first-floor flat pressing all the buzzers at four in the morning until someone let them in. It was too warm for vagrants to be looking for places to spend the night, and even a dozen of them wouldn't make the stairwell smell any worse than it already did. Wrinkling his nose against the spray of too many tomcats, he climbed the stone steps up to the top floor.

The answering machine flashed a single message as he closed the door and dropped his keys on the table. He pressed the button and listened to his old flatmate suggesting they meet in the pub. If it hadn't been for the flashing light he might have thought it an old message – Phil phoned at least twice a week with the same suggestion. Just occasionally he even took up the offer. Smiling, he went to his bedroom and stripped off, dropping his clothes into the laundry basket before walking through to the bathroom. A long, cool shower soaked away the sweat of the day, but it still couldn't wash the memories clear. He thought about going for a run, or maybe hitting the gym, as he towelled down and pulled on a T-shirt and loose cotton trousers. An hour of hard exercise might help, but he didn't want the company of driven executives. He needed to be with people who were relaxed and having fun, even if he was just on the outside watching. Maybe Phil's idea wasn't so bad after all. Slipping on a pair of loose shoes, he grabbed his keys, banged shut the door and headed out to the pub.

The Newington Arms wasn't the best place to drink in Edinburgh, not by anyone's measure. But it made up for that by being the nearest to his home. McLean pushed through the swing doors, bracing himself for the onslaught of noise and smoke, then remembered that the wise men in the parliament down in Holyrood had banned smoking. It was still noisy, though no doubt they'd ban that next. He bought himself a pint of Deuchars and looked around for any familiar faces.

'Oi, Tony! Over here.' The shout coincided with a lull in the noise as the juke box paused between selections. McLean located the source, a group of people huddled around a table over by the large window looking onto the street. Post-grad students, by the sight of them. Lording it over them all, and beckoning him to join them, Professor Phillip Jenkins beamed a beer-fuelled smile.

'How's things, Phil? I see you've got your harem with you tonight.' McLean sat down in the space made as the students shuffled up the bench.

'Can't complain.' Phil grinned. 'The lab's just had its funding renewed for another three years. And increased, too.'

'Congratulations.' McLean lifted his beer in mock-salute, then drank whilst his old friend regaled him with tales of molecular biology and the politics of private funding. From there the conversation split off into all manner of inconsequential stuff, the idle chat of folk in the pub. He joined in from time to time, but mostly he was happy just to sit and listen. For a little while he could try and forget all the insanity, the mutilation, the job. Not like going out with the lads from the station after shift; that was a different

35

kind of unwind, one that usually meant a heavy head the next morning.

'So what are you up to these days, Tony? We've not seen you around much.'

McLean looked across at the young woman who had spoken. He was fairly sure her name was Rachel, and she was writing up her PhD in something he almost certainly couldn't spell. She looked a bit like the SOC officer who had worked the burglary scene and Smythe's murder, only about ten years younger and with flame-red hair that probably owed as much to a bottle as to nature. Even post-graduate students seemed impossibly young these days.

'Now, now, Rae. You mustn't go asking the inspector questions. He might have to arrest you. Might even have to put you in handcuffs.' Phil smirked into his pint, a wicked grin that McLean remembered all too well from the many years they had shared a flat.

'I can't discuss current investigations anyway,' McLean said. 'And you really wouldn't want to know about them. Trust me.'

'Gruesome, are they?'

'Not especially. It's not like *CSI* or whatever nonsense they put on the telly these days. Mostly it's dull old burglaries and street crime. And there's way too much of that going on. And anyway, I don't get to do much real investigation anymore. That's the problem with being an inspector. You're expected to manage people, direct things, sort out the overtime and balance the budgets. Look at the bigger picture. Not much different from what Phil does these days, I guess.'

McLean wasn't sure why he lied, even if it was only a half-lie. There was far more paperwork and far less legwork now he was an inspector. Maybe it was because he had come to the pub to get away from work. Whatever the reason, the question had spoiled the moment. He couldn't get Barnaby Smythe's dead eyes out of his mind; couldn't forget the agony on the young girl's face.

'Another round, I think.' He lifted his glass, choking slightly as he drained rather more from it than he'd been expecting. No one seemed to notice the awkward moment as he escaped to the bar.

'For a policeman, you're a very poor liar, Detective Inspector McLean.'

McLean turned from the bar to see who had spoken, realised he was standing far too close in the huddle of the crowd, but couldn't back off even if he wanted to. She was about his height, with straw-blonde hair cropped at neck length – a bob, if he had the terminology right. Something about her face was familiar, but she was older than the thicket of students who had been clamouring around Phil.

'I'm sorry. Do I know you?'

The puzzled look that must have been plastered over his face brought a smile to hers that sparkled mischievously in her eyes.

'I'm Jenny, remember? Jenny Spiers. Rae's sister? We met at Phil's birthday party.'

The party. He remembered now. Too many students getting horribly drunk on cheap wine, Phil holding court like some modern day King Arthur. He'd dropped off a very expensive bottle of whisky, had a glass of something that had made his teeth itch, and then left early. That had been the day they'd been called round to the tenement down in Leith. Neighbours complaining about someone's dog making an awful racket. You could hardly blame the poor beast, its owner had died in her bed at least a fortnight before and there hadn't been much left of the old girl worth eating. It was entirely possible he had met this woman at that party, but it was hard to get past the image of chewed flesh and gnawed bones rotting into a sunken mattress.

'Jenny, of course. Sorry, I was miles away.'

'I think you probably still are. And not somewhere nice. Bad day at the office?'

'And then some.' McLean caught the eye of the barman and waved him over. 'Can I get you something?'

Jenny glanced back across the bar to the crowd of students laughing at their professor's jokes. It didn't seem to take her long to make up her mind where she'd rather be.

'Sure, white wine. Thanks.'

An uncomfortable, noise-filled silence hung in the air between them as the drinks were poured. McLean tried to look at his unexpected companion without it being obvious. She was older than her sister, considerably older. Her blonde hair was streaked with fine white hairs she'd not bothered to conceal. Neither did she appear to be wearing any kind of make-up, and her clothes were simple, perhaps a little old-fashioned. Not dressed up for a night on the town like the crowd she'd come with. No war paint and attitude.

'So Rachel's your sister,' he said, all too aware of how stupid it sounded.

'Mum and dad's perfect little mistake, aye.' Jenny smiled at some personal joke. 'Seems to have caught your friend Phil's eye. You used to share a flat, I hear.'

'Back in my university days. Long time ago.' McLean took a gulp of his beer, watched Jenny sip her wine.

'Am I going to have to drag the story out of you?'

'I . . . No. Sorry. You caught me at a bad time. I'm not the best of company right now.'

'Oh, I don't know.' Jenny nodded over at the rowdy band of

students egging their professor on to ever more stupid behaviour. 'Given the alternative, I'll take moody and introverted any day.'

'I –' McLean started to complain but was interrupted by an unfamiliar vibration from his trouser pocket. He pulled out his phone just in time to see a missed call from the hospital. As he stared at it in confusion, the screen faded, then died completely. Pressing the buttons prompted a few half-hearted flashes and squeaks, but nothing more. He pushed it back into his pocket and turned back to Jenny.

'I couldn't borrow your phone, could I? The batteries in mine keep on dying.'

'Someone's thinking negative thoughts about you. Drains the life out of any electrical gadgets you rely on.' Jenny guddled around in her handbag before pulling out a slim smartphone and handing it over. 'Least, that's what my ex would say, but he's a loony. Work calling?'

'No, it was the hospital. My gran.' McLean found his way to the keypad and thumbed in the number from memory. He'd phoned so many times, knew all the nurses so well it took only moments to get through to the right ward. The call was over in a matter of seconds.

'I have to go.' McLean handed back the phone and headed for the door. Jenny made to follow, but he stopped her. 'It's OK. She's fine. I just need to go and see her. Stay and finish your wine. Tell Phil I'll call him this weekend.'

McLean pushed his way through the happy crowd and didn't look back. He was, after all, a very poor liar.

The back of the driver's head oozed in fleshy rolls from his bald pate down into his shoulders without any definable neck, giving him a curiously melted appearance. McLean sat in the back of the

39

taxi, staring at the pig-skin stubble through the open loop of the headrest and willed the man not to speak. The street lights strobed orange as they made good progress across the midnight city towards the hospital, the view streaked by a sudden shower of rain blown in off the North Sea. The touch of it was still on his skin from the walk to the taxi rank, dampening his hair and making his overcoat smell like an old dog.

'You want the main reception or A and E?' The taxi driver spoke with an English accent, South London possibly. A long way from home. It jarred McLean out of something that might have been sleep. He focused through the grimy windscreen, seeing the hulk of the hospital glittering and wet.

'Here's fine.' He handed over a ten pound note, told the driver to keep the change. The walk from the street across the near-deserted car park was enough to wake him up, but not enough to clear his head. Was it really just yesterday he'd been here looking at her? And now she was gone. He should feel sad, shouldn't he? So how come he felt nothing at all?

The corridors at the back of the hospital were always quiet, but at this time of the night it was almost as if the place had been evacuated. McLean found himself treading carefully so as not to make too much noise, his breathing shallow and ears pricked for the slightest sound. If he'd heard someone coming, he might well have tried to hide in an alcove or storage room. It was almost a relief to arrive at the coma ward unnoticed. Not quite sure why he was so loath to meet anyone, he pushed open the door and stepped inside.

Thin drapes blanked off his grandmother's bed from the other inhabitants, something he had never seen before. The familiar beeps and whirrs were there still, keeping everyone else alive, but the pulse of the place felt different. Or was that just in his head?

Taking a deep breath, as if about to plunge into the ocean, McLean pulled aside the curtain and stepped inside.

The nurses had removed all the tubes and wires, wheeled away the machines, but left his grandmother behind. She lay in the bed unmoving, her sunken eyes closed as if asleep, hands above the blankets and crossed neatly over her stomach. For the first time in eighteen months she looked something like the woman he remembered.

'I'm so very sorry.'

McLean turned to see a nurse standing in the doorway. The same nurse who'd spoken to him before, the one who'd cared for his grandmother all these long months. Jeannie, that was her name. Jeannie Robertson.

'Don't be,' he said. 'She was never going to recover. Really this is for the best.' He turned back to the dead woman lying on the bed, saw his grandmother for the first time in eighteen months. 'If I keep telling myself that I might even start believing it.'

7

Early morning and a crowd of officers jostled around the entrance to one of the larger incident rooms. McLean poked his head through the door, seeing the chaos that always marked the start of a major investigation. A clean whiteboard ran the length of one wall, and someone had scrawled 'Barnaby Smythe' on it in black marker. Uniformed constables arranged desks and chairs, a technician was busy wiring up computers. Duguid was nowhere to be seen.

'You helping out on this one, sir?' McLean looked around. A broad-shouldered PC pushed his way through the throng, carrying a large cardboard box sealed with black and yellow evidence tape. Andrew Houseman, or Big Andy to his friends, was a competent officer and a far better prop forward. But for an unfortunate injury early on in his career, he would probably have been playing for his country right now, instead of running errands for Dagwood. McLean liked him; Big Andy might not have been bright, but he was thorough.

'Not my case, Andy,' he said. 'And you know how much Dagwood likes my help.'

'But you were at the scene. Em said you were there.'

'Em?'

'Emma. Emma Baird? You know, the new SOC officer. So high, spiky black hair, always looks like she's wearing too much eyeliner.'

'Oh aye? You two got something going on, have you? Only I'd not want to get on the wrong side of that wife of yours, Andy.'

'No, no. I was just over at HQ getting this evidence from the scene.' The big man blushed, hefting the box to illustrate his point. 'She said she'd seen you at Smythe's house, hoped you'd catch whatever sick bastard killed him.'

'Just me? On my own?'

'Well, I'm sure she meant all of us.'

'I'm sure she did, Andy. But this investigation will have to do without me. It's Dagwood's call. And anyway, I've got my own murder to solve.'

'Aye, heard about that. Creepy.'

McLean was about to answer, but a rumbling voice echoing down the corridor heralded the arrival of the chief inspector. He had no intention of getting sucked into another investigation, particularly one headed by Charles Duguid.

'Gotta go, Andy. The chief superintendent wants to see me, and it doesn't do to keep her waiting.' He ducked around the large man and headed off towards his own incident room as what looked like half of the region's officers filed in for the morning briefing on the murder of Barnaby Smythe. Nice to see the alloca-tion of resources spread so evenly. But then Smythe was an important man, a city benefactor, a prominent member of society. No one had noticed his dead girl in her basement for over fifty years.

Grumpy Bob was nowhere to be seen when McLean reached the incident room; it was far too early in the morning for that. Consta-ble MacBride was hard at work, however. Somehow he had managed to find three chairs, and more miraculously, a laptop com-puter. He looked up from the screen as McLean entered the room.

'How's it going, constable?' He pulled off his jacket and hung it on the back of the door. The radiator under the window was still belting out heat.

'I've almost finished going through these burglary reports, sir. Think I might have spotted something.'

McLean pulled up a chair. One of its casters was missing. 'Show me.'

'Well, sir. These are all just random as far as I can tell. Not much skill, probably junkies feeding a habit and we got lucky with forensics.' MacBride hefted the bulk of the reports, piled up on one side of the desk, and put them back in their cardboard box. 'These ones, however. Well, I think there may be some connection between them.' He lifted a slim pile of folders, perhaps four or five, then dropped them back on the table.

'Go on.'

'All of them are skilled burglaries. Not just a brick-through-the-window job; no sign of forced entry at all. They all had alarm systems that were circumvented without any obvious sign, and in each case the burglar only took small items of high value.'

'Were they kept in safes?'

'No, sir. The safe-breaking's new. But there's one other common factor. In all of these cases, the home owner had recently died.'

'How recently?'

'Well, within a month.' MacBride paused, as if trying to make up his mind whether to say something or not. McLean kept quiet.

'OK, one of the burglaries happened eight weeks after the old woman died. But the other four were all within a fortnight. Last week's one happened on the day of the funeral. I need to check the others against burial dates, but we've not got that information on file.'

44

'Mrs Douglas's funeral was advertised in the paper, and she had an obituary printed beforehand.' McLean picked up the files, looking at the names and dates on the front of them. The most recent, apart from the case they were investigating, was almost a year ago; the oldest one five years past. They were all still open, nominally. Unsolved. All under the watchful eye of his most favourite chief inspector. He doubted Duguid would even remember their names.

'Let's see if we can't put a bit of flesh on the bones.' He passed the files back to MacBride. 'Find out some more about these people. Did they have obituaries? Were their funerals advertised, and if so, what paper?'

'What about the alarms?' MacBride asked. 'It's not easy getting round some of these systems.'

'Good point. OK. We need to check out where these people were when they died. Were they at home, hospital, in care?'

'You think our burglar got that close? Isn't that a great risk?'

'Not if your victim's dead before you carry out the burglary. Think about it. If our burglar works in a care home, he'd be able to charm the elderly, gain their trust and confidence. Then once they'd told him all he needed to know, he just had to wait for them to die.'

Even as he said it, he realised it was far-fetched, but a knock at the door stopped McLean from digging himself in further. He looked around to see a uniformed sergeant poking her head into the room, as if she didn't want to commit herself any further lest some awful fate befall her.

'Ah, sir, I thought I might find you here. The chief superintendent would like a word.'

McLean stood wearily, reaching for his crumpled jacket as the sergeant disappeared.

'Let's work the obituary angle first. Get onto the next of kin. Whoever was interviewed when the burglary was reported. Find

45

out how well known these people were. When Grumpy Bob gets in, the both of you can contact everyone in those files, see if there's a common theme. I'd better go and see what Her Majesty wants. And Stuart?'

The young detective looked up from the open case file.

'Well done.'

McLean remembered Jayne McIntyre from when she had been an ambitious sergeant on a fast track up the promotion ladder. Even back then she'd made time for those beneath her in the hierarchy. She didn't socialise much with her peer group, preferred to hob-nob with the inspectors and the chief constable, but if you needed her help, she'd give it. Always wise not to piss people off on your way up, in case you met them again on your way down. Somehow McLean didn't think that would be a problem in McIntyre's case, both because she was almost universally respected and because she was heading for the very top. She was only eight years his senior, and yet here she was, chief superintendent, running the station. There was little doubt that she would take the deputy chief constable's job when he retired in eighteen months' time. She understood the politics, knew how to impress the important people without laying on the bullshit. That was maybe her greatest skill, and McLean didn't begrudge her the success it had brought. He just wished he could keep under her radar.

'Ah, Tony. Thanks for popping in.' McIntyre stood as McLean knocked on the open door. That was a bad sign already. She walked around her desk, holding out a hand to be shaken. She was short, perhaps only just the minimum height for an officer. With her long brown hair tied back in an aggressive bun, he could see streaks of grey beginning to show around her temples. The foundation around her eyes couldn't hide the lines when she smiled.

'Sorry I didn't come earlier, I had a bit of a rough night.'

'Never mind. Have a seat.' She motioned towards one of two armchairs set in the corner of the spacious office, then settled into the other one herself.

'Chief Inspector Duguid spoke to me this morning. He tells me you were sniffing around the Barnaby Smythe scene the other night.'

So that was what it was about. A terrible thing, professional jealousy. 'I was in the neighbourhood, I saw that something was up and thought I might be able to help. I grew up around there, I know some of the local residents. DCI Duguid invited me in to see the crime scene.'

McIntyre nodded her head as McLean spoke, her eyes never leaving his face. He always felt with her like he was a naughty schoolboy being hauled up in front of the headmistress. Without warning, she stood up and walked across the room to a low wooden sideboard with a percolator on it.

'Coffee?' McLean nodded. McIntyre busied herself with measuring ground coffee from a Kilner jar into the filter, pouring in the exact amount of water required for two cups, and clicking the machine on.

'Barnaby Smythe was a very important man in the city, Tony. His murder's caused a lot of anxiety at high levels. Questions are being raised in Holyrood. Pressure is being brought to bear. We need to get a result on this one, and we need it fast.'

'I'm sure DCI Duguid will be very thorough. I see he's got a substantial team helping him with the investigation already.'

'It's not enough. I need my best detectives on this case, and I need them to co-operate with each other.' Thin brown liquid began to drip from the percolator into the glass jug beneath.

'You want me on the investigation?'

McIntyre walked back to her desk and picked up a manila folder, opening it on the table in front of him. There were a couple of dozen large colour photographs inside, taken in Barnaby Smythe's library. Close-ups showed his opened chest; his staring dead eyes and blood-stained chin; his hands resting on the arms of the chair; his entrails pooled up in his lap. McLean was glad he'd not yet eaten.

'I saw all this already,' he said as McIntyre poured two mugs of coffee and brought them over, settling herself back down in her armchair.

'He was eighty-four years old. Over the course of his life, Barnaby Smythe contributed more to this city than anyone I can think of, and yet someone did that to an old man. I need you to find out who did it, and why. And I need you to do that before they decide to cut open some other prominent citizen.'

'And Duguid? He's happy to have me on his team?' McLean sipped at his coffee, then wished he hadn't. It was hot, but weak, and tasted of dirty water.

'Happy's not the word I'd use, Tony. But Charles is a senior detective. He won't let personal animosity get in the way of something this important. I'd like to think you'll be the same.'

'Of course.'

McIntyre smiled. 'So how are your other cases coming along?'

'Constable MacBride's come up with a good theory about the burglary. He reckons there's a connection with several earlier ones, going back about five years. We've still no identity on the dead girl, though the doctor reckons she was killed about sixty years ago. I've a meeting with the builder later this morning.'

McLean went through his caseload quickly, but he could see that the chief superintendent was only half-listening. This was the show; pretending to be interested, pretending to be his friend. It was a good sign, because it meant she thought he could be of use to her. But he wasn't so stupid as to miss the subtext. He was on the Smythe investigation because there was a possibility it might fail. There might be other murders of prominent people, or worse, the killer might disappear and never be found. But if it did go wrong, it wouldn't be Chief Superintendent McIntyre's fault. Neither would DCI Duguid feel the heat. No, he was being invited into the investigation so that Lothian and Borders Police would have someone expendable to throw to the wolves if that should become necessary.

8

McLean decided he didn't like Tommy McAllister within two minutes of meeting the man.

It didn't help that neither of his two assigned officers were about when he had extricated himself from the superintendent's office. He'd wasted several minutes searching for them before remembering he'd told them to interview the earlier burglary victims. The station was almost deserted of uniforms, everyone seemed to have been drafted onto the Smythe investigation, but eventually he tracked down a young constable and persuaded her it would be in her interests to find him a pool car. She was standing in the corner of the room now, notebook in hand, visibly nervous. She'd have to work on that if she wanted to make detective.

'Can I get you some coffee, inspector? Constable?' McAllister slouched in a high-backed black leather executive chair he no doubt thought made him look important. He was dressed in a suit, but the jacket had been thrown over a nearby filing cabinet. His shirt was crumpled, sweat darkening the cotton around his armpits. Loosened tie and rolled up sleeves gave the impression that he was relaxed, but McLean could see the nervous darting of his eyes, the way he played with his fingers and bounced his feet.

'Thank you, but no,' he said. 'We shouldn't be long here. I just wanted to clear up a few facts about the house in Sighthill. Is Mr Murdo here?'

A scowl passed across McAllister's face at the mention of the name. He leant forward, hitting a button on the ancient intercom on his desk.

'Janette, can you put a call out for Donnie.' He lifted his finger off the button and looked back up at McLean, jerking his head backwards to the window behind him. 'He's out in the yard somewhere, I think.'

A woman's voice, muffled by the glass, announced over the tannoy for Donnie Murdo to come to the office. McLean looked around the room, seeing nothing that looked particularly out of place. It was cluttered, overstocked with filing cabinets. Safety notices, bills, post-it notes and other detritus covered the walls. One corner was piled up with tripods, striped poles and other surveying equipment.

'Who owns the house?' McLean asked.

'I do. Bought it for cash.' McAllister settled back into his chair, a look of something like pride on his weathered face.

'How long have you owned it?'

'About eighteen months, I'd say. Janette could give you the full details. It's taken long enough to get planning through. Time was you could do pretty much what you wanted, if you knew the right people to talk to. But now it's all committees and reviews and appeals. It's getting so a man can hardly make a living, if you know what I mean.'

'I'm sure I do, Mr McAllister.'

'Tommy, please, inspector.'

'Who did you buy the house from?'

'Oh, some new bank that's just set up in the city. Mid-Eastern Finance, I think they're called. I don't really know why they wanted to sell it. Probably decided it was time to get out of property and back into shares. Don't think they'd owned it long themselves.' McAllister leaned forward again, jabbing the intercom button.

'Janette, can you dig out the paperwork on Farquhar House.' He didn't wait for a response.

'It's a bit of a change of direction for you, isn't it, Mr McAllister,' McLean said. 'Renovating an old house, I mean. You made your money putting up all those boxes in Bonnyrigg and Lasswade didn't you?'

'That's right, aye. Good times they were. But it's getting that hard to find cheap development land round the city these days, ken? People moan about us ruining the countryside, then they complain about house prices going through the roof. You can't have it both ways, can you, inspector. Either we build more houses, or there's no' enough for everyone and the price goes up.'

'Then why not knock down that old house and put an apartment block in its place?'

McAllister looked like he was about to answer, but a tap at the door stopped him. It opened and a surly faced man stood uncertainly in the doorway.

'Come in, Donnie, have a seat. Don't be shy.' McAllister didn't get up. Donnie Murdo looked at McLean, then at the constable, a trapped expression on his face. He was a man who had come up against the law many times before in his life. He held himself defensively, shoulders hunched, arms hanging loose at his sides, legs slightly flexed as if ready to run at the slightest prompting. His hands were huge and across his knuckles faded tattoos read love and hate.

'Here's the file you wanted, Tommy.' The secretary who had shown them in earlier bustled past and laid a thick folder down on the desk. She looked at McLean with silent disapproval, then stalked out of the office, closing the door behind her.

'You were working at the old house in Sighthill the night before last, Donnie?' McLean watched as the foreman's eyes darted across to his boss. McAllister was sitting upright now, his arms resting on his desk. The nod was almost imperceptible.

'Aye. Ah wiz there right enough.'

'And what exactly were you doing there?'

'Well, we wiz clearing oot the basement, see. Goin' tae put a gym doon there.'

'We? I thought you said you were alone when you discovered the hidden room.'

'Aye, well, ah wiz. True enough. The lads were helpin' oot earlier, like. But ah sent them hame. Ah wiz jest cleanin' up like. Finishin' the job so's they could get started on the plasterin' in the morning.'

'It must have been quite a shock, seeing the body like that.'

'Ah didnae see much, ken. Jest a hand is all. That's when ah called Mr McAllister here.' Donnie inspected his hands, picking at his fingernails, eyes down so as not to have to make contact with anyone in the room.

'Well, thank you, Donnie. You've been very helpful.' McLean stood, offering his hand to the foreman, who looked momentarily startled, then took it.

'Is there anything else I can do for you, inspector?' McAllister asked.

'If I could get a copy of the title deeds, it would be useful. I need to try and track down who owned that house when the poor girl was murdered.'

'It's all in there. Take it, please.' McAllister motioned towards the file with an upturned palm, but didn't get out of his chair. 'If it's no' safe with the polis, then where is it safe, eh?'

McLean picked up the file and handed it to the constable.

'Well, thank you for your co-operation, Mr McAllister. I'll make sure you get this back as soon as possible.'

He made to leave, and only then did McAllister stand. 'Inspector?'

'Mr McAllister?'

'You wouldn't know when we can get back onto the site now, would you? Only we've had enough delays with the project as it is. It's costing me money every day now, and we can't do anything.'

'I'll have a word with the forensic people. See what we can do. It shouldn't be more than a day or two more, I'm sure.'

Outside, McLean climbed into the passenger seat of the pool car, letting the constable drive. He didn't say anything until they were on the road.

'He's lying, you know.'

'McAllister?'

'No. Well, yes. He's a property developer and they're always hiding something. But right now he just wants to get his building site back. No, the foreman. Donnie Murdo. He might have been in the cellar last night, but he wasn't working. Not hefting a hammer anyway. His hands were way too soft. Don't reckon he's done any hard graft in years.'

'So someone else uncovered the body. Who?'

'I don't know. And it's probably not relevant to the murder, either.' McLean popped open the folder and started to leaf through the random jumble of legal papers and letters. 'But I intend to find out.'

'Don't you ever switch on your bloody mobile?' A fat vein pulsed at Chief Inspector Duguid's right temple; never a good sign. McLean fished in his jacket pocket, dug out his phone and flipped it open. The screen was blank; pressing the power button elicited no better response.

'Battery's gone again. That's the third this month.'

'Well, you're an inspector now. You've got your own budget. So get yourself a new phone. Preferably one that works. You might even consider an airwave set.'

McLean shoved the offending article back into his pocket, then handed the folder to Constable Kydd, the PC who had accompanied him to McAllister's building yard and who now looked like she wanted to escape before she was dragged into an argument between two senior officers.

'Can you take that to DC MacBride. And tell him not to lose it. I don't want to end up beholden to Tommy McAllister in any way.'

'Who's McAllister? Another one of your dodgy informants?' Duguid looked past McLean's shoulder at the retreating constable, no doubt wondering why she wasn't working on his investigation.

'He owns the house where they found the young woman's body.'

'Ah, yes. Your ancient ritual sacrifice. I'd heard. Well that should be right up your street, I guess. Rich folk and their unseemly perversions.'

McLean ignored the jibe. He'd heard worse.

'What did you want to see me about, sir?'

'This Smythe case. You've spoken with Jayne, I understand, so you know how important it is that we get a result, and fast.'

McLean nodded, noting Duguid's casual use of the chief superintendent's first name.

'Well, the post-mortem's in half an hour and I want you there. I want you to keep on top of all the forensic information as it comes in; attack the problem from that direction. I'll be interviewing the staff, trying to find out who might have had a grudge against someone like Smythe.'

It made sense to split the investigation up that way. McLean was resigned to the fact that he was going to have to work with Duguid, and decided it would probably be best to try and get off on the right foot.

'Look, sir. About the other night. I'm sorry I stuck my nose in; it was out of line, I know. This is your investigation.'

'It's not a competition, McLean. A man's dead and his killer's walking the streets. That's the only thing that's important right now. As long as you get results, I'll tolerate you on my team. OK?'

So much for building bridges. McLean nodded again, not trusting his mouth to speak only the words Duguid should hear, rather than the ones he was thinking.

'Good. Now get down to the mortuary and see what your ghoul of a friend Cadwallader's come up with.'

Dr Sharp looked up from her desk as McLean walked in. She smiled at him then went back to the game of solitaire on her computer. 'He's not back yet. You'll have to wait,' she said to the screen.

McLean didn't mind, really. Watching dead bodies being cut up wasn't much fun at the best of times, but the building had air conditioning that worked.

'Did you get back any results on the dead girl yet, Tracy?' he asked.

Sighing, she clicked off the screen and turned to an overflowing in-tray. 'Let's see . . .' She leafed through the mess, pulled out a single sheet of paper. 'Here we are. Hmm. More than fifty years ago.'

'Is that it?'

'Well, no. She was killed less than three hundred years ago, but because it was more than fifty years ago we can't pin it down any closer, I'm afraid. Not with carbon dating, anyway.'

'How's that work then?'

'Thank the Americans. They started doing nuclear testing in the forties, but the really big stuff happened in the fifties. Filled the atmosphere with unnatural isotopes. We're full of them, you and me. Anyone alive after about 1955's full of them too. And once they die, the isotopes begin to decay. We can use that to tell how long ago death occurred, but only back to the mid-fifties. Your poor wee girl died before then.'

'I see,' McLean lied. 'What about the preservation? What was used to do that?'

Tracy shuffled in the tray until she came up with another sheaf of papers.

'Nothing.'

'Nothing?'

'Nothing we can detect. As far as the tests go, she simply dried up.'

'It can happen, Tony. Especially if all the blood and bodily fluids have already been removed.' McLean looked around to see Cadwallader walking into the room. He held a small brown paper bag out to his assistant. 'Avocado and bacon. They didn't have any pastrami left.'

Tracy grabbed the bag, delving into it and pulling out a long brown baguette. The sight of it made McLean's stomach gurgle. He realised he hadn't eaten anything all day. Then he remembered what he was here for, and decided food was probably not the best idea.

'Are you here for any particular reason, or did you just drop by to chat up my assistant?' Cadwallader pulled off his jacket and hung it on the door, changed into a clean set of green scrubs.

'Barnaby Smythe. I understand you're examining him this afternoon.'

'I thought he was Dagwood's case.'

'Smythe had a lot of powerful friends. I reckon McIntyre would pull every officer on the force in if she thought it would get the case solved more quickly. Pressure from above.'

'There must be if she's put you and old misery-guts together again. Oh well, let's see if his remains yield up any clues.'

The body awaited them in the post-mortem room, laid out on a stainless-steel table and covered with a shiny white rubber sheet. McLean stood as far back as he could whilst Cadwallader set about Barnaby Smythe, finishing the job that the killer had begun. The pathologist was meticulous in his work, examining the pale, firm flesh and inspecting the gaping wound.

'Subject is in exceptionally good health for his age. Muscle tone suggests he took regular exercise. No signs of bruising or rope marks, suggesting he wasn't tied whilst he was being cut open. This is consistent with the scene in which he was found. Hands are free of cuts and abrasions; he didn't struggle or try to fend off his attacker.'

He moved towards Smythe's head and neck, prising back the neat scar that ran around from ear to ear. 'Throat has been cut with a sharp knife, probably not a medical scalpel. Could be a Stanley knife. There's some tearing, which would indicate the cut was from left to right. Judging by the angle of entry, the killer stood behind the victim while he was seated, held the blade in his right hand and . . .' He made a slashing motion with his hand.

'Was that what killed him?' McLean asked, trying not to imagine what it might have felt like.

'Probably. But he should have been dead from all this.' Cadwallader motioned towards the long slash that ran from Smythe's groin up to his chest. 'The only way his heart could still have been pumping after someone had hacked away at him would be if he had been anaesthetised.'

'But his eyes were open.' McLean remembered the dead stare.

'Oh, you can anaesthetise someone completely and still leave them lucid, Tony. But it's not easy. Anyway, I can't say exactly what was used on him until the blood tests come back. Should know by the end of the day, early tomorrow morning at the latest.'

The pathologist went back to the body and began removing organs. One by one the internals came out, were inspected, placed into white plastic buckets that looked suspiciously like they might have had raspberry ripple ice cream in them in a previous life, and finally handed to Tracy to be weighed. McLean watched with increasing disquiet as Cadwallader peered closely at a bright pink pair of lungs, prodding them with his gloved fingers, almost caressing them.

'How old was Barnaby Smythe?' Cadwallader asked as he held up something brown and slippery. McLean dug out his notebook, then realised it didn't have any useful information on the case in it.

'I don't know. Old. Eighty at least.'

'Yes, that's what I thought.' The pathologist put the liver in a plastic bucket and hung it on the scales. Muttered something under his breath. McLean knew that mutter and felt a twinge in the pit of his stomach that was nothing to do with a lack of food. He knew all too well that sense of dread, of uncovering too many complications in what should have been a straightforward part of the investigation. And Duguid would blame him, even if it wasn't his fault. Shoot the messenger.

'But there's a problem.' It wasn't a question.

'Oh, probably not. I'm just being fanciful, I guess.' Cadwallader brushed aside his concerns with a nonchalant wave of his blood-caked hand. 'It's just such a shame. He must have worked hard all his life to keep this fit and healthy, and then some evil bastard goes and cuts him open.'

9

The Smythe murder incident room was a hive of activity when McLean passed its open door on his way back from the mortuary. Peering in, he could see at least a dozen uniforms tapping information into computers, making phone calls and generally keeping themselves busy, but no sign of Duguid. Thanking small mercies, he carried on down the corridor, stopping only to persuade a vending machine to give him a bottle of cold water on his way to the small incident room he had commandeered for his own investigation. He twisted off the top of the bottle, draining half of the liquid in three long gulps. It hit his stomach with a heavy weight, making it gurgle as he pushed open the door.

Grumpy Bob sat behind one of the tables, his head in his hands as he read a newspaper. He looked up as McLean entered, and guiltily pulled a brown report folder over.

'What've you got there, Bob?'

'Er . . .' Grumpy Bob looked down at the folder, then turned it through a hundred and eighty degrees so he could read what was written on it. Finally he flipped it over, realising that he had been looking at the back. 'It's a report into a break-in at the house of a Mrs Doris Squires. Back in June of last year. Me and the boy went to see her son this morning. He was quite surprised to hear from us. Wondered if we'd found his mother's lost jewellery.'

'Where is Constable MacBride?' McLean looked around the room, but there really wasn't anywhere to hide.

'I sent him on a doughnut run. He should be back any minute.'

'Doughnuts? In this heat?' McLean pulled off his jacket and hung it on the back of the door. He drained the rest of the water, feeling slightly light-headed as the cold liquid washed his throat. His mind jumped back to Barnaby Smythe. A knife opening up his carotid artery, blood spilling out over his ruined body. Knowing he was dead. He shook his head to try and dislodge the image. Perhaps a bit of food would be a good idea after all.

'Did you get anything useful from Mr Squires, then?' he asked.

'Depends what you mean by useful. I think we can safely say old Mrs Squires didn't divulge the alarm code to anyone.'

'They did have an alarm, then?'

'Oh yes. Penstemmin Alarms, remote system. All the bells and whistles you could ask for. But Mrs Squires was very blind and a bit doolally. She never knew the code. Her son always set it. And she died at home, in her sleep. The burglary happened about two weeks later. The day she was buried. There was a note in the paper and an obituary too.'

'Not a care worker, then. But still, it was a Penstemmin alarm system. I guess we'd better check them out. Find out who's their liaison officer at HQ.'

Grumpy Bob's complaint at being given more work to do was cut short by a sharp knock at the door. Before either of them could do anything, the handle dropped and it swung open to reveal a large cardboard box floating in mid-air. Closer inspection revealed the box to have blue-trousered legs beneath it. Small hands clasped at the edges of it and a muffled female voice came from behind.

'Inspector McLean?'

McLean reached out, taking the box. Behind it a red-faced Constable Alison Kydd stood catching her breath.

'Thank you, sir. I'm not sure I could have carried that much longer.'

'What is it, Alison?' Grumpy Bob asked, standing as McLean dumped the box down on the table and on top of Doris Squires.

'The forensics team sent them up. Said they'd run all the tests they could and come up with nothing.'

The opened box revealed a heap of evidence bags, all neatly tagged and labelled; the items found in the hidden alcoves along with thick files of forensic reports and crime-scene photographs. The organs in their preserving jars were still at the mortuary, but there were photographs and test results confirming they were all from the girl. McLean lifted the first bag out, seeing a plain gold tie-pin and a piece of folded card. He leafed through the photographs until he found one of the two items in-situ, set in front of a cracked jar.

'Have we got the other photos from the scene?' he asked. Grumpy Bob shuffled around the table, bent down in the corner and straightened back up again with a cracking of joints and a thick folder. He handed the latter over and McLean opened it up to reveal dozens of glossy A4 prints. 'Right, let's try and get this all in order. Constable . . . Alison, could you give us a hand?'

The constable looked a bit sheepish. 'I'm supposed to be processing actions back in the Smythe incident room, sir.'

'And I'm meant to be collating the forensic reports, but this will probably be more fun. Don't worry. I won't let Dagwood give you a hard time.'

They had all the bags out of the box, arranged around the floor with accompanying photographs, when DC MacBride returned bearing a greasy brown bag full of doughnuts. There had been six alcoves in the round wall of the hidden room, and each had contained a different preserved organ, along with a piece of folded card bearing a single word written in black ink, and one other item. The tie-pin had been found with the jar that had contained the sludgy remains of the girl's kidneys and accompanied by the word 'Jugs'. Placing the evidence bags on top of the photo of the alcove, McLean sorted through the box until he had the next items; a photograph of the perfectly preserved liver, a small silver pill box with some residue of aspirin in it and the word 'Wombat'. Next came the cracked jar that had contained the lungs, a jewel-studded cufflink and the word 'Toots'; then to go with the well-preserved spleen, a Japanese netsuke box containing a few flakes of dried snuff, and the word 'Professor'. Another unbroken specimen jar came next in the circle, containing the dead girl's ovaries and womb. It had been found with a pair of plain wire-framed spectacles and the word 'Grebo'. And finally, placed in an alcove in line with the girl's head, her heart, the word 'Skipper' and a slim silver cigarette case.

An uneasy silence hung over the room as the last pieces of the puzzle were laid out. Of the six specimen jars, two had mysteriously been damaged. Had they been walled up that way? Was it intentional, or just a coincidence?

McLean stood up, his knees popping in protest. 'OK. Who wants to go first?'

A long pause like the schoolroom when teacher's asked a trick question.

'Could they be nicknames?' It was the young Constable Kydd who broke the spell, her voice hesitant.

'Go on,' McLean said.

'Well, there's six of them. Six personal items. Six organs taken from the victim. Six people?'

McLean shuddered. It made sense that there had to be more than one person involved in the killing; it would have been too difficult to hide otherwise. But six?

'I think you're right. There has to be some twisted reason for this; Christ alone knows what. But if there were six people involved and they needed to be associated with the ritual in some way, then if each of them left some token of themselves behind, and took a part of the girl . . .'

'That's . . . disgusting. Why would anyone do that?' Grumpy Bob asked.

'The Fore people of Papua New Guinea used to eat their dead.' All eyes turned on DC MacBride, who turned red around the cheeks at the sudden attention.

'What's that got to do with anything, lad?'

'Well, I don't know. They believed that if you ate someone you took their strength and power for yourself. They used to have big funeral feasts and everyone would get a bit of the body. The chief and the important men would get the best bits, and the women and children were left with the offal and brains.'

'Just how is it you know this, Stuart?' McLean asked.

'Well they all started to die from this mysterious wasting disease. Kuru, I think they called it. It almost completely wiped them out. Scientists reckon one of the ancestors got a form of mad cow disease. You know, Creutzfeldt–Jakob's? And when they ate him, it was passed on to the next generation.'

'A fount of useless information. How's this relevant to our poor wee murdered girl, eh? Nobody's eaten her, have they?' Grumpy Bob said.

'Well, if they each of them took a part of her, then maybe the idea was to . . . I don't know . . . have a bit of her youth for themselves or something.'

'Sounds a bit far-fetched,' Grumpy Bob said.

'Go easy on him, Bob. Right now we've absolutely no idea as to why this girl was murdered. I'm open to suggestions no matter how off the wall they might seem. But I think we should concentrate our efforts on the physical evidence first.' McLean pulled the last bag out of the box. It contained the floral print dress, neatly folded as if it were about to be put on the shelf in Marks & Spencer's.

'Let's see if we can't narrow down the time of her death a bit.'

Detective Chief Inspector Charles Duguid stood in the centre of the Smythe murder incident room, directing operations like a conductor before a particularly inept orchestra. Reluctant officers sidled up to him with actions for approval, or more often ridicule. McLean watched from the doorway for a moment, wondering if the whole thing wouldn't run more smoothly if Duguid weren't actually there.

'No, don't waste your time on that. I need solid leads, not idle speculation.' The chief inspector looked up, saw McLean. 'Ah, inspector.' He managed to make the word sound like an insult. 'Good of you to join us. And Constable Kydd, you might want to check with your commanding officer before swanning off to help out with other investigations.'

McLean was about to defend the constable, but she ducked her head in apology and scurried off to join the line of uniforms working away at computers. He remembered all too well Duguid's man-management skills. Bullying and shouting were high up on the list. Any officer with a sense of self-preservation learnt early on to accept it, and never answer back.

'Well? How did the autopsy go?'

'Death was most likely from blood loss due to the cut throat. Dr Cadwallader's not sure, but he thinks Smythe may have been anaesthetised before he was cut open. There's no sign of struggle, and nothing to suggest he was strapped down. Given that he wasn't dead until after his spleen was removed, he must have been sedated in some manner.'

'Which means the killer would have to have some degree of medical knowledge,' Duguid said. 'Do we know what they used?'

'Blood tests should be complete by this evening, sir. I can't do much more until then.'

'Well, chase them up, man. We can't afford to waste a moment here. The chief constable's been on the phone to me all day asking for updates. The press are going to start reporting this death tonight, and we need to be on top of it.'

So it was important the case be solved quickly to avoid embarrassment to the CC, not because there was a madman out there who liked to cut out people's organs and shove bits of them in their mouths. Interesting set of priorities.

'I'll get right on it, sir,' McLean said, turning to leave.

'What've you got there? Anything important?' Duguid was pointing at the bag in McLean's hand, his tone that of a man grasping at straws. McLean wondered if a day's interviewing had turned up so little. Or maybe the chief inspector just didn't know where to start.

'The Sighthill case. It's the dress the young girl was wearing when she was murdered.' He held up the plastic bag, but Duguid didn't take it. 'I'm going to show it to someone who might know when it was made. Try and narrow down our time of death a bit.'

For a moment McLean thought Duguid was going to shout at him; the way he had when he'd still been a sergeant. The chief inspector's face reddened and a vein started to tick on the side of his forehead. With visible effort, he calmed himself.

'Good. Well, yes. Of course. But don't forget how important this case is.' He swept the room with one hand. 'Chances are your killer's long dead. We need to find a living one.'

He couldn't remember when the shop had first opened. Sometime in the mid-nineties, probably. It was confusing because it looked like one of those places that had always been there. Clerk Street was full of them, catering to the impoverished students who made up more than half of the area's inhabitants. It specialised in second-hand clothing, particularly party dresses and evening wear made in a time when quality mattered. McLean had been in a few times, looking for something different to the mass-produced dark business suits that were his daily uniform since passing his detective exams. But nothing had caught his eye. It was all too contrived, really. In the end he'd been to a bespoke tailor and had a couple of suits made to measure. One of them still hung in his wardrobe unused, the other had been binned after a particularly bloody crime scene had stumped even the most expensive dry-cleaners. Now he wore cheap suits from the high-street chains, and put up with the poor fit.

The woman on the till wore a 1920s flapper-girl outfit, with a long feather boa that must have been sweltering in the late summer heat. She eyed him with suspicion as he approached the desk. He doubted many people his age shopped there. And very few men.

'Do you know much about these clothes?' He waved at the racks, lined up in their decades. 'The styles, when they were popular?'

'What yer wannae know?' The accent quite spoiled the effect of her outfit. Close-up, he revised woman to girl. She couldn't have been much over sixteen, but the outfit aged her.

'When this was made, possibly. Or at least when it might have been worn.' McLean placed the evidence bag on the till. The assistant picked it up, turning it over.

'You trying tae sell it? We don't take stuff like this.'

McLean showed his warrant card. 'I'm conducting an investigation. This was found at the scene of a crime.'

The assistant dropped the bag as if it were a live snake, 'I'll get Mam. She knows more about this stuff 'n me.' She flounced off to the back of the shop, disappearing behind the racks of clothing. A few moments later another woman came out. She was older, though not as old as the clothes she wore, which would have been more appropriate perhaps a century earlier. And there was something very familiar about her.

'It's Jenny. Jenny Spiers, isn't it? I almost didn't recognise you in those clothes.'

'It's all right. We all dress up in our favourite decades. You should see Rae when she's in one of her hippy outfits. How's your gran, by the way?'

McLean looked around the shop, seeing the different eras laid out. He couldn't imagine much of the stuff coming out of the sweatshops of India and Bangladesh these days surviving to take their place in a couple of decades.

'I didn't realise you worked here.' It sounded a bit pathetic even as he said it. Avoiding the question like a politician.

'I own it, actually. Ten years now. Well, technically the bank owns it, but . . .' Jenny tailed off, embarrassed. 'But you didn't come here for a chat, did you, inspector?'

'Tony's fine, really. And I was wondering if you might be able to tell me anything about this dress.' He lifted the plastic once more.

'Can I open the bag?' Jenny asked. McLean nodded and watched as she deftly pulled out the garment, laying it along the wide counter and inspecting it minutely. Her fingers paused, shaking slightly as she saw the faded blood stains.

'It's home-made,' she said finally. 'Hand-stitched by someone very skilled with a needle and thread. The lace was probably bought in, but it's difficult to tell. Very similar in cut to something I've seen before. Let me see.' She went off into the depths of the shop, pushing her way down a narrow aisle between two rows of dresses swathed in plastic and hanging from long racks. Swift hands shuffled their way through the garments before alighting on one, which she brought back to the counter with an air of triumph.

'This is a cocktail dress from the late 1930s. Something rich society girls would have worn just before the war. Your dress you've got here is very similar, almost as if it's been copied. But the fabric's cheaper, and as I said it was hand-stitched. There's no label, either, which suggests to me it was made by someone who couldn't afford to buy.'

'So when might it have been made? How long could it have been worn?'

'Well, it wouldn't have been made in this style much before 1935. Hems were lower before then, and the neckline's all wrong. It's been worn quite a bit; there's some skilled patching around the back and the fabric's thin in places. I'd say it could have been ten years old. They had to make do and mend over the war years.'

The mid-1940s then, the end of the Second World War. McLean wondered what chance there was that anyone connected with the murder would be still alive.

10

He was halfway across the entrance hall of the station when the duty sergeant flagged him down.

'Do you know a chap called Jonas Carstairs?'

McLean racked his brain. The name was familiar.

'Well, he's been calling you all day and leaving messages.'

'Did he say what he wanted?'

'Something about your grandmother. How is the old girl anyway? Any improvement?'

The blood drained from his face. It wasn't as if he had forgotten, exactly. More that he'd compartmentalised her illness for so long, her death hadn't really had time to sink in. He'd managed to duck the question with Jenny Spiers, but there were no secrets in a police station, not for long anyway. And, of course, the quickest way to let everyone know was to tell the duty sergeant. It would only get around quicker if he said it was a secret.

'She passed away last night.'

'Jesus, Tony. What're you doing coming into work then?'

'I don't know. I guess there wasn't a lot else I could do, really. It's not as if it was sudden or anything.' Although, in a way it was. He had grown so accustomed to her being there, comatose, in the hospital. He'd known that she would die sooner or later; there were even times when he had hoped it would be sooner. But he'd expected there to be signs that she was going. He thought he'd have time to prepare.

'Did he leave a number? This Carstairs?'

'Yeah, and he asked if you could call back as soon as possible. You know it wouldn't hurt for you to turn your mobile on from time to time.'

McLean reached into his pocket, pulling out his phone. It was still dead.

'I do, but the batteries keep going flat on me.'

'What about an airwave set then? I don't know why you detectives think you shouldn't have to use them.'

'I've got one somewhere, Pete, but it's even worse. Nothing holds a charge unless it's plugged into the wall. Kind've defeats the point of a mobile, really.'

'Yeah, well. Get something that works, aye?' The sergeant handed McLean a scrap of notepaper with a name and number scribbled on it and buzzed him through into the station.

McLean had an office all to himself; one of the perks of being an inspector. It was a dismal place, with one small window that was obscured by the nearby tenement buildings and so let in very little light. Filing cabinets still full of his predecessor's case notes took up most of the available space, but some genius at geometry had also managed to squeeze in a desk. A pile of folders sat on top of this, a yellow Post-it with 'Urgent!' scribbled on it and underlined three times pasted to the first. He ignored them, sliding round the edge of the desk until he could sit down. Picking up the phone, he dialled the number, glancing at his watch as he did so. It was getting late for office hours, but he had no idea if this was an office number.

'Carstairs Weddell, how may I help?' The swift response and polite tone of the receptionist put him off his stride. McLean recognised the name of the firm of solicitors who had been dealing with his grandmother's affairs since her stroke. He felt a bit of a fool for not remembering.

71

'Oh. Err. Hello. Could I speak to Mr Jonas Carstairs, please?'
Previously he'd only ever dealt with a junior clerk, Perkins or
Peterson or something like that. It seemed odd that the senior
partner would contact him in person.

'May I ask who's speaking, please?'

'McLean. Anthony McLean.'

'One moment, inspector. I'll put you right through.' Once
again he was caught out by someone knowing more about him
than he did about them. He had no time to be any more than
surprised. The brief holding music was cut off by a click.

'Detective Inspector McLean, Jonas Carstairs here. I'm so
sorry to hear about your grandmother's passing. She was a great
woman in her time, Esther.'

'I take it you knew her, Mr Carstairs.'

'Jonas, please. And yes, I've known her a long time. Far longer
than I've been acting as her solicitor. That's what I wanted to talk
to you about. She appointed me as executor of her will. I'd appreciate it if you could drop by my office sometime soon to sort a
few things out.'

'OK. Would tomorrow be all right? Only it's getting late and I
didn't really sleep last night.' McLean rubbed at his eyes with the
heel of his free hand, realising as he voiced the thought just how
exhausted he was.

'Of course. I understand. And don't worry about the arrangements. I've got everything in hand. There'll be an announcement
in the *Scotsman* tomorrow; they'll probably run an obituary too.
And Esther didn't want a church funeral, so it'll just be a simple
memorial service at Mortonhall. I'll let you know as soon as we
can get a slot booked. Would you like me to organise a wake? I
know how busy you officers of the law can be.'

McLean only half took in what was being said. He had thought about all the little things that needed to be done now that his grandmother had actually died, but there was so much else going on in his head it was easy to lose track. The cocktail dress with its floral pattern, securely wrapped in its evidence bag, lay on the desk in front of him, and for a moment he couldn't remember what it was there for. He needed food, and then he needed sleep.

'Yes, please,' he said finally. He thanked the solicitor and arranged to go to the firm's offices at ten the next day, then hung up. The evening sun painted the tenements outside a warm ochre, but little of the light made it into his tiny office. It was too stuffy, and as he leant back in his chair to stretch, resting his head against the cool wall behind him, McLean closed his eyes for just a moment.

She is naked as the day, a skinny thing with bone-thin legs and arms. Her hair hangs lank from her skeletal head, her eyes sunk deep in their sockets. As she walks towards him, she holds out her hands, reaching forward, begging him to help her. Then she stumbles, and a wound appears in her belly, ripping upwards from her crotch to her cleavage. She stops, grasps at her entrails as they start to drop to the ground, scooping them back with one arm, still reaching for him with the other. She shuffles forward again, slower this time, her dark eyes pleading.

He wants to look away, but he is trapped, immobile. He can't even close his eyes. All he can do is watch as she falls to her knees, spilling her innards on the ground, still trying to crawl towards him.

'Inspector.'

Her voice is pain. And as he hears it, her face begins to change, her skin drying, stretching even tauter over her cheekbones. Her eyes draw further back into her head and her lips curl in a grimace, a parody of a smile.

'Inspector!'

She is right beside him now, her free hand reaching out to his shoulder, touching him, shaking him. Her other hand struggles to keep her intestines inside, like a lonely housewife answering the postman's knock in her dressing gown. Bits of her start to fall out; her kidneys, her liver, her spleen.

'Tony, wake up!'

With a snap, McLean opened his eyes, almost falling out of his chair as his perceptions shifted from the dream back to reality. Chief Superintendent McIntyre stood beside his desk, looking down at him with a mixture of irritation and concern across her face.

'Sleeping on the job now? That's not the kind of behaviour I expected when I recommended you for promotion.'

'I'm sorry, ma'am.' McLean shook his head slightly, trying to dislodge the disturbing image of the eviscerated girl. 'It's this heat. I only closed my eyes for a moment. I . . .' He stopped when he realised McIntyre was trying to suppress a smirk.

'I'm just joking, Tony. You look done in. You should go home and get some rest.' She sat herself down on the edge of the desk. There was room in the office for one other chair, but it was piled high with box files. 'Sergeant Murray told me about your gran. I'm very sorry.'

'She died a long time ago, really.' McLean felt slightly uneasy with the chief superintendent perched above him. He knew he should stand, but to do so now would be even more awkward.

'Maybe, but you have to deal with it now, Tony. And I know you miss her.'

'You know my folks died when I was four, right? Gran raised me as if I were my dad. It must have been hard for her having me around as a reminder of him.'

'And what about you? I can't imagine what it must have been like, to lose both your parents at such a young age.'

McLean leant forward on the desk, rubbing at his eyes. These were old wounds, long since healed over. He really didn't want to be picking at the scars. But his grandmother's death was going to do just that. Perhaps one more reason why he was finding it hard to accept she was really gone.

He reached out for the evidence bag and the floral dress, as much for something to do with his hands as anything else.

'We've managed to pin down the time of death to the mid-1940s.'

'I'm sorry?' McIntyre looked at him blankly.

'The dead girl in the house in Sighthill. Her dress was probably ten years old, and couldn't have been made before 1935. Carbon dating puts her death before 1950. Best guess is sometime around the end of the Second World War.'

'So chances are her killer is dead already.'

'Killers. Plural. We reckon there were six of them.' McLean summed up the investigation as far as it had progressed. McIntyre sat on the edge of his desk, silently listening as he marshalled his thoughts so far. It was very little to go on.

'What about Smythe?'

The question threw him. 'You think there's a connection?'

'No, no. Sorry. I meant what about the Smythe investigation. How are we getting on with that?'

'The PM confirms he was murdered and that probable cause of death was blood loss. I'm still waiting on toxicology reports – whoever did this must have used some powerful anaesthetic. That alone should narrow down our suspect list. Duguid was concentrating on interviewing; I've not had a chance to catch up with him yet.'

'OK. We can pull it all together at the briefing tomorrow. But I want you to concentrate on Smythe as much as possible. Your young woman's trail's not going to get any colder now. Not after sixty years.'

It made sense, of course; far more important to catch a killer who had struck just twenty-four hours ago. Why then did he feel the need to concentrate on the girl's murder? Was it simply because he didn't like working with Dagwood? McLean stifled a yawn, trying not to look at the pile of papers on his desk requiring his urgent underlined-three-times attention. They had the suspicious look of overtime forms and expenses claims to be ratified with his budget for the quarter. He started to reach for the top one, but McIntyre stopped him. Her hand was soft; her grip firm.

'Go home, Tony. Have an early night. Get some sleep. You'll be fresher in the morning.'

'Is that an order, ma'am?'

'Yes, inspector. It is.'

11

His mind is a whirl of confusion. He doesn't know this city, doesn't understand the harsh language they speak here. He feels sick, right down to his core. His breathing is ragged, and every gasp hurts in his throat, his chest burning. Once he was strong, he knows this even though he can't remember his name. Once he could carry a dozen sheaves of grain at a time, clear a whole field in an afternoon under the hot sun. Now his back is bent, his legs weak and faltering. When did he become old like his father? What happened to his life?

Noise spills out from a nearby building. Its tall glass windows are frosted, but he can see the colourful shadows of people moving about inside. The central door swings wide and a young woman staggers out, closely followed by two more. They are laughing, jabbering away at each other with words he doesn't recognise. Drunk and happy, they don't see him watching from the other side of the street. Their high heels clatter on the pavement as they stagger away, their short skirts riding up their legs, crop-tops revealing flaccid white flesh.

He catches glimpses of memory. Someone doing terrible things. More pale flesh, parted by a sharp knife. Blood welling up from the edges of the cut. Rage at an ancient injustice. Something dark and wet and slippery underneath. These are not his memories. Or maybe they are. He no longer knows what is real.

The air is warm; a heavy moist blanket under the dark night

sky. Orange street lamps reflect off dull clouds overhead, casting everything in a hellish light. He is slick with sweat and his head pounds to the rhythm of his heart. His throat feels suddenly dry and he knows now what the building across the road is.

The noise stabs at him as he pushes open the heavy door. It envelops him in a smell of unwashed bodies, deodorant, perfume, beer, food. There are hundreds of people standing, sitting, shouting at each other to be heard over the tuneless music that fills everything. No one seems to notice him as he steps into the throng.

He looks at his hands, so familiar. These are hands that have built walls, caressed lovers, held a tiny baby whose name is as forgotten to him as his own. These are hands crusted with dried blood, worn into the wrinkles and underneath the short fingernails. These are the hands that wielded the knife. That violated another man so completely. The hands that sought vengeance for all the wrongs done to him and his kind.

He sees the sign, understands one small thing in this foreign place. Is it the sickness that has weakened him, or the terrible images flooding his mind that drives him there? Either way, he is in the toilet, hunched over the bowl, vomiting. Or at least trying to vomit. Nothing but dry heaves, his stomach empty.

He grabs paper, wipes his face and hands, flushes. When he stands up, the world seems to tilt dangerously. He is breathless, unknowing. There are other people in the toilet, laughing at him. Moving around him like bullies in the schoolyard. He can't focus, can only remember the terrible feel of the knife in his hand, the power that flowed through him as he used it, the righteous fury. He can feel it again, heavy against his palm.

They're not laughing now. A silence has fallen on the place. Even the droning thump of the music outside is still. He looks around, noticing for the first time the long mirror in front of him. It's hard to make out anything past the images of carnage filling his mind. But he can see a man he doesn't recognise, haggard and gaunt, dressed in filthy clothes, hair matted and grey. He watches, fascinated, terrified, as the man reaches up with one hand. A fist is clamped around a short builder's knife, the blade angled inwards towards his exposed throat. He has done this before, he thinks, as he feels the welcome touch of cold steel on his flesh.

Blood sprays across the mirror.

12

The station was in turmoil when McLean came in the next morning. A take-away curry and an early night had left him feeling much better than the previous day's brain-dead zombie. He was half an hour early for the morning briefing on the Smythe case, and had hoped he might use the time to make a start on his outstanding paperwork. As he approached the incident room on his way to the stairs, he could hear Dagwood's distinctive voice rumbling out through the open door.

'Bloody marvellous. Can't keep the buggers out, and when they come here they're all nutcases . . .'

He peered around the door frame, hoping to get the lay of the room before stepping past. The chief inspector took the same moment to break off from his conversation with a pair of uniformed sergeants and look around.

'Ah, McLean. Good. Glad to see you're in early. You can help with the tidying up.'

'Tidying up, sir?' McLean looked around the room and saw constables busy packing things into boxes, pulling photographs from the walls and rubbing down the whiteboards.

'Yes, Tony. We got him last night. No doubting his guilt, his prints were all over Smythe's library.'

'You caught the killer?' McLean was finding it hard to reconcile the point they had reached in the investigation yesterday evening with what he was being told. He hoped his mouth wasn't gaping open. 'How?'

'Well, I wouldn't say exactly caught,' Duguid said. 'This man walked into a pub just off St Andrew's Square about half eleven last night. Went into the gents' and cut his own throat. It was even the same knife he used on Smythe.'

'Is he all right?'

'No of course he's not all right, you idiot. He's dead. Do you think we'd be taking this all down if we had him in the cells waiting for interrogation?'

'No, sir. Of course not.' McLean watched the dismantling of the incident room proceed apace. 'Who was he?'

'Illegal immigrant. Name of Akimbo or something. I can never tell how you're supposed to pronounce these foreign names.'

'Who identified him?'

'Some wifey from SOC; Baird, I think she's called. The fingerprint search came up blank, but then she had the bright idea to try the illegal immigrants register. This chap should have been locked up. He was due to be shipped back to Fuzzistan or wherever it is he came from.'

McLean tried to ignore Duguid's casual racism. The chief inspector was a walking reminder of all that was wrong with the force. The sooner the man retired, the better.

'I guess the chief super will be happy, no doubt the chief constable too. I know there was a lot of pressure for a quick result.'

'Quite right. Which is why we need the report typed up and on Jayne's desk by the end of the day. I don't think the procurator fiscal will want to take it any further, but we've got to go through the motions. You'll need to attend the post-mortem, just to make sure there's no nasty surprises. But the evidence is pretty compelling.

He had Smythe's blood type on his clothes. DNA results will confirm it, I'm sure. He's our man.'

Oh great. Another chance to watch a dead body being cut up. 'What time's the PM, sir?' McLean looked at his watch. Seven o'clock in the morning.

'Ten, I think. You'd better phone and check.'

'Ten. I'm supposed to be meeting –' But McLean stopped. He knew there was no point in complaining to Duguid. It would only provoke the man into one of his tirades. 'I'll reschedule.'

'You do that, McLean.'

The small incident room was empty when McLean finally managed to escape from Duguid and make his way to the back of the station. Grumpy Bob's newspaper lay on one of the two tables; Constable MacBride had piled a neat stack of files on the other. He flicked through them quickly, burglary reports stretching back five years. Post-it notes with questions on them poked out between the pages. Well, at least someone had been busy.

The photographs of the organs and other artefacts from the walled-up basement were pinned to one wall, arranged in a circle just as they had been found. A full-on A3 photograph of the girl's twisted, violated body hung in the middle of the circle. He was staring at it still some minutes later when the door nudged open.

'Morning, sir. Hear the news?' DC MacBride looked like he had scrubbed himself pink. His hair was still slightly damp from showering and his smooth, round face held an expression of innocent hope and excitement.

'News? Oh, Smythe's killer. Don't you think it's a bit odd?'

'How so, sir?'

'Well, why'd he do it? Why did he break into some old man's

82

house and cut him open? Why shove his spleen in his mouth? And why kill himself just days later?'

'Well, he was an illegal immigrant, wasn't he?'

McLean bristled. 'Don't start on that, please. They're not all coming to rape our women and steal our jobs, you know. It's bad enough hearing that nonsense from Dagwood.'

'That's not what I meant, sir.' MacBride's face went pinker still, the lobes of his ears turning almost blood-red. 'I meant he might have had a grudge against Smythe because he was chair of the Immigration Appeals Board.'

'Was he? How'd you know that?'

'Alison . . . Er, Constable Kydd told me, sir.'

It was McLean's turn to feel the warmth of embarrassment. 'I'm sorry, Stuart. I didn't mean to snap at you. What else do you know about Smythe that I missed?'

'Well, sir, he was eighty-four but still worked every day. He sat on the boards of a dozen different companies and owned controlling interests in at least two biotech start-ups. He took over his father's merchant bank just after the war and built it into one of the largest financial institutions in the city before selling out just before the dotcom bubble burst. Since then he's been mostly setting up charitable trusts for various good causes. He had a permanent staff of three at his city house, all of whom had been given the night off when he was killed. Apparently that wasn't unusual; he quite often sent them away for the evening so he could be alone.'

McLean listened to more potted history, noting as he did that the constable seemed to have committed the detail to memory. Apart from the tenuous connection with illegal immigration and repatriation, there was absolutely nothing to connect Smythe with the man who had murdered him.

'What was the killer's name again?'

This time MacBride pulled out his notebook, licking the tip of his finger before leafing through the pages.

'Jonathan Okolo. Apparently he came from Nigeria. Applied for asylum three years ago but was turned down. He was being held in a secure facility until April, "awaiting repatriation", the records say. No one's quite sure how he escaped, but there's been a few others disappear from there in the last year or so.'

'Do you have their names?'

'No, sir. But I'm sure I could find them out. Why?'

'I don't know, really. Duguid's going to want to wash his hands of this whole thing as soon as possible. Quite likely the chief constable and all the top brass will be happy to let it lie too. If I had half a brain I'd do the same. But I've a nasty feeling we haven't heard the last of Jonathan Okolo yet. I wouldn't mind being one step ahead of the game when his name pops up again.'

'I'll do some digging, sir.' MacBride made a note in his book, putting it carefully away. McLean wondered what he had done with his own notebook; it was probably upstairs in his office. Along with all that paperwork which wouldn't do itself.

'What have you got lined up for today then, constable?'

'Detective Sergeant Laird and I are meant to be interviewing some of these burglary victims, sir. Just as soon as he gets in.'

'Well, Grumpy Bob always was more of a night-shift person.' From the look on MacBride's face McLean reckoned he'd never heard the sergeant referred to as Grumpy Bob before. 'I tell you what, constable. You tell him when he gets in that he can do those interviews on his own. He can take a uniform with him if he feels lonely. I want you to spend the next hour tracking down what you can about Okolo and his friends. Then you and me're going to take a trip down to the Cowgate and watch Dr Cadwallader cut him open.'

'Um, do I have to sir?' MacBride's ruddy complexion paled to a pasty green.

'You've been to post-mortems before haven't you, constable?'

'Yes sir, I have. A couple. That's why I'd rather be somewhere else.'

He found his notebook where he had last left it, sitting under the evidence bag containing the dead girl's floral dress, on his desk. McLean slipped it into his pocket, reminding himself to take the dress back down to the incident room. The scrap of paper with Carstairs' number on it was still lying beside the phone. He rang through, rearranging their meeting for later in the afternoon, then switched on his computer and pulled the pile of papers towards him. He understood the need for full accounting and proper procedure; he just wished someone else could do it for him.

It was mind-numbing work, requiring just too much concentration for him to mull things over in his mind whilst he was doing it. And all the while, out of the corner of his eye, he could see the dress. Finally when he had reached a point optimistically halfway down the pile, he took out his notebook, pushed his chair back from the desk and flicked through the pages.

He came almost immediately to the strange swirling patterns he had seen in the basement room, or at least had thought he had seen. They had suggested that the murder was some form of ritual sacrifice, but the hidden alcoves had revealed far more obvious and tempting clues. So he had concentrated on the names, the preserved organs and the personal items. But as his old mentor had always told him, it was usually the least obvious things that were the key. McLean glanced at his watch; it was half-past nine. He logged off the computer, grabbed the dress and headed back down to the tiny incident room. Grumpy Bob was there, reading the paper again. Constable MacBride concentrated on the screen of his laptop , tapping furiously at the keys.

'Morning, sir,' Grumpy Bob folded his paper and stuck it in a box under the table.

'Morning, Bob. You got the photos from the murder scene?'

Grumpy Bob looked over at MacBride but got no response, and so had to fetch the box from the corner himself. He sat it down on the table and pulled out a handful of glossy prints.

'What were you looking for, sir?'

'There should be a series of pictures of the floor about a foot or so in from the wall.'

'Aye, I wondered why the photographer took those.' Grumpy Bob guddled around some more, coming out with a handful of sheets. He started to lay them out on the table, occasionally refer-ring to numbers printed on the backs.

'I asked him to.' McLean studied the first of the photos, then the next and the next. They all looked the same; washed-out with the flash, the floor was smooth, featureless wood with absolutely no markings on it at all. He pulled out his notebook and looked at the shapes he had drawn. The shapes he was certain he had seen.

'Is this all of them?' he asked Bob when he had studied every picture and come up with nothing.

'Far as I know.'

'Well get onto the SOC team and double-check will you, Bob? I'm looking for pictures of the floor that show markings like this.' He showed the images in his notebook to the sergeant.

'Can't Constable MacBride do it?' Bob complained. 'You know he's much better at all this technical stuff than me.'

'Sorry, Bob. He's coming with me.' He turned to the constable. 'You finished there?'

'Just about, sir. One moment.' MacBride tapped a couple of

keys, then folded the notebook flat. 'I'll run past the printer and pick that up on our way out. Unless you'd prefer Sergeant Laird to go with you to the post-mortem, sir?' There was hope in his voice.

McLean smiled. 'I suspect Bob's only just had his breakfast, constable. And I for one have no desire to know what it was.'

13

'That's three times in forty-eight hours, inspector. If I didn't know better I'd say you were stalking me.' Dr Sharp was waiting for them as they walked into the mortuary. 'Who's your handsome sidekick?'

'This is Detective Constable MacBride. Go easy on him, it's his first time.' McLean ignored MacBride's reddening face. 'Is the doctor in?' he asked.

'Just getting prepped,' Tracy said. 'Go right ahead.'

The examination room was not much changed from the day before. Only the body laid out on the slab was different. The pathologist greeted them as they walked in.

'Ah, Tony. I can see you've not got the hang of delegation yet. Normally when you send a junior officer to do something for you, it's because you're not intending to come along yourself. Why'd you think Dagwood sent you in the first place.'

'Because this place reminds him too much of home?'

'Well, quite.' Cadwallader smirked. 'Shall we get down to business?'

As if she had been waiting for the cue, Tracy appeared from the little room that served as their office. She had donned a set of scrubs and long rubber gloves and wheeled a steel trolley on which had been laid out various instruments of torture. McLean could feel Constable MacBride tense beside him, rocking slightly on his heels.

'Subject is male, African, six foot two. At a guess I'd say late fifties.'

'Forty-four.' MacBride's voice was slightly higher than usual, and there'd been no cutting yet.

'I'm sorry?' Cadwallader put his hand over the microphone hanging above the table.

'He was forty-four, sir. It says so in his file.' MacBride held up the sheaf of papers he had retrieved from the printer on their way out.

'Well, he doesn't look it. Tracy, have we got the right body?'

The assistant checked her paperwork, looked at the tag on the dead man's foot, then went over to the racks of cold cabinets, opening a couple and peering inside before coming back.

'Yup,' she said. 'Jonathan Okolo. Brought in late last night. Identified by fingerprints from his immigration file.'

'Well, that is odd.' Cadwallader turned back to his patient. 'If he's only forty-four, I hate to think what kind of life he's had. OK, let's continue.' He went on, examining the body minutely.

'His hands are rough, fingernails chipped and short. He has a couple of recent scars consistent with splinters in his palms and fingers. Manual labourer of some kind, though I can't imagine he'd be much good at it, given his health. Ah, here we go.' The pathologist turned his attention to the dead man's head, reaching into his thinning, tight-curled, grey hair with a pair of forceps. 'Specimen jar, please, Tracy. If I'm not mistaken, that's plaster. His hair's full of it.'

McLean noticed movement out of the corner of his eye and turned to see Constable MacBride furiously scribbling down notes. He smiled; all of this would be typed up and presented to them within the day, but a little enthusiasm never hurt. And besides, it might distract the constable from what was coming next.

There was a certain elegance to the way a skilled pathologist opened up a body. Cadwallader was perhaps the best McLean had ever watched. His deft touch and quiet banter with his assistant went some way towards making the whole process bearable. Even so, he was glad when it was all over and the job of stitching up began. It meant they could get out of the examination room, which in turn meant they could soon leave the building.

'What's the verdict, Angus? Can you save him?' McLean saw the joke raise a flicker of a smile, but it was soon replaced with a worried frown.

'I'm surprised he lived long enough to kill Smythe, let alone himself,' Cadwallader said.

'What do you mean?'

'He has advanced emphysema, acute cirrhosis of the liver, his kidneys are diseased. Christ alone knows how a heart with so much scar tissue on it could possibly beat regularly enough to let him walk.'

'Are you suggesting he didn't kill Smythe?' A cold shiver ran down McLean's spine.

'Oh, he killed him all right. His clothes were soaked in Smythe's blood and there are traces of it under his fingernails. That Stanley knife is a perfect fit for the notches in his neck vertebrae. He's definitely your man.'

'Could he have had an accomplice?' McLean had that dull sensation in the pit of his stomach. He knew he'd be unpopular for even mentioning the possibility, but he couldn't ignore it.

'You're the detective, Tony. You tell me.'

14

Carstairs Weddell occupied the entirety of a large Georgian terraced house in the west end of the city. Where the more modern and progressive law firms had moved into purpose-built offices on the Lothian Road or further out towards Gogarburn, this one small partnership had held out against the tides of change. McLean remembered a time, not so long ago, when all the old Edinburgh family firms, the lawyers and stockbrokers, merchant bankers and importers of fine wares had their offices in the grand old houses of the west end. Now the streets were full of basement restaurants, boutique shops, health clubs and expensive apartments. Times changed, but the city always adapted.

He was an hour early for his appointment, but the secretary told him that she didn't think it would be a problem. She left him waiting in an elegant reception room, lined with portraits of stern-faced men and furnished with comfortable leather armchairs. It was more like a gentleman's club than anything else, but at least it was cool compared with the ever-rising heat outside.

'Inspector McLean. It's good to see you again.' McLean looked around at the voice. He'd not heard the door open, but now a white-haired man with thin round metal-rimmed spectacles stood with his hand outstretched. McLean shook it.

'Mr Carstairs. Have we met before?' There was something familiar about him. It was always possible that he had been in court whilst

McLean was giving evidence, of course. Perhaps he had been cross-examined by the lawyer.

'I should think so. It's been quite a few years, though. Esther used to hold such wonderful parties, but she stopped around the time you went off to university. I never did find out why.'

McLean pictured the string of people who had frequently turned up at his grandmother's house. The only thing he could remember about most of them was that they had been very old. But then, so had his grandmother so that was hardly surprising. Jonas Carstairs was old now, but he would have been too young surely to have been part of that set.

'I think she always wanted to be a recluse, Mr Carstairs. She just thought it would be good for me to meet people. When I left home and moved to Newington, she stopped.'

Carstairs nodded, as if that made perfect sense to him. 'Please, call me Jonas.' He pulled a pocket watch from his waistcoat, flipped it open to see the time, then carefully slid it back again in a fluid, practised motion.

'What would you say to a spot of lunch? There's a new place opened up just around the corner from here and I've heard it's very good.'

McLean thought about the pile of papers on his desk waiting to be sorted; the girl dead so long that a few more hours would make no difference. Grumpy Bob had the burglary investigation in hand, and MacBride would be busy ferreting out whatever information on Jonathan Okolo he could find. He'd really only be getting in the way.

'That sounds like a good idea to me, Jonas. But if I'm off duty, you'll have to stop calling me inspector.'

It wasn't the kind of eating establishment McLean was used to visiting. Newly opened, and tucked into a basement, it was quite busy, filled with the subdued noise of contented customers enjoying a leisurely lunch. They were shown to a small table in an alcove with a window that looked out onto a recess below the pavement level. Looking up towards the sky, McLean realised he could see up the skirt of any women who walked past, and concentrated instead on the menu.

'They do fish rather well, I'm told,' Carstairs said. 'I expect the wild salmon will be good at this time of year.'

McLean ordered the salmon, suppressing the urge to ask for chips with it, and restricted himself to sparkling mineral water. It arrived in a blue tear-drop shaped bottle with something written on it in Welsh.

'In the old days, apothecaries kept poisons in blue bottles. That way they knew not to drink them.' He poured himself a glassful and offered the same to the lawyer.

'Well, Edinburgh has its fair share of poisoners, as I've no doubt you know. Have you been to the Pathology Museum at the Surgeons' Hall?'

'Angus Cadwallader showed me around it a couple of years back. When I was still just a sergeant.'

'Ah yes, Angus. He has a distressing habit of leaving the theatre halfway through a performance. The job, no doubt.'

They talked about police work, legal matters and those few mutual friends and acquaintances they could identify until the food arrived. McLean was only half disappointed to find his salmon poached rather than battered and deep fried. It wasn't that he didn't appreciate fine food, more that he rarely had the time for it. He couldn't remember the last time he'd been to a restaurant like this one.

'You're not married, Tony?' Carstairs' question was innocent enough, but it brought an uncomfortable silence as McLean realised he did remember the last time he'd been to a fine restaurant like this one. His companion then had been far younger, prettier and completely unaware of the life-changing question he had been screwing up his courage to pop.

'No,' he said, aware that his voice was flat, unable to do anything about that.

'Seeing anyone?'

'No.'

'A shame. Young man like you should have a wife to look after him. I'm sure Esther would have –'

'There was someone. A few years back. We were engaged. She . . . she died.' McLean could still see her face, eyes closed, skin as smooth as alabaster and just as white. Lips blue and long black hair splayed out around her, tugged by the icy, sluggish flow of the Water of Leith.

'I'm so sorry. I didn't know.' Carstairs' voice cut through his reminiscing, and McLean knew, somehow, that the old lawyer was lying. There couldn't be many people in the city who didn't remember the story.

'You said you needed to see me about my grandmother's will,' he said, latching on to the first subject he could think of.

'Yes, indeed I did. But I thought it might be nice to catch up with an old family friend first. You won't be surprised to learn that Esther left everything to you, of course. She had no one else to give it to.'

'I'd really not given it much thought, to be honest. I'm finding it hard to come to terms with the fact that she's gone. Have to keep reminding myself I don't need to stop by the hospital and visit her this evening.'

Carstairs said nothing, and they continued to eat in silence for a while. The lawyer cleaned his plate, wiping at his face with the soft white napkin. Only then did he speak.

'The funeral will be on Monday. Ten o'clock at Mortonhall. A notice went in today's *Scotsman*.'

McLean nodded, abandoning the rest of his meal. Delicious though it was, he had quite lost his appetite.

Back at the office, Carstairs led him through to a large room at the rear of the building, overlooking a well-tended garden. An antique desk angled into one corner of the room, but Carstairs indicated to McLean to sit in one of the leather armchairs beside the empty fireplace before taking the other for himself. It reminded the inspector of his chat with the superintendent the day before. Formal informality. A thick folder tied together with black ribbon waited on the low mahogany table that sat between them. Carstairs leant forward, picking up the folder and untying the ribbon. McLean couldn't help but notice that he moved with remarkable agility and grace for a man of his age. Like a younger actor playing the role of an old man.

'This is a summary of your grandmother's estate at the time of her death. We've administered her affairs for many years now, since your grandfather died, in fact. She had quite a large portfolio of shares as well as her property.'

'She did?' McLean was genuinely astonished. He'd known his grandmother was comfortable, but she'd never shown any signs of being rich. Just an old lady who'd inherited the family home. A doctor who'd worked hard and retired on a comfortable pension.

'Oh yes. Esther was quite the shrewd investor. Some of her recommendations surprised even our own finance department, but she rarely lost money.'

'How is it I knew nothing of this?' McLean didn't know whether he was shocked or angry.

'Your grandmother gave me power of attorney long before she had her stroke, Anthony.' Carstairs' voice was soft, calming, as if he knew that the news he was bringing might be disturbing. 'She also asked me specifically not to disclose her assets to you before she died. She was quite old-fashioned in her thinking, was Esther. I suspect she thought you might be distracted from pursuing a career if you knew you stood to inherit a large estate.'

McLean couldn't argue. That sounded so like his grandmother he could almost picture her, sitting in her favourite armchair by the fire, lecturing him about the importance of hard work. She also had a mischievous sense of humour, and somewhere right now she was laughing her head off. He was surprised to find a smile forming on his lips as he thought about her. It was the first time in months he'd remembered her as a vibrant, living person, rather than the worse-than-dead cabbage she had become.

'Do you have any idea what it's all worth?' The question sounded mercenary to his ears, but he couldn't think of anything else to say.

'A valuation on the property is a best estimate from our conveyancing department. The shares are priced as of the close of the market the day after she died. Obviously there are sundry other items; I suspect the furnishings and pictures in the house are worth something, and there's a few other bits and bobs. Esther always did have a good eye.' Carstairs took a single sheet from the top of the file and placed it on the table, twirling it around so that McLean could read it.

He picked it up with trembling fingers, trying to take in all the different columns and figures, until his eyes lighted on a total underlined and in bold at the bottom.

'Bloody hell.'

His grandmother had left him a large house and a portfolio of shares worth considerably more than five million pounds.

15

Force HQ was almost on the way back to the station from the offices of Carstairs Weddell. Near enough that McLean felt justified in taking the detour. That the longer he delayed his return the greater the chance of missing Duguid had nothing to do with his decision, of course. He needed to talk to someone about crime-scene photographs, that was it. At least that's what he told himself.

As usual, the SOC section was almost completely empty. The bored receptionist buzzed him through to deserted corridors, but at least in here the air conditioning worked. Down in the basement, lit by narrow windows high in the walls, he found the photography lab, its door propped open with a metal stool. He knocked, shouted 'Hello', and wandered in. The room was filled with quietly humming machinery, none of whose function he could begin to guess. A wooden counter ran along the far wall, under the high-set windows, and a row of computers with enormous flat-panel monitors flickered and whined. At the furthest, a lone figure sat hunched in front of a blurred picture. She seemed completely absorbed in whatever task she was performing.

'Hello?' McLean said again, then noticed the white earphone leads. He approached slowly, trying to catch the officer's attention. But the closer he came, the more he could hear the racket coming from her earphones. There was no easy way to do this.

'Jesus! You nearly gave me a heart attack.' The woman clutched one hand to her chest, pulling out her earphones and dropping them onto the desk. The cord snaked into the computer in front of her. McLean recognised her now; she had been at the burglary scene looking for fingerprints, and at Smythe's house too.

'I'm sorry. I tried shouting . . .'

'Yeah. OK. I guess I was playing it a bit loud. What can I do for you, inspector? It's not often we get one of the high heidyins down here in the basement.'

'It's cooler than my incident room.' McLean didn't complain at being accused of seniority; as the most recently promoted inspector on the force, he was more often treated as the new boy. 'And I was wondering if you had the originals of those crime-scene photos from the house in Sighthill.'

'Sergeant Laird mentioned something about that.' She reached for the mouse, clicking several windows closed in quick succession. McLean thought he saw a page of thumbnails from Smythe's crime scene amongst the images, but before he could be sure it was gone. Then the screen filled up with a series of pictures all looking identical.

'Forty-five high-resolution digital images of a piece of floor. I remember Malky complaining about that; you made him go back into the room with the dead body. Odd, really. It's not as if he hasn't photographed dozens over the years, maybe hundreds. Sorry, I'm blethering. What was it you wanted to see?'

McLean took out his notebook, flipping the pages until he found the first sketch. He cast his mind back to the scene, tried to remember what he had told the photographer to shoot first.

'I saw markings on the floor, near where the wall had been knocked in. They looked like this.' He showed her the picture. She clicked on the first image and it zoomed to fill the screen. There was the smooth wooden floor, a bit rubble-strewn at the edge, but no markings, no sigils.

'That's definitely where I saw them. Could the flash have washed them out?'

'Let's see.' The SOC officer clicked her mouse, bringing up menus and making selections with bewildering speed. Whatever program she was using, she was completely at home with it. The picture greyed, faded, brightened, lost its contrast and then went negative. Still it was roughly the same. There was nothing more to see than in the original.

'Nothing, I'm afraid. Are you sure it wasn't just shadows? The arc lights can throw some pretty odd ones, especially in an enclosed space.'

'Well, it's possible I suppose. But the positioning made me think there was a circle, with six points marked on it. And you know what we found hidden in the walls at each of those points.'

'Hmmm. Well, there's one more thing I could try. Pull up a seat. It'll take a minute or two to process.'

'Thanks . . . umm, it's Ms Baird, isn't it?' McLean settled himself into the next chair along, noting that it was far more comfortable than either one in his office, and made those in the tiny incident room feel like splinter-covered wooden stools. SOC obviously had a better equipment budget than CID. Or a more creative accountant.

'Miss, actually. But aye, it is. How'd you know that?'

'I'm a detective. It's my job to work these things out.' He noticed her face redden slightly under her unruly mop of jet black hair. She scratched her button nose in an unconscious, reflex gesture, her eyes darting back to the screen where an unconvincing hourglass was emptying and turning, emptying and turning.

'Well then, tell me this, Mr Smarty-Pants Detective. If you're so observant, how come you didn't notice the sign on the door over there. The one that says "No Unauthorised Access" on it?'

McLean looked back over his shoulder to the far side of the room. The door was wide open to the corridor beyond, held back by a chair wedged under the handle. There was no sign on it apart from a room number – B12. He looked back, puzzled, to a wide smile.

'Gotcha. Ah, here we are.' She turned back to the screen, clicking the mouse again to focus on one corner of the newly processed picture. 'Let's try and enhance . . . Yes, there you go. You were right.'

McLean peered at the screen, screwing his eyes up against the glare. Whatever the SOC officer had done, it had rendered most of the image almost pure white. The rubble of the broken wall seemed to float above the floor, etched in the air with sharply contrasting thin black lines. And just past them, the palest shade of grey over the white, something of the swirling sigil patterns.

'What did you do?'

'Would you understand it if I told you?'

'Probably not.' McLean looked down at his notebook then up at the screen. He had begun to doubt what he had seen, and really didn't like where that line of thinking took him.

'Can you run that program on all the other photos?'

'Aye, sure. Well, I'll make a start, then I'll get Malky to do the rest when he comes back in. He'll be chuffed he didn't take them all in vain.'

'Thanks. You've been a great help. I thought for a moment I was going mad.'

'Well, maybe you are. You shouldn't have been able to see those marks, whatever's made them.'

'I'll be sure and ask my optician next time I'm in for an eye test.' McLean pushed himself up off his seat, pocketed his notebook and made to leave.

'I'll send the files over to your printer. Should be waiting for you by the time you get there.'

'You can do that?' Wonders never ceased.

'Aye, no bother. Beats driving them across town. Mind you, I'll be heading up your way soon anyway. You'll be going to the pub with all the others, won't you?'

'Pub?'

'Aye, Duguid's standing everyone on the Smythe investigation a drink. I'm told it's not often he puts his hand in his pocket, so I guess the place'll be packed.'

'Dagwood buying drinks?' McLean shook his head in disbelief. 'Now that I have to see.'

16

True to Miss-not-Ms Baird's word, a stack of freshly printed photographs awaited McLean when he returned to the station. He carried them down to the small incident room, empty and quiet in the late afternoon. On the wall, the dead girl still stared back at him, screaming her sixty-year silent scream, accusing him of not doing enough, not finding out who she was and who had killed her. He stared at her, then down at the photos, each almost completely white. Thin black lines showed the edges of the floorboards and circled the occasional knot in the wood. Barely distinguishable under the fluorescent lights, a sinuous pattern of pale grey snaked through each photograph.

McLean found a permanent marker pen with a narrow tip and tried to trace the edges of the pattern on the first photograph. It was almost impossible to make out, but as he worked his way through the pile, the repeats became more obvious and the task easier. He moved the tables back against the walls, trying to make as much room on the floor as possible, then spent half an hour arranging the photographs in a circle around the centre of the room. As he put the last piece of the jigsaw in place and looked over what he had done, a cloud passed over the setting sun outside and the air turned suddenly cold.

He stood in the middle of a complex circle made up of six intertwining ropes. At six points equidistant around the circumference, they coiled into fantastic knots, impossible shapes that seemed almost to writhe like snakes as he looked at them. He felt trapped, his chest constricted as if it were wrapped tight in bandages. The lights dimmed, the ever-present rumble of the city outside quietened to almost nothing. He could hear his breath passing through his nose, feel his heart beating slowly, rhythmically. He tried to shift his feet, but they were glued to the floor. All he could move was his head.

A sense of panic filled him, a primal fear, and the ropes began to slowly unravel in front of his eyes. Then the door opened, knocking some of the photographs out of line. The lights snapped back on. The tightness in his chest disappeared and his head felt suddenly light. Somewhere in the distance what sounded like a howl of rage echoed in the night. His invisible restraints broke and McLean lurched forward, off-balance, as Chief Superintendent McIntyre walked into the room.

'What was that?' She cocked her head slightly, as if listening for an echo that never came. McLean didn't answer. He was too busy getting his breath back.

'Are you all right, Tony? You look like you've seen a ghost.'

He crouched down and pulled the photographs towards him, starting with the knotted sigil that had been unravelling. On the glossy paper it was nothing more than a few lines in green marker pen, but it still chilled him to look at.

'I just stood up too quickly,' he said, and even as he said the words, it started to make sense.

'Well, what were you doing down there anyway?'

McLean explained about the photographs, the markings he had seen and how they had led him to the hidden alcoves. He said nothing of his strange hallucination. Somehow he didn't think the chief superintendent would be all that sympathetic, and besides, it was fading from memory, becoming little more than a vague feeling of disquiet.

'Let's have a look at those.' McIntyre took the photos from him, leafing through them, pausing at the ones showing the six marked points.

'Do they mean anything to you?'

'I don't really know.'

'I thought it might be some kind of circle of protection.'

'What?'

'You know, circle of protection. Five-pointed star, candles, traps the demon inside when you summon it, kind of thing.'

'I know what a circle of protection is, I'm just not sure how you go about arresting a demon. There's this little problem that they don't actually exist outside the imaginations of pulp novelists and thrash-metal fans.'

'I know that, ma'am. Christ knows our job's hard enough as it is without supernatural forces intervening. But just because demons don't exist, it doesn't mean someone can't believe in them enough to kill.'

'Aye, I guess you're right.'

'Doesn't make it any easier trying to track down just which brand of lunacy gave birth to this, mind you.' McLean rubbed at his eyes and face in a vain attempt to chase some of his weariness away.

'Well if it's magic circles and demon worship you want to know about, then you need to talk to Madame Rose, down on Leith Walk.'

'Err . . . I do?'

'Trust me. There's not many know more about the occult than Madame Rose.'

From the way she spoke, McLean couldn't really be sure whether he was having his leg pulled or not. If he was, then he needed to remember never to play poker with the chief superintendent. He decided that if she was going to play it straight, then he would too.

'I'd better pay her a visit then. I could do with having my fortune told.'

'You do that, Tony. But it can wait for now.' McIntyre shuffled the photographs together and placed them firmly on the table. 'I didn't come looking for you to talk about raising demons. Not this kind, anyway. Charles has been bending my ear about the Smythe case. Did you sanction DC MacBride to requisition information from immigration services?'

McLean hadn't in as many words, but he wasn't about to punish the lad for his initiative.

'Yes, I did. I thought it was important to establish motive, and maybe corroborate that with some of Okolo's co-internees. His post-mortem threw up some difficult questions.'

'Which is precisely why you should do as Chief Inspector Duguid requested, and let it alone. We know Okolo had been in repatriation proceedings for over two years. It's not nice being locked up, especially if you don't think you've done anything wrong. Smythe was a frequent visitor, so everyone there would have known him. Okolo escaped, tracked down the man he felt was responsible for his torture and murdered him in a frenzy. End of story.'

'But there were other men who escaped. What if they've got the same idea? What about the other members of the Immigration Appeals Board?'

'All the other escapees have been captured and returned. Two of them have been repatriated already. Okolo was a lone madman. We might have driven him to madness, but that's not the point. There's no direct evidence to suggest anyone else was involved in this murder. I can't afford the manpower, and frankly I think it's a waste of time pursuing the investigation any further.'

'But . . .'

'Just let it go, Tony.' McIntyre looked at her watch. 'And why aren't you at the pub anyway? It's not often Charles offers to buy everyone a drink.'

'Chief Inspector Duguid neglected to inform me of the arrangements.' McLean knew it sounded petty even as he said it.

'Oh don't be such a pompous ass. I saw Constable MacBride and Sergeant Laird heading out earlier, and they weren't even on the case. Pretty much the whole day shift's gone. What do you suppose the junior officers are going to think of you, holed up in here with your strange photos? Too good to be seen with the likes of them now you've been made up to inspector?'

Put like that, McLean could see how unreasonable he was being.

'I'm sorry. I guess I just let the case get to me sometimes. I really don't like loose endings.'

'And that's why you're a detective inspector, Tony. But not for more than twelve hours a day, not in my station at least. And certainly not the day after your grandmother has died. Now go to the pub. Or go home. I don't care. But forget about Barnaby Smythe and Jonathan Okolo. We'll worry about the report for the PF tomorrow.'

The pub was like a police convention gone wrong. McLean pitied any regulars who had nothing to do with the force, though looking around in the crowd he couldn't see any faces he hadn't already seen in the station earlier that day. The party was obviously well under way; small groups had split off and taken all the available tables, the friendships and alliances clear, the enmities and dislikes even more so. Duguid was at the bar, which presented McLean with something of a dilemma. He didn't want to be in a position where the chief inspector could refuse to buy him a drink, and neither did he particularly want to accept one if the man offered. But it was a bit daft to come in and not have a pint.

'There you are, sir. I was beginning to think you'd bailed on us.' McLean looked around to see Grumpy Bob making his way back from the gents'. He pointed to a table in a dark corner, a suspicious-looking crew huddled around it. 'We're over here. Dagwood only put a fifty down on the bar, cheapskate. Wasn't even enough for a half pint each.'

'I don't know what you're complaining about, Bob. You weren't on the investigation.'

'Well, that's not the point. You can't promise to stand everyone a drink and then only pay for a half.'

They reached the alcove before McLean had time to argue. Constable MacBride sat in the far corner, Constable Kydd beside him. Bob pushed his way past the imposing bulk of Andy House-man and plunked himself down in a seat, leaving McLean to squeeze onto the narrow bench beside Miss-not-Ms Baird.

'You've met Emma? She's come doon tae us frae the giddy heights o' Aberdeen.' Grumpy Bob rolled out the name of the town in a ridiculous parody of a Doric accent.

'Aye, we've met.' McLean slid onto the bench.

'You made it then,' Emma said as Grumpy Bob picked up a full pint of fizzy lager and handed it to McLean, then helped himself to the only other one on the table.

'Get your teeth around that, sir.'

'Cheers.' McLean raised his glass to everyone, then took a sip. It was cold and wet and fizzy. More than that he couldn't tell, as it had no discernible flavour.

'I got your photos, thanks for that.' He turned to the SOC officer.

'All part of the service. Were they any use? I couldn't see anything but white on them myself.'

'Yeah, they were . . . OK.' McLean shuddered, remembering the strange sensation of helplessness, the odd echoing howl of rage. It felt like a dream, or his imagination running overtime. No, he'd just stood up too quickly after so long crouching on the floor.

'Are you two talking shop? You are, aren't you.' Grumpy Bob grinned in triumph, his pint glass all but empty. He slapped Constable MacBride on the chest. 'That's ten quid you owe me, lad. I said the inspector'd be last in and first to forfeit.'

'What's this?' Emma asked, a crease of concern on her forehead. McLean sighed and took his wallet out of his jacket pocket. He was going to get the next round in anyway. Not as if he couldn't afford it.

'Talking about work in the pub's not allowed, under pain of forfeit. It's an old tradition dating back to when Grumpy Bob was just a beat constable, which would mean sometime between the wars, wouldn't it Bob?' He pulled out a twenty pound note and slapped it down on the table, ignoring Grumpy Bob's protests. 'Stuart, do the honours will you?'

'What? Why me?'

'Because you're the youngest.'

Grumbling, Constable MacBride extricated himself from his cosy corner, grabbing the money and heading for the bar.

'And make sure it's decent beer this time.'

109

It was a good deal later that McLean waved off a taxi filled with inebriated constables and scene-of-crime experts. Big Andy had left earlier, headed home to his wife and young child, leaving just Grumpy Bob to walk McLean home, and judging by the state of him, sleep in the spare room. It wouldn't be the first time, and it wasn't as if Mrs Bob was waiting up for him either; she'd walked out many years since.

'She's a nice girl, that Emma, don't you think?'

'Don't you think you're a bit old to go getting hitched again, Bob?' McLean expected the playful punch to the shoulder, and wasn't disappointed.

'No' for me, you loon. I'm talking about you.'

'I know you are, Bob, and yes, she's nice. Odd taste in music, but that's only a minor point. d'you know anything about her?'

'Only that she transferred in a few months back. She's frae Aberdeen.' Grumpy Bob rolled out his terrible Aberdonian accent again.

'Yeah, you said that already.'

'Not much else to know. The SOC crowd think well enough of her, so she must be good at her job. And it's nice to have a pretty face around the place instead of the usual bunch of sourpusses.'

They fell silent for a while, walking up the street in step, like a grizzled old sergeant and his not-so-young constable pounding the night beat. The air was cool, the sky overhead dark with a hint of orange; you could never see the stars anymore, too much light pollution. Without warning, Grumpy Bob stopped in mid-stride.

'I heard about your gran, Tony. I'm sorry. She was a great woman.'

'Thanks, Bob. You know, I find it hard to believe she's really gone. I feel I should be wearing black and tearing my hair. Perhaps wailing and gnashing of teeth might be in there somewhere too. But it's odd. I feel more relieved than sad. She was in a coma so long.'

'You're right. It's a blessing really.' They resumed walking, rounding the corner into McLean's street.

'I saw her solicitor today. She left me everything, you know. It's quite a tidy sum.'

'Christ, Tony, you're no' going to leave the force are you?'

The thought hadn't occurred to him until that moment, but McLean took all of five seconds to answer.

'God no, Bob. What would I do? And besides, if I left, who'd cover for you while you were reading the paper all day?'

They reached the front door to the tenement block and McLean noticed the same strategically placed stone defeating the lock.

'You all right for getting home, Bob, or d'you want the spare bed?'

'Nah, I'll have a bit of a walk, get some air. Who knows I might even be sober by the time I get home.'

'OK then. Sleep well.'

Grumpy Bob waved without turning as he walked away down the street. McLean wondered how far he'd get before he decided to flag down a taxi.

17

Penstemmin Security Systems occupied a large area of reclaimed land down on the edge of the Forth between Leith and Trinity. The building itself was a featureless modern warehouse. It could have been a DIY store or a call centre, although those weren't usually surrounded by razor-wire fences, motion sensors and more CCTV cameras than the average prison. The walls were painted in battleship grey, and a strip of darkened glass ran around the whole building, just under the eaves of the wide, shallow roof. In the near corner it extended down to the ground, and a small entrance foyer.

Constable MacBride parked the pool car in the only space marked 'Visitors'. The white Vauxhall Vectra looked very much out of place alongside the shiny BMW and Mercedes four-by-fours. The director, McLean noticed, could afford to come to work in a brand new Ferrari.

'Looks like we're in the wrong business.' He followed the constable across the car park, enjoying the cool morning breeze coming in off the Firth. MacBride's face was pale, his eyes hooded after the previous night's celebratory excess. No doubt the tequila slammers he'd been matching with PC Kydd had robbed him of a few million functioning brain cells. He looked bemused at first, then finally noticed the collection of expensive machinery.

'I never imagined you as a petrolhead, sir. They say you don't even own a car.'

McLean ignored the desire to investigate just who 'they' were. There were worse things to have said behind one's back. 'I don't, but that doesn't mean I don't know anything about them.'

Having already checked in at the gate to the whole fenced-off complex, they had to confirm their identities through an intercom and CCTV system before they could enter the building. They were met, finally, by a smartly dressed young woman with aggressively short hair and a pair of heavy-framed rectangular spectacles so narrow she must have seen the world as if peering through a letterbox.

'Detective Constable MacBride?' She held out her hand to McLean.

'Er, no. I'm Detective Inspector McLean. This is my colleague, DC MacBride.'

'Oh, I'm sorry. Courtney Rayne.' Hands were shaken and then the young woman led them through a series of security doors and into the heart of the building. It was a vast cavern of a place, open up to a ceiling supported by a spider-web trellis of beams high overhead. Industrial-strength air-conditioning units pumped frigid air into the huge space, sending a shiver down McLean's spine.

The room was divided into small squares by office partitioning boards. In each one, a dozen or more people sat at individual computer screens, telephone headsets strapped to their heads, talking to small microphones that hovered like picnic wasps in front of their lips. The noise was a loud hubbub, punctuated by occasional bursts of action as a team leader bustled over to one workstation or another.

'Our centre monitors over twenty thousand alarm systems throughout the central belt,' Ms Rayne said. McLean decided that she was definitely a 'Ms', even if she was married.

'I'd no idea Penstemmin was such a large organisation.'

'Oh, they're not all Penstemmin systems. We run monitoring services for perhaps two dozen smaller companies. The pods on the far side of the hall are dedicated to Strathclyde police region, these two here are monitoring all alarm systems in Lothian and Borders.'

'Pods?'

'It's what we call our teams, inspector. Each group is a pod. Don't ask me why, I haven't a clue.'

Ms Rayne led them through the middle of the great hall, along a wide aisle that separated the two great cities of Scotland like their enmity of old. McLean watched the pasty-faced teleworkers at their consoles. As the sleek-suited woman strode past, they ducked their heads, feigned busyness even if they had been doing nothing beforehand. It didn't feel like a happy place to be working; he wondered what the staff turnover was like; if any left bearing a grudge and classified information.

At the far side of the hall, a set of stairs led up to a long balcony. Glass-fronted offices ranged the length of the building, their single occupants no doubt the owners of the flash motors in the car park outside. The poor sods on the floor would likely get the bus to work, or park in the street outside the complex.

Having walked the length of the building to reach the stairs, they now made their way back towards the front. McLean suspected that there was a quicker way which would have brought them swiftly from the front reception area up to this outer office, but for some reason Ms Rayne had wanted to show them the great hall. Perhaps it was just a way of impressing the police force with their professionalism; if so it had failed. McLean was tired of Penstemmin Security Systems already, and he hadn't even begun his questioning.

114

They reached a large frosted-glass door, set in the middle of a frosted-glass wall that angled across the corner of the building. Their guide paused only long enough to tap lightly, then pushed the door open and announced their arrival.

'Doug? I've Inspector McLean from Lothian and Borders CID here. You know? The constable who called?' By the time McLean had crossed the threshold, the man she addressed had risen from his seat behind a huge desk and begun his trek across the empty expanse of his office. Never mind pods, they could fill this with water and keep a half dozen whales in here.

'Doug Fairbairn. Pleased to meet you, inspector. Constable.' He was all smile; flashing white teeth in a sun-browned face. He wore a loose shirt with heavy gold chain-links at the cuffs, a tie neatly tied around his neck. His jacket hung over the back of his chair, and his suit trousers were expensively tailored to hide a growing paunch.

'Mr Fairbairn.' McLean took the proffered hand and shook it, feeling a firm hold. Fairbairn oozed confidence. Or arrogance; too early to tell which. 'Is that your Ferrari outside?'

'F430 Spider. You like cars, do you inspector?'

'Used to go to Knockhill and watch the racing as a lad. Don't have the time for it now.'

'She's too powerful for Knockhill. I have to go down south for my track days. Took her to the Ring last year. Here, have a seat.' Fairbairn gestured towards a low leather sofa and armchairs, grey in a minimalist style. 'What can I do for you, inspector?'

No offers of tea and biscuits. Just self-absorbed banter.

'I'm investigating a series of burglaries. Professional jobs, you might say. Certainly not your average smash and grab. At the moment we've only got a tenuous link between them all. But in each of the last three cases Penstemmin alarms have been fitted.

And in each of those cases the alarms have been circumvented without anyone being the wiser.'

'Courtney, the file please.' Fairbairn nodded to the stern businesswoman, who had remained standing, close to the door. She left, returning moments later with a single manila folder.

'I presume this is about the recent break-in at the home of Mrs Douglas. Most regrettable, of course, inspector. But I've had a full systems analysis run and there's nothing to suggest that the alarm was tampered with.'

'Does your system log when the alarm was set, sir?' DC MacBride had his notebook out, pencil poised.

'Yes, it does, constable. Mr Douglas had a top of the range installation. Our computer system has the alarm set at . . .' Fairbairn opened the folder and pulled out a printed sheet '. . . Ten-thirty a.m. on the date in question. It was switched off again at a quarter to three in the afternoon. Monitoring recorded a few electrical spikes during that time, but there's nothing unusual there. The city's supply is notoriously dirty.'

'Could someone have bypassed the alarm? I don't know, reset the monitor log?'

'Technically it's possible, I suppose. But you'd need access to our mainframe, which is behind a foot-thick steel door in the basement. That means you'd have to get in here first, which I can assure you isn't easy. And you'd have to know our systems inside out, plus know the latest passwords. Even then you'd likely leave a trace. We've had the whole system tested by the best computer security experts in the business. It's virtually foolproof.'

'So if the system was bypassed, then it would have to be an inside job?' McLean enjoyed the look of panic his words brought to Fairbairn's face.

'That's not possible. Our staff go through a rigorous vetting

116

process. And no one has access to all parts of the system. We take great pride in our integrity.'

'Of course you do, sir. Can you tell me who installed Mr Douglas's system?'

Fairbairn looked through the folder, flicking the pages nervously. He didn't seem so confident now.

'Carpenter,' he said after a while. 'Geoff Carpenter. He's one of our better fitters. Courtney, can you see if Geoff's out on call right now? If not, get him to pop in will you?'

Ms Rayne disappeared once more from the room. The sound of a muted telephone conversation came through the still-open door.

'I assume you want to talk to him,' Fairbairn said.

'It would help, certainly,' McLean replied, fixing the man with a stare. 'Tell me, Mr Fairbairn. Ms Rayne says you provide monitoring services for several other alarm companies from this centre. Could you give me a list of their names?'

'That's very confidential information, inspector.' Fairbairn hesitated for a moment, playing with his fingers much less skilfully than Grumpy Bob. Finally he wiped his palms on his expensive silk trousers. 'But I dare say I could let you know. After all, we work in close partnership with all the police forces in Scotland.'

'I'll make it easier for you. Do the names Secure Home, Lothian Alarm Systems and Subsisto Raptor mean anything to you?'

Fairbairn's look of alarm increased. 'I . . . Er, that is, yes, inspector. We monitor Edinburgh installations for all three of those companies.'

'How long have you had this arrangement with them, Mr Fairbairn?' Constable MacBride flipped over a page in his notebook and licked the tip of his pencil. The lad had been watching too many cop shows on the telly, McLean thought, but the effect was amusing to watch.

'Oh, um, let me see. We actually bought out Lothian just a couple of months ago, but we'd been running their back-operations for them for about five years. Secure Home would have started using us the year before last. Subsisto Raptor came on board about eighteen months ago. I can dig out the exact dates if you want. These are your similar incidents, I take it?'

'They are indeed, Mr Fairbairn.'

'I hope you're not trying to imply –'

'I'm not implying anything, Mr Fairbairn. Merely investigating a line of enquiry. I don't think your company is systematically trying to rip-off its customers. That would be stupid. But there's a leak somewhere in your system and I aim to find it.'

'Of course, inspector. I'd expect nothing less. But please realise, our reputation is everything. If it got out that our system was failing, we'd be out of business within the year.'

'You know that's not really in my interests, Mr Fairbairn. Companies like yours make our job a lot easier, generally speaking. But I will catch whoever's doing this.'

'I'm missing something, constable.'

'Sir?'

'Something obvious. Something I should have seen from the start.'

'Well, Fairbairn's not telling us everything, that's for sure.'

'What? Oh, no. Sorry. I was thinking about the dead girl.'

They were driving up Leith Walk, headed back to the station. Away from the coast and blocked in by the tall buildings on either side, the growing heat of the day made the car oppressive. McLean had the window open, but their progress was too slow to create a meaningful breeze, the traffic brought to a standstill by something up ahead.

'Take the next left.' McLean pointed to a narrow side street.

'But the station's up ahead, sir.'

'I don't want to go back there just yet. I want to have another look at that basement.'

'In Sighthill?'

'We'll get there a lot quicker if you stop asking damn fool questions.'

'Yes, sir. Sorry, sir.' MacBride pulled the car into the bus lane, crept forward and took the turning. McLean regretted snapping at him, unsure why he was suddenly bad tempered.

'What do we know about this girl?'

'Um, what do you mean, sir?'

'Well, think about it. She's young, poor, dressed in her best. What was she doing when she was killed?'

'Going to a party?'

'Hold that thought. A party. Now let's assume the party was in the house where we found her. What does that suggest?'

Silence as they negotiated the warren of roads around Holyrood Palace.

'That whoever owned that house when she was killed knew about the murder?'

'And who owned the house?'

'It belonged to Farquhar's Bank. The title deeds showed that they acquired it in 1920, and kept it until they were bought out by Mid-Eastern Finance eighteen months ago.'

'OK, let me rephrase that. Who lived in the house? For that matter, who ran Farquhar's Bank before it was sold?'

'I'm not sure, sir. Someone called Farquhar?'

McLean sighed. There was definitely something he was missing.

'We need to talk to Mid-East Finance. They must have some

staff from the old bank on their payroll. Or at least have records of who worked there. See if you can set something up when we get back to the station.'

'You want to go back there now, sir?'

'No. I want to go and look at the house again. Sooner or later I'm going to have to let McAllister get on with his work. I know SOC have wiped the place clean. But I need to see it for myself one more time.'

A deserted building greeted their arrival, the portacabins locked. Heavy plywood boards filled the ground-floor windows and a solid hasp and padlock denied entry through the door. McLean told MacBride to get on the phone for a key, then set off around the grounds to see what he could find.

Unusually for a house of this type, the ornamental tower was at the back. From the number of broken slates and flaked-off plasterwork lying in the overgrown garden, McLean guessed no one had lived in the house for many years. Brambles twined their way up the damp walls towards the broken first-storey windows, and what must once have been a lawn was dotted with substantial saplings from a nearby sycamore. The whole was surrounded by a high stone wall topped with broken glass set in crumbling mortar. A well-worn path led to a small, arched gateway. The old wooden door lay in the undergrowth, rotting, the gap it left now filled with more thick plywood. Tommy McAllister was obviously less welcoming of Sighthill's addicts and vandals than Farquhar's Bank.

It took only ten minutes for a car to arrive with keys; the young constable who had guarded the site the night the body had been uncovered.

'You going to be finished with this place soon, sir? Only I've had that Tommy McAllister on the phone three times a day, bending my ear about paying workmen to do nothing.' She unlocked the padlock and pocketed the key.

'I'll bear that in mind, constable, but I'm not conducting this investigation for Mr McAllister's convenience.'

'Aye, I know that, sir. But you don't have to listen to him, do you.'

'Well if he complains, tell him to come to me,' McLean said.

'I'll do that, sir. And I'll leave you to lock up after you're done.' The constable turned away, heading back to her squad car. McLean shook his head and stepped into the old house, realising as he did that he still didn't know her name.

Police tape barred entry to the basement, but when he stepped under it and went down the stone stairs, McLean was certain someone had been in and cleared up. The plaster debris around the hole that revealed the hidden chamber was all gone, only clean-swept flagstones now. It was possible that SOC had tidied before they left, but that would have been a first.

Pulling out his torch, he stepped through the small hole and into the room. It felt very different, now that the poor tortured body had been removed. There were the six neat holes, spaced at regular intervals around the smooth plastered wall. He peered into every one of them in turn, not expecting to see anything much. They were simple alcoves made by removing some of the bricks that lined the whole basement. Beneath each, a small pile of plaster and wood spokes showed how they had been concealed.

'Is this where she was found?' McLean looked around to see DC MacBride standing in the entrance, blocking the light from the bare bulbs outside. He hadn't been to the crime scene before, McLean realised.

'This is it, constable. Come in and have a look around. Tell me what you see.'

MacBride had a larger torch than his own, McLean noticed. It might have been part of the pool car's standard equipment, but he doubted it. The constable walked slowly around the room, playing his light on the ceiling, then the floor and the four small holes where the nails had been driven in. Finally he looked at the walls, running his hand over the plaster.

'It's a nightmare plastering a round room,' he said. 'Whoever did this was a skilled builder.'

McLean stared at him. Then looked back at the alcoves and the arch of the original doorway that had been bricked up to conceal the horrible crime. How could he have been so stupid?

'That's it.'

'That's what?'

'The work that's been done here. Concealing the alcoves, bricking up the doorway. You'd need a builder to do that.'

'Well, yes.'

'And if we're going with the ritual theory, that would suggest educated men. If they came to parties at places like this, then wealthy men, too.'

'So?'

'So sixty years ago, wealthy men didn't do DIY. They wouldn't know a plasterer's trowel from a pick-axe.'

'I don't see –'

'Think about it, constable. The organs were hidden in the alcoves, which means the plastering happened after the girl was killed. Whoever did this, they had to employ someone to finish all this off. And that person must have seen what was in here. Now how do you suppose the killers stopped him from talking about what he'd seen?'

'Killed him after he'd done the job?'

'Exactly. There's no way they could have let him live.'

'But how does that help? I mean, if he's dead, then . . . Well, that's it. And if they hid his body?'

'You're forgetting something, constable. We can't begin to trace the girl through missing persons because we don't know anything about her. She could have been a vagrant, a foreigner, anything. But whoever plastered this room, hid these alcoves. He was a tradesman, and probably a local.'

'But couldn't he have been one of them? One of the six, I mean.'

McLean paused, his train of deduction derailed by MacBride's remorseless logic. Then he remembered the items placed in the alcoves. A gold cufflink, silver cigarette case, netsuke box, pill case, tie-pin. Only the spectacles might have belonged to a labourer in the 1940s, and even then it was unlikely, wasn't it?

'It's possible,' he conceded. 'But I think it's unlikely. And for now it's the best line of investigation we've got. We might have to go through twenty years of paper records, but there'll be something about a missing plasterer. Find him and we can find who he worked for.'

18

'Oh, Mr McLean. Just a minute, I've a package for you.'

McLean paused at the bottom of the stairs, trying not to breathe in the smell of cat piss. Old Mrs McCutcheon must have been sitting in her little inner hall, waiting for him to come in. She left her door open whilst she disappeared back into the depths of her apartment. No sooner had she gone, than a slim black cat came snaking out, head bobbing as it sniffed the air. For a moment McLean had a mad fancy that the old woman was a witch and had turned into this creature. Perhaps she made a habit of wandering the night-time streets of Newington, peering in windows and seeing what everyone was up to. That would certainly explain how she knew so much about what was going on.

'I was so sorry to hear about your grandmother. She was a good woman.' Mrs McCutcheon came back out with a large parcel clutched in her wrinkled and shaky hands. The cat twined around her legs, threatening to topple her over. So much for that theory.

'Thank you, Mrs M. That's very kind of you.' McLean took the parcel before she dropped it.

'Mind you, I'd no idea she'd done so much with her life. And to lose her son like that and . . . Oh.' Mrs McCutcheon's eyes met his for a moment, then she dropped her gaze to the floor. 'Oh I'm so sorry. Of course. He must have been your father.'

'Please, Mrs M. Don't worry about it,' McLean said. 'It was a long time ago, after all. But how did you find out about it?'

'Och, it's in the paper.' She disappeared back into the apartment, appearing moments later with that day's edition of the *Scotsman*. 'Here, you can keep it. I've read it all now.'

McLean thanked her again, then climbed the winding stone stairs to the top floor and his own flat. The answering machine was flashing a big red number two; he hit the button, putting down the parcel and paper as the tiny tape rewound.

'Hi Tony, Phil here. Put your handcuffs away and meet us in the pub at eight. Jen tells me you've been cross-dressing and I want to know all the details.'

The machine beeped, then played the second message.

'Inspector McLean? It's Jonas Carstairs here. Just confirming that the funeral is set for midday on Monday. I've arranged for a car to pick you up at eleven. Call me if you need anything else. You've got my home and mobile numbers. Oh, you should get a package over the weekend. It's just copies of all the legal papers and other stuff relating to your grandmother's estate. Thought you might like to have a look through it all. We can discuss the details later. '

McLean looked at the parcel. It was stamped with the postmark of Carstairs Weddell. He opened it and pulled out a thick wad of papers, still smelling slightly of the photocopier. The top sheet bore a flowery script reading 'Last Will and Testament', and he was about to read it when the answering machine beeped once more.

'Please help me. Please find me. Please save me. Please. Please.'

The voice sent a shiver up his spine. It was a young woman, maybe a girl. Her accent was strange to him. Scottish, east coast, but not Edinburgh. He looked at the answering machine; the red LED said '2'. Two messages. He hit play again, waiting impatiently as the tape spooled back. Phil's cheery voice came on, then

Jonas Carstairs. Then nothing. The machine clunked and stopped.

He rewound and played the messages twice more. Still only two. Going through into his study, he fished around in his desk for an old dictation machine, then spent ten minutes looking for batteries for it. He put the tape from the answering machine in it, played it from the start. There was the outgoing message; did his voice really sound so dreary and bored? Then a short gap followed by Phil's message. Another short gap then Jonas. A bunch of old messages that hadn't been overwritten by new ones yet, but nothing that sounded remotely like what he had heard before. Or what he thought he'd heard. And then silence. He let it play a bit more, then hit fast forward. The Dictaphone would play anything that had been recorded, but at fast speed. He should have been able to hear the girl. But there was just a gap and then a succession of very old messages stretching out for a few minutes. Then silence.

Had he imagined it? It seemed an odd hallucination if that was the case. And yet the tape sped forward silently until it reached the end. He pulled it out, turned it over, hit play.

'Hi, this is Tony and Kirsty's phone. We're far too busy righting wrongs and fighting crime to answer it right now. You'll just have to make do with leaving a message after the tone.'

McLean sank slowly to his knees, the muscles in his legs no longer prepared to hold his weight. He was dimly aware of the room around him, but it was a darker place, indistinct. Her voice. How many years had it been since he'd heard her voice? That final, fateful, lying, 'See you later'? And all the while it had been on this tape in this stupid machine.

Without thinking, he hit rewind and played the message again. Her words echoed in the empty flat, and for a time it felt as if the city noise melted away. He looked around the room, seeing the same old pictures on the wall; the rug, a little threadbare now, covering the pale sanded floorboards; the narrow table beside the door where the telephone lived, and his keys. They'd bought that in the old architectural salvage place down in Duddingston. Nest-building, Phil had called it. So little of his flat had changed since Kirsty had died. She'd gone so suddenly, she'd even left her voice behind.

The door buzzer startled McLean out of his melancholy. For a moment he considered not answering, pretending to be out. He could spend an evening listening to her voice and believing she might come back. But he knew that was impossible. He'd seen her cold dead corpse laid out on the slab. Watched her coffin slide behind the final curtain. He picked up the intercom.

'Yes?'

It was Phil. McLean buzzed open the door, realising as he did that the students downstairs must have stopped propping it open with rocks. He cracked open his own front door and listened to the sound of footsteps clambering upwards. More than one set, so Phil must have brought Rachel with him. That was ominous; his old flatmate always came to visit alone.

They burst into the flat, Phil, Rachel and Jenny, laughing at some joke they'd shared on the way up. The laughter died all too quickly.

'Jesus, Tony. You look like you've seen a ghost.' Phil stepped into the hallway like he still lived there; the two young women stood uncertainly in the doorway. For a moment, McLean felt bitter resentment at their presence. He wanted to be alone with his misery. Then he realised just how daft that was. Kirsty was gone. He had come to terms with that long ago. Hearing her voice had just taken him by surprise.

'You caught me at a bad moment, sorry. Ladies, come in. Make yourselves at home. I know Phil does.' He slipped the Dictaphone into his pocket, then pointed towards the living room door, hoping that it was tidy. He couldn't remember the last time he'd been in there. 'Would anyone like a drink?'

It was strange to have women in his flat. McLean was used to the dubious company of Grumpy Bob after a particularly heavy post-investigation celebration, and Phil came round occasionally, usually when he'd just split up with one of his students and needed to find solace in a bottle of malt whisky. But he couldn't remember the last time he'd entertained guests. He liked living alone, preferred to do his socialising in the pub. Which was why his kitchen was ill-stocked with any kind of food. He'd found a large packet of dry-roasted peanuts, but it was approaching the first anniversary of its sell-by date and bulged ominously, like a dead man's stomach.

'What's up, Tony? If I didn't know better I'd say you were trying to avoid us.' He turned to see Phil standing in the doorway.

'Just looking for something to eat, Phil.' McLean opened a cupboard by way of demonstration.

'It's me, Tony. Your ex-flatmate, remember? You might be able to bullshit the stress councillor at work, but I've known you long enough. Something's up. Is it your gran?'

McLean looked at the packet of papers. He'd dumped them on the kitchen table along with the burglary reports and a file on the dead girl. Another reason why he preferred not to have guests. You never knew what they might find.

'It's not my gran, no Phil. I lost her eighteen months ago. I've had plenty of time to come to terms with that.'

'So what's bothering you then?'

'I found this. Just before you got here.' McLean fetched the

128

Dictaphone out of his pocket, set it down on the counter and hit play. The colour drained from Phil's face.

'Jesus, Tony. I'm sorry.' He sat down heavily in one of the kitchen chairs. 'I remember that message. God it must be ten years ago. How on earth . . . ?'

McLean began to explain, only then remembering the strange girl's voice that had prompted him to investigate the answering-machine tape in the first place. He must have imagined it, but now it merged with Kirsty's words into a desperate plea from someone long dead, far beyond his reach. He shivered at the thought.

'You look like you could do with some company, mate.' Phil lifted the suspect bag of peanuts, prodding its tumescence before carrying it across to the bin and dropping it into the otherwise empty depths. 'And if Rache and me are going to help drink your extensive wine collection, we'll be needing pizza.'

'So it's serious then, you and Rachel?'

'I dunno. Maybe. I'm not getting any younger. And she's put up with me far longer than most.' Phil shuffled his feet, stuck his hands in his pockets and did a good impression of an embarrassed school-boy. McLean couldn't help but laugh, and he felt instantly better for it. At almost the same instant music exploded from the living room. The Blue Nile belting out 'Tinseltown in the Rain' far too loud, then quieting to a still-unfriendly level. McLean rushed through, meaning to ask them to turn it down, then remembered the nights he'd been kept awake by the students downstairs. It was Friday evening; every-one in the tenement except Mrs McCutcheon would be out enjoying themselves, and she was as deaf as a post. Why should he bother about being quiet?

Rachel sat perched on the edge of the sofa, looking slightly uncomfortable. She brightened up when Phil entered the living room just behind McLean. Jenny squatted down in front of the shelves that lined one wall, leafing through his record collection. Back turned, and with the music playing loud, she didn't notice them come in.

'Tony being a hopeless bachelor, there's no food in the house at all, only drink,' Phil said over the noise. 'So we're going to order pizza.'

'I thought we were going to the pub,' Rachel said. At her voice, Jenny looked up, turning. She reached for the volume control on the stereo, turned down the music.

'I'm sorry. I shouldn't have. I . . .' She flustered, turning pink.

'It's OK,' McLean said. 'You need to play them from time to time or the music fades away.'

'I don't think I know anyone who owns a record player any more. And so many records. They must be worth a fortune.'

'That's not a record player, Jen,' Phil said. 'That's a Linn Sondek sound system worth slightly more than the gross domestic product of a small African dictatorship. Tony must like you a lot. He'd cut my hands off just for touching it.'

'Come off it, Phil. I know you used to play that old Alison Moyet record of yours whenever I was out.'

'Alison Moyet! You insult me, Detective Inspector McLean. I shall have to challenge you to a duel, sir.'

'The usual weapons?'

'Of course.'

'Then I accept your challenge.' McLean smiled as Jenny and Rachel looked on bemused. Phil disappeared from the room, returning moments later with two loofahs from the bathroom. They were brittle dry and covered with cobwebs, untouched in many years.

'Rachel will be my second. Jen, would you do the honours for

130

our host?' Phil bowed, handing her one of the loofahs. 'In the hall, I think.'

'You're serious about this, aren't you?' Rachel said. In the background, Neil Buchanan had started to sing 'Stay', his mournful tones at odds with the growing hilarity.

'Of course I am, my lady. Honour has been slighted, and now it must be regained.' He strode out into the hallway, and McLean followed.

'Umm, what are you doing?' Jenny asked him as he rolled up the rug and pushed it into one corner of the long, narrow hallway.

'Duelling with loofahs. It's how we used to settle arguments when we were students.'

'Men.' She rolled her eyes, handing the weapon over and retreating to a safe distance as Phil took his place at the kitchen door.

They were clearing up the mess when the pizza delivery man arrived. McLean was unsure who had won, but he felt better than he had done in days. The cynical detective in him realised that Phil had engineered the whole situation. Normally his old friend would have come round much later in the evening, most likely alone. They'd have listened to depressing music and drunk malt whisky, moaning about life and the terrible effects of getting old. By bringing the two sisters round with him, he'd turned it into more of a party. A vigil for Esther McLean, and in a manner his grandmother would have heartily approved.

Quite what she'd have made of Jenny, he wasn't so sure. She was a good bit older than her sister, which made her probably the same age as him. She'd changed from the outfit she'd been wearing in the shop, dressed casually in jeans and a plain white blouse. Without the make-up that was no doubt part of her working face, she was attractive in a slightly worn around the edges way. He wasn't really sure why he'd not noticed when they'd met before. Possibly because the lighting in the Newington Arms was hardly flattering; more likely because his mind had been full of mutilated bodies.

'Penny for them.' The object of his musing leaned over, helping herself to another slice. Phil and Rachel were deep in conversation about some film they'd seen.

'Eh? Oh. Sorry. I was miles away.'

'I could see that. You're not often here, are you. So where were you, inspector?' She used the title as a joke, but it was painfully close to the bone. Even here, with wine and pizza and good company, the job was in the background, never leaving him alone.

'Just wondering if your sister's going to make an honest man out of my old friend.'

'Oh, I doubt that. She's always been a very corrupting influence.'

'Is there something I should be warning Phil about?'

'I think it's too late for that.'

'Aren't you worried about her hooking up with an older man?'

'Nah, she always had a thing for her big brother's friends, and Eric's probably older than you are.'

'A well-spaced family then.'

'Rae was what might be called a happy accident. I was ten when she was born, Eric was fourteen. So what about you then, Tony? Have you got any brothers hidden away?'

'Not that I know of, no. I'm sure my gran would've told me if there were any other McLeans lurking out there.'

'Oh, I'm sorry. That was insensitive of me. Phil told me about her . . . passing.' Jenny sat up straight, clasping her hands primly in her lap, embarrassed.

'Not at all. I'd much rather talk about her than pussyfoot about the subject. She had a stroke eighteen months ago. It put her in a coma and she never recovered from it. She's been dead for over a year, really, only I couldn't bury her and get on with life.'

'You were very fond of her, though.'

'My parents died when I was four. I don't think I ever heard my gran complain about having to raise me. Even though she'd lost her only son. She was always there, even when —' But he was interrupted by the phone ringing out in the hall. For a moment he thought about leaving it for the answering machine. Then he remembered taking the tape out and a flood of other memories washed through him. 'Excuse me, I'd better get that. It could be work.'

McLean glanced at his watch as he picked up the phone. Just past eleven; where had the evening gone?

'McLean.' He tried not to let the irritation in his voice show. There was only one thing anyone could possibly be ringing him about at this hour.

'You're not pissed are you?' Duguid's nasal tones were made worse by the tinny phone. McLean considered his intake, maybe half a bottle of wine spread over three hours or more. And he'd eaten, too, which was unusual for him.

'No, sir.'

'Good. I've sent a car round to pick you up. Should be there any moment.' As if by perverse magic, the doorbell buzzed.

'What's this about, sir? What's so important it can't wait until the morning?' He knew the question was stupid even as he said it. Maybe he had drunk a little too much.

'There's been another murder, McLean. Is that important enough for you?'

19

Constable Kydd said nothing as they drove across the city, which made McLean suspect she was not meant to be on duty either. He thought about asking her for more information than Duguid had offered, but he could feel the waves of resentment boiling off her, and didn't want to offer himself as a target.

As it was, their destination was only a few minutes from his flat. Patrol cars flashed blue lights on the cobbles of the Royal Mile just across from St Giles' Cathedral as uniforms fended off curious Friday-night revellers, keen to get an eyeful of whatever was happening. The constable parked in the middle of the cordoned-off road and McLean walked across to the SOC van. It was backed up as close as possible to a narrow alleyway between two shop fronts. Dim lighting showed a line of wheelie bins tucked away behind a cast-iron security fence and gate. Beyond them, a set of shallow stone steps led up to a tenement door.

'Where's Chief Inspector Duguid?' McLean showed his warrant card to one of the constables rolling out blue and white tape.

'No idea, sir. I've not seen him here. SOC and the doctor are upstairs.' The man looked up and pointed to the top of the five-storey building.

Bloody marvellous, McLean thought. Just like Dagwood to send him out after hours rather than shifting his own sorry arse. He stomped past the SOC van and down the alleyway, was just about to step up into the building when a loud voice rang out over the night noise.

'Oi! Where the bloody hell d'you think you're going?'

McLean froze, looking round to see a white-boilersuit-clad figure stepping down out of the dark recesses of the SOC van. When she stepped into one of the weak pools of light, he recognised Miss-not-Ms Emma Baird. She nearly dropped the bag she was carrying.

'Oh-my-god. I'm sorry, sir. I didn't realise it was you.'

'It's OK, Emma. I take it you've not finished examining the scene then?' Stupid of him. He should have checked before marching in.

'At least put a boilersuit and gloves on, sir. The boys won't be happy if they have to take samples from everyone's clothes for elimination.' She went back to the van and fetched out a white bundle. McLean struggled into the suit, pulling white paper covers over his shoes and latex gloves over his hands before following the young woman up a narrow winding staircase.

A full-length glass canopy in the roof would have lit the wide landing at the top of the stairs by day. This late at night two wall lights provided illumination, one mounted beside each of the apartment doors. Both of these were open, and smears of blood on the white-painted walls made it impossible to guess which was the correct one. McLean opted to continue following the SOC officer, but she stopped at the door she was entering and pointed to the other one.

'Witness fingerprints for elimination, sir. Your body's in there.'

Feeling like an idiot for not knowing anything about the crime scene, or for that matter the crime, McLean nodded his thanks, turned and crossed the landing. He could hear low voices inside the apartment and peered through the door. Sergeant

Andy Houseman stood in the hallway. He wasn't wearing overalls.

'Andy, what have you got for me?' McLean winced as the big sergeant almost jumped out of his skin.

'Jesus! You nearly gave me a heart attack.' The big man looked around, saw who it was and relaxed. 'Thank Christ, a detective at last. I've only been on the bloody radio for the last two hours.'

'Well I only got the call about twenty minutes ago, Andy. So don't go blaming me. It's meant to be my weekend off.'

'Sorry, sir. It's just . . . Well, I've been stuck in here all that time, and it's not a nice place to be.'

McLean looked around the hallway of the apartment. It was expensively decorated, with antique furniture cluttering up the living space. The walls were covered with an eclectic mix of paintings, leaning towards the modern in style. One nearby caught his eye and he peered more closely.

'It's a Picasso, sir. Least I think it is. I'm no expert.'

'OK, Andy. Assume that I know exactly nothing about this crime. Fill me in.'

'Me and Constable Peters were patrolling the High Street when we got the call, sir. That would have been about twenty-one hundred hours. Break-in and violent assault. We proceeded to this address and found the gate and front door open. We followed the trail, found old Mr Garner up on the top landing in his dressing gown.'

'Mr Garner?'

'The neighbour, sir. He and Mr Stewart were good friends. Well, if you ask me I think it maybe went a bit further than that, but that's none of my business, sir.'

'Mr Stewart?' McLean felt like a complete idiot and cursed Duguid for his predicament.

'The victim, sir. A Mr Buchan Stewart. He's in there.' The sergeant pointed to the only open door in the hallway, but made no sign of going anywhere near.

'OK, Andy. I'll take it from here. But don't go too far. I still need a full briefing.' McLean watched the sergeant leave the apartment, then stepped into the room.

The smell hit him first. It had been there, lingering, all the while. But outside it was muted. Here it was a full iron tang, the scent of recently spilled blood. The room was the private study of a wealthy man, filled with yet more antique furniture and modern art. Mr Buchan Stewart had been catholic in his tastes; there was something for everyone. But none of it would do him any good now.

He sat in a Queen Anne chair facing into the room. He had been wearing pyjamas and a long velvet dressing gown, but someone had removed all his clothes and laid them neatly on the desk. Blood matted and stained the wiry grey hair on his chest, oozing from a wound that had opened up his neck from ear to ear. His head tilted back, staring blindly at the ornately plastered ceiling, and yet more blood smeared around his mouth, dribbled over his chin.

'Ah, McLean. It's about time a detective showed up.' McLean's eyes flicked down towards the dead man's lap, and he suddenly noticed the white boilersuited pathologist and his assistant hunkered down on the floor. Dr Peachey was not his favourite among the city's forensic experts.

'And a good evening to you too, doctor.' He stepped forward gingerly, aware of the pool of blood spreading out in a dark stain around Buchan Stewart's chair. 'How's the patient?'

'I've been here an hour and a half waiting for one of your lot to show up so we could get this body out of here. Where the bloody hell have you been?'

'At home, with some friends, sharing a bottle of wine and some pizza. I got the call exactly half an hour ago, doctor. I'm sorry if your evening's been ruined, but you're not the only one. I guess Mr Stewart here's not exactly thrilled at the way events have turned out either. So why don't you just tell me what's going on, eh?'

Dr Peachey looked up at him with narrow eyes, a fierce debate raging across his pale face. It would have been easier with Angus, McLean thought. Just my luck to get Dr Bolshy.

'Cause of death is most likely massive blood loss.' Dr Peachey spoke in short, clipped sentences. 'Victim's throat has been cut with a sharp knife. The rest of the body shows no signs of imme-diate injury, except the groin.' He heaved his bulk up from the floor and moved to one side so that McLean could get a better look. 'Penis and scrotum have been removed.'

'Are they gone? Did the killer take them?' McLean felt the pizza weigh heavy in his stomach; the wine go sour. Dr Peachey reached for an evidence bag that lay beside his open medical case, lifting it up to the light for him to see. It contained what looked remarkably like the bits you find shrink-wrapped inside a Christ-mas turkey.

'No, he left them behind. But he shoved them in the victim's mouth before he went.'

20

Timothy Garner was frail and shaky. His skin had that translucent quality you only see in the very old, like rice-paper covering yellow muscle and blue veins. Constable Kydd sat with him in his tidy apartment; she looked up with hope in her eyes when McLean entered the room. He had watched the undertakers remove Buchan Stewart's body to the mortuary, seen the SOC officers pack up and leave, taking all the wheelie bins outside. Someone was going to have fun. Sergeant Houseman was organising a half dozen uniforms to interview the tenement owners on the lower floors, which just left the witness who had reported the incident in the first place.

'Mr Garner. I'm Detective Inspector McLean.' He held out his warrant card, but the old man didn't look up. He was staring at nothing, his hands slowly smoothing the folds of his dressing gown over his thighs.

'You couldn't rustle up a cup of tea, could you, constable?'

'Sir.' The constable stood up like someone had jabbed a fork in her arse and scurried out of the room. Mr Garner's company must not have been the most pleasant. McLean took her seat close by the old man.

'Mr Garner, I need to ask you some questions. I can come back later, but it's best if we do it now. While the memories are still fresh.'

Still the old man didn't respond, didn't look up. Just kept

smoothing his hands over his thighs, slowly. McLean reached out and placed his fingers on the back of one of Garner's hands, stopping him. The contact seemed to break whatever trance he had fallen into. He looked around, his eyes gradually focusing on the inspector. Tears welled up in the puffy, wrinkled lids.

'I called him a cheating bastard. That was the last thing I said to him.' His voice was thin and high, tinged with a soft Morningside accent that clashed with the swear-word.

'You knew Mr Stewart well, Mr Garner?'

'Oh yes. Buchan and I first met in the fifties, you know. We've been in business together ever since.'

'And what line of business is that, sir?'

'Antiques, art. Buchan has an eye, inspector. He can spot talent, and he always seems to know where the market's going.'

'So I've seen from his apartment.' McLean looked around Garner's living room. It was well-furnished but not with the same opulence as his business partner. 'And what of you, Mr Garner? What did you bring to the relationship?'

'Brilliant men need their foils, inspector, and Buchan Stewart is a brilliant man.' Garner swallowed, his prominent Adam's apple bobbing in his thin, sinewy neck. 'I should say *was* a brilliant man.'

'Can you tell me what you argued about?'

'Buchan was hiding something from me, inspector. Of that I'm sure. Just these past few days, but I've known him long enough.'

'And you thought he was cheating. What, setting up a business with another man?'

'You might call it that, yes, inspector. I very much suspect there was another man involved.'

'The man who killed him, perhaps?'

'I don't know. Maybe.'

'Did you see this man?'

'No.' Garner shook his head, as if reinforcing the answer in his mind, but there was uncertainty in his voice. McLean kept silent, letting the doubt do its work.

'I can't expect you to understand, inspector. You're young still. Perhaps when you're as old as me you'll know what I'm talking about. Buchan was more than just my business partner. He and I, we were . . .'

'Lovers? There's no crime in that, Mr Garner. Not any more.'

'Aye, but there's shame still, isn't there. There's still the way people look at you in the street. I'm a private man, inspector. I keep to myself. And I'm too old to be interested in sex these days. I thought Buchan was too.'

'But now you think he was seeing someone else? Another man?'

'I was sure of it. Why else would he be so secretive? Why would he lose his temper and send me away?'

McLean said nothing for a moment. In the quiet he could hear a kettle boiling, the clink of teaspoon on china.

'Tell me what happened this evening, Mr Garner. How did you find Mr Stewart.'

The old man paused. His hands started their rhythmic movements again, and he clenched them into fists to stop himself.

'We'd had a row. This afternoon. Buchan wanted me to go away for a couple of weeks. There's a big art fair in New York and he thought it would do me good to go. He'd even organised the tickets, hotel, everything. But I retired from the business years ago. I told him I didn't have the strength to travel that far, let alone work an auction when I got there. I told him I'd rather stay and let him go. He always had so much more energy than me.'

'So you'd argued. But you went back over to his apartment to talk to him later, is that right?' McLean saw the old man beginning to wander off topic and gently steered him back.

'What? Oh, yes. It would have been around nine, maybe quarter past. I don't like leaving an argument unresolved, and I'd said a few harsh words, so I thought I'd go and apologise. Sometimes we'd sit up late, maybe have a wee brandy and talk about the world. I've a key to the apartment, so I could let myself in. But I didn't need it; the door was wide open. I smelled something bad. Like the sewers had backed up. So I went in and . . . Oh God . . .'

Garner started to sob. Constable Kydd chose that moment to come back in bearing a tray with three china cups and a teapot on it.

'I know this is hard, Mr Garner, but please try and tell me what you saw. If it's any consolation, saying it out loud can often help to lessen the shock.'

The old man sniffed, accepting a cup of tea with shaky hands and sipping at the milky liquid.

'He was sitting in there, naked. I thought he'd been doing something to himself. I couldn't understand why he was so still, or why he was staring at the ceiling. Then I saw the blood. Don't know how I could have missed it before. It was everywhere.'

'What did you do then, Mr Garner? Did you try to help Mr Stewart?'

'What? Oh. Yes. I . . . That is, no. I went over to him, but I could see he was dead. I dialled 999, I think. The next thing I knew there was a policeman here.'

'Did you touch anything? Other than the telephone.'

'I . . . I don't think so. Why?'

'The officer who came to see you earlier? She took your fingerprints so we can separate them from any we find in Mr Stewart's apartment. It helps us if we know where you went.' McLean lifted his teacup to his mouth. Garner did the same, taking a long sip. The old man shuddered as the warm tea slipped down his throat, that prominent Adam's apple bobbing up and down again with each swallow. They sat in silence for a while longer, then McLean put his cup back down on the tray. He noticed that Constable Kydd hadn't drunk any of hers either.

'We'll need you to come down to the station and make a statement, Mr Garner. Not now, tomorrow will do,' he added as the old man made to stand up. 'I can send round a car to pick you up and bring you back. Shall we say ten o'clock?'

'Yes, yes. Of course. Earlier if you want. I don't think I'll sleep much tonight.'

'Is there someone we can call to keep you company? I'm sure we could spare a constable.' McLean looked across at Constable Kydd and received a withering stare in return.

'No. I'll be fine, I'm sure.' Mr Garner put his hands back down on his thighs, but only to lever himself up out of his chair. 'I think I might have a bath, though. That usually helps me sleep.'

'Thank you. You've been very helpful.' McLean stood with greater ease, offering his hand to the old man. 'There'll be a constable on duty outside Mr Stewart's apartment all night. If you've any worries, let him know and he can radio in to the station.'

'Thank you, inspector. That's very considerate.'

The landing was quiet outside Mr Garner's apartment. The door opposite stood open, but there was no sign of anyone within. McLean clumped downstairs and out onto the street, where a few uniforms were still busying themselves. He accosted Sargeant Houseman manning the barrier outside the gate; the SOC van had long disappeared.

'How'd you get on with the other tenements?'

Big Andy pulled out his notebook. 'Most of them are empty. Seems they belong to a leasing company. They put foreign executives and the like in them. The ground floor's got two flats in it; neither of them heard anything until we arrived. Oh, and there's a basement flat too. He got home with his girlfriend about half an hour ago and was rather abusive when we told him he couldn't go in unescorted. Sergeant Gordon got a bloodied nose and Mr Cartwright's going to be spending some time in the cells.'

'Drunk and disorderly?'

'Possession, sir. Probably with intent to deal. You'd think with a pound of hash on his person he'd steer clear of the police.'

'You would indeed. You were right by the way.'

'I was? About what?'

'Buchan Stewart and Timothy Garner. Odd arrangement, though. Living in separate apartments just across from each other.'

'The world's full of odd people, sir. Sometimes I think I'm the only normal man alive.'

'That's a fact, Andy.' McLean looked at his watch, it was getting on for two in the morning. 'I think we've done pretty much all we can here tonight. Put two men on guard duty. We have a potential witness. I don't want our murderer coming back to try and silence him.'

'You don't think he's a suspect, then? Garner?'

'Not unless he's a very good actor, no. My gut tells me there's more to this than a lovers' tiff turned bad, but Garner's in no state to be interviewed tonight. I don't think he'd do too well in a cell either.' McLean looked up to the high windows, light spilling out into the night. 'He's not going anywhere in a hurry. Best let him calm down a bit and I'll talk to him in the morning. Let whoever draws the short straw for guard duty know he's there. If he wants to go anywhere, we'll get a DC round to go with him. OK?'

'Right you are, sir.' Big Andy lumbered off, shouting orders at the few remaining policemen on the scene. McLean turned to Constable Kydd, who stifled a yawn.

'I thought you were on day shift.'

'I am.'

'Then how'd you get roped into this assignment?'

'I was using one of the interview rooms at the station to study, sir. My folks aren't the quietest at the best of times. Friday nights it's best to be somewhere else if you want a bit of peace.'

'And let me guess, Duguid found you and sent you after me. Any idea why he couldn't attend himself?'

'I wouldn't like to say, sir.'

McLean stopped himself from interrogating the constable any further. It wasn't her fault they'd both had their evening ruined. He'd find out sooner or later why the case had been handed over to him.

'Well get yourself home now, and get some sleep. And don't worry about coming in a bit late tomorrow. I'll square it with the desk sergeant, get the rosters juggled.'

'Thank you, sir.' The constable smiled a weary smile. 'Do you need a lift home?'

'No thanks.' McLean looked down the High Street. There were still people wandering about even at this late hour. Revellers on their way home from the pub, people spilling out of nightclubs, late-night kebab and burger bars doing a roaring trade. The city never really slept. And somewhere out there was a killer with blood on their hands. A killer who had cut off a part of his victim and shoved it in their mouth. Just like Barnaby Smythe. Copycat? Coincidence? He needed time, air, distance to consider it all.

'I think I'll walk.'

21

Saturday should have been his day off. Not that he'd made any plans, but whatever he'd intended doing, sitting in his office at the police station at half past eight in the morning hadn't been high on the list of options. Not after less than four hours' sleep. McLean clicked through the digital photographs from the Stewart crime scene on his computer. He'd need to get them printed out; it was impossible to work off the tiny screen. Selecting the whole batch, he sent them to the shared printer down the corridor, hoping it would have enough paper and toner in it for a change.

The flat had been thankfully empty when he'd let himself in, having walked the mile and a half back from Buchan Stewart's apartment. It wasn't that he didn't like company, but he preferred to lose himself in a crowd. One to one, without the crutch of his professional persona, was just too fraught with possibilities and difficulties to be ever truly enjoyable. Even if he hadn't just come back from a violent crime scene, he preferred his own company. Just him and his ghosts.

'Ah, Tony. I was hoping to catch you in this morning.'

Startled, McLean looked up to see Jayne McIntyre advancing down the corridor towards him. Her uniform didn't flatter her much, and he wondered idly if she'd put on weight.

'Ma'am?'

'You took on the Stewart case last night. Thank you.' She fell in beside him as they carried on walking.

'I did wonder why there was no one else to take it.'

'Ah. Yes. Well, Chief Inspector Duguid did want the case, but as soon as I heard about it, I had to insist he pass it on to someone else.'

'Why?'

'Buchan Stewart is . . . was his uncle.'

'Ah.'

'So really you should be flattered that he chose you to conduct the investigation. I know the two of you don't see eye to eye.'

'That's the polite way of putting it, ma'am.'

'Well, I have to be tactful in my line of work. And I have to make sure my senior officers can work together. Do a good job on this, Tony, and whatever Dagwood's got against you, I'm sure he'll let it slide.'

It was the first time he'd ever heard McIntyre use the chief inspector's nickname. He smiled at her attempt to be conspiratorial with him, but she'd got the nature of their animosity all wrong. He didn't much like Duguid because the chief inspector was a sloppy investigator. Duguid didn't like him because he knew it.

'So what have you got so far?' McIntyre asked.

'It's early days, really. But I'm leaning towards jealousy as motivation. Nothing obvious had been stolen, so it wasn't burglary. And Stewart was naked, which suggests he may have been expecting sex. He was homosexual, and could have recently found a new partner. I'd finger him as our prime suspect. If I had to make a guess, I'd say a younger man, maybe considerably younger.'

'Any witnesses? CCTV?'

'No one in the tenement saw anything. I've got DC MacBride going over the tapes from last night, but it's a bit of a camera black spot. We'll hopefully narrow things down a bit once the pathologist has given us a more accurate time of death.'

147

'What about the man who phoned it in?'

'Timothy Garner. Lived next door. He was Stewart's partner for years, business and, um, personal.'

'Could he have done it?'

'I don't think so. It just didn't feel like that kind of case. He's meant to be coming in later this morning to make a statement anyway, but I think I might head over there and interview him at home. He'll be more at ease there.'

'Good idea. It'll help to keep things low profile too. I suspect DCI Duguid would appreciate that.' McIntyre gave him a conspiratorial wink. 'See Tony, you can do diplomacy if you try hard enough.'

The blood smear on the stairwell wall looked paler and less ominous in the daylight flooding from the glass canopy overhead. A constable stood on guard outside Buchan Stewart's flat. He looked bored to tears, but snapped to attention when he saw the inspector coming up the stairs. Constable Kydd trailed behind, once more his driver for the day.

'Anyone coming or going, Don?' McLean asked.

'Not a peep, sir.'

'Good.' He knocked gently on the door to Garner's apartment. 'Mr Garner? It's Inspector McLean.'

No answer. He knocked a little harder.

'Mr Garner?' McLean turned back to the constable on duty. 'He didn't pop out, did he?'

'No, sir. I've been here since seven and no one's moved since then. Phil . . . Constable Patterson was on before me. Said the place was quiet as the grave.'

McLean knocked once more, then tried the door handle. It clicked open onto a darkened entrance hall.

'Mr Garner?' A shiver ran down his spine. What if the old man had died of a heart attack? He turned back to Constable Kydd. 'Come with me,' he said and stepped inside.

The apartment was silent save for the tick, tick, ticking of an old grandfather clock in the hallway. As McLean went to the living room where they had interviewed Garner earlier in the morning, Constable Kydd headed down a narrow corridor that he assumed led to the kitchen. The old man was not in the seat where they'd left him, neither was he in his study, which McLean found through the next door off the hallway. The room was neat and tidy, the desk empty save for a green-glass-shaded library lamp, which was switched on and pointed downwards to illuminate a single sheet of paper.

He crossed the room, his mind racing. Bending down, he could read the words written on the paper in neat pen.

I have killed my soulmate, my lover, my friend. I did not mean to but fate has made it so. I could no longer live with him, but now I find I cannot live without him. To whomsoever finds this note . . .

A loud gasp echoed through the silent apartment. McLean hurried out of the study.

'Constable?'

'Sir! In here.'

He rushed across the hallway and down the narrow corridor, but he knew what was coming. Constable Kydd stood in the doorway to the bathroom, her face white, her eyes staring. He gently moved her out of the way and stepped past.

Timothy Garner had taken his bath. And then he'd taken a razor to his wrists.

22

'That was quick, Tony. You might even have beaten Duguid's record.' DCS McIntyre perched herself on the edge of the desk; there was nowhere else in the room to sit other than the chair McLean was already occupying. She looked pleased for once; there was nothing like a quick result for boosting the clean-up statistics, after all. Just a pity he couldn't share her enthusiasm.

'I don't think he did it, ma'am.'

'Didn't he leave a confession?'

'Yes, he left a note.' McLean picked up the A4 print of the digital photograph which was all he had of Timothy Garner's last words, handing it to McIntyre. SOC had taken the original away to 'do tests'. He could have told them not to bother; they would show it had been written by Garner, using his normal handwriting. The paper would yield no fingerprints other than those of the dead man, but analysis of the liquid that had splashed the last paragraph might well reveal it to have been his tears.

'"I have killed my soulmate, my lover, my friend." What part of that isn't a confession? You already said they'd rowed because Garner thought Stewart was getting a bit on the side. It was a brutal attack, sure. But crimes of passion often are. And then, when he realised what he'd done, he couldn't live with it.'

'I don't know. It doesn't feel right. And his words are so flowery. He could just be blaming himself for not being there with Stewart when it happened.'

'Come on. He had the motive, he had the weapon.'

'Did he? Forensics couldn't match his cut-throat to the knife that killed Stewart. They just said it was razor sharp.'

'Drop it, Tony. OK? You've been through the CCTV tapes for the time of the murder. No one enters or leaves that building half an hour either side of the time of death. There were no witnesses to the murder and the person most likely to have committed it has confessed. Don't go raking over the coals when you don't need to.'

McLean slumped back in his uncomfortable chair and looked up at his boss. She was right, of course. Timothy Garner was the most obvious choice of suspect.

'What about the fingerprints? They couldn't match all of them to Garner.'

'That's because they were so smeared they couldn't match them to anyone. And they found traces of Stewart's blood in Garner's basin where he washed his hands. His clothes were spattered in it too. They'd probably have found it in his bath if he hadn't filled it with his own.' McIntyre dropped the copy of the suicide note back onto McLean's desk, followed by the slim brown folder she had brought in with her; the report on the murder of Buchan Stewart. 'Face it, Tony. Your report as good as says Garner killed Stewart and then committed suicide, and that's what's going to the prosecutor. Case closed.'

'Is this being hushed up so Duguid doesn't have to explain to the world about his gay uncle?' McLean knew as soon as the words were out that he shouldn't have said them. McIntyre stiffened, then stood up from the desk, straightening her uniform.

'I'll pretend I didn't hear that, detective inspector. The same way as I'm ignoring the fact that you left Garner at home on his own when by all rights he should have been down in the cells, or at the very least with an FLO to keep him company. Now sign off that report and get out of here. Isn't there a funeral you're meant to be attending?' She turned and left.

McLean sighed, pulling the slim folder towards him. He could feel his ears burning slightly at the rebuke and knew that he had lost the superintendent's good will, at least for the next few days. But he couldn't help thinking there was much more to the death of Buchan Stewart. Nor could he stop blaming himself for Timothy Garner's suicide. He should have insisted someone stay with the old man overnight. Hell, he should have taken the man into custody as a suspect. Exactly why hadn't he done that?

Glancing out the window, the pale blue morning sky cast the tenements behind the station into deep shade. He stifled a yawn, stretching until the muscles and joints in his back started to protest. He was meant to have the weekend off, but instead it had been long and for the most part dull as he waited for the results of Buchan Stewart's post-mortem, the forensic and fingerprint reports. Everything pointed to Garner being the culprit, and yet McLean couldn't accept it. Something in the pit of his stomach squirmed as he remembered sitting with the old man, touching his hand to wake him from his trance, listening to his story. He had been eighty years old, frail. How would he have had the strength to kill? And to mutilate a man so?

In the end, it didn't matter. Chief Superintendent McIntyre had told him to close the case. She might have been trying to protect Duguid, or pressure might have been applied from higher up the food chain. It didn't matter. Unless he could show irrefutable evidence of a third party being involved in the crime, then as far as everyone else was concerned it was solved. A big plus point on the annual statistics and a cheap investigation to boot. Everyone happy. Except poor old Buchan Stewart, lying on a cold slab with his manhood in a plastic bag beside him. Except Timothy Garner, pale and drained of blood like a stuck pig.

Except him.

Pushing aside the thought, he opened up the folder, glancing up at the clock on the wall. Just gone nine; half an hour until the car came to collect him. He clicked on his computer and began to type. If McIntyre wanted a whitewash, he wasn't going to waste a lot of time on it.

He is confused, hungry, anxious. Pain fills his head, making it hard to concentrate, hard to remember who he is. His hands are raw, rubbed almost to the bone with washing, and yet still he feels dirty. Nothing gets him clean anymore.

There was a place he used to go every day. They had water there, and food. Images tumble through his mind, and one sticks. Hands rubbed together with soap, under a tap running warm water. The rhythmic ritual of fingers sliding between each other, palms gliding together, thumbs massaging. He knows this place and it is near. He must go there. He can be clean there.

The streets are canyons, tall buildings rising high on either side, blocking out the light but letting the heat build like an oven. Cars rumble past, their tyres thrumming on the cobbles. They ignore him and he ignores them in return. He has a destination now, and once he is there, everything will be all right. He just needs to wash his hands.

Steps lead up from the street. They are like mountains to his exhausted, pain-wracked legs. What has he been doing to feel this way? Why can't he remember where he has been? Why can't he remember who he is?

The door is made of glass, and it slides away from his approach as if he is too terrible to be faced. The room beyond is light and

153

airy, cooler than the foetid heat of outdoors. He steps uncertainly from stone to polished floor, glances around, trying to remember where those taps are, that soap. He looks down at his hands, suddenly frightened by them, by what they can do. He shoves them in his pockets and the right one feels something hard, smooth; grasps it instinctively.

Someone is talking to him, an insistent voice that he cannot understand. He looks around, the room suddenly too bright, the light like daggers in his eyes. A woman sits behind a desk, her face white, eyes wide. He thinks he should know her. Behind her, men in pale suits stand like puppets with their strings cut. He thinks he should know them too. He takes his hand out of his pocket, meaning to wave to them, show them his stained hands, to reassure them that all he wants to do is wash. But the smooth, hard object comes too, brings with it a memory.

And he knows what it is he must do.

23

Mortonhall Crematorium probably didn't hold happy memories for many people. Maybe the gardeners who tended the grounds were proud of their work, and the staff who so efficiently ushered through the mourners in their half-hour slots might have taken grim satisfaction in their polite competence. But for everyone else it was a place of grief, of final goodbyes. McLean had visited it far too often in his work to be much moved by the place. Instead he noted with a clinical eye how little it had changed over the years.

There wasn't much of a turnout for his grandmother. Given her age, and his tendency for solitude, it was hardly surprising. Phil sat with Rachel next to him at the front of the room, and Jenny had come too, which was unexpected but not unwelcome. Grumpy Bob was there, the only representative from Lothian and Borders Police, and Angus Cadwallader had bustled in to the back at the last minute. Jonas Carstairs sat impassively, head up and staring into the distance as a community celebrant tried to say comforting words about a woman he had never known. A few elderly friends McLean half recognised sat in little groups around the empty hall. It should have bothered him that so few people had come to say farewell, but he found he was more comforted that anyone had turned up at all. And of course he could console himself with the thought that his grandmother had outlived all her friends.

The service was mercifully swift, and then the curtains pulled around the coffin, the edges not quite joining together enough to conceal its motorised passage through to the business end of the crematorium. He remembered the first time he had been here; a bewildered four-year-old boy watching two wooden boxes and only dimly understanding that his parents were inside them; wondering why they wouldn't wake up. His grandmother had been beside him then, holding his hand and trying to be a comfort while she mourned her own loss. She had explained to him, in her careful, logical way, all about the business of death. He understood why she had done that, but it hadn't helped. When the curtains began to close, he had expected to see a door open to a furnace, watch the flames leap towards their new source of fuel. The nightmares had stayed with him for years.

They exited through the front doors; a large party had already gathered at the rear, eager to send off the next dead. Outside, the morning was growing hot, the sun risen over the tall trees that surrounded the site. McLean shook hands with everyone and thanked them for coming, an act which took all of five minutes. Jenny Spiers hung back, he noticed, unwilling to commit herself to the line. In the end he went over to her instead.

'It was good of you to come.'

'Wasn't sure if I should, to be honest. I never met your grandmother, after all.' Jenny flicked aside a stray bang of hair. She'd come straight from the shop, if her outfit was anything to go by. Sombre, as befitted the tone, but probably the sort of thing McLean's grandmother would have worn to a funeral when she was in her twenties. He wondered whether the choice was on purpose. It suited her, though.

'I always say these things are about the living, not the dead. And anyway, if you hadn't come, the average age of the people here would have been well into three figures.'

'It's not that bad. Rae's here, and she's only twenty-six.'

'Fair point,' McLean conceded. 'You coming over for a cup of over-stewed tea and a fish-paste sandwich?' He nodded in the direction of the Balm Well across the road, then stuck out his arm for her to take. Several elderly people in dark suits and dresses were trying to dodge the traffic, intent on getting their fill of the late Esther McLean's final hospitality. Together they helped them across the road and into the pub.

Jonas Carstairs had organised a decent wake; it was just a shame he'd overestimated the catering numbers by an order of magnitude. Old people, McLean noticed, had very small appetites too. He just hoped that the pub could find someone else to feed all the leftovers to. Paying for it didn't bother him so much as the thought that it would end up in the bin. His gran would have been horrified too, were she not past caring.

He left Jenny with Phil and her sister, worked his way around the small band of mourners with as much grace as he could muster. Most of them said the same things about his gran; a few mentioned his parents. It was a duty he had to perform, but it was also a chore and quite frankly he'd rather be back at work, helping DC MacBride plough his way through a stack of Mis-Per reports that were so old no one had bothered to digitise them. Or trying to find out who had lived and partied in Farquhar House in the 1940s.

'I think it's gone well enough, all things considered.' McLean turned away from the last wheelchair-bound friend of his gran, whose name he had forgotten almost as soon as it had been spoken, and stood up to face Jonas Carstairs. The lawyer had a large whisky in his hand, took a long sip.

'Perhaps overestimated the numbers coming?' McLean asked.

Something like a haunted look passed over Carstairs' face. He glanced over his shoulder and for some inexplicable reason, McLean got the feeling he was looking for someone rather than appraising the numbers. As if he had been expecting another mourner who hadn't turned up.

'It's always difficult to gauge these things.' Carstairs took another swig from his glass.

'Looking for one more in particular?'

'I sometimes forget the young boy turned into a detective inspector.' Carstairs grinned mirthlessly. 'There was someone. Well, he might have come. Maybe he didn't know.'

'Anyone I'd know?'

'Oh, I doubt that very much. This was someone your grandmother knew before she married your grandfather. They were close.' Carstairs shook his head. 'For all I know he died ages ago.'

McLean was about to ask the name of this long lost friend, but something else occurred to him at the same time. 'Did you ever do any work for Farquhar's Bank?'

Carstairs choked a little on his whisky. 'What makes you ask that?'

'Oh, just a case I've been working on. I'm trying to find out who was living in Farquhar House at the end of the Second World War.'

'Well that's easy enough. That would be old man Farquhar. Menzies Farquhar. He set up the bank at the turn of the century. I knew his son, Bertie. You'll have heard of him.'

McLean shook his head. 'Doesn't ring a bell.'

'I forget how long ago it was, of course. Before you were even born. Poor old Bertie.' Carstairs shook his head. 'Or perhaps I should say stupid old Bertie. He crashed his car into a bus stop, killed half a dozen people. I think things would have been worse

158

for the family if he hadn't had the decency to kill himself at the same time. Old man Farquhar was never the same after that, though. He shut up Farquhar House and moved out to his place in the Borders. As far as I know it's been empty ever since.'

'Not for much longer. Some property developer's bought it. Going to turn it into luxury apartments or something.'

'Really?' Carstairs went to take another swig only to discover that he'd already finished his drink. He put it down carefully on a nearby table, pulled a white handkerchief out of the breast pocket of his jacket and daubed at his lips. 'Who on earth would want to do that? I mean, it's not exactly the most desirable of locations, is it.'

'No, not really.'

'Mr Carstairs, sir?'

McLean turned around at the interruption. A dark-suited man stood a polite distance behind him, his eyes fixed on the solicitor.

'Can it not wait, Forster?'

'I'm afraid not, sir. You did say to let you know if he got in touch.'

Carstairs stiffened, a hunted look darting across his face like a startled deer. He recovered quickly, but not so quickly that McLean didn't notice.

'Something come up?'

'The office, yes.' Carstairs patted his suit jacket as if looking for something, saw the empty glass tumbler on the table beside him, picked it up as if to finish his drink then seemed to realise what he was doing. 'A very important client. I'm so sorry, Tony, but I'll have to go.'

'Think nothing of it. I'm just grateful that you came at all. After all your hard work organising things.' McLean reached out and shook Carstairs by the hand. 'I'd very much like to talk some more. You obviously knew my gran better than I did. Perhaps I could give you a call?'

'Of course, Tony. Any time. You've got my number.' Carstairs smiled as he said the words, but as the lawyer walked away, McLean couldn't shake the feeling he didn't really mean what he said.

24

It was a long way home once the wake had wound itself down, but McLean turned down the car that Carstairs had organised. He preferred solitude, the chance to think that only came with the rhythm of his feet on the pavement. It was only after he'd been walking for half an hour that he realised they were taking him towards his grandmother's house and not back to the flat in New-ington. He made to change direction, then stopped. He'd not been back since the day they'd found Barnaby Smythe's body.

Before she'd suffered her stroke, McLean had often gone to his grandmother for advice, for help with problems he just couldn't get his head around. Usually she'd just talked him around the sub-ject until he'd worked it out for himself, but he'd always valued her input. Once she had gone into hospital, the house had lost its appeal. He went there because he had to. Had to check the meters, collect the mail, make sure no one had broken in. But it had always been a chore. Now, with his grandmother's ashes in the ground, going back to her house – his house as soon as the paperwork was done and the taxman had taken his pound of flesh – felt like the right thing to do. Perhaps it might even help him with some of the many intractable problems that even a good long walk couldn't unravel.

The late afternoon faded to evening, and further from the city centre the noise dwindled away to nothing more than a distant background hum. When finally he turned into the street where the house stood, it was almost like stepping into the countryside. The big sycamore trees that broke up the pavement also damped down the city noise and darkened the summer evening light. Most of the houses were silent hulks set back from the road in their mature gardens. Only occasional signs of life, a slammed door, a spill of voices through an opened window, showed him that he wasn't completely alone. For a while, the black cat kept stride with him on the other side of the road, waiting until it was sure he had seen it before disappearing over a high stone wall just as he reached his destination.

The gravel drive gave a reassuringly familiar crunch beneath his feet. Ahead, the house looked dead, empty, like a ghost rising out of the overgrown borders, but as soon as he left the street, he smelled the familiar scent of home. McLean let himself in the back door, going straight to the alarm console and tapping in the code to disarm all the sensors. Seeing the Penstemmin logo reminded him that he still needed to interview the installer who had fitted old Mrs Douglas's alarm. Another case he was no nearer to solving.

It was amusing to see just how many finance companies were keen to offer personal loans and credit cards to the deceased. He leafed through the pile of junk mail that had accumulated at the front door in the few days since his last visit, sorting out the few letters that looked important and binning the rest. The hallway was dark with falling evening, but when he went through to the library, the red-orange glow of the setting sun reflected off high clouds, painting the room.

McLean spent a few minutes pulling off all the white sheets that covered the furniture, folding them neatly and stacking them by the door. His grandmother's desk sat in one corner, the sleek flat-screen monitor and keyboard looking incongruous amongst the antique furniture. The solicitors had been looking after her affairs, and he'd been quite happy with that arrangement, but at some point he'd have to go through her files, both paper and electronic. Put everything in order. Just thinking about it made him weary.

He poured himself a decent measure from the crystal decanter in the drinks cupboard artfully concealed behind a panel of false books, then realised that the bottled water was at least eighteen months old. He sniffed the top; it seemed OK, put just a dash in his whisky and sipped the pale amber liquid. Islay, without a doubt. And strong. Adding more water, he remembered his grandmother's fondness for Lagavulin and wondered if this was one of the cask-strength bottlings from the Malt Whisky Society. It was a while since he'd drunk anything so refined.

Dram in hand, McLean settled down into one of the high-backed leather armchairs beside the empty fireplace. The library was warm; those long windows trapped all the afternoon and evening sun. This room had always been his favourite. It was a sanctuary, a haven of peace and quiet where he could escape from the madness of the city outside. Head tilted against the soft leather back of the chair, McLean closed his eyes and let the weariness wash over him.

He woke to total darkness. For a moment he didn't know where he was, but then memory seeped back. McLean was about to reach for the lamp sitting on the table with the letters and his unfinished whisky when he realised what had woken him. There had been a noise, just the slightest of creaks in the floorboards, but he was certain it had been there. Someone else was in the house.

He sat motionless, straining his ears to hear, trying to ignore the loud thumping of his own heart. Had he imagined it? The house was old, and full of creaking boards that shifted and groaned as the temperature changed. But he was used to those noises; he'd grown up with them. This was different. He let out his breath then held it, feeling the house around him. Had he shut the back door properly? It was a latch, he knew, but what if it hadn't clicked closed?

Something metallic clinked against china. Out in the hallway there were two large ornamental vases. McLean could almost picture a stealthy intruder brushing one with a ringed hand. Now he had a focus for the sound, he could hear more: quiet breathing; the swish of loose-fitting clothes; the gentle touch of a hard object being put down very carefully on a wooden surface. The noises were purposeful, quiet by habit rather than design. Whoever was in the hall expected the house to be empty. He looked at the door, peering around the edge of the high-winged chair. No chink of light came from underneath, so the person on the other side either felt by touch, or was using some kind of night-vision device. He reckoned on the latter, and that gave him a plan.

There was scant light in the library. Its dark, book-lined walls didn't reflect much of the dull glow that filtered in from the city outside. But there was enough for him to make out the large furniture. He also knew where the loose floorboards were, clustered around the doorway and the fireplace. McLean took a moment to slip off his shoes, then trod as quietly as he could around the outside of the room until he reached the door. Outside he could hear more noises as the intruder moved methodically around the hall. He waited patiently, holding himself still, breaths shallow and regular.

It seemed to take for ever for the intruder to work his way around to the library, but finally McLean saw the brass handle begin to twist. He waited until the door was half open. A head, half obscured by heavy goggles, peered through the gap. With a silent flick, McLean switched on the lights.

'Argh! Bastard!'

The figure was closer than McLean had expected, hands reaching up to a heavy headpiece, trying to tear it off before the night-vision apparatus burned out his retinas. Not waiting to let the burglar get his bearings, McLean reached forward and grabbed him by the front of his T-shirt, pulled hard as he stuck a foot out. They both fell to the floor, McLean ending up on top, wrestling to try and get the burglar into an arm-lock.

'Police. You're under arrest.'

It never worked, but the lawyers insisted. For his pains, McLean got an elbow to the gut, driving the wind out of him. The burglar kicked out, arched his back, still struggling with one hand to tear off the night-vision goggles. He was strong, wiry under tight black T-shirt and jeans, and very reluctant to come quietly. McLean got a hand around his neck, a knee in his back, just like they taught you in police college. It didn't do him much good as the burglar writhed like a bagful of eels. He slid around until he was facing McLean like a lover, drawing up his knees in a manner that was surely anatomically impossible.

'Oof!' Feet drove the wind out of McLean's lungs as he pushed away. He crashed into one of the chairs, rolled off it and scrambled to his feet as the intruder made a leap for the doorway.

'Oh no you don't.' McLean lunged forward, catching the man in a perfect rugby tackle. Their combined momentum carried them both forward too fast and with a horrible cracking sound, the burglar's head connected with the edge of the open door. He dropped like someone had switched him off, and McLean, unable to stop himself, landed heavily on top, getting a face-full of burglar's buttock.

165

He scrambled up, spluttering and coughing, grabbed the intruder's arms and twisted them behind his back. 'You are fucking nicked,' he said between gasps for breath, but it was academic. The man was out cold, his expensive night-vision goggles smashed to one side of his head and a large bruise flowering across his face.

25

Tuesday morning and Interview Room 3 was stuffy and airless. It had no window, just a vent in the ceiling that was meant to pump fresh air but didn't. A plain white-topped table sat squarely in the middle, a few cigarette burns marking the Formica. On the far side of it from the narrow door, a plastic chair had been bolted to the floor just too far away for its occupant to lean his elbows comfortably. He had tried, several times, and now slumped back, his cuffed hands in his lap.

McLean watched him for a while, not saying a thing. So far the burglar had refused to give his name, which was a nuisance. He was a young man, late twenties to early thirties at a guess. Fit, too. McLean had a nice bruise on his right side where he'd wrestled him to the ground, but it was nothing compared to the mess that was the other guy's face.

The door banged open and Grumpy Bob pushed in. He carried a tray with two mugs of tea and a plate of biscuits on it. Setting the whole lot down on the table, he handed one mug to McLean and took the other for himself, dunking a rich tea biscuit in the hot milky liquid.

'What about me? Do I no' get anythin'?' The young burglar's accent was broad Glaswegian, making him seem like some ned from the schemes. But McLean wasn't fooled. Anyone with the skill to pick a lock and the nous to use night-vision goggles was a cut above your average drug-addict burglar.

'Let me see.' He pretended to think for a while, sipping from his own mug of tea. 'No. You don't. Here's how it works. You co-operate, we'll be nice.'

'How about a ciggy then? I'm gasping here.'

McLean pointed to the No Smoking sign fixed to the wall. The effect was slightly marred by the heavy biro marks erasing the word 'No'.

'One of the few good things to come out of Holyrood, that. You can't smoke anywhere in this building. Not even the cells. And you're going to be spending a long time in the cells if you don't co-operate.'

'You can't keep me locked up in here. I know my rights. I want to see a lawyer.'

'Got that off the telly, did you?' Grumpy Bob asked. 'Think you know all about the polis because you watch *The Bill*? You don't get a lawyer until we say so, sunshine. And the longer you piss us about, the longer that'll be.' He took another biscuit from the plate and bit into it, sending a shower of crumbs to the floor.

'OK. Let's start with what we know.' McLean took off his jacket, hanging it on the back of his chair. He fished in one of the pockets, coming out with a pair of latex gloves which he slowly pulled on, snapping the rubber and smoothing the fingers. All the while the burglar watched him with wide, grey eyes.

'You were found last night in the house of the late Mrs Esther McLean.' McLean bent down and lifted a cardboard box from the floor, dumping it on the table. He pulled out a heavy canvas duffle bag, wrapped in plastic. 'You were carrying this bag, and wearing these.' He took the mangled/broken night-vision goggles from the box and placed them on the table. They too were encased in a clear plastic evidence bag.

'Inside the bag, we found several items taken from the house.'

He lifted out a set of silver ornaments that had been in a display cabinet in the hall. It felt odd to be handling his grandmother's possessions like this, even wrapped up. 'You were also carrying a set of lock-picking tools, a stethoscope, a high-speed electric drill and a set of clothes a man of your age might wear to a nightclub.' He laid the offending articles out on the table. 'Oh, and this set of keys, which I assume is to your house. There were BMW car keys on the ring as well, but my colleague Detective Constable Mac-Bride has taken them to the nearest franchised garage to get the code checked against their owner's database.'

As if on cue, there was a knock on the door, it opened a fraction, and MacBride popped his head in. 'Something for you, sir,' he said, handing over a sheet of paper and another clear evidence bag. McLean looked at it and smiled.

'Well, Mr McReadie, it seems we won't be needing your co-operation after all.' He stared at the burglar, looking for signs of discomfort and finding them writ large.

'Take him back down to the cells, Bob. And tell the duty sergeant no fags, OK?' He picked up the evidence bag with the keys in it and shoved them in his pocket. 'Stuart, round up a couple of constables and meet me at the front. I'm going to see about getting a search warrant organised.'

*

For a ned, Mr Fergus McReadie had done rather well for himself. His address was a large warehouse conversion down in Leith Docks. Twenty years earlier, it would have been the haunt of prostitutes and drug dealers, but with the Scottish Office relocation and HMY *Britannia*, Leith was upmarket these days. Judging by the cars parked in their allocated bays, the development wasn't cheap either.

'How the other half live, eh, sir?' Constable MacBride said as they took the lift to the loft floor, five storeys up. It opened onto a spotless hallway with just two apartment doors leading off. McReadie's was the one on the left.

'I don't know. Can't really call it a tenement if it doesn't smell of stale piss.' McLean pointed at the other door. 'See if the neighbours are home. With any luck they might know a bit about our cat burglar's other life.'

As the constable buzzed on the right-hand door, McLean let himself into McReadie's apartment. It was a vast hangar of a space, old wooden beams criss-crossing the ceiling. The loading doors had been converted into full height windows, overlooking the docks and out onto the Firth of Forth. One corner of the room formed an open-plan kitchen, and at the far end, spiral steps led up into the rafters and a sleeping platform. Underneath it, two doors suggested more partitioned space.

'OK, people. We're looking for anything that might be stolen goods, any information about Mr McReadie we can find.' He stood in the middle of the room as Constable Kydd and Grumpy Bob started to rummage around, opening doors and looking under cushions. A huge plasma TV screen dominated one wall, and beneath it neatly arranged shelves of discs. McLean looked at some of the titles; they were mostly Japanese manga and kung-fu films. Tacked on the end, almost as if they were an afterthought, was the complete set of Pink Panther movies. The boxes were battered and worn, as if they had been watched many times. Except the last one, which still had its cellophane wrapping around it.

'Sir?'

McLean looked around to see DC MacBride standing in the open doorway. A woman stood behind him, her long blonde hair tousled as if she had been asleep, her eyes wide as she watched the policemen search the flat. He hurried over.

'This is Miss Adamson,' MacBride said. He looked slightly stunned. 'She lives next door.'

On closer inspection, McLean could see that Miss Adamson was dressed only in a long silk dressing gown. Her feet were bare.

'What's going on? Where's Fergus? Is he in trouble?' Her voice was soft, thick with sleep, and with the faintest trace of American mixed in with the Edinburgh.

'Miss Adamson. Detective Inspector McLean.' He held up his warrant card for her to see, but she hardly seemed able to focus. 'I'm sorry to disturb you, but I wonder if you could answer a few questions for us.'

'Sure. I s'pose. I'm not in trouble, am I?'

'Not at all, miss. No. I'm interested in what you know about your neighbour, Fergus McReadie.'

''Kay. Come over and I'll put some coffee on.'

Miss Adamson's apartment was smaller than McReadie's but still large enough. She stepped lightly round a stainless steel counter that separated her kitchen from the bulk of the living space, busying herself with beans and grinder. Soon the air filled with a powerful aroma.

'So what's Fergus done then, inspector? I always thought there was something slightly creepy about him.'

McLean settled himself on one of the tall stools that were arranged along the length of the counter. Behind him he could sense Constable MacBride's unease.

'I can't exactly say, not until he's been charged. But we caught him red-handed, Miss Adamson.'

'Vanessa, please. Only my agent calls me Miss Adamson.'

'Vanessa, then. Tell me. Have you known Fergus McReadie long?'

'He was there when I moved in about, what, two years ago? I'd see him in the elevator, we'd say hello. You know how it is.' She plunged the coffee then poured it into three mugs, turning to pull a large carton of fat-free milk from the enormous fridge behind her. McLean couldn't help noticing that, apart from a couple of bottles of champagne, it was pretty much empty. 'He tried to hit on me a couple of times. But he wasn't my type. Too geeky, and that accent just used to get on my nerves.' Her own voice was soft, with the faintest trace of American mixed in with the Edinburgh.

'Do you know what he does for a living, then?' McLean accepted the proffered drink, unsure quite why MacBride was so reluctant to come forward and claim his.

'He's some sort of computer security expert, I think. He tried to explain it to me once. My mistake for inviting him to the party, I guess. He made it sound glamorous, like he spent his life trying to break into banks and stuff. You know, so he could show them where their weaknesses were? I got the impression most of it involved sitting in front of a computer watching numbers scroll past.'

There was a light tapping at the door. McLean looked round to see Constable Kydd framed in the doorway. Her gaze shifted from him to Vanessa and her eyebrows shot up. He looked back at his hostess, wondering what he was missing.

'Oh, do come in, officer. There's plenty more coffee.' Miss Adamson stooped for another cup and McLean averted his eyes as the dressing gown parted to reveal perhaps more than was intended.

'That's very kind, ma'am,' the constable said, not moving from the doorway. 'But I think the inspector should come see what we've found.'

'No rest for the wicked, eh?' McLean levered himself off the stool. 'Constable MacBride, stay here and get as much detail as you can about our burglar. Vanessa, thank you for your help. I'll be back for the rest of that coffee if you don't mind.'

'Not at all, inspector. It's quite the most exciting thing that's happened to me all summer. And who knows when I might have to play the part of a policewoman. This is a wonderful opportunity for research.'

As he turned to leave, McLean was almost certain he saw Constable Kydd mouth a silent, questioning 'Vanessa?' to MacBride, but her expression dropped back to its normal not-quite-angry self before he could be sure. He followed her out, across the hall and back into McReadie's apartment. One of the two doors at the far end stood open.

'Am I missing something, constable?' McLean asked as they crossed the huge space.

'You didn't recognise her, sir? Vanessa Adamson? Won a Bafta last year for her role in that BBC period drama? Oscar-nominated for that Johnny Depp movie?'

He hadn't seen either, but he'd seen her on the news, now that he thought about it. McLean felt the tips of his ears heat up. No wonder she'd looked a bit familiar.

'Really? I thought she was taller.' He took refuge from his embarrassment in the room through the open door, a large study, lit by a single floor-to-ceiling window. A wide, glass-topped desk supported a laptop computer and a phone, but nothing else. Grumpy Bob sat in the black leather executive chair, spinning it from side to side.

'Found something, Bob?'

'I think you'll like this, sir.' He stood up and reached for a book on the top shelf behind him. When he pulled it out, the whole shelving unit clicked, moved forward and slid sideways on silent runners. Behind it, there was another set of shelves, glass this time and lit from above and below. They were stacked with a bewildering collection of jewellery.

'How on earth did you find that?' McLean walked around the desk, peering into the hoard.

'I was looking at the titles, sir. Saw one that McReadie'd written himself. Thought I'd have a look at it, see if there was a biography in it. Only he hadn't written it, had he. It was his little joke.'

'Well, ten out of ten for observation. Eleven out of ten for jammy luck.'

'It gets better, sir. I found these too.' Bob reached down and pulled a couple of newspapers out of the bin beneath the desk. Copies of the *Scotsman* from the previous week. He unfolded them both and spread them out. One had been left open at the announcements page, the other at the obituaries. Both had circles of black biro on them. McLean recognised the grainy black and white photograph of his grandmother, taken forty years earlier. Grumpy Bob beamed the smile that had earned him his nickname so many years before.

'I think this just might be our obituary man, sir.'

26

'McLean! Where the fuck were you yesterday morning? Why weren't you answering your phone?'

Chief Inspector Duguid marched down the corridor towards him, face livid red, hands clenched into ugly fists. McLean struggled for a moment to remember what he had been doing, so much had happened since. Then it all clicked back into place.

'I had the day off, sir. I was burying my grandmother. If you'd spoken to Chief Superintendent McIntyre she'd doubtless have told you. She might also have let you know that I came in early anyway to finish up the report on your uncle's death and his killer's suicide.'

Duguid's face went from livid red to ghostly white in an instant. His piggy little eyes widened and his nostrils flared like a bull pawing the ground ready to charge.

'Don't you dare mention that in here, McLean.' Duguid's voiced hissed out through tight lips and he looked around nervously to see if anyone had heard. There were a number of uniforms going about their business, but they had enough of a sense of self-preservation to avoid eye contact with the chief inspector. If they had heard anything, they weren't showing it.

'Was there something you wanted, sir?' McLean kept his voice level and steady. The last thing he needed was to have Duguid raging at him; not after the day had started so well.

'Too bloody right I do. Some lunatic called Andrews walked into a busy office in the city centre yesterday and opened up his neck with a cut-throat razor. I want you to find out who he was and why he did it.'

'Is there no one else available? I've got quite a full case-load as it is —'

'You wouldn't know the meaning of full bloody case-load if it bit you in the arse, McLean. Stop whingeing and do the job you're paid to do.'

'Of course, sir.' McLean bit his tongue trying not to argue. There was no point when Duguid was in a rage. 'Who conducted the initial investigation?'

'You did.' Duguid looked at his watch. 'In the next half hour if you've any sense. There's a report on your desk from the sergeant who attended the scene. You do remember your desk, don't you inspector? In your office?' And on that sarcastic note, he stalked off, muttering under his breath.

Only then did Grumpy Bob come out of his hiding place behind the photocopier.

'Bloody hell. What's crawled up his arse and died?'

'I don't know. Probably found out his uncle left all his money to the animal sanctuary or something.'

'His uncle?' So Bob hadn't been listening.

'Forget it, Bob. Let's go find out about this suicide. It'll take a while for forensics to process all that jewellery. We can't match anything with the other burglaries until then.'

'What about McReadie? You want to charge him?'

'I guess we better had. But you know he's going to have a wea- sel lawyer get him out on bail before the end of the day. You saw his apartment; he's got money coming out of his ears. He can buy his freedom and he knows it.'

'I'll leave it until the last minute then. Better check with the duty sergeant when you logged him in.'

Grumpy Bob sauntered off towards the front desk; McLean headed for his office. Sure enough, on the top of a huge pile of overtime sheets, a slim manila folder contained a single typed sheet reporting the apparent suicide of Mr Peter Andrews. There were names and addresses of a dozen witnesses, all employees of the same financial management company, Hoggett Scotia. Andrews had been an employee there himself. He'd apparently walked into the front reception area, looking like he'd slept in his clothes for the past two days, pulled out a cut-throat razor blade from his pocket and, well, cut his throat. And all this had happened almost twenty-four hours ago. Since which time the police had done bugger all.

McLean sighed. Not only was it likely to be a fruitless task investigating the suicide, he was also going to be met with hostility and anger that it had taken so long for him to do anything about it. Bloody marvellous.

Grabbing the phone, he dialled the number for the mortuary. Tracy's chirpy voice answered.

'Did you get a suicide in yesterday? Name of Andrews?' McLean asked after she had tried her usual flirtation.

'Mid-morning, yes,' she confirmed. 'Dr Cadwallader was planning on doing him late afternoon. About four.'

McLean thanked her, said he'd see her there, then hung up. He looked at the notes again; at least the address wasn't far to walk. Interviews first, then the post-mortem. With a little bit of luck, by the time he got back from that the jewellery they'd found in McReadie's apartment would be back from forensics. Then they could have endless fun trying to match it to the lists of stolen items.

He picked up the file, ignoring the pile of overtime sheets that needed to be processed, and went off in search of Detective Constable MacBride.

'You've been keeping us busy this last week, Tony.'

McLean grimaced at the pathologist. 'Good afternoon to you, too, Angus. And thanks for coming yesterday, by the way.'

'Think nothing of it. The old girl taught me a thing or two. Least I could do was make sure she was seen off properly.' The pathologist already wore his scrubs, long surgical gloves pulled tight over his hands. They went through into the autopsy room, where Peter Andrews lay in his pale glory on the stainless steel table. Apart from the ragged mess of his throat, he looked strangely clean and peaceful. His hair was dishevelled and grey, but his face looked young. McLean would have put him in his late thirties to early forties. It was difficult to tell from such a pale, pasty corpse.

Cadwallader began with a thorough inspection of the body, looking for signs of injury, drug abuse or disease. McLean watched, only half listening to the quietly spoken commentary and wondering what could bring a man to commit suicide in such a violent and messy way. It was all but impossible to understand the broken thought processes that made killing yourself seem better than life. He'd known despair himself, more than once, but he had always imagined the anguish and alarm of the people who might find his dead body, the mental scars that might leave. Perhaps that was the difference between the suicidal and the depressed; you had to no longer care how other people felt.

If that was the case, then maybe Andrews was a good candidate after all. According to his boss, he had been a ruthless business-man. McLean didn't quite understand the ins and outs of fund management, but he knew enough to know that by deciding to remove a stock from his portfolio, Andrews could well destroy a company. But whilst that ruthlessness might make him the sort of man who could kill himself, the rest of his life spoke of someone with everything to live for. He wasn't married, had no girlfriend to tie him down. He was rich, successful, doing a job he seemed to enjoy. In fact no one at Hoggett Scotia had a bad word to say about him. There was still the matter of his parents to interview; they lived in London and were heading north that afternoon.

'Ah, now that's interesting.' Cadwallader's change in tone cut through McLean's thoughts. He looked up and saw that the pathologist had begun his internal examination.

'What's interesting?'

'This.' He pointed to the shiny mess of entrails and other bits. 'He has cancer, well, everywhere. Looks like it started in his bowel, but it's spread to every organ in his body. If he hadn't killed himself he'd have been dead within a month or two. Do we know who his doctor was? He should have been on serious drug therapy for this.'

'Don't chemo patients usually lose their hair?' McLean asked.

'Good point, inspector. I guess that's why you're a detective and I'm just a pathologist.' Cadwallader bent close to the dead man's head, tweaking some of his hairs out with a pair of forceps. He placed them in a steel dish held out by his assistant. 'Run a spectrographic analysis on those will you, Tracy. I'm willing to bet he wasn't on any medication at all stronger than ibuprofen.' He turned back to McLean. 'Chemo leaves other, more subtle changes in the body, Tony. This man shows none of them.'

'Could he have refused treatment?'

'I can't see what else he could have done. He must've known what was happening to him. Otherwise why kill himself?'

'Why indeed, Angus. Why indeed?'

27

Duguid was nowhere to be seen when McLean walked back into the station. He raised a silent prayer of thanks and hurried down to the tiny incident room. Heat boiled out of the open door, the combined effects of the afternoon sun on the window and the radiator gurgling away, thermostat stuck on full. Both DC Mac-Bride and Grumpy Bob had removed their jackets and ties. Sweat sheened the constable's forehead as he tapped away at his laptop computer.

'Remind me to ask you how you got hold of that machine some-time, Stuart.' MacBride looked up from his screen.

'Mike Simpson's my cousin,' he said. 'I asked him if they had anything spare hanging around.'

'What, Nerd Simpson? The forensic IT guy?'

'The same. And he's not such a nerd really, sir. He just looks that way.'

'Aye, and when he speaks, I understand each of the words he's using, but somehow the meaning of them all together goes straight over the top of my head. So he's your cousin, eh?' Could be useful. Had already been useful judging by the state of the laptop MacBride was using. It might even have been new. 'Have you asked him to take a look at McReadie's computer?'

'He's working on it right now. I don't think I've ever seen him so excited. Apparently McReadie's something of a god in the hacker community here in Edinburgh. Goes under the handle Clouseau.'

McLean remembered the Pink Panther discs in the burglar's collection. All well-played except the last one.

'I'm surprised he picked that name. You'd think he'd associate himself more with the David Niven character.'

Detective Constable MacBride's expression eloquently described his complete lack of understanding.

'The Pink Panther, constable. He played the part of Sir Charles Lytton, the gentleman thief. A cat burglar.'

'Oh, right. I thought he was a cartoon character.'

McLean shook his head and turned away, his eyes falling on the photographs of the dead girl still pinned to the wall behind Grumpy Bob.

'That reminds me. You get anywhere with Mis-Per about that builder?'

MacBride tapped a couple more keys before answering. 'Sorry, sir. I spoke to them, but the computer records only go back to the sixties. I need to go to the archives for anything older. I was going to get onto it this afternoon.'

'Builder?' Grumpy Bob asked.

'The constable's idea, really.' McLean nodded at MacBride, who reddened about the cheeks and ears. 'Our killers were educated men; they wouldn't have known how to lay bricks or set plaster. Someone had to, though, to cover up the alcoves and brick up that room. They'd have needed a builder to do it.'

'But no builder would cover up that,' Grumpy Bob said. 'I mean, he must have seen her body. He'd have seen the jars, too. If it'd been me, I'd've refused. I'd've kicked up merry hell.'

'Ah, but you're not a working-class builder born at the beginning of the twentieth century, Bob. Sighthill was little more than a village back then, the people deferred to the local laird like he was their king. And I wouldn't put it past our killers to threaten his family, either. These people aren't exactly squeamish.'

'The laird?'

'The place belonged to Menzies Farquhar. Set up Farquhar's Bank.'

'So you think he did it? Bullied some local builder into covering it up, then got rid of the builder after he'd finished?' Grumpy Bob looked sceptical to say the least, and as he outlined the theory, McLean could hardly blame his old friend. What had seemed obvious in the unsettling atmosphere of the crime scene looked far-fetched in the warmth of the tiny incident room. It was thinner than a schoolboy's excuse, but it was all they had.

'Not Menzies Farquhar, no. But it could have been his son, Albert.' McLean recalled his brief conversation with Jonas Carstairs at the wake. Could it really be that easy? No. It never was. 'But it's all too circumstantial at the moment. We don't really know anything about the family, less about anyone who might have worked for them around about the war. It's unlikely anyone's going to be alive to talk to. There's certainly no Farquhars left to lock up, if it was them. But if nothing else, I'd like to put a name to our victim, and our best shot at the moment is a missing builder.' He turned back to the constable. 'Stuart, I want you to dig up everything you can on Menzies and Albert Farquhar. Once you've done that you can go and help Bob over in the archives.'

'Oh aye? And what am I going to be doing in there?' The old sergeant looked decidedly shifty, as if he didn't already know.

'You're going to dig out all the unsolved Mis-Per reports for skilled builders living in the Sighthill area. Forty-five through to fifty should cover it. If we don't find anything we can widen either end.'

'From 1945? You've got to be kidding.' Grumpy Bob looked horrified.

'You know they keep records further back than that, Bob.'

'Aye, in the basement, in great big dusty file boxes.'

'Well take a constable with you to help then,' McLean said as Constable Kydd knocked on the open door. 'See, you don't even have to look for one.'

'Sir?' The constable looked from Grumpy Bob to McLean and then back again, worry furrowing her brow.

'Never mind,' McLean said. 'What can we do for you?'

She stepped into the room, pulling a trolley behind her. It was laden with cardboard boxes. 'It's the haul from McReadie's apartment, sir. Forensics have been over them. Apparently they're cleaner than DC Porter's soul, whatever that's supposed to mean.'

'He's a Jehovah's Witness, constable. Hasn't he tried to convert you to the cause yet?'

'Um, no sir. I don't think so. And I've a message from the front desk, too. They've been trying your office but getting no answer and your mobile's going straight to message.'

McLean hefted his phone. He was sure he'd charged it overnight. The screen was blank now, and pressing the power button elicited no response.

'Bloody battery's gone flat again. Why didn't they just phone through to here? No, forget that.' He looked at the lone phone perched on the desk by the laptop. It might have worked, but he'd never seen anyone using it. 'What's the message?'

'Apparently there's a Mr Donald Andrews to see you. Something about identifying his son.'

'Oh crap.' McLean threw his phone to MacBride. 'Lend us your airwave will you, constable. I've got to go back to the mortuary.'

Donald Andrews didn't look much like his son. Angular cheekbones and a pointed nose sharpened his features like he'd spent too long in a high wind. He wore his hair cropped close, a little grey showing at the temples. His eyes were bright blue and piercing and he spoke with a clipped Home Counties accent. McLean commandeered a squad car and driver to take them across town to the mortuary. He left the constable with the car outside, hoping they wouldn't be long.

Dr Sharp had prepared the body for viewing. He was fully shrouded, laid out on a table in a small room set aside from the main examination hall. When they arrived, she showed them in, then carefully folded down the shroud, revealing the dead man's head but hiding the ragged gash in his neck. Donald Andrews stood silent, stock still for long minutes, staring at the pale white face, then slowly turned back to McLean.

'What is this?' he demanded. 'What the hell happened to my son?'

'I'm sorry, sir. This is your son, Peter Andrews, isn't it?' McLean felt a sudden coldness grip his stomach.

'I . . . Yes . . . That is, I think so. But . . . Can I see the rest of his body, please.' It wasn't a question.

'Sir, I'm not sure you want to do that. He's –'

'I'm a surgeon, dammit! I know what's been done to him.'

'I'm sorry, sir. I didn't realise.' McLean nodded to Tracy, who rolled back the rest of the shroud. It was most likely she who had sewn up the body after Dr Cadwallader had finished his examination. McLean was impressed by her skill and thoroughness, but there was no getting past the fact that Peter Andrews had been cruelly filleted. Whereas most fathers might have been horrified, Donald Andrews instead pulled out a slim pair of spectacles and bent closer to inspect his son.

'It's him,' he said after a few minutes. 'He has a birthmark and a couple of scars I'd recognise any day. But I don't understand what's happened to him. How did he get this way?'

'What do you mean, sir? This is how he was when he died.' McLean swallowed. 'They did tell you how he died, didn't they?'

'Yes, and that itself I find hard to believe. Peter had his faults, but depression wasn't one of them.'

'Did you know he had terminal cancer, sir?'

'What? But that's impossible!'

'When did you last see your son, sir?'

'Back in April. He came down to London for the marathon. He did it every year to raise money for the Sick Kids hospital.'

McLean looked at the ravaged body lying naked on the table. He knew that all kinds of people took part in marathons; some even took days to walk the course rather than running. Peter Andrews looked like he'd have needed to take a taxi. His legs were wasted, his spine crooked. The stitching made it hard to see what condition he'd been in before the post-mortem examination, but McLean could remember the swell of a paunch.

'He must have cared for the hospital a great deal, to go to all that effort. Did he raise much?'

'It wasn't about the money, inspector. He did it for the running. You need a charity behind you to get a place in the London marathon these days.'

'I'm sorry, sir, are you saying your son was a regular runner?'

'Since he was about fifteen. He nearly went professional.' Donald Andrews reached out and stroked his dead son's hair. Tears brightened his accusing eyes. 'He finished the last race in two and a half hours.'

185

28

The unfamiliar sound of the airwave set going off in his pocket distracted him as he walked back to the station.

'McLean,' he said, after remembering how to use the machine. It was bulkier than a mobile phone, and more complicated, but its battery hadn't gone flat. Not yet at least.

'Ah, hello, inspector. I was wondering if I was ever going to be connected.' McLean recognised the voice of his grandmother's solicitor.

'Mr Carstairs, I was going to get in touch. About Albert Farquhar.'

A pause, as if the lawyer had been caught off guard. 'Of course. Actually, that's not what I was calling about. I have your grandmother's papers all in order; just need you to sign some forms and then we can begin the tedious process of transferring title deeds and so forth.'

McLean glanced at his watch. The afternoon was getting away from him, and there was a mountain of paperwork on his desk even before he could get to the interesting task of sorting through McReadie's trophies. 'I'm quite busy right now, Mr Carstairs.'

'Of course you are, Tony. But even detective inspectors need to eat sometime. I wondered if you might be interested in a touch of supper. Say around eight? You can sign the papers then and we'll sort out the rest for you. Esther entrusted me with various personal messages to pass on to you after she died, too. It didn't seem quite appropriate to do so at her funeral. And I can tell you all about Bertie Farquhar if you want, although it's a rather distasteful subject.'

It was probably the best offer he was going to get, and would beat a carry-out on the way home close to midnight, which was how the evening looked to be shaping up. And if he could find out a bit more about Farquhar, well, it was almost like work anyway.

'That's very kind, Jonas.'

'Eight o'clock then?'

'Yes, fine.'

Carstairs reminded him of his address, then hung up, by which time McLean had almost reached the station. He was still holding the airwave set trying to work out how to turn it off when he pushed in through the front door.

'Well, miracles never cease,' the desk sergeant said. 'A detective inspector with an airwave set.'

'It's not mine, Pete, I borrowed it off a constable.' McLean shook the thing, prodded the buttons on the front, all to no avail. 'How do you turn the damn thing off?'

Downstairs, chaos ruled the tiny incident room. The boxes Constable Kydd had wheeled in on her trolley were piled all over the place, some opened, others still taped up. In the middle of the whirlwind, DC MacBride knelt with a sheaf of papers, leafing through them hopefully.

'Having fun, constable?' McLean looked at his watch. 'Actually, shouldn't you have gone home by now?'

'Thought I'd make an early start on identifying these pieces, sir.' MacBride held up a clear plastic bag containing a jewel-encrusted gold egg of singular vulgarity.

'Well, I've got about an hour to kill. Chuck us one of those sheets and I'll give you a hand. You had any success yet?'

187

MacBride pointed to a small pile of items on the desk. 'Those were on Mrs Douglas's list. And according to the inventory they were on the bottom shelf, furthest to the right. They were all next to each other too. I'm working on the hypothesis McReadie did things methodically. He's a computer expert, after all.'

'Sounds like a good strategy.' McLean looked around the boxes, checking their labels with his list. 'So this should be the top shelf, working from the left; his first burglary. Major Ronald Duchesne.'

He opened up the box, looking through the clear plastic bags within and trying to tally them against the items reported stolen. It was unlikely they'd all be there; McReadie would probably have sold the pieces that didn't appeal to him, and victims of theft almost always added things to the list of stolen goods. But the box contained nothing that even partially matched. Having pulled everything out and placed it neatly on the floor around him, McLean was about to put it all back again and start on the next box when he noticed one more bag inside. He reached it out, held it up to the light.

A cold shiver ran down his spine.

On the wall, blown up large and pinned in a circle, were the images of the six items found in the alcoves along with the dead girl's preserved organs. Right now he was focusing on the photograph of a single, ornately carved gold cufflink, set with a large ruby. Lying in the bottom of the clear plastic evidence bag was its identical twin.

29

She can't understand what's wrong with her. It all started . . . when? She can't remember. There was shouting, people running around. She'd been scared, a little sick even. But then a warm blanket fell over everything, even her mind.

Voices whisper to her, chiding and comforting, pushing her on. Somehow she has walked for miles, but she has no memory of the distance. Only a dull ache in her legs, her back, the pit of her stomach. She is hungry. So hungry.

The smell catches her nose and drags her along as surely as any rope. She is powerless to resist its call, even though her feet feel like bloody scars on the end of her legs. There are people around, going about their business. She feels ashamed to be seen by them, but they ignore her anyway, moving aside as she staggers along. Just another stupid binge drinker.

She is angry with them for assuming that weakness in her. She wants to hit out, to hurt them, to show them up for the petty-minded fools they are. But the voices calm her, take her anger and bottle it for later. She doesn't ask what later means, only walks towards the smell.

It's like a dream. She leaps from one still image to the next without the boring motion in between. She is in a busy street; she is in a quiet lane; she is standing in front of a large house set back from the road; she is inside.

He sees her standing there, turns towards her. He is old, but youthful in his movements as he walks towards her. Then his eyes meet hers and something in her dies. There is an arrogance in his posture that awakens her anger once more. The whispering voices become a tumult, a rage undammed. Memories hidden for a lifetime blossom like black flowers, rank and rotting. Old men sweating and thrusting, pain enveloping her. Make it stop. God, please make it stop. But it never does. On and on, night after night after night. They did things to her. He did things to her, she is sure of it now, even as she forgets everything else that she ever was.

Something cold and hard and sharp is in her hand now. She has no idea how it got there, no idea where she is, who she is. But she knows why she came here, and what she has to do.

30

'Where's McReadie? Which cell is he in?' McLean burst through the doors into the duty sergeant's office like an explosion. The sergeant looked up from his mug of tea, the late-shift admin staff turning to see what the noise was all about.

'McReadie? He left here a couple hours ago.'

'What?'

'I'm sorry, sir, we left it as late as we could. But we had to charge him with the burglary eventually. Soon as we did, his lawyer was down here like a shot. There was no reason to oppose bail.'

'Damn. I need to speak to him.'

'Can't it wait until tomorrow, sir? You go rushing after him and he'll start claiming harassment. You don't want him getting off on a technicality do you?'

McLean tried to calm himself. It could wait. The young girl wasn't going to get any less dead.

'You're right, Bill,' he said. 'Sorry I banged in like that.'

'No problem, sir. But while you're here, could you do something about that pile of overtime sheets on your desk? Only, month end's coming up and we need to sort out the roster.'

'I'll get them done,' he promised, backing out of the control room. But instead of heading up to his office, he went back to the small incident room, clutching the clear plastic evidence bag all the while. DC MacBride was still there, searching through a different pile of cardboard boxes.

'Found it yet?'

'It's in here somewhere, sir. Ah, here we go.' The constable straightened up, holding another clear evidence bag, also containing an ornate, jewelled cufflink. He handed it over and McLean held them side by side. There was no doubting that they were a pair, though the one found in the basement alcove was cleaner and bore fewer scratches, as if whoever had left it behind had continued to wear the other. Until it had somehow ended up in the collection of Mr Fergus McReadie.

He glanced at his watch. A quarter to eight. Neither of them should be in the station now. It was frustrating to be so close and yet still have to wait. But the duty sergeant was right; he couldn't haul McReadie in this soon after his release without it looking like harassment. Not after having taken so bloody long to charge the man. It would have to wait until morning.

'How's your cousin Mike getting on with the computer?' McLean asked.

'Last I heard he said he hoped to have cracked it by tomorrow.'

'OK, go home, Stuart. We'll run with this tomorrow. I'm not sure what you're doing here this late anyway.'

The constable reddened under his mop of blond hair and muttered something about waiting for someone else to finish their shift at nine.

'Well, as a special treat then, you can do some real policing work for a change.'

'I can?' MacBride's face lit up like Christmas had come early.

'Yes, you can. Go up to my office and sort through the overtime sheets. I'll sign them off when I get in tomorrow.' McLean didn't wait to hear the constable's thanks.

It was a short walk from the station down to Inverleith and the Colonies. The sun had disappeared behind the buildings and exhaust haze somewhere in the north-west, but it was still light. Proper darkness wouldn't come for another couple of hours at least at this time of year. They'd pay for it in the winter, of course.

Over the Water of Leith, the streets changed from Georgian terraces to large detached houses as he approached the Botanical Gardens. The address Carstairs had given him was an imposing three-storey building in a narrow side street blocked off at one end to stop it being a rat-run for commuter traffic. It was pleasantly quiet and clean away from the main road, and reminded him of the street where his grandmother's house stood, on the other side of the city. Edinburgh was full of these pockets of gentility, hiding silently among less salubrious neighbourhoods.

As he walked towards the house, McLean caught a glimpse of a young woman, drunk before the evening had even started, weaving down the pavement away from him. With the Festival and Fringe in full swing, it wasn't that odd to see revellers at all hours, so he gave it little thought. A heavy lorry rattling past the street-end snatched his attention away momentarily, and when he looked back, she was gone. Shaking the image from his head, he climbed the half dozen wide stone steps that led to Carstairs' front porch, and lifted his hand to the bell-pull.

The door was already open.

Somewhere in the distance, a clock chimed the hour. McLean stepped inside, reasoning that Carstairs was expecting him. He may well have left the door open on purpose. A small lobby held an umbrella stand with three umbrellas and a couple of walking sticks in it. A row of elderly overcoats hung from cast iron hooks. Another door, open too, led into the central hall of the house.

'Mr Carstairs?' McLean raised his voice to just below a shout. He had no idea where his host might be within such a large house. Silence greeted him as he stepped onto the black and white tiled floor. It was darker in here, light filtering through a tall window at the back, halfway up the stairs and obscured outside by a large tree.

'Mr Carstairs? Jonas?' He looked around, noting the dark wood panelling, the fireplace, empty now but no doubt very welcoming to winter guests. Large oil paintings of sombre gentlemen lined the walls; an ornate brass chandelier hung from the high ceiling. Something smelled odd.

It was a smell he had encountered recently, and as it worked its way into his memory, McLean found himself looking down at the chequerboard floor. A trail of dark stains meandered across from the entrance lobby to a half-open door on the left of the hall. He followed them, careful not to tread in anything.

'Jonas? Are you in there?' McLean spoke the words, but he already knew the answer. He nudged the door with his foot. It swung easily on silent, well-oiled hinges, releasing an overpowering smell of hot iron and shit. He had to grab a handkerchief, shove it over his nose and mouth to stop from retching

The room beyond was a small study, lined with books and with a neat, antique desk in the centre. Sitting at the desk, his head tilted back to the ceiling, was Jonas Carstairs. His lower half was thankfully obscured from view by the desk. His upper body was a naked, bloody mess.

31

When the first squad car arrived five minutes later, McLean was sitting on the stone steps outside, breathing the fresh city air and trying not to think about what he had seen. He set the two PCs to secure the area, knowing full well that the back door was locked, and carried on waiting for the police doctor to arrive. Meanwhile the SOC van rumbled up the street and half a dozen officers piled out. He was surprised to find himself pleased at seeing the smiling face of Miss-not-Ms Emma Baird, her digital camera already out of its case and slung around her neck. Then he remembered what she'd be photographing.

'You've got another dead body for us, inspector. This is becoming something of a habit, isn't it?'

McLean let out a half-hearted laugh by way of a reply, watching the SOC team clamber into their white paper overalls and grab their cases from the back of the van.

'What've you touched?' the senior technician asked, passing a set of overalls to McLean.

'The front door, the inner door and the back door. I had to use the phone, too. To call it in.'

'Don't they give inspectors mobiles any more?'

'Battery's dead.' McLean lifted the offending article out of his pocket, waved it in front of the technician and put it back again, then started to pull on the overalls. As they were getting ready, a battered old VW Golf rattled up, parked itself in the middle of the street and disgorged an enormous man in an ill-fitting suit. He pulled a medical bag from the passenger seat and waddled over. Dr Buckley was an amiable fellow, as long as you didn't ask him stupid questions.

'Where's the body then?'

'You'll need to suit up, doc,' McLean said, knowing it would get him a scowl and not being disappointed. There was a scramble to find a pair of overalls that would fit, but finally they were able to re-enter the house. He led them straight to the study. If anything the smell was worse. Lazy houseflies buzzed around the body.

'He's dead,' Dr Buckley said, without even entering the room. He turned to leave.

'Is that it? You're not going to examine him?' McLean asked.

'Not my job, and you know it, inspector. I can see from here that his throat's been cut. Death would have been near instantaneous. Dr Cadwallader will be able to give you more details when he gets here. Good day.'

McLean watched the fat man waddle out of the house, then turned back to the SOC team. 'OK, I guess you can start on the room, but don't touch the body until the pathologist gets here.'

They moved in like a small but efficient swarm of ants. The flash on Emma's camera popped away as McLean finally entered the room. The first thing he noticed was the pile of clothes, neatly draped over the back of a leather armchair in the corner. Shirt, jacket, tie. He looked back at the body and realised it was undressed from the waist up. Moving behind the desk, he winced as he saw the mess of entrails spilling into the lawyer's lap, draping to the polished wooden floorboards. His chair had been pushed back from the desk a small distance, and he sat upright, almost posed, with his hands dropping to either side. Blood had trickled down his bare arms, dripping from the ends of his fingers to form twin pools beneath. A short-bladed Japanese kitchen knife lay on the desk in front of him, smeared in blood and gore.

'Good God, Tony. What the hell's been going on here?'

McLean looked round to see Angus Cadwallader standing in the doorway. He had already pulled on a paper overall, and Dr Sharp stood nervously behind him.

'Does any of this look familiar to you, Angus?' McLean stepped aside to let the pathologist get a closer look.

'Superficially, yes. It's obviously a copy of the Smythe and Stewart killings.' Cadwallader bent down close to the body, prodding the gash in Carstairs' neck with his gloved fingers. 'But I can't say here what came first, the throat cut or the evisceration. Hard to see if anything's missing, either. Ah, what's this?' He stood, leaning over the corpse and prising open its mouth.

'Bag please, Tracy, and a pair of forceps.' Cadwallader took the instrument and started to fish around. 'You wouldn't have thought it would all fit in there. Ah, no, it's been cut in half. That would explain it.'

'Explain what, Angus?' McLean stifled a belch. Christ but it'd be embarrassing to throw up. It wasn't as if he was some fresh-faced PC seeing his first corpse. But then he'd come here to have supper with Carstairs.

'This, inspector, is what we doctors call the liver.' Cadwallader lifted up a long, slimy purple-brown strip of material, pincered in his forceps, then dropped it into the waiting bag. 'Your killer's cut a strip of it and shoved it in his victim's mouth. I can't tell from here whether it's his or not, but I can't think of any other reason for tearing him up like that.' He pointed at the mess that had once been Carstairs' stomach and chest. 'Let's get him back to the mortuary, shall we. See what secrets he has to reveal.'

32

'I'm sorry, Tony, but I'm going to have to give the investigation to Chief Inspector Duguid.'

McLean stood in front of Chief Superintendent McIntyre's desk, not quite at attention, but neither relaxed. She'd summoned him the moment he'd arrived at the station that morning, bright and early after a night of fitful sleep and horrible nightmares. He clenched his teeth against the retort he wanted to make, willed himself to relax. Losing his temper with the boss was never going to help.

'Why?' he asked, finally.

'Because you're too close to Carstairs.'

'What? I hardly knew the man.'

'He was executor of your grandmother's estate. As I understand it you're the sole beneficiary. He attended her funeral. You were going round to have dinner with him. He was, in short, a family friend. I can't let that jeopardise what is a very important investigation. Have you any idea what Carstairs did for this city whilst he was alive?'

'I . . . No.'

'Well, various very important people have been phoning me up since five this morning to tell me. The chief constable used to play golf with him; the first minister used to invite him on fishing holidays; he was instrumental in writing the constitution for the new parliament.'

'Why Duguid? Can't Chief Inspector Powell take the case? Or one of the other inspectors?'

'Charles is a highly experienced detective, Tony. And he impressed everyone with his handling of the Smythe case.'

Except me, McLean thought. 'But he over-simplifies things.'

'And you needlessly complicate them. It's a shame you can't work together. You'd cancel each other out.'

'So that's it then. I'm to have nothing to do with the case?'

'Not exactly. I'll want you to give your input where it can help, but you're not leading this. Besides, there's a more pressing side of the investigation that you can work on. You attended the Smythe crime scene, and you were the first to see Carstairs after he'd been killed. How likely do you think it is that their similarities are just coincidence?'

'But we know Smythe's killer is dead. He killed himself less than twenty-four hours afterwards.'

'Exactly. And we've not released details of the murder to the press. The coverage just said that he'd been brutally attacked. Which means whoever killed Carstairs had access to detailed crime-scene reports. That's not a leak I can tolerate. Find it, Tony, and stop it.'

'Um. Isn't that a job for Professional Standards?'

McIntyre rubbed at her temple with a tired hand. 'You really want them all over everything you, Duguid, everyone in CID has been doing for the last God knows how many months? It may come to that, Tony, but for now I want someone I can trust to start looking into it.'

*

She watches the rising sun with a sense of awe. It sits on the eastern horizon, a great fat red orb of power, filling her with its heat.

The voices sing to her of great deeds and she knows she is their tool of vengeance. It was good to do their work.

She looks at her hands, stained and bloody, and feels once more the warmth and wetness of the man's skin; red welling up as the knife parted flesh to reveal the pulsing life beneath. She had held it in her hands, cut it from him and forced him to eat. His last meal on earth before she ripped his soul out for the voices to devour.

But she is tired, so tired. And still the hunger courses through her belly. The pain in her legs is a constant ache, her back a twist of agony with every step. The voices still comfort her, still urge her on. There is more work to do, more vengeance to take. He was not the only one to defile her, after all. The others must pay too.

But it is hard, so hard, to do their bidding anymore. If she can just reach the sun. Just tap the smallest part of its immeasurable strength for herself. Then she can obey the voices. And she longs for the thrill of obeying them. She wants nothing more than that. How she has longed all her life to be the tool of vengeance.

Somehow she is on top of the world. Wind whistles around her like a crowd screaming in alarm. She ignores it. There is only her, only the sun, only the voices she wants to serve.

Spreading her arms wide, she leaps into the sky.

33

Waverley Station was busy at the best of times. With the Festival and Fringe in full flow, it was a nightmare of milling backpacks, horn-tooting taxis and lost tourists. Throw in an ambulance, a couple of squad cars and a halt on all train movements and the chaos was complete.

McLean saw all this from the walkway that linked the steps down from Princes Street beside the Balmoral Hotel to Market Street on the other side. Before they'd built the railways, this had all been a rank, foetid loch, filled with the refuse and sewage of the Old Town. Sometimes he wished they'd let it flood over again.

Dr Buckley had beaten him to the scene this time. The portly fellow was bent low over the tracks, studying a crumpled mess. Closer up, McLean realised that once it had been a human being, possibly female. The fall from North Bridge, through the reinforced glass roof of the station and into the path of the night train from King's Cross hadn't left much to go by.

'This one dead too?'

The doctor looked up at his words. 'Ah, inspector. I thought it might be you who showed up. Yes, she's dead. Probably as soon as she hit the glass, poor thing.'

McLean searched for a uniform who looked like he might be in charge. Two constables were busy keeping the gawkers away, but other than that there was no one around.

'Who called you in?' he asked the doctor.

'Oh, Sergeant Houseman was here a minute ago. I think he was first on the scene.'

'Where's he got to now?'

'I'm a doctor, not a detective, inspector. I think he went to talk to the station manager.'

'Sorry, doc. It's been a frustrating morning.'

'Tell me about it. Ah. Here he is now.'

Big Andy pushed his way through the crowd, closely followed by Emma Baird and her camera. Both of them jumped down from the platform and picked their way across the tracks.

'Andy, can we get a tent over her or something,' McLean said, as camera-phone flashes flickered around him. 'I'm not happy with the ghouls on the platform.'

'Already on it, sir.' Big Andy pointed to where a couple of ScotRail employees struggled with a maintenance shelter. They seemed reluctant to approach, so in the end McLean and the sergeant had to wrestle it into position themselves. Baird began to photograph the scene and McLean had a sudden, nasty thought. She was the official SOC photographer. Who else would have easy access to scene-of-crime photographs from Barnaby Smythe's murder?

Just about any of the hundred or so officers Duguid had drafted in to the case, and any of the admin staff who'd had a reason to go into the incident room during the short duration of the investigation. He shook the thought from his head.

'What's the story?' he asked.

'Not much to tell, sir. Happened about half an hour ago, apparently. I've two constables up on the bridge getting names of witnesses, but there's not many people prepared to admit they were watching. Looks like she climbed up on the parapet and jumped. Bad luck that she hit a pane square on and broke through, worse luck that the train was coming into the station at the time. What're the chances of that, eh?'

'Pretty damn small, I'd say. What about witnesses down here?'

'Well, there's the train driver for one. A few people were on the platform, but it's chaos in here. As many would've run away as come forward to get a better look.'

'Yeah, I know. Well, do the best you can, OK? See if you can't get a room somewhere to conduct interviews. I don't think there's much we'll glean from the witnesses, but we've got to go by the book.'

'The station manager's clearing us an office right now, sir. I could do with a couple more constables if that's all right.'

'Call the station and have them send anyone who's stupid enough to be hanging around. I'll sanction the time. We need to get her moved before the whole city grinds to a halt.'

McLean knelt by the broken mess that had once been a human being. She was wearing what appeared to be office clothes: knee-length skirt in sensible beige cotton; once-white blouse, its lace exposing the edge of her bra beneath; sharp-edged jacket with heavy shoulder-padding, some of which had torn loose in great long synthetic hairs. Her legs were bare, snapped and cut, but recently shaved. She wore a pair of high-heeled black leather ankle boots of the type that had been fashionable in the late eighties and were no doubt making a comeback. It was impossible to tell what her face might have looked like; her back was twisted well past snapping point and her head was ground into the coarse gravel between the sleepers. Blood matted her long auburn hair; her hands smeared with it.

'Christ but I hate jumpers.'

McLean looked up as Cadwallader knelt down beside him. The pathologist looked tired as he peered at the dead body, examining her exposed skin with gloved fingers. He stooped low and peered under the arch of her twisted spine.

'OK to move her?' he asked. Cadwallader stood, stretching his back like a cat.

'Sure. I can't tell you anything from here except that she died before getting most of these injuries. There's not enough blood loss. Some people are dead before they even hit the ground.' He looked up. 'Or in this case the roof. With any luck she was one of them.'

McLean turned and nodded to the waiting ambulance driver. He jumped down, bringing his stretcher and an assistant. Together they lifted the dead woman away from her little pit. He was relieved to see that nothing fell off as they put her in a black body bag and zipped it up. Emma Baird zoomed in on the indentation in the gravel, the flash on her camera bleaching it with light. The pathologist was right; there was no blood staining the ground, only oil. A scrubby weed with a single yellow flower rose up in the middle.

'Where's the train?' he asked of no one in particular. A short man bustled up, his thinning hair lifted in a greasy comb-over and his moustache just millimetres away from being Hitler. He wore a bright orange safety jacket and clutched a walkie-talkie.

'Bryan Alexander.' He offered a fat hand for McLean to shake. 'I'm the operations manager. Is this going to take long, inspector?'

'A woman's dead, Mr Alexander.'

'Aye, I know.' He had the decency to look a little ashamed. 'But I've ten thousand others alive an' waiting on their trains.'

'Well show me the one that hit her, will you?'

'You're just here, inspector.' Mr Alexander pointed down the track towards England. About twenty yards away a sleek, red intercity train leant slightly to one side, the bulk of its carriages curving away around a bend. From this angle it looked absurdly like it had a flat tyre.

'We had to back her up. Lucky she was almost at a stop anyway. I've worked the railways for near on thirty years now, and I can tell you a moving train doesn't leave much of a body it hits.'

McLean walked up to the locomotive. He'd never realised just how big they were. It towered over him close up, smelling of heat and diesel oil. A thin bloodstain smear on the pointed glass front marked where the woman had hit the windscreen full on. Most likely she had bounced onto the rails and then been pushed to her final resting place. He turned around and shouted, 'Miss Baird!'

She came trotting up.

'Pictures, please.' He pointed to the front of the train. 'Try and get one showing the point of impact.'

As the SOC photographer got to work, McLean noticed Mr Alexander glance at his wristwatch. Cadwallader approached at the same time, appraising the train.

'Not much blood here either.' He looked up to the glass ceiling and the one broken pane. 'Can we get up there?'

'Aye, if you'll follow me.' The operations manager led them to the end of the platform, back towards the central building. Emma Baird took a couple more photographs and then scurried to join them as they entered through a side door marked 'Authorised Personnel Only'. They climbed a narrow flight of stairs and then stopped at the top by another locked door whilst Mr Alexander searched for the right key.

Stepping out on the station roof was a strange experience. It was a completely new vista of the city, looking up at the underside of North Bridge and the lower basements of the North British Hotel. McLean always thought of it as the North British. As far as he was concerned, Balmoral was a castle in Aberdeenshire.

Cast-iron railings flanked the walkway across the glass roof. It was like some giant Victorian greenhouse, only the glass was thick, reinforced and opaque. The broken pane was alongside the walkway, much to McLean's relief. He didn't much fancy trusting his weight to the glass, even if it was meant to be more than strong enough. It had failed once, and that was too often.

Cadwallader knelt beside the hole, peering through to the tracks below. 'No blood here at all,' he said finally, as Baird took more photographs; she was nothing if not thorough. McLean looked up to the parapet of the bridge, trying to judge the height.

'Are we all done here?' Mr Alexander asked. McLean decided he really didn't like the man, but he was also aware of the need to get the station running again as soon as possible. He didn't want a bollocking from McIntyre when ScotRail put in a complaint.

'Angus?' He looked at the pathologist.

'I'm guessing the impact here killed her. Probably snapped her neck. The cuts are most likely from the train. If she was already dead when she hit it, that would explain why there's so little blood on the ground.'

'I can hear a but coming,' McLean said.

'Well, if she didn't bleed profusely after the train hit her, and there's barely any skin fragments here, then why is her hair matted with blood, and why is it all over her hands?'

34

McLean left Grumpy Bob at Waverley to co-ordinate the investigation. He walked through the crowds of blithely ignorant tourists and shoppers back to the station, considering the various investigations he was juggling. They were all important, but try as hard as he might, it was always the dead girl in the basement who grabbed the lion's share of his attention. It didn't really make sense; she was a cold case, after all. Chances were very slim of finding anyone alive who could be made to pay for her death. And yet the fact that the injustice done her had festered for so long somehow made it worse. Or maybe it was because nobody else seemed to care that he felt the need to go that extra mile?

'I need to see McReadie, find out where he nicked those cufflinks from. Sort out a car and let's pay our cat burglar a visit.'

DC MacBride was hard at work tapping at the keys on his shiny laptop down in the incident room. He stopped, closed the folder he'd been transposing, paused before answering.

'Er, that might not be wise, sir.'

'Why not, constable?'

'Because Mr McReadie's lawyer's already lodged a formal complaint alleging that his client was shown undue force when he was arrested, and that he was held without charge longer than necessary.'

'He's what?' McLean almost exploded with rage. 'The little bastard breaks into my grandmother's house on the day of her funeral and he thinks he can pull a stunt like that?'

'Aye, I know. He'll not get away with it. But it might be an idea to stay away from him a while.'

'I'm investigating a murder, constable. He's got information that could lead me to the killer.' McLean looked at MacBride, seeing the discomfort written plainly on his face. 'Who told you this, anyway?'

'Chief Superintendent McIntyre, sir. She asked me to tell you to steer clear of McReadie if you knew what was good for you.' He held up his hands in defence. 'Those were her words, sir, not mine.'

McLean rubbed at his forehead with a tired hand. 'Great. That's just fucking great. Have you got the cufflinks there?'

MacBride shuffled some papers on the table, then handed the two evidence bags over. McLean shoved them in his jacket pocket, heading for the door.

'Come on then,' he said.

'But I thought . . . McReadie . . .'

'We're not going to see Fergus McReadie, constable. Not now, anyway. There's more than one way to skin this particular cat.'

Douglas and Footes, Jewellers to Her Majesty the Queen, occupied an unprepossessing shopfront in the west end of George Street. It looked for all the world like it had been there even before James Craig had drawn up his master plan for the New Town. Its only concession to the ills of modernity was that, despite the 'Open' sign, the door was locked; now you had to ring a buzzer to be allowed in. McLean showed his warrant card and they were ushered into a room at the back that could have been the butler's pantry in an old country mansion, sometime around the turn of the nineteenth century. They waited for a few minutes in silence, then were greeted by an elderly man in an equally dated black pinstripe suit, a slim leather apron tied around his waist.

'Inspector McLean, how nice to see you. I was so sorry to hear about your grandmother. Such an intelligent lady, and a good judge of quality too.'

'Thank you, Mr Tedder. That's very kind.' McLean took the proffered hand. 'I think she rather enjoyed coming in here; she often complained that the shops in the city weren't what they used to be, but you could be sure of good service in Douglas and Footes.'

'We do our best, inspector. But I don't suppose you came here to exchange compliments.'

'No, indeed. I was wondering if you might be able to tell me anything about these.' He pulled the bags from his pocket and handed them to the jeweller. Mr Tedder peered at the cufflinks through the plastic, then reached over to the nearby counter and switched on a large anglepoise lamp.

'May I take them out?'

'By all means, only don't get them muddled, please.'

'Unlikely, I think. They're quite different.'

'You mean they're not a pair?'

Mr Tedder pulled a small eyeglass out of his pocket, wedged it in his eye and bent over the first cufflink, rolling it around in his fingers. After a minute, he dropped it back in its bag and repeated the process with the other one.

'They're a pair, all right,' he said finally. 'But one's been used regularly, the other's almost as new.'

'So how do you know they're a pair, sir?' DC MacBride asked.

'The hallmarks are the same on each one. Made by us, as it happens, in 1932. Exquisite craftsmanship, bespoke, you know. These would have been part of a set given to a young gentleman, along with matching shirt studs and possibly a signet ring.'

'Have you any idea who they might have been given to?'

'Well now, let me see, 1932.' Mr Tedder reached up to a dusty shelf full of leather-bound ledgers, running his fingers along them until he found what he was looking for. He pulled out a slim volume.

'Not a lot of people commissioning pieces in the early thirties. The depression, you know.' He laid the ledger down on the counter, carefully opened it at the back and consulted an index written in neat copperplate writing, the ink slightly faded with age. His finger scanned the lines far faster than McLean could read the narrow, angular script. Then he stopped, flicked the pages back one by one until he found what he was looking for.

'Ah, yes. Here it is. Gold signet ring. Pair of gold cufflinks, set with brilliant round-cut rubies. Matching set of six shirt studs, also gold set with rubies. They were sold to a Mr Menzies Farquhar of Sighthill. Oh yes, of course, Farquhar's Bank. Well, they didn't suffer much between the wars. If I remember correctly, they made a lot of money financing the rearmament.'

'So these belong to Menzies Farquhar?' McLean picked up the cufflinks in their bags.

'Well, he bought them. But here it says there's to be an inscription engraved on the presentation case. "Albert Menzies Farquhar, on the reaching of his majority, August 13th 1932."'

'I want a word with you, McLean. In my office.'

McLean stopped in his tracks. Duguid had stepped out of McIntyre's room just as he and Constable MacBride had walked past. He turned slowly around to face his accuser.

'Is it urgent? Only I've got an important new lead on the ritual killing.'

'I'm sure someone who's been dead for sixty years can wait a day or two longer for justice, inspector.' Duguid's face was flushed red, never a good sign.

'Ah, but her killers aren't getting any younger. I'd like to catch at least one of them before he dies.'

'Nevertheless, this is important.'

'OK, sir.' McLean turned back to MacBride, handing him the bagged cufflinks. 'Take these back to the incident room, constable. And see what you can dig up about Albert Farquhar. There should be a report about his death.'

MacBride took the bags and hurried off down the corridor. McLean watched him go for just long enough to make his point, then followed Duguid to his office. It was bigger by far than his own tiny space, with room for a couple of comfortable chairs and a low table. Duguid shut the door on the empty, quiet corridor, but didn't sit down.

'I want to know the exact nature of your relationship with Jonas Carstairs,' he said.

'What do you mean?' The room seemed to shrink on him as McLean stiffened, his back to the now-closed door.

'You know damned well what I mean, McLean. You were the first on the scene, you discovered the body. Why did Carstairs invite you round to his house?'

'How do you know he did that, sir?'

Duguid picked up a piece of paper from his desk. 'Because I have here a transcript of a phone conversation between the two of you. Made, I should add, just hours before his death.'

McLean began to ask how Duguid had come by the transcript, then remembered that Carstairs' call had been routed from the station through to DC MacBride's airwave set. Of course it would have been recorded.

'If you've read the transcript, sir, then you'll know that Carstairs wanted me to sign some papers regarding my late grandmother's estate. He invited me around to supper I assume because he realised

211

I'd have difficulty finding time to drop round the office during the day.'

'Does that seem normal behaviour for a solicitor? He could have just couriered the papers over here for you to sign.'

'Is it normal behaviour for the senior partner in a prestigious law firm to personally handle the execution of a will, sir? Would you expect him to attend the funeral? Mr Carstairs was an old friend of my grandmother. I suspect he saw it as his personal duty to make sure all her affairs were put in order.'

'And these messages that your grandmother entrusted.' Duguid read from the sheet. 'What's all that about?'

'Is this a formal interview, sir? Only if it is, shouldn't we be taping it? And shouldn't there be another officer present?'

'Of course it's not a bloody formal interview, man! You're not a suspect. I just want to know the circumstances of the discovery.' Duguid's face reddened.

'I don't see how my grandmother's last will and testament has anything to do with it.'

'You don't? Well, perhaps you can explain why Carstairs changed his own will, just a couple of days ago.'

'I honestly have no idea what you're talking about, sir. I only met the man a week ago. I hardly knew him.'

Duguid put the transcript sheet down on his desk and picked up another piece of paper. It was a photocopy of the front page of a legal document, the letters smudged by the fax machine. At the top of the sheet was the fax number and name of the sender: Carstairs Weddell Solicitors.

'Then why do you suppose he left the entirety of his personal wealth to you?'

35

Grumpy Bob was reading his newspaper, feet up on the table amongst the evidence bags when McLean finally stumbled back into their tiny incident room.

'You all right, sir? You look like you just found half a maggot in your apple.'

'What? Oh, no. I'm fine, Bob. Just a little shocked is all.' He told the sergeant his news.

'Jings. Your boat's certainly come in. Don't suppose you could lend me a few quid?'

'It's not funny, Bob. He left me everything except his business assets. Why the hell would he do that?'

'I dunno. Maybe he didn't have anyone else to leave it to. Maybe he always had a thing for your gran and decided he'd rather leave it to you than the animal shelter.'

A thing for your gran. Bob's words brought back a memory suppressed by the rush of recent events. A series of photographs in an empty bedroom. A man not his grandfather who nevertheless looked just like his father. Just like him. Could that have been a young Carstairs? Could he have? No. His grandmother would never have. Would she?

'But he changed it just last week.' McLean answered his own question and Bob's both. He tried to remember the few conversations he'd had with the old lawyer since that first telephone call the day after his grandmother had died. He'd been friendly enough, almost avuncular at first. But at the funeral he'd seemed distracted, expecting someone else. And then the strange conversation the afternoon before the lawyer had been killed. What was that all about? What messages had his grandmother left for Carstairs to deliver after her death? Or was it something Carstairs himself wanted to say? Something had rattled the old man. Now he'd never know what.

'I don't know what you're complaining about, sir. It's not often a lawyer gives you money.'

McLean tried to smile at the joke, but found it hard. 'Where's DC MacBride?'

'He went off to the *Scotsman*. Something about searching their archives.'

'Finding out about Albert Farquhar. Good. How are we getting on with McReadie?'

Grumpy Bob put down his paper, moved his feet off the table and sat up straight. 'We've found items from the five burglaries we were looking into. Not everything reported missing's here, but certainly enough to put McReadie away for a good stretch. The IT boys have pretty much sorted out his computer, too. I don't think he's going to weasel out of it, even if he has got himself a fancy lawyer.'

'Good. What about the cufflink? Did IT come up with an address for that piece yet?'

Grumpy Bob shuffled through the pile of bags on his desk, retrieving a slim sheaf of papers, leafing through them until he found what he was looking for.

'That was taken from an address in Penicuik about seven years ago. A Miss Louisa Emmerson.'

'Do we know if the theft was ever reported?'

'I'll check, sir.' Grumpy Bob shuffled over to the laptop, tapped at a few keys. 'There's nothing against that address or that name on the database.'

'I didn't think there would be. Grab us a car, Bob. I fancy a trip out to the countryside.'

Penicuik nestled in a valley ten miles south of the city and was cut in two by the meandering River Esk. McLean had faded half-memories of weekend road trips to the Borders with his parents, stopping off at Giapetti's for ice cream on their way to visit historic sites. He'd been bored to tears by cold ancient buildings, but he'd loved sitting in the back seat of his father's car, watching the bleak and wild countryside go by, falling asleep to the rhythm of tyres on tarmac and the thrum of the engine. And he'd loved the ice cream too. The town had spread since then, sprawling up the hillsides and north towards the army barracks. The main street was pedestrianised now, Giapetti's long since disappeared under the bulk of a faceless supermarket.

The house they were looking for was a little way out of the town, heading along the old church road towards the Pentland Hills. Set back from the road in a large garden, surrounded by mature trees, it was built of dark red sandstone, with tall, narrow windows and a high-pitched roof; most likely a manse from the days when ministers were expected to have dozens of children. As the car drove up the long gravel drive and pulled to a halt in front of the heavy stone porch, a flurry of small dogs came flying out of the doorway, all high-pitched barks and excitement.

'You sure it's safe?' Grumpy Bob asked as McLean started to open the door. A sea of wet noses and excited yelps greeted him.

'It's when they make no noise at all you need to worry, Bob.' He bent down and offered his hand as a sacrifice to be sniffed and licked. The sergeant stayed where he was, seat belt firmly on, door tightly closed.

'Don't mind the dogs, they only bite when they're hungry.'

McLean looked up from the throng to see a portly lady in wellingtons and a tweed skirt. She was perhaps in her late fifties and held a pair of secateurs in one hand, a wooden trug draped over her arm.

'Dandie Dinmonts, aren't they?' He patted one of the beasts on the head.

'Indeed they are. It's nice to see someone with a bit of education. How can I help you?'

'Detective Inspector McLean. Lothian and Borders Police.' He produced his warrant card, then waited whilst the woman retrieved a pair of spectacles from a chain around her neck and placed them on her nose, peering first at the tiny photograph, then rather disconcertingly at him. 'Have you lived here long, Mrs . . . ?'

'Johnson, Emily Johnson. I'm not surprised you don't recognise me, inspector. It's been, what, over thirty years since I last saw you?'

Not quite thirty-three years, and he'd been not yet five. Putting his mother and father to rest in a corner of Mortonhall Cemetery. Christ, but the world could be small sometimes.

'I thought you moved to London after the plane crash.' It was a random piece of information he had picked up many years later. That awkward teenage phase when he'd obsessed about his dead parents, collecting every scrap of information he could find about them, and about the people who had died on the plane with them.

'You're right. I did. But I inherited this place about seven years ago. I was growing tired of London, so it seemed the ideal time to move.'

'And you never remarried. You know, after . . .'

'After my father-in-law killed my husband and your parents in that damn-fool aeroplane of his? No. I didn't have the stomach to go through all that again.' A grey frown passed over the woman's face, almost a scowl. 'But you didn't come here to reminisce, inspector. You weren't expecting to find me here at all. So what did bring you here?'

'A burglary, Mrs Johnson. Just after a Miss Louisa Emmerson died at this house.'

'Louisa was Toby's cousin. She was married to Bertie Farquhar. Old man Menzies bought them this house as a wedding present. Can you imagine that? She dropped her married name when Bertie died. That would have been the early sixties, I think. It was all a bit messy really. Got blind drunk and piled his car into a bus stop. She lived out here on her own until she died. I only found out afterwards that she'd left it to me. Guess there was no one else in the family to pass it on to.'

'So Albert Farquhar's belongings would have been here?'

'Lord, yes. Most of them still are. The Farquhars never really needed to sell things off to pay the coal bill, if you know what I mean.'

McLean looked up at the large house, then over at a lower building set a bit away; a converted coach house. A brand new Range Rover poked its nose out of a wide garage. Money just seemed to cling to some people; they were so rich they didn't even notice being robbed. Was he like that? Would he get that way?

'Did you know that the place had been burgled, Mrs Johnson?'

'Goodness, no. When did you say it happened?'

'Seven years ago. March the fourteenth. The day Miss Emmerson was buried.'

'Well, it's the first I've heard of it. I didn't get the house until

217

July of that year; there was a mountain of paperwork to sort through. That's what brought me back to Scotland, and once I was here, well, I realised how much I'd grown to hate London.' Mrs Johnson paused for breath, then narrowed her eyes. 'But how do you know there was a burglary, inspector?'

'We caught the burglar trying to steal from another house. He kept records of where he'd been, and mementos from each job.'

'How very stupid of him. What did he take from here?'

'A number of small items, including a gold cufflink we can now positively identify as belonging to Albert Farquhar.'

'And is that important?'

'It could well be the clue that solves a particularly nasty murder.'

'Sounded like you'd met before. Did you get what you were looking for?'

McLean studied the road as he drove the pool car back towards the city. Grumpy Bob hadn't moved from the car during the whole conversation.

'Mrs Emily Johnson was married to Andrew Johnson, whose father Tobias was flying the plane that crashed into the side of Ben MacDui on its way from Inverness to Edinburgh, killing himself, his son and my parents in 1974.' He stated the facts simply, wondering why it was that they kept on coming back to haunt him. 'The last time I saw her was at their funeral.'

'Jesus. What're the chances of that happening?'

'Greater than you'd think, Bob.' McLean explained the tortuous, convoluted relationships that linked the current owner to Bertie Farquhar.

'So you reckon Farquhar's your man, then?'

'One of them. I asked Mrs Johnson if she recognised the nickname "Toots", but it meant nothing to her. She said she'd have a search through the attic for any old photographs and stuff, though. And she came up with one other interesting piece of information.'

'Oh, aye. What's that then?'

'Farquhar and Tobias Johnson were old friends. They served in the army together during the Second World War. Some special forces group based in West Africa.'

They fell silent after that, as McLean drove the car past the turning down to Roslin and its enigmatic chapel; past Loanhead and the blue-box Ikea warehouse, its car park overflowing with eager shoppers; under the bypass and through Burdiehouse; and finally up the hill towards Mortonhall, Liberton Brae and on into the city. As they passed the entrance to the crematorium, he hit the brakes, darting in through the gates to a blare of horns from the car behind. Grumpy Bob grabbed the dashboard, slamming his feet into the passenger foot well.

'Christ! Give us a bit of warning, will you.'

'Sorry, Bob.' McLean pulled into a space in the car park, killed the engine and threw the keys to his passenger. 'Take the car back to the station, will you. There's something I have to do here.'

36

McLean watched the car pull away, then went in search of the manager. Moments later he was walking away from the cremato-rium building and into the grounds that surrounded it, clutching a tiny, plain terracotta urn. It didn't take long to reach the spot he was looking for. He felt a twinge of guilt that he hadn't visited it in at least three years. The headstone had developed a lean, prob-ably from the action of tree roots. It bore his grandfather's name and dates, then a wide gap had been left. Beneath that his mother and father's names. Two years separated their birth dates, but their deaths had occurred on the same day. At the same instant when the aeroplane they had been flying in had hit the side of a moun-tain south of Inverness. He liked to think they might have been holding hands when it happened, but in truth he hardly knew them at all.

Someone had dug a neat, small hole at the base of the head-stone, and for a moment he felt a sense of outrage that his parents' final resting place could be desecrated so. Then he realised why he was here. What he had come to do. He looked at the urn. It was simple, functional and unadorned by decoration or embellish-ment. Much like the woman whose remains it contained. He suppressed the urge to pull open the top and peer at the contents within. This was his grandmother. Reduced to a tiny pile of ash, but it was still his grandmother. The woman who had raised him, fed him, nurtured him, loved him. He had thought that he'd come to terms with her death a long time ago, when he had accepted that she would never recover from her stroke. But seeing the family grave, the names on the headstone and that space waiting for hers to be added, he finally understood that she was gone.

The ground was dry under the trees as he knelt and placed the jar in the hole. The removed earth had been piled up alongside, covered over with a sheet of green tarpaulin lest the sight of bare soil offend or upset the bereaved. No doubt someone would come along later and fill in the hole, but that felt wrong somehow. Disrespectful. McLean looked around for a shovel, but whoever had dug the hole had taken his tools away with him. So he carefully removed the tarpaulin, then, kneeling on the ashes of his dead parents, he shifted the soft, dry earth back into the hole with his bare hands.

'She was a fine woman, Esther Morrison.'

McLean stood and turned in one swift motion that sent a tweak of pain up his spine into his neck. An elderly gentleman stood behind him, dressed in a long black coat despite the August heat. He held a dark, wide-brimmed hat in one gnarled hand, and leant heavily on a walking stick. His head was topped with a profusion of thick white hair, but it was his face that caught McLean's attention. Once proud, strong features had been marred by some terrible accident, and now it was a mess of scar tissue and ill-matched skin-graft. It was a face you wouldn't have thought it possible to forget, those piercing eyes as much as the scarring. But though it was hauntingly familiar, for the life of him, McLean couldn't put a name to it.

'Did you know her, Mr . . . ?' He asked.

'Spenser.' The man pulled off a leather glove and offered his hand. 'Gavin Spenser. Yes, I knew Esther. A long time ago. I even asked her to marry me, but Bill beat me to that prize.'

'In all my life I don't think I've ever heard anyone refer to my grandfather as Bill.' McLean wiped his palms on his suit, then took the proffered hand. 'Anthony McLean.' He added.

'The policeman, yes, I've heard about you.'

'You weren't at the funeral.'

'No, no. I've been living abroad for years now. America mostly. I only heard the news the day before yesterday.'

'So how'd you know my gran?'

'We met at university in, oh, it must have been '33. Esther was the brilliant young medical student everyone wanted to be with. It quite broke my heart when she chose Bill over me, but that's ancient history.'

'And yet you came all this way to pay your respects?'

'Ah yes, of course. The detective.' Spenser smiled, his scarred face creasing in all the wrong ways. 'Actually I had some business that needs tidying up. You know how it is when you delegate; you always spend twice as much time sorting out the mess left behind.'

'I've known some people like that, but mostly my colleagues are quite reliable.'

'Well, you're a lucky man, inspector. I seem to spend most of my time correcting other people's mistakes these days.' Spenser chuckled. He reached into the pocket of his coat and drew out a slim silver case. Inside it were some business cards and he handed one to McLean. 'This is my home in Edinburgh. I should be around for a week or two. Look me up and we can have a chat about your . . . grandmother, eh? Who'd have thought it.'

'I'd like that, sir,' McLean said, shaking the man's hand again.

'Well, I'll be off now,' Spenser said, shifting his hat back onto his head. 'Business to attend to. You'll be wanting some time alone here anyway.' He walked off with surprising swiftness and agility for a man of his years, swinging his cane in time to a tuneless whistle.

McLean hitched a ride into town in a squad car out of Howden-hall nick. The PC driving offered to take him all the way to the city centre, but he knew there would be nothing but a big pile of overtime sheets to be dealt with. Fallout from closing Waverley Station for a morning. He needed time to think, needed a bit of space, so he had the squad car drop him off in Grange and walked the rest of the way to his grandmother's house. With his mobile still refusing to hold a charge for more than half an hour, there was a chance he might have some peace and quiet for a while. He'd pay for it later, of course, but wasn't that always the way?

As soon as he opened the back door, he knew something was different. The hairs on the back of his neck stiffened. There was a smell he couldn't identify; perhaps the merest whiff of a per-fume, or just a hole in the air where someone had passed through it recently. Nobody should have been in here since the team who had arrived to take McReadie to the station. He'd locked up after them, and there hadn't been time to come back since. Hadn't been time to arrange to get the locks changed, either. And McReadie was a free man right now. A free man with a grievance. Damn. McLean stood silent and still, listening for the faintest sign that someone might be in the house, but there wasn't a sound to be heard.

He followed his nose, gently sniffing that almost imperceptible odour. It was stronger in the hall, but he couldn't smell anything in the library or the dining room. Upstairs, he moved quietly around the empty house, looking into rooms that were unchanged since the last time he had visited them, and yet utterly different. His own bedroom, the place where he had grown up, was exactly the same as he remembered it. That bed seemed too narrow for comfortable sleep, and those faded posters on the wall were an embarrassment, even if they were in large glass clip-frames.

The solid furniture, dresser, chest of drawers, large hanging cupboard, all took up the spaces he expected them to, but the wooden chair that should have been neatly tucked in under his desk was pulled away at a slight angle. Had he really left it that way? Come to that matter, when had he last been in here?

The bathroom smelled strongest, still faint, but enough of an odour to stir a vague memory. Reflexively, he went to his jacket pockets, looking for a pair of latex gloves to pull on before he touched anything. Finding none, he used his handkerchief and careful fingertips to avoid disturbing any potential prints. The bathroom cabinet held everything he might need for an overnight stay, though he couldn't be sure quite how old the toothbrush was. A bottle of painkillers from a few years back when he'd stayed with his gran whilst recuperating from the gunshot wound that had got him promoted to sergeant, but otherwise nothing worth mention. Just that smell.

McLean lifted the toilet seat, but there was nothing in the bowl except stale water, limescale rings showing where it had evaporated down over the months. Instinctively, he went to flush the handle, then stopped, a horrid certainty creeping into his mind. A thin layer of dust coated the edge of the bath and the toilet seat, but the lid of the cistern was clean and shiny. He went back into the bedroom and fished another handkerchief out of the drawers, the reek of cedar and mothballs obliterating the other more subtle smell completely. Using both handkerchiefs to protect his fingers, he carefully lifted the lid off the cistern and placed it on the floor, then looked inside.

Nothing. What had he been thinking? That someone would go to the trouble of planting something incriminating in his grandmother's house? Try to frame him? It was just the pressure of work getting to him. Paranoia born of tiredness.

Only when he went to pick up the porcelain lid did he notice that it didn't sit squarely on the floor. He turned it over slowly.

A brown plastic-wrapped package was taped securely to the underside.

37

'Woa, sir. This is some palace you've got here.'

Detective Constable MacBride stood in the hallway, looking up the wide stairwell at the glass dome in the ceiling two storeys above. McLean let him goggle for a while, turning to Grumpy Bob with a low whisper.

'Are you sure it's a good idea involving him in this?'

'You think he can't be trusted, sir? He's a good lad.'

'It's not that,' McLean said, though he had his reservations. He should really have been involving the drugs squad, the chief super-intendent and anyone else he could think of. But if he let the official channels take over, then he'd be at the very least suspended from active cases for the foreseeable future. Until his name was cleared. And even then it would hang around his neck for the rest of his career – the detective inspector with a kilo of cocaine hidden in his toilet cistern. Far better if as few people knew about this as possible, and he'd investigate it himself, though he had a shrewd idea exactly who was behind it.

'I'm more concerned about his future as a detective if it gets out he's been here.'

'Oh, and I don't count any more.' Grumpy Bob feigned an affronted look. 'Don't worry about the lad. He volunteered.'

McLean looked back to the young detective constable, wondering what it was he'd done to earn such loyalty.

'I'll make it up to him, if I can. To both of you,' McLean said. Grumpy Bob just laughed and nudged him in the ribs.

'OK, sir. Where is it then? We're missing valuable drinking time here.'

'Upstairs.' McLean led the way. They all trooped through his bedroom and into the bathroom beyond. The cistern lid with its suspicious package attached lay on the floor untouched.

'Did you manage to get a fingerprint kit?' McLean asked as Grumpy Bob handed out latex gloves.

'Should be here any minute,' Bob answered. As if on cue, the doorbell rang.

'Who?'

'That'll be Em,' Grumpy Bob said.

'Em? Emma Baird? You told her about this?'

'She's a trained fingerprint expert and she can get her hands on the kit without anyone being suspicious. What's more, if she finds something she can run it through the database, too. And she's new. No axes to grind, no allegiance to anyone in particular. Well, not yet anyway.'

The doorbell rang again, and though the chime was exactly the same as before, it sounded somehow more insistent, as if demanding an answer. McLean liked having her involved even less than DC MacBride, but he trusted Grumpy Bob. Apart from the obvious mistake that was Mrs Bob, his judgement was generally sound. And it was true they needed someone with forensic expertise. He levered himself up again and went to answer the door.

'Didn't realise inspectors got paid so well. All right if I come in?' Emma was dressed in street clothes; faded denim jeans and a loose-fitting T-shirt. Slung over one shoulder was her camera bag, not quite managing to counteract the weight of the heavy battered aluminium fingerprint case.

'Thanks for coming. I really appreciate it. Here, let me give you a hand with that.' McLean took the case and led her across the hall towards the stairs. As she followed, her footsteps clacked noisily on the floor tiles. Turning, he saw that she was wearing black tooled-leather cowboy boots; not exactly regulation crime-scene attire.

'Bob said it was urgent. Should I have changed?'

'No, you're OK like that. Just didn't peg you as the line-dancing type.' McLean felt the tips of his ears flush with heat. 'It's this way.' He started up the stairs.

'Straight to the bedroom. I like a man who's direct.' Emma looked at the bed as they passed through. 'A bit narrow for my tastes, though.' In the bathroom, Grumpy Bob had the packet open and was peering at the contents with a puzzled frown on his face.

'It looks like cocaine, sir. Can't be sure without a tester kit, but unless you've a habit of keeping your talc in the cistern, that's what it's most likely to be. But this is a lot of money here. Tens of thousands of pounds' worth. Who'd waste that just to set you up?'

'I'm keeping an open mind, but someone who can afford a luxury warehouse conversion in Leith is high on my suspect list.'

'Good point. Well we're going to need to find out where this has come from, and that means it's going to have to be found somewhere.'

'Maybe not,' Emma said. 'I should be able to get a sample tested without being registered on the system. There's people in the labs owe me more than a few favours, and we can run it through as a calibration test.'

'You'd do that for me?' McLean wasn't quite sure why she had chosen to side with him, but he was grateful nonetheless.

'Sure, but it'll cost you.'

'Did you have anything in mind?' He looked down at the tight-wrapped package on the floor beside the cistern. There were some things he wouldn't do, even if his job was on the line. Even if his liberty were at stake. Emma followed his gaze, then laughed.

'How about dinner?'

McLean was so relieved that she wasn't after the drugs, it took him a while to realise what she'd asked instead. Beside him, Grumpy Bob stifled a titter, and DC MacBride looked distinctly uncomfortable. This probably wasn't how he had imagined detective work was done.

'OK. But not tonight, I'm afraid. Unless you count pizza and beer shared with these two reprobates as dinner.'

'That wasn't quite what I had in mind.'

'No, I didn't think it would be.'

It was after midnight before they had finished going over the house from top to bottom. Not content with hiding cocaine in his cistern, McLean's unknown benefactor had also hidden a bag of cash in the cold water tank in the attic; used twenties and tens amounting to several thousands of pounds, their waterproof packaging unmarked.

Emma had found half a dozen partial fingerprints, mostly around the back door and up in the bathroom. One promising half-smear came off the gloss white surround to the door leading up to the attic, close by a protruding nail head that might have ripped a latex glove. It looked like someone had tried to wipe it away with a rough cloth, which roused suspicions. Otherwise, the house was full of prints, mostly McLean's.

'This place is alarmed, right?' Emma asked as they sat around the kitchen table, munching on pizza and drinking the last bottles of beer from the cellar. Like pretty much everything else in the house, they were eighteen months out of date, but nobody seemed to care much.

'Yeah, but I'm not exactly convinced it's any good. The last I heard, Penstemmin's in a bit of a muddle trying to sort out what McReadie did to their system. I'm beginning to wish I'd never caught the bastard.'

Grumpy Bob slumped back in his chair, letting his breath out in a long sigh. 'You think he hates you that much he'd do all this? Christ, the man's not poor, but that's taking it a bit far, isn't it?'

'Can you think of anyone else?'

The silence that descended on the table was answer enough.

'Well, I'll check those partials against him first thing tomorrow.' Emma looked at her watch. 'That's to say today. I really should be going.' She pushed back her chair and stood up. McLean followed her to the door.

'Thanks for this, Emma. I know you've put yourself on the line to help me.'

'Too right I have, but I know coke addicts and you're not the type. And as for the cash, you've got this place, what d'you need it for?'

'Yeah, well hopefully I won't have to prove that to anyone else. I'm sure you understand how awkward this could be if it got out. For all of us.'

She smiled, the corners of her eyes creasing slightly. 'Don't worry, my lips are sealed. But you owe me dinner, and there'd better be candles.'

Grumpy Bob and DC MacBride joined him at the front door as she drove off.

'You'd best be careful with that one,' Bob said. 'She's got a reputation, you know.'

'You're the one who brought her here,' McLean began to say, but he could see the smile breaking out on Grumpy Bob's face and stopped himself. 'Go on, both of you. Get yourselves home.'

He watched them drive off into the night, then went back to the kitchen. The cocaine and the money sat on the table with the leftover pizza. The one would probably be OK cold for breakfast, but the other was more of a problem. McLean looked at the clock on the kitchen wall; it was late, but not too late. Not for this. And besides, what were friends for if you couldn't wake them up by calling in the wee small hours?

The phone rang three times before answering. Phil sounded slightly out of breath; McLean didn't want to speculate given his ex-flatmate's legendary dislike of exercise.

'Phil. Sorry for calling so late. I've got a favour to ask.' McLean hefted the cling-film wrapped brick of cocaine in one hand. 'I was wondering if I might borrow that incinerator you've got in your state-of-the-art lab.'

*

Rachel was with Phil when they met outside the back door to the lab complex, which surprised McLean. He'd no doubt she'd been there when he'd called his friend, but there was no need for her to come along, surely? At this time of the morning she'd have been comfier tucked up in bed, even alone.

'Thanks for this, Phil.' McLean hefted the bag over his shoulder. It was surprising just how much a kilo of cocaine and fifty thousand pounds in unmarked bills could weigh. Particularly when you were carrying them through the city's streets in the wee small hours. He'd thought about getting a taxi, then decided it was better if there were as few witnesses as possible.

'Not even sure what it is,' Phil said. 'You've got us both on tenterhooks here, Tony.'

'Aye, well. Can we go in?' He nodded at the door, anxious to be away from the ever-present glare of the security cameras.

'Yes, of course.' Phil tapped a code into the keypad by the door, which obligingly clicked open. Inside, the back end and store rooms for the lab were in semi-darkness. They walked in silence up two flights of stairs, across a room filled with expensive machinery humming and whirring to itself and finally into Phil's office. Only once the door was closed did McLean begin to relax a little. He dumped the bag down on the desk and told them the tale.

'Um, shouldn't you be reporting this to the police?' Rachel broke the uncomfortable silence that fell once he was finished.

'Best case scenario, I'd be suspended for six months while Professional Standards looks into everything about me. Even if they don't find anything untoward, I'll be known for the rest of my career as the copper with a kilo of coke and fifty grand in cash stashed away.'

'It's not that bad, surely?' Phil asked.

'You don't know coppers, Phil. And this sort of thing goes on your permanent record no matter the outcome. I don't have any dirty secrets to hide either, but that doesn't mean PS won't find some. If this was left at gran's, then there'll be other stuff at my flat. Probably any number of snitches willing to waste a bit of police time claiming I've done all manner of things that'll turn out to be lies in the end.'

'But . . . why?' Rachel pushed herself away from the wall where she'd been leaning, opened the bag and hefted the wad of money.

'I haven't got a bastard clue.' McLean shrugged, perhaps a little too theatrically. 'I must have pissed someone off, though.'

'So you want to burn it?' Phil asked. 'You want to burn fifty thousand pounds of untraceable cash?'

'I want to destroy the drugs. That's for certain. I'd rather the cash was gone, too. To be honest, I've no idea whether it's stolen or what. It's not marked, but other than that?'

'It just seems such a waste. I mean, what if it really is untraceable? That would really piss off whoever planted it if it was never found and used to incriminate you.'

McLean looked at the money in Rachel's hands. He'd come here intending to destroy everything, didn't really need the money himself. But then it might be put to good use somewhere else, and there'd be a certain irony if he managed to get away with it.

'OK. Give me a handful.' The bundle of money was tightly wrapped, and still peppered with grey dust where Emma had searched it for fingerprints. He carefully unwrapped it and pulled out the first paper-bound wad. 'Rachel, can you write down a few serial numbers if I read them out?'

It took them ten minutes before McLean was certain he had enough. He pulled out a random wad of notes to have checked for forgery, then wrapped the whole bundle up again and handed it to Phil. Rachel handed him the sheet of serial numbers.

'I'll get these checked as soon as possible against any known robberies,' he said. 'Also make sure they're real. Until then, no one's to touch any of those notes. Hide them somewhere you know they won't be accidentally found. You really don't want to be caught in possession of dodgy money. If they turn out to be clean, then use them to pay for your wedding.'

'Don't you want them?' Phil asked.

'Not really, no. And congratulations, by the way.'

233

'What?'

'On your engagement. I notice you didn't deny it when I mentioned your wedding.'

'Phil, it was meant to be a secret until I got my PhD.' Rachel's face turned a furious red and she thumped him across the shoulders.

'Don't worry, Rachel. My lips are sealed until you make an official announcement.' McLean grinned, feeling cheerful for the first time in twenty-four hours. 'Now let's go and burn some drugs.'

38

Dawn had been greying the sky for some time when McLean let himself in through the front door to the Newington tenement. His eyes were dry with a lack of sleep that had left him drained and cranky. Burning a kilo of cocaine, even in an incinerator designed for the safe disposal of bio-hazardous waste, took a surprisingly long time. Along with finding somewhere suitable to hide the cash until he could run a trace on it, he'd managed exactly no sleep. He'd hoped the walk across town would perk him up, but instead he just felt even worse.

'Did your friend find you all right?'

McLean started at the voice, turning to see old Mrs McCutcheon standing in her half-opened doorway at the bottom of the stone stairs leading to the other apartments. He wasn't really in the mood for idle chit-chat with the tenement gossip, just wanted a shower and then perhaps a couple of hours' kip before heading in to work. He smiled at her automatically, nodding and feeling guilty as he made for the steps. Then what she had said finally sank in.

'My friend?'

'What was it, night before last I think. Quite late, but you policemen are always coming and going at odd hours.'

The night before last. When someone had planted evidence in his grandmother's house. Not long after Fergus McReadie had been released on bail. Not long after Jonas Carstairs had been murdered.

'Did you speak to him, Mrs McCutcheon? Did he tell you his name?'

'Oh no, dear. I was just sitting in the front room doing my knitting. You know how it is when you get old. Sleep's something young people do. I don't know what time it was, but the buses had stopped, so it must have been well past midnight. This young man comes up the path and rings your buzzer.'

'How'd you know it was my buzzer?'

'Och, they all sound different you know. Anyway, he came straight in and headed up the stairs. I thought it was odd because I didn't hear you open the door. Then I remembered the students leave it wedged open when they go out to the pub. But they'd come home already, and I'm sure they'd shut it properly. But, oh, I don't know.'

'Did he stay long?'

'Oh no. He only got halfway up the stairs when one of them students came out and started shouting at him. Ye ken what they're like when they've been at the drink, aye?'

McLean did. Many was the time he'd had to remind unruly tenants that there was a policeman living on the top floor who took unkindly to having his sleep disturbed.

'He came scuttling back doon the stairs sharpish. I don't think he saw me, he was going that fast. I was putting one of the cats out. Gave me quite a turn.

McLean looked at the old woman. She'd been living in the ground-floor flat when he'd moved in. She'd probably been there all her life. He'd never met Mr McCutcheon, and assumed the man had died some years earlier. Truth was, he didn't really know very much about her other than she was old, liked to know what was going on, and was beginning to look very frail indeed.

'Don't worry about it, Mrs M,' he said, trying to calm her down.

'All that's really important is that someone came round in the early hours of yesterday morning. That's what you're saying, right?'

The old lady nodded.

'And you saw him? You saw his face?'

She nodded again.

'Do you think you might recognise him from a photograph?'

Mrs McCutcheon paused, her normally cheerful and positive self replaced by an older, more uncertain one.

'I'm no' sure I could leave the hoose for very long,' she said after a while. 'The cats . . .'

McLean knew that the cats were perfectly capable of looking after themselves, but he wasn't about to say so.

'Perhaps I can bring the photographs to you, Mrs M. But it would be really helpful if you could identify this man for me.'

'I can't let you bring McReadie in again. Not unless you've got something specific you can charge him with.'

McLean stood just inside Jayne McIntyre's office, not trusting himself to get any closer. His first action on arriving at the station had been to ask the duty sergeant to arrange for McReadie to be brought in for questioning. He probably shouldn't have shouted at Pete when he'd refused, the poor man was only following orders from the boss, after all.

'He stole Bertie Farquhar's cufflink. I need to know what else he took from there.'

'No, Tony. You don't.' McIntyre remained seated behind her desk. Annoyingly calm and logical, damn her. 'You know where he got it from, and besides, as I understand it you'd identified who the cufflink belonged to anyway. That was good work, going to the jewellers.'

'He's been hanging around my flat.'

'You don't know that. You've just the word of a confused old woman that someone who may or may not have been McReadie came looking for you.'

'But I need –' He needed to ask him if he planted a kilo of cocaine in his grandmother's house. What he left at his flat that he'd not been able to find.

'You need to leave him alone, is what you need.' McIntyre pulled off her reading spectacles and rubbed at her eyes. Perhaps she'd had no sleep either. 'We've got him bang to rights now. Caught red-handed and with a stash of stolen goods in his home. But he's already filed an official complaint against you for using undue force, and his lawyer's been picking at the terms of the search warrant, too.'

'He –' McLean's brain caught up with his mouth. 'He's what?'

'If he can make either stick then we've got a very thin case indeed. The PF might even decide to go with receiving stolen goods. Bloke like him, that's a suspended sentence.'

'But he can't do that. The little bastard broke into my gran's house.'

'I know, Tony. And if I could have my way, he'd be stewing in remand until he came to trial. But he's got a lot of money for the best lawyer, and worse he's got connections. You wouldn't believe how high up the pressure's coming from.'

'He's not getting away with this. You're not going to cut a deal.'

McIntyre grimaced. 'Not a bloody chance. I do not like being dictated to by suits. But I can't have you riding roughshod over this one just because McReadie's pissed you off. That's precisely what he wants and I'm not going to give him the satisfaction.'

'But . . .'

'No buts, Tony. It's not even your case any more. You're the victim, for God's sake. You can't be involved. Get on with your other cases, why don't you? You've not even been to see that occult expert I told you about yet, have you.'

Bugger. And the worst of it was she was right. McLean knew damned well he shouldn't even have interviewed McReadie the first time. It should have been handed over to someone not directly involved.

'Please tell me you're not going to give it to Duguid.' It sounded like a pitiful, spiteful whinge.

'Actually I thought Bob Laird would be better suited.' McIntyre slid her spectacles back up her nose with a little smirk. 'You can tell him yourself.'

McLean met Constable Kydd on his way down to the incident room. She had a heavy load of box files and a heavier expression of dread on her face. Headed in the direction of the incident room recently cleared of the Barnaby Smythe investigation and now being hastily re-filled as Detective Chief Inspector Charles Duguid rose once more to the challenge of royally fucking things up.

'Let me guess, Dagwood's got every able-bodied person in the station seconded to his team?'

Constable Kydd bobbed her head in unhappy agreement. 'There's a lot of pressure from high up.'

'There's always a lot of pressure from high up.' But of course there really would be for someone like Carstairs. Same as Smythe. Important men had important friends. It was just a shame the little people couldn't get such support. Like the poor girl mutilated in the basement of some rich and influential man, part of some sick fantasy ritual.

'You're photo-fit trained, aren't you, constable?' McLean asked, dredging up the information from a conversation half remembered.

'Um, aye.' Constable Kydd offered the confirmation with great reluctance.

'How would you fancy doing a bit of detective work then? I heard you were studying for the exams.' Well, McIntyre wouldn't let him interrogate McReadie without good reason. What could be better than proving the man had been sniffing around McLean's tenement just hours after being released on bail?

'I'm a wee bit busy, sir.' Kydd hefted the box files, an unhappy gloom settling on her features.

'Don't worry. I'll square it with Dagwood. I've got some other stuff to do this morning anyway, but if you can sign out a laptop with photo-ID software on it, maybe rustle up some random mugshots too. And chuck in the ones we took of Fergus McReadie when he came in the other night. I'll get a car sorted for two.'

'I –'

'I know the chief super said I wasn't to hassle him.' Christ, had she told everyone in the station? How impetuous did she think he was? 'I'm not going anywhere near him. Trust me.'

39

The sign on the door said 'palms read, tarots, fortunes told'. McLean had always figured the place as a front for something else, prostitution most likely, but this was the address McIntyre had given him. He'd asked around too, and word was that Madame Rose was as honest as the day, in as much as she did exactly what she said she did. Everything else was a lie, of course, a pandering to the gullible. There wasn't a large market in Edinburgh for this particular brand of fool-and-his-money enterprise, but enough people wanted to believe that an enterprising soul could make a crust at it.

'Why are we here, sir?' Detective Constable MacBride had drawn the short straw and was tagging along on this particular dead-end in the ever-growing list of cases. Grumpy Bob had the even more fun task of trying to identify the Waverley jumper whilst gathering together all the evidence against Fergus McReadie for the Procurator Fiscal. That just left the investigation into the potential leak of crime-scene information that was the most obvious explanation for the disturbing similarities between the murders of Jonas Carstairs and Barnaby Smythe. And the dead girl, of course. All in a day's work, really.

'We're here to find out about human sacrifice and demonic ritual. Apparently Madame Rose is something of an expert on the occult. All this magic-show stuff is just a front. Or so I'm told.' McLean pushed open the door to reveal a narrow hallway with stairs leading straight up. Threadbare carpet, more stain than pattern, released an aroma of chip-fat and mould into the air; a curious smell of hopelessness. Up the stairs, through a once-sparkly bead curtain turned dull with grease and discarded skin, they found themselves in a small room that desperately wanted to be described as a boudoir but really couldn't even merit reception room. The same carpet as the stairs ran wall to wall, more stains spreading out like mushroom fairy rings. In places they had even begun to colonise the walls, competing with nasty flock wallpaper and cheap prints of vaguely oriental and mystic scenes. Looking up, McLean wasn't at all surprised to see spots marking the ceiling too. The heat of the day wasn't helping either, that cooking smell and damp fug made mouth-breathing preferable, though only slightly. And people came here of their own volition?

A low sofa leant against the outside wall, under the only window in the room. Sitting on it was probably not a good idea. Two rickety wooden chairs flanked a low table covered in elderly copies of *Reader's Digest* and *Tarot Monthly*. In the opposite corner to the stairwell, someone not very good at DIY had built a narrow counter, behind which stood a closed door. A scruffy piece of paper tacked to the wall showed a menu of prices for services rendered. Ten pounds for a basic palm reading, twenty for consulting the cards. Some mad punters might even fork out over a hundred for something called a 'Full Karmic Workout'.

'Oh. I thought I felt something in the aether. Magnificent.' A deep, husky voice, the product of too many cigarettes, too much whisky. The words were out even before McLean had registered the door opening. An enormous woman swept through, halving the size of the reception room with her presence. She wore what appeared to be a red velvet tent, pulled around her body like the swaddling on a once-fat mummy. Her hands were like tired, gold-studded pink balloons, fleshy fingers squeezed into cheap, ornate rings, nails painted a slightly different shade of red to her dress.

'I simply must see your palms.' Madame Rose grabbed McLean's hands with surprising speed, flipping one over and tracing the lines with a soft caress. He tried to pull away but the woman's grip was like iron.

'Oh, such a tragic life already. And, dear me, so much more to come. You poor, poor boy. And what's this?' She let go as suddenly as she had grabbed him. Took a theatrical step back, one hand to her ample breast, splayed fingers reaching up to her wattle-skin throat. 'You've been marked out for things. Great things. Terrible things.'

'Enough of the show.' McLean held up his warrant card. 'I'm not here for any mumbo-jumbo.'

'I assure you, detective inspector, I do not deal in mumbo-jumbo. Why, I felt your aura the moment you stepped through the front door.'

'And do you know why we've come calling then?' It was Mac-Bride who asked the question, but only because he beat McLean to it.

'Of course, of course. You want to know about ritual killing. Nasty business. Never works, at least not in my experience, but it's worse than alcohol for bringing out the devil in people, if you know what I mean.'

'How did you . . . ?' MacBride's mouth hung open as the words escaped.

Madame Rose let out a snort of most unlady-like laughter. 'The spirit world talks to me, detective sergeant. And Jayne McIntyre from time to time.'

'I don't have a lot of time, and even less patience.' McLean shoved his warrant card back in his pocket. 'I was led to believe you knew something about occult practices. If that's not the case then I'll not waste any more of your time.'

'Touchy, isn't he.' Madame Rose winked at MacBride, who reddened about the face and ears. She turned back to McLean. 'Come on through to the office then. It's a slow day anyway.'

The office turned out to be a sizeable room at the back of the building, one tall window looking out onto a grey courtyard filled with limp washing on sagging lines. The contrast with the front reception area, and the receiving room through which they had passed to get here, could not have been more marked. Where they were seedy and loaded with kitsch trinkets of the sort you would expect an old gypsy fortune-teller to collect, the few artefacts on show in this room looked both genuine and unsettling.

All four walls were lined with bookshelves reaching up to the high ceiling, most packed with a seemingly random assortment of ancient and modern books. Two shelves, either side of the large antique desk, held glass cases housing a wildcat and a snowy owl. Both had been given the full benefit of the taxidermist's art, posed in the act of killing their respective preys. On top of the desk, mounted on a dark wooden shield, what looked suspiciously like a withered human hand had been pressed into service as a book stand. Other things lurked in dark corners. Sinister when glimpsed through the corner of your eye, they turned out to be perfectly innocent items when given full attention: a coat stand with a bowler hat, greatcoat and umbrella had been a dark assassin; the artfully discarded stole on the back of the moth-eaten high-back leather armchair had been a living fox, a witch's familiar fixing him with an evil eye. McLean blinked, and the stole blinked back, then yawned a great fang-baring snarl, stretched and leapt from the chair onto the floor. Not a fox, but a cat, thin as a toast rack and with a tail that curved like a great shaggy question mark as it stalked across the room to inspect the new intruders.

'So, Detective Inspector McLean, Detective Constable Mac-Bride. You want to know about human sacrifice, why people might try to do it, that sort of thing?' Madame Rose pulled a pair of pince-nez out of her décolletage, where they had been hanging from a silver chain, and pushed them onto her nose.

'Pretty much. I'm trying to get a handle on a particular ritual. We think there was probably more than one person involved.'

'Oh there usually is. Otherwise it's just attention-seeking.'

'I meant more than one killer, actually. Six, possibly.' McLean outlined what they had found in the walled-up basement, keeping the details as sparse as possible.

'Six?' Madame Rose leant forward in her chair. 'That's . . . unusual. Mostly it's a solitary affair. Two people if you include the victim. The kind of people who go in for ritual killing don't socialise well, you understand.'

'Why do they do it?' MacBride asked. McLean hadn't actually told the constable not to say anything, so he tried not to let his annoyance show.

'A very pertinent question, young man,' Madame Rose said. 'Some have speculated that it gives them a sense of importance lacking in their everyday lives. Others suggest that childhood experiences, usually violent and at the hands of close family members, cause the individual to conflate attention with love and thus mete out their own love accordingly. Many come from a strict religious upbringing where the child has not been spared the rod. Ritual is important to them, as is its subversion. For myself I think they mostly do it because they're bonkers.'

'You don't believe it works, I take it,' McLean said.

'Oh, but of course I do. And so did your six madmen. Well, they must have done or they wouldn't have killed the girl. Or at least one of them must have believed, and had the other five completely in his thrall.'

'You think that's possible? That people would kill like that just because someone told them to?'

'Of course. If the leader's charismatic enough. Look at Waco, Jonestown, Al Qaeda. Most cult followers don't really believe what they're being peddled. They just want to be told what to do. It's easier that way.'

OK. Not quite what he'd been expecting when he'd come here. 'So this ritual isn't anything special, then. It could just be any random nutter with a god delusion.'

'I didn't say that, inspector.' Madame Rose reached for a book that looked like it had only recently been fetched from the shelves to her desk. She flicked it open at a page already marked. 'Six organs, six artefacts, six names. Arranged at the cardinal points around the body. Tell me, were there markings on the floor? A circle of protection, perhaps?'

She spun the book around, showing the page to McLean. It was a crude black and white line drawing, done in a medieval style, showing a female figure lying with her arms and legs splayed. A slit opened up her torso with nothing but black ink inside. All around her, a twining circle of vines twisted together, clumping in knots at her hands, feet, head and the space between her legs. Beneath the picture were etched the words 'Opus Diaboli'. McLean pulled the book towards him, but Madame Rose tweaked it away.

'That's seventeenth century. Probably worth more than your young constable here earns in a year.'

246

'Where did you get it?' McLean asked.

'Interesting choice of question, inspector.' Madame Rose ran a careful finger across the page. 'I bought it from an antiquarian book dealer down on the Royal Mile. Many, many years ago. I believe he acquired it and several others from the estate of the late Albert Farquhar. Quite the occult enthusiast was Bertie Farquhar, or so I've heard.'

Another piece in the puzzle. 'And what is the ritual supposed to do?'

'That's where it gets interesting.' Madame Rose slid her finger under the page, turning it carefully over before handing the book back. McLean looked at a new chapter, momentarily confused by the elegantly illuminated dropped capital. Then he noticed the ragged edge of a page torn out. The frayed edges were not fresh.

'It was like that when I bought it, in case you were wondering.' Madame Rose took the book back, carefully closed it and laid it back down on the desk, patting the cover like a good pet. 'I've spent the last twenty years looking for another copy.'

'So you've no idea what that . . .' McLean waved a hand at the book and the grisly image it contained. 'What it was supposed to achieve.'

' "Opus Diaboli", inspector. The work of the devil.'

It wasn't until he stepped out onto the street that McLean realised it had been cold in Madame Rose's study. Shade from being on the north side of the building, perhaps, but it felt more than that. As if the place lived in its own dimension. He looked back at the door, but the sign still said 'palms read, tarots, fortunes told'. The stonework was still dirty, the window sill rotting away for want of a lick of paint. He shook his head, a judder passing through his body as it adjusted to the warmth of the sun.

247

'She was a bit weird.' DC MacBride stated the obvious.

'And some.' McLean shoved his hands in his trouser pockets as they started the walk back to the station. 'But I think it would probably be fairer to say he.'

'He?' MacBride took three more strides. Possibly four. Turned to face McLean. 'You mean she was a . . . He was a . . .'

'You don't often see an Adam's apple like that on a woman, Stuart. Or hands that big. I'd wager that ample bosom owed more to padding than nature, too.'

'So Madame Rose really is a charlatan. In more ways than one.'

'Oh, I wouldn't knock the old fortune-telling. Anyone fool enough to part with their money for that sort of thing deserves to be poorer, if you want my opinion. And she . . . he has helped us, after all.'

MacBride cradled in his arms the package in which Madame Rose had carefully placed the book. She had insisted on getting a receipt for it when McLean had asked if he could take it as evidence. The five-figure sum mentioned as its value might have been an exaggeration but the constable wasn't taking any chances.

'We already have the cufflink though,' he said. 'Do we really need the book as well? We know Bertie Farquhar did it.'

'It's always nice to have confirmation.' And besides, there was something about that book. He wanted a chance to study it some more, even if the really crucial page was missing.

'There's one thing that bothers me, sir.'

'Only one?'

'Aye, well.' MacBride paused a while, collecting his thoughts or unsure of himself. 'This book. Madame Rose back there. She, he, whatever, had it lying there on the desk. She'd even marked the page.'

'I had noticed.'

'But how did she know what we were looking for?'

40

'That looks a bit like him, but maybe a bit darker? No, this one. Or maybe this?'

McLean had never been in Mrs McCutcheon's inner sanctum before, even though he'd lived in the same tenement block as her for more than fifteen years. As it was, nothing in the room surprised him; it was exactly how he might have imagined. The layout of the living room was not unlike his own three floors up, but there the similarity ended. She had trinkets everywhere, mostly of the twee, Victorian chocolate box and tartan-tat variety, and the large room was made small by the sheer amount of stuff. That and the cats. He'd given up counting after ten, unsure whether he had doubled up on some. They stared down from shelves, peered up from chairs, twisted around his legs until he didn't dare move. Sitting down was out of the question.

'I don't know, dear. They all look a bit grim, don't they? Haven't you got anyone smiling? The chap I saw had a wide grin on his face.'

Constable Kydd sat alongside the old woman on a sofa that may well have pre-dated both of them. The back had been covered in a delicate lace antimacassar, with similar on the two matching high-back armchairs currently occupied by suspicious eyes and quivering whiskers. Despite the cats, everything about the cluttered room was neat and tidy; there was just too much of it. Surprisingly it smelled only of wood polish and age. But then judging by the smell in the main landing, outside the apartment, Mrs McCutcheon had trained her cats to go elsewhere.

'This one. Now I think it could be him.' The old lady was peering through half-moon spectacles at the laptop Constable Kydd had brought with her. It was loaded with mugshots as well as photo-fit software. So far it had been just an exercise in looking through pictures, McReadie's strategically placed amongst them, and trying to remember not to drink the tea. McLean had seen it being made when they arrived. A bag each and one for the pot, as Mrs McCutcheon had said. A shame the pot was only big enough for about a pint of water.

'Yes. I'm certain of it. He had those funny eyes. Too close together. Made him look a bit, well, glaikit.'

McLean smiled at the word, stooped forward to see the screen for himself. Kydd angled it up, her own face a picture of triumph.

'It's him,' she said, but McLean didn't need telling. Gurning up from the laptop was the image he'd been wanting to see. Fergus McReadie.

'We need to get on to the station. I want McReadie picked up as soon as possible. The little bastard's not getting out on bail this time.'

They were walking down towards the Pleasance, heading back to the city centre. It had taken longer than McLean liked to get out of Mrs McCutcheon's apartment, and all the while he'd been trying to suppress the thought of Fergus McReadie in his BMW, doing a runner to somewhere with too much sun and an unhelpful attitude towards extradition of known felons.

'You want me to call it in, sir?' Constable Kydd fumbled with the laptop bag slung over her shoulder, trying to get it out of the way so she could reach her airwave set. McLean stopped, turned to face her.

'Here, give me that. No, the laptop. I haven't got a clue how to work the other one.' He took the bag and slung it over his own shoulder. Kydd pulled her airwave set out, thumbed a few buttons and raised it to her ear.

'Yeah, Control? This is two-three-nine . . . Oh my God. Look out!'

It happened too fast to even think. Kydd let go of the airwave set, launched herself at McLean, catching him in the stomach with her shoulder and knocking him sideways. He fell backwards, feet tripping over the stone steps leading up to an open tenement doorway. His knees buckled as he windmilled his arms in a futile attempt to stay upright. He hit the flagstone floor with enough force to jar his spine and drive the wind out of his lungs. The question formed on his lips. 'What?' But it was answered before he could finish thinking it.

A white Transit van mounted the pavement, sending a street bin flying into the road. Constable Kydd was caught in its path like a rabbit in the headlights. For an instant that was for ever, she stood there, half bent as she tried to recover her balance, eyes wide in astonishment more than fear. And then the van hit her, lifted her off her feet, threw her into the air like a child's discarded doll. Only then did McLean hear the tortured roar of an engine at full throttle, the thud of a body hitting the ground, glass shattering. Screeching brakes.

Fighting for breath, he forced himself to his feet, back out of the doorway that had offered him protection. The van careened back onto the street, fighting a way through the traffic like a drunk boxer. He couldn't see any number plate on the back of it and in seconds it was gone around a corner, off in the direction of Holyrood Park.

Constable Kydd lay twenty feet away from the doorway, her body twisted cruelly. McLean looked around for the airwave set, seeing only pieces of broken electronics spilled into the road. His own mobile was useless. Why the fuck wouldn't it hold a charge? He pulled out his warrant card, ran into the path of the nearest car, slammed his hands down on the bonnet.

'You got a phone?'

The startled driver pointed at something in a holder suction-mounted to the windscreen.

'I wasnae using it. Honest.'

'I don't give a fuck. Hand it over.' McLean grabbed the phone even before the driver had it out of the window. He keyed in the number for the station. Didn't wait for the preamble that he knew would be coming.

'Pete? McLean. I'm just opposite the Pleasance. There's been a hit and run. Constable Kydd's down. I need an ambulance five minutes ago. And put out an APB on a white Transit, plate unknown. It's going to have a bloody great dent in its bonnet though. Probably broken windscreen too. Last seen heading down the Canongate towards Holyrood.'

Still clutching the phone, McLean ran to where Constable Kydd was lying. Blood was leaking from her mouth and nose, bright and bubbly. Her hips shouldn't have been able to twist the way they were, and he didn't want to know about her legs. Her eyes were still open though, glazed over with shock.

'Stay with me, Alison. There's an ambulance on the way.' McLean took one cut hand in his, unwilling to move her any more than necessary, even though he doubted she would ever walk again. If she even made it the next five minutes.

Somewhere in the distance, a siren started to wail.

41

The cheap plastic chair was uncomfortable, but McLean hardly noticed the numbing in his buttocks as he stared across the empty waiting room at the noticeboard and its unseen leaflets. Even now the journey across town in the ambulance was jumbling into a confused series of flash-images. A paramedic talking to him in a voice he couldn't hear; kind but firm hands prising his grip from Constable Kydd's; trained professionals working what scant miracles they could, fitting neck brace, back brace; lifting the twisted figure into the ambulance, so small, so young; a journey across town to a hospital he'd hoped never to see again; serious faces with serious words like operation, emergency surgery, quadriplegic. And now the slow wait for the news he knew could only be some shade of dreadful.

A soft rustling in the air as someone sat down beside him. McLean didn't need to turn to know who it was, he'd know that perfume anywhere. A mixture of paperwork, worry and just the tiniest dab of Chanel.

'How is she?' Chief Superintendent McIntyre sounded tired. He knew how she felt.

'The doctor's aren't quite sure how she was still alive when she got here. She's in surgery right now.'

'What happened, Tony?'

'It was a hit and run. Deliberate. I think they were trying to get me.' There. He'd said it. Given voice to his paranoia.

McIntyre took a deep breath, held it a moment as if daring herself to go on. 'Are you sure of that?'

'Sure? No. I don't think I'm sure of anything any more.' McLean scrubbed at the dryness in his eyes. Wondered if tears would be misconstrued. 'She saw it coming. Constable Kydd. She pushed me out of the way. Could have saved herself, but her first instinct was to save me.'

'She's a good copper.'

McLean noticed that McIntyre didn't add, 'She'll go far.' Chances were she wasn't going anywhere ever again. Not without wheels.

'What were you doing there, anyway?'

And now the difficult part. 'We were on our way back to the station. Constable Kydd was helping to ID someone who came to my apartment the other night when I was out. My neighbour saw him acting suspiciously.' God, he sounded pathetic.

'McReadie?' There was the slightest hint of question in McIntyre's voice, but McLean could tell she wasn't expecting an answer. He nodded anyway.

'So why wasn't Sergeant Laird carrying out the investigation? I told you, Tony. Steer clear of McReadie. He's playing with you.'

'He's trying to kill me, is what he's doing.'

'Are you sure of that? Don't you think it's a bit extreme?'

No, because the bastard planted fifty grand and a kilo of cocaine to try and set me up, but I didn't do what he expected me to, so now he's taken the direct option.

'It'd be very hard for me to testify against him in court if I was dead.'

'Give it a rest, Tony. Melodrama really doesn't suit you. And anyway, according to the duty sergeant, at four o'clock this afternoon when you called in the accident, Fergus McReadie was being interviewed at the station, along with a lawyer so sharp he probably cuts himself getting dressed in the morning.'

'He wouldn't have done something like this himself. He'd've paid someone. I bet you he volunteered to come in this afternoon, too. Make himself the perfect alibi.'

McIntyre let out a long, slow breath, slumped her head against the wall.

'You're not making this easy for me, Tony.'

'I'm not making it easy?' He turned to face his boss but she wouldn't return his stare. Talked instead to the empty waiting room.

'Go home. Get some sleep. You can't do anything here.'

'But I need –'

'You need to go home. If you're not in shock already it's going to hit soon enough. Do I need to make it an order?'

McLean slumped back in his chair, defeated. He hated it when the chief superintendent was right. 'No.'

'Good, because this next bit is an order. I don't want you coming in to work until next week.'

'What? But it's only Wednesday.'

'Next week, Tony.' McIntyre finally looked at him. 'You can write me a statement detailing exactly what happened this afternoon. Then I don't want to hear a squeak out of you until Monday.'

'But what about McReadie?'

'Don't worry about him. You've got a witness says he was round your place, that sounds like a clear breach of his bail conditions.' McIntyre pulled out her phone but didn't dial. 'He won't be bothering anyone for a while.'

'Thank you.' McLean let the back of his head bang lightly against the wall. 'Are you sure there's –'

'You keep out of this. If you're right and someone's out to get you, then I can't have you investigating. Same as I can't have you hassling McReadie at every turn. Due process, Tony. Leave it alone. I'll be leading this investigation myself, so I'll know if you start poking your nose where it's not welcome.'

'I –'

'Home, inspector. Not a word more.' McIntyre stood up, her hands automatically smoothing out the creases on her uniform as she turned and walked away. McLean watched her go, then went back to staring at the wall.

Police Constable Alison Kydd was moved from surgery into intensive care at a quarter past one in the morning. Eight hours of surgery might have saved her life, but the doctors were keeping her in a medical coma just in case. It was a certainty she would never walk again, unless someone came up with a way to re-grow a severed spinal cord. Only time would tell if she had the use of her arms, or even control of her bladder. And there was always the chance that she might never wake up.

The doctor who had told McLean all this looked too young to have been long out of medical college, but she seemed to know what she was doing. She was cautiously optimistic; better than fifty–fifty had been her words. Said as if that was a good thing, with a tired smile to back it up. They haunted him all the way home in the rain-swept taxi, smile and words both. Stayed with him as he got started on his report for the chief superintendent and a bottle of single malt whisky. It was dawn before he had finished the one, realised the other wasn't really helping. Getting blind drunk on his own just wasn't his style; he needed a few good friends to do that with. And all the while he kept telling himself it wasn't his fault. Say it enough, he might even start believing it.

256

He called the hospital at six to be told there hadn't been any change, nor was there likely to be for the foreseeable future. The nurse at the other end of the line hadn't said as much, but McLean could tell from her tone that she wouldn't be as polite if he phoned again soon. He should have been tired, hadn't slept in twenty-four hours, but the guilt and the anger wouldn't let him sleep. Instead he showered, read through the report and made a couple of changes before emailing it off. Not his fault. No way he could have anticipated what happened.

But it was his fault, after a fashion. Like McIntyre had said, it should have been Grumpy Bob who took a constable round to visit Mrs McCutcheon. McReadie could have had his hired goon run down McLean somewhere entirely different, where there was no one about to sacrifice themselves so that he might live. Jesus, what the fuck was that about? Why had that stupid little . . . ?

His fist was nearly at the pane of glass before McLean realised he'd even clenched it. Pulling the punch, he slammed his palm into the window frame instead, feeling a hot sting of tears in his eyes that had nothing to do with the pain. Not the physical pain, anyway. That faded away in moments. If only the other kind would too.

He was so bloody-minded sometimes. Maybe if he listened to what other people told him, perhaps even delegated from time to time, this would never have happened. And now he was stuck here, climbing the walls for the best part of a week because he'd been told to stay away and just couldn't help himself. Christ, what a mess.

There was too much to do, too many other cases that needed his attention. McIntyre couldn't really expect him to do nothing until Monday, could she? He'd be OK as long as he kept well clear of the station and anything to do with McReadie or the search for the van that had run Alison down. That still left the dead girl and the two suicides, not to mention the leak of crime-scene details.

Leaving the flat felt like sneaking round the back of the bike shed for an illicit smoke, but he had to go to the shops for food, if nothing else. And when all else failed, there was nothing like a good walk to help him think.

'Inspector. What a pleasant surprise.'

McLean turned at the voice, seeing a very shiny black Bentley sliding along the road, one window down like a late-night kerb-crawler trawling the streets for some negotiable virtue. Not that you'd find anyone working the pavement in this neighbour-hood, but it wouldn't have surprised him if one of these elegant, large houses catered for the more upmarket kind of intimate escort. Bending slightly, he caught a glimpse of gloved hand, dark overcoat and scarred face before the car came to a silent halt. The door clicked open, swinging wide to reveal soft red leather, the kind of interior that Freud would have had paroxysms over. Inside, Gavin Spenser beckoned towards him.

'Can I offer you a lift?'

McLean looked up the empty road, then back the way he had come. Half an hour of concentrated walking had failed to throw off his guilt and self-pity. Or his frustration.

'I wasn't really going anywhere.'

'Then perhaps you'd join me for coffee. It's not far.'

Why the hell not? He wasn't exactly doing anything else. McLean climbed into the car, nodding at the huge hulk of a driver squashed in behind the wheel, and sank into the soft leather arm-chair next to Spenser. Nothing as sordid as a bench seat in the back of this car. They moved off with barely a whisper from the engine, no noise at all from the street outside. How the other half live.

'Nice car.' It was all McLean could think of to say.

'I can't drive any more, so I favour comfort over power.' Spenser nodded at the back of the chauffeur's shaven head. 'I dare say Jethro takes her out and canes her from time to time.'

Viewed in the mirror, McLean saw the chauffeur's mouth twitch at the edge in the most minimal of smiles. No glass screen for privacy, so Spenser obviously trusted his man.

'The last time I saw your grandmother she was driving about in that dreadful Italian thing. What was it?'

'The Alfa Romeo?' McLean hadn't thought about it for a long time. Chances were it was still laid up at the back of the garage, unused since his gran had finally decided she was too old and blind to drive any more. She'd never sell it, and he couldn't remember the last time he'd been to look. 'That was my father's car. Gran spent a fortune keeping it going. New engine, resprays, the number of body panels that got replaced down the years, it was a bit like George Washington's axe.'

'Ah yes, the famous McLean thrift. She was a canny woman, was Esther. Ah, here we are.'

The Bentley pulled through a stone gateway and up a short drive to one of those surprisingly large mansions that lurk in unexpected corners of Edinburgh. It was surrounded by land a property developer would kill for; at least enough to build twenty executive homes and all given over to mature trees, beautifully tended gardens. The house itself was Edwardian, large but well-proportioned, and set high enough up to have stunning views across the city, taking in the castle, Arthur's Seat and the sea of spires and rooftops between them. Jethro was unbelted, out of his seat and opening Spenser's door before McLean had even registered they had stopped. The old man climbed out with an agility that was at odds with his appearance. No creaking joints

259

and difficulty straightening out here. McLean felt almost jealous as he hauled himself out, feet crunching on deep gravel, and popped a few vertebrae in his own spine.

'Come,' Spenser said. 'It's a bit more sheltered round the back.'

They walked around the house, Spenser pointing out interesting features as they went. At the back, a large orangery grew out from the house, surrounded by a raised patio that had to have been a 1970s addition. The crazy paving was immaculately maintained, however naff it might appear, and in the middle of it a table and chairs awaited. All that was missing was a swimming pool, but no, there it was, nestling between a tennis court and a croquet lawn of perfect flatness. A lot of effort had gone into maintaining this place, but then Spenser wasn't short of a bob or two.

A taciturn butler brought them coffee in silence. McLean watched it being poured, declined milk and sugar, sipped the finest brew he'd tasted in a very long time, breathed in the delicious aroma of perfectly roasted Arabica beans. How the other half live.

'You said you knew my grandmother when she was at university. No offence meant, but that must have been a while back.'

'Nineteen thirty-eight, I think it was.' Spenser scrunched up his face as if trying to recall, the creases of his scars turning livid red and yellowy white. 'Could have been thirty-seven. The memory goes, after a while.'

McLean very much doubted that. Spenser was sharp as one of those pins they hide in the tails of new shirts.

'Did she . . . ? Were you . . . ?' Why was it so hard to ask the question?

'An item, as I believe you youngsters have it?' Spenser frowned, and a whole new set of shapes fought across his ruined flesh. 'If only. We were good friends. Close. But Esther wasn't one for playing around, and she had to work twice as hard as the rest of us.'

'Oh? I always thought she was bright.'

'She was. Quite the most brilliant mind I've ever encountered. Razor-sharp, could learn anything easily. But she had one huge handicap: she was a woman.'

'They had women doctors in the thirties.'

'Oh yes. A few intrepid souls. But it wasn't easy getting there. It wasn't enough to be as good as the men, you had to be better. Esther, well, she relished that kind of challenge, but it did make her quite single-minded. I'm afraid that for all my charms, I just couldn't compete.'

'It must have been very galling then, when my grandfather came along.'

'Bill?' Spenser shrugged. 'He was always there. But he was a med student too, so he got to spend more time with Esther than the rest of us.'

'Rest of us?'

'Are you interrogating me, inspector?' Spenser smiled. 'Or may I call you Tony?'

'Of course. Sorry. For both. I should have said. And it's a habit, I'm afraid. All part of being a detective.'

'That surprised me, when I heard.' Spenser drained his coffee and put the cup down on the table.

'Me being a detective? Why?'

'It's an odd choice. I mean, your grandmother was a doctor, Bill too. Your dad was a lawyer. Would've been a good one if he'd had the chance. Why did you decide to join the police?'

'Well, I never had the brains to be a doctor for one thing.' McLean could picture his grandmother's resigned disappointment each time he came home with yet more poor results in his science subjects. 'As to being a lawyer, it never really occurred to me. My father wasn't exactly a great influence on my life.'

Something like sadness passed over Spenser's face, though it was difficult to tell through all the reconstructive surgery.

'Your father. Yes. John was a bright lad. I remember him well. I was very fond of him.'

'It seems you know more of my family than I do, Mr Spenser.'

'Gavin, please. Only my employees call me Mr Spenser, and even then only when I'm in earshot.'

Gavin. It didn't feel right. Like calling his gran Esther or his grandfather Bill. McLean swilled the coffee dregs around the bottom of his cup, eyed the cafetiere in hope of a refill, unsure whether it was because the coffee was so good or just that he needed a prop to overcome his discomfort. And that was the problem. Why was he uncomfortable in this man's presence? Apart from his disfigurement, and it couldn't be that, Spenser was nothing if not the perfect gentleman. An old family friend helping out at a time of grieving. So why were McLean's guts telling him something wasn't right.

'Actually, that brings me to another thing,' Spenser said. 'How would you like to come and work for me?'

McLean almost dropped his coffee cup. 'What?'

'I'm serious. You're wasted in the police, and if what I've heard is true, you're not going to get much further up the greasy pole. Not a politician, am I right?'

McLean nodded his head, unsure quite what to say. It seemed he wasn't the only one playing detective here.

'Whereas I don't give a damn about that kind of thing. It's a person's capabilities that I'm interested in. Like Jethro there. Most people wouldn't have given him a first chance, the way he's built, the way he talks. Not good with words, is Jethro. But he's brighter than he looks and he gets the job done. You get the job done, Tony. That's what I've heard about you. I could use a man with your skills. And let's face it, your training as well.'

'I don't really know what to say.' Except that Grumpy Bob would kill him if he left the force. And why was he even considering it? He loved being a detective, always had. But it wasn't as much fun being an inspector as he'd imagined it would be when he was still a sergeant. And then there were times when the endless stream of shit started to wear you down, it was true. It would be nice to do something where you could stop occasionally and view your achievements with a sense of pride. Nowadays there was barely time to catch a breath before you had to plunge straight back into the shit.

'It'd be a troubleshooting role, mainly. We've got operations all over the world, and sometimes you need an outsider to go in and stir them up a little. Especially when the revenues start to flag?'

'It sounds . . . interesting?'

'Just think about it, aye?' Spenser smiled again, and something familiar ghosted across his disfigured face. Something in those dark eyes, made deeper still by the livid pink and white of the scar tissue surrounding them. What terrible accident had befallen this man to leave him so disfigured? What would it be like to work for a man who had carried that with him for so long? And what harm was there in thinking about the offer? It wasn't as if he was going to take it up, after all.

'OK, Gavin. I will.'

42

The car was still there, lurking at the back of the converted coach house that served as garages. He'd walked straight here from Gavin Spenser's house, mind working overtime at the strange offer the old man had made. It was still just a philosophical question, of course. There was no way he'd leave the force. But it was interesting nonetheless to imagine travelling around the world, troubleshooting problems in the far-flung empire that was Spenser Industries. Except that he had no real idea what it was that Spenser Industries did, beyond the vague memory of a company logo on some computer equipment and the occasional snippet of information read in a paper or seen on the news that for whatever reason had lodged in his mind.

Shaking his head, McLean turned his attention to the other mystery the conversation had brought him. He had to move the old lawnmower and several boxes before he could get close enough to pull off the tailored cover, but when he did, the car beneath brought back so many memories.

It was a darker red than he had remembered, the paintwork glossy like new. The tiny mirrors, heart-shaped grille and hubcaps were shiny chrome, though winter road salt had pitted some of the metal. He ran a hand over the roof, tried the door handle. The car was locked, but the keys were on their hook in the box screwed to the wall by the door into what had once been a tack room. The stiff lock resisted at first, then gave with a creaking that spoke of expensive restoration bills to come, which was when he realised he, like his grandmother before him, was going to keep this car alive, the last memento of his long-dead father. What was it Mac-Bride had said when they'd visited Penstemmin Alarms? 'They say you don't even own a car?' Well, he did now.

Inside, the black leather seats seemed impossibly small and thin compared to the bulky padded things he was used to finding in the faceless pool cars he drove most days. The steering wheel was thin as he sank down behind it, metal spokes pointing to a tiny central boss designed in a time when airbags were a fantasy, and the waiting list for donated organs much shorter. Even seat belts had been an optional extra. That much he remembered his father telling him; a memory he'd not thought about in decades. Those childhood weekends when his parents had taken him out on long trips to the Borders.

He took a deep breath. It smelled exactly as he had remembered. He put the key in the ignition, turned it one click. Nothing. Well, that was hardly surprising. The car had been stood unused for well over two years. He'd have to dig out the number of that garage out in Loanhead where it used to go for its servicing. Get them to recommission it or whatever it was you did with old cars. Check the brakes, put new tyres on, that sort of thing. Reluctantly, McLean climbed out of the car, put everything back the way he'd found it and locked up the garage.

*

The folder for the car was in the filing cabinet exactly where it should have been. McLean was surprised to see that it had been taxed and insured at the time of his grandmother's stroke. He wondered if the solicitors had kept up the payments; they'd probably sent him a note about it at some point and he'd filed it in the things-to-do pile. There was a lot of stuff in that pile and sooner or later he was going to have to wade through it. Bad enough the paperwork at the office. Did he really have to deal with that shit at home too? Of course he did. That was life, and there was no getting around it.

The phone ringing sent a shock through him as if he'd been wired up to the mains. It had been so quiet in the garage, and now in the house. And who would be phoning him here anyway? Not many people even had the number. He picked the phone up quickly, barked into it louder than he'd intended.

'McLean.'

'That's not a very friendly telephone manner, inspector.' He recognised the voice.

'Sorry, Emma. It's been a long day.'

'Tell me about it. Some of us have been trying to match cocaine samples with known supplies all day. Have you any idea how many different chemicals get mixed in with the average line of blow?'

There'd been a briefing some time last year. Drug Squad trying to show the little detectives how much more important and difficult their job was. It was a war, after all. McLean vaguely recalled some technical stuff about how cocaine was made, and all the shit it got mixed with between the Colombian forests and the end user with his rolled-up ten pound note. 'Don't think I don't appreciate it. You get anywhere?'

'Nope. Well, that's not exactly true. It doesn't match any known profile in the UK, but then that's hardly surprising, since it's pure.'

'Uncut?'

'Totally. I've never seen anything like it. You can double whatever you thought it was worth. Just as well you're not a coke-head too. A couple of lines would have killed you.'

Very reassuring. 'What about the prints? You get anything off them?'

'Sorry, no. Too degraded. I checked them against McReadie first, but there's just not enough detail to make a watertight case. If I had to guess I'd say they were his, but it'd never stand up in court.'

McLean flicked through the folder on the desk in front of him before realising it was the paperwork for the car.

'Oh well. You tried. Thanks for that. I owe you.'

'You do indeed, inspector. Dinner if I recall. And as I understand it, you're at a loose end right now.'

Forward. That's what Grumpy Bob had said. Well, he couldn't fault the sergeant's character analysis any more than he could fault Emma's logic. McLean glanced at his watch – seven o'clock – and wondered what had happened to most of the day.

'Where are you now? HQ?'

'No, I'm at the station. Just been delivering some stuff to the evidence store. Dropped by your office, but they told me you were . . . well.'

Policemen were nothing if not gossips. No doubt his temporary suspension was all over Lothian and Borders by now. Bloody marvellous.

'OK. I'll meet you in an hour shall I?' He suggested a convenient restaurant, then hung up. Stared at the wall for a while. Outside, across the city, people were gearing themselves up for another night of Festival and Fringe, bustle and having fun. He wasn't sure his mood could take much exposure to that. His nice, comfortable, boring, safe old life was slowly unravelling, and he was powerless to do anything about it. His instinct was to hide away. He fought against it. Take control of the situation, that was the answer.

The folder lay open still on the desk in front of him. Well, there was always tomorrow to deal with that. He shuffled the papers together to put them away, and that was when he noticed the photograph tucked into the back. It must have been taken when the car was brand new, the colours slightly unreal, vivid, as if the intervening years had faded the world to what he saw now. His mother and father stood in front of the Alfa, parked in front of an old-fashioned garage forecourt. He was there too, short trousers and tidy jacket, one hand clutching a teddy bear, the other enveloped in his mother's grip. He flipped the photo over, but there was nothing except the watermark of the paper manufacturer. Back to the image again and as he stared at it the vaguest stirrings of memory. Could he really remember that day, that hour, that second? Or was he just constructing a possible scenario around the fact of the photograph?

He laid it back down on top of the rest of the paperwork, closed the folder. He didn't know these people, no longer felt any emotion when he saw them. But as he stood, put the folder back in the filing cabinet and pushed the drawer closed, he couldn't shake the image from his mind, couldn't help but see the smile in his father's dark eyes.

43

They went to a Thai restaurant close to the station. McLean had eaten there often before, mostly with large groups of hungry policemen.

'What's good? I don't think I've ever eaten Thai.' Emma took a sip from her beer; she'd ordered a pint, he noticed.

'That depends. Do you like spicy, or would you prefer something a bit easier?'

'Spicy, always. The hotter the better.'

McLean smiled; he enjoyed a challenge. 'OK, then. I'd suggest you start with gung dong and follow up with a panang. See if you've got room for one of their coconut cream puddings after that.'

'Are you this knowledgeable about everything, inspector?' Emma raised an inquisitive eyebrow and shook her short black hair out of her face. McLean knew she was teasing him, but couldn't help taking the bait.

'I'm told even inspectors get to clock off now and then. Besides, I'm on leave until Monday. And you can call me Tony, you know.'

'So what does an inspector do when he's not at work, Tony?'

For the past eighteen months, since he'd found her unconscious in her favourite armchair, visit his gran in hospital. Or at work, or just maybe at home asleep. McLean couldn't remember the last time he'd been to the cinema or a show. He hadn't been on holiday for more than a couple of days at a time and even then all he'd done was take his old mountain bike out into the Pentland Hills, wondering why they were so much steeper every time.

'Mostly I go to the pub,' he said, shrugging. 'Or Thai restaurants.'

'Not alone, I hope,' Emma laughed. 'That would be very sad.'

McLean didn't say anything, and Emma's laughter died away to embarrassed silence. It had been far too long since he'd done anything like this; he didn't really know what to say.

'I brought my gran here once,' he finally managed. 'Before she had her stroke.'

'She was very special to you, wasn't she.'

'You could say that. When I was four years old, my parents were killed in a plane crash just south of Inverness. Gran raised me as if I were her own child.'

'Oh Tony, I'm so sorry. I didn't realise.'

'It's all right. I got over it a long time ago. When you're four you adapt quickly. But gran dying, well to me that felt a lot more like I'd imagine losing a parent would feel. And she was in a coma for so long. It was horrible seeing her just waste away like that.'

'My dad died a few years back,' Emma said. 'Drank himself to death. Can't really say me or my mum were that sad to see the back of him. Is that wrong?'

'I don't know. No. I wouldn't have thought so. Was he a violent man?'

'Not really, just careless.'

'You have any brothers or sisters?' McLean tried to move the conversation away from the maudlin.

'No, there's just me.'

'And what does an SOC officer do with her spare time. Assuming she has any, that is.'

Emma laughed. 'Probably no more than a detective inspector. It's very easy to get absorbed by work, and being on twenty-four-hour call-out plays havoc with your social life.'

'Sounds like you've had a few bitter experiences.'

'Haven't we all?'

'So you're not seeing anyone at the moment?'

'You're the detective, Tony. Do you think I'd be sitting in here drinking beer and eating curry with you if I was?'

'Sorry, stupid question. Tell me about cocaine and all the strange things dealers think of to mix it with.'

It was perhaps a little sad, but he found it easier to talk about work than anything else. Emma seemed happier on that topic too, and he suspected that her father had been more than just careless. All lives are defined by the endless little tragedies.

By the time their food arrived, they were deep in conversation about the need for absolute cleanliness in the lab. The meal passed in a succession of anecdotes about work colleagues and before long he'd paid the bill and they were stepping out into the night.

'That pudding was gorgeous. What was it called again?' Emma slipped her arm through his, leaning close as they walked slowly up the street.

'Kanom bliak bun, at least I think that's how they pronounce it.' Where they were going, McLean had no idea. He had approached the meal as a chore, an obligation in repayment for a favour. It was something of a surprise to him to find the company so enjoyable. And he really hadn't planned anything. The night had turned chill, a north-easterly breeze coming in off the sea. Her body was warm against his side. Years of practice at being alone urged him to push her away, to keep his distance, but for the first time in as long as he could remember, he ignored it. 'D'you fancy a nightcap?'

They started off in the Guildford Arms because it was close and served decent beer. After that, Emma suggested they try and find a Fringe comedy show that wasn't sold out. McLean suspected she knew where she was going all along, but he was happy to be led. The bar they eventually managed to get into was tiny and packed with sweaty people. It was an open mic night and a series of hopeful comedians braved a hostile and inebriated audience for their scant minutes of fame. Some of them were quite good, others so bad they raised more of a laugh anyway. By the time the last act had finished and the bar emptied, it was two in the morning and the street outside was noticeable for a complete lack of taxis. McLean fumbled in his pocket for his mobile phone, pulling it out and staring at the screen in consternation.

'Damned battery's dead again. I swear I'm jinxed when it comes to these bloody things.'

'You should talk to Malky Watt in the SOC office. He's got a theory about people's auras and how some can suck the life out of electrical devices. Especially if someone powerful is thinking negative thoughts about you.'

'He sounds a right nutter.'

'Yup. That'd be about right.'

'It never used to happen to me. Just the last month or so. I've tried changing phones, new batteries, everything. Bloody thing's useless unless it's plugged into the wall, which kind of defeats the point.'

'I see what you mean.' Emma looked at the blank screen on the phone. 'Never mind. My flat's only five minutes from here. You can phone for a taxi from there.'

'Oh, right. I was going to try and get one for you, not me. I can walk back to Newington from here, no bother. I kind of like the city late at night. Reminds me of when I was on the beat. Come on, I'll walk you home.' McLean held out his arm and Emma took it once more.

Her flat was in a terrace of stone houses down in Warriston, backing onto the Water of Leith. McLean shivered as they reached the road-end.

'Cold, inspector?' Emma reached around him with her arm and pulled him against her. He tensed.

'No, not cold. Something else. I'd rather not go into it.'

She looked at him strangely. 'OK.' Then continued to walk. McLean kept up with her, but the moment had gone. He couldn't stop himself from looking back to the bridge where he'd found Kirsty's dead body, all those years ago.

They reached her door after a couple of hundred yards. Emma fished around in her bag for a set of keys. 'You want to come in for a coffee?'

He was tempted, sorely. She was warm and friendly, she smelled of carefree days and fun. For the whole evening she had chased away his ghosts, but now they were back. If she'd lived in any other street, he might have said yes.

'I can't.' He made a show of looking at his watch. 'I've got to get back. It's been a long day today, and it looks like tomorrow's going to be even worse.'

'Liar, you're supposed to be on leave. You can sleep in as late as you like. You've no idea how much I envy you.' Emma punched him playfully on the chest. 'But it's all right. I've got to be in the lab for eight. This was fun, though.'

'Yeah, it was. We should do it again.'

'Is that a date, Inspector McLean?'

'Ah, I don't know about that. If it was a date, I'd have to cook for you.'

'Fine. I'll bring the wine.' Emma stepped close to him, leaned forward and kissed him lightly on the lips, backing away and darting up the steps before he had time to react. ''Night, Tony,' she shouted as she unlocked the door and disappeared inside.

It wasn't until he was halfway back to Princes Street that McLean realised he hadn't thought about Constable Kydd all evening.

44

A harsh buzzing sound filtered in from the edges of his dreams, bringing McLean back to the land of the living. He opened an eye to stare at his bedside alarm. Six o'clock and he felt like death. It seemed rather unfair, after such a pleasant time the night before. And he'd been looking forward to that lie-in, too.

Reaching out, he hit the snooze button on the alarm. The buzzing continued and now he realised it was coming from the top of the chest of drawers on the other side of the room. Stumbling out of bed, he reached his crumpled jacket just as the noise stopped. Underneath it, plugged into its charger, his phone flashed a single text message for him to contact the station. He was just about to call in when his home phone started to ring out in the hall.

Stomping out in his boxers, McLean reached the handset just as it too rang off. He'd still not replaced the tape in the answering machine. Perhaps he'd go and buy a new one. Something digital that wouldn't preserve the voices of the dead. He looked down at the text message on the phone in his hand, hit the speed-dial number and asked to be put through. Ten minutes later he was showered, dressed and out the front door. Breakfast would have to wait.

A chill morning wind cut down the narrow street, sharpened by the tall buildings on either side. Lazy wind, his gran would have called it; goes straight through you rather than making the effort to go round. McLean shivered in his thin summer suit, still cold from no breakfast, too little sleep and a sudden, rude awakening with news he could have done without. Sometimes the life of an office worker seemed very attractive indeed; shift end and knock off. Go home safe in the knowledge that no one was going to call in the middle of the night asking you to come in and process a few more reports, or whatever it was people in offices with normal jobs did.

Detective Constable MacBride was waiting for him at the entrance to the city mortuary, nervously loitering in the street like some fresh-faced first-year student wondering if he had the nerve to go alone into one of the Cowgate's more notorious pubs. He looked even colder than McLean felt, if that was possible.

'What's the story, constable,' McLean asked, flashing his warrant card to a young uniform carefully rolling out black and yellow tape around the vehicle entranceway.

'It's the young girl, sir. The one from the house in Sighthill. She . . . Well, I think you'd be better off talking to Dr Sharp.'

Inside the building it was unusually busy. A SOC team were dusting everything in their search for fingerprints and other clues, watched by a nervous pathology assistant.

'What's happening, Tracy?' McLean asked. She looked relieved to see him, a familiar face in the chaos.

'Someone broke in here and stole one of our bodies. The mutilated girl. They took her preserved organs, too.'

'Anything else gone?'

'Gone, no. But they've been at the computers. We've got password protection, but when I came in mine was switched on. I could have sworn I turned it off last night. Didn't think much of it until we noticed the body gone. Nothing's been deleted as far as I can tell, but they could have made copies of any of my files.'

'And the other bodies in storage?' McLean looked out through the glass panes that separated the office from the autopsy theatre. Emma was popping away with her flashgun. Stopped when she saw him and gave a cheery wave.

'Don't appear to have been touched. Whoever did this, they knew what they were looking for.'

'Chances are SOC won't find anything, then. It looks like this has been very well planned. Are you sure it went last night?'

'I can't be a hundred per cent. It's not like we took her out every day to check. But the organs were stored in the secure room over there.' She pointed to a heavy wooden door with a small reinforced glass window in it at head height. 'They were there last night when I put the suicide victim's clothes away; gone this morning when I went to get another box of specimen jars. As soon as I noticed, I checked the drawers and she wasn't there.'

'What time did you leave last night?'

'About eight, I think. But there's someone here twenty-four hours a day. We never know when a body's going to come in.'

'I'm assuming not just anyone can walk in off the street in here.' McLean knew already the security measures in place. They weren't perfect, but they had seemed more than adequate before now. Enough to stop people coming in without authorisation. 'How do you suppose someone would take a body out of here? I mean, you can't exactly throw it over your shoulder and walk out onto the Cowgate.'

'Most bodies are brought here by ambulance or undertakers. Maybe they took her away that way?'

'Makes sense, I guess. How many bodies came in last night?'

'Let me check.' She turned to her computer, then paused. 'Is it OK to use this?'

McLean grabbed a passing SOC officer and asked the same question.

'Dusted it for prints, but it's unlikely we'll get anything off it. There's none on the security keypad, and nothing on the chiller doors. My guess is whoever did this was wearing gloves.'

'Go ahead then,' McLean nodded to Tracy. She clicked a few keys.

'We had your suicide logged in at half-past one. A suspected heart-attack victim came in at eight. Yes, I remember them bringing him in. Nothing else after that. Must have been a quiet night.'

'And the night desk can confirm that?'

'I'll ask.' Tracy picked up the phone without asking a SOC officer if that was all right. She spoke briefly, scribbling down a number, then hung up and dialled it. Silence for a long while. Then finally, 'Pete? Hi, it's Trace at work. Yeah, I'm sorry, I know you're on nights. We've had a break-in though. Police all over the place. No, I'm not joking. They're going to want to talk to you. Look, did you process any bodies after Mr Lentin came in yesterday evening?' Pause. 'What? You're sure? OK. OK. Thanks.' She put down the phone.

'An ambulance came in at two this morning. Pete swears he logged it in, but there's nothing on the system.'

'That would be the system you found switched on when you came in yourself?' McLean had to admire the thoroughness of the thief. It was a professional job from top to bottom. But why would anyone want to steal a sixty years dead corpse they still hadn't been able to identify?

'You were right, you know.'

'I was? What about?' McLean stood in the doorway of Chief Superintendent McIntyre's office. It was famously always open, but he was reluctant to commit himself. Her weary, resigned sigh at seeing him there had been enough to know he was pushing his luck.

'McReadie. He wasn't due in for interview for another day, but his lawyer phoned up and persuaded Charles to move him up the schedule. That's why he was in here when Constable Kydd was run down. Won't do him any good. He's on his way to Saughton right now.'

That wouldn't be much solace for poor bloody Alison. 'I phoned the hospital.'

'Me too, Tony. No change, I know. She's a tough kid, but they almost lost her on the operating table. I don't need to tell you how slim her chances are.' Or how much of a life she's going to have even if she does pull through. McLean watched as McIntyre rubbed a tired palm against her face. Let her get to the point in her own time. 'Now what exactly are you doing here. You're meant to be on leave.'

He told her about the missing body. 'We know that Bertie Farquhar was one of the killers, but I think at least one of the others is still alive.'

'You think they took it?'

'At least arranged for it to be taken. Farquhar would have been in his nineties if he hadn't crashed his car. I'm guessing anyone else involved would have been much the same age. Not exactly the type of people to go breaking into the city mortuary.'

'More likely they'd be wheeled in.' McIntyre tried to raise a smile without much success.

'Whoever it is, they've got influence. Or money. Both, really. We've not exactly been public about the body, but someone knew we'd found it, and where we were keeping it. I'm guessing they're trying to cover their tracks.'

'You do know I said Monday. You shouldn't be here.'

'I know. But I can't leave this to DS Laird. Not with everything else he's got going on. And I'll go mad if I have to sit at home knowing the killer's out there erasing every last shred of evidence we have.'

The chief superintendent said nothing for a while, leaned back in her chair and stared at him. McLean let her have as much time as she needed.

'What are you going to do?' She asked finally.

'I'm trying to trace Bertie Farquhar's friends. Constable Mac-Bride's already gone through the archives, and we've asked for his war record. I was going to see if Emily Johnson's come up with anything else. She was going to have a search through the attic for any of Farquhar's old photo albums or stuff.'

'Why do I get the feeling you'd have been paying Miss Johnson a visit today anyway?' McIntyre waved away McLean's protestation of innocence. 'Go, Tony. Find your missing dead girl and her geriatric murderer. But stay away from McReadie. I hear you've been anywhere near him and it'll be Professional Standards, you understand?'

45

Grumpy Bob looked perfectly happy as he perched on the edge of an elderly, hair-covered sofa. The Dandie Dinmonts were locked away in the kitchen, he had tea and he had biscuits. At this time of the day, McLean knew, the sergeant could want for little more.

Emily Johnson had welcomed them in, announcing that she'd been up in the attic going through old trunks of stuff. Now they were all in the living room, flicking through endless black and white photos.

'I think I might have to get a professional valuer in,' she said. 'There's so much stuff up there just mouldering away. I thought maybe I'd have a charity auction. Give everything to the sick kids. It's not as if I need the money, and none of it has any sentimental value.'

McLean thought about his own situation, suddenly awash with old family heirlooms he had no great liking for and no desire to keep. Maybe that was the way to go; auction it all and use the proceeds to set up some charitable fund.

'I'd be grateful if you'd give us time to go through Albert's things before you start disposing of them, Mrs Johnson.' The last thing he wanted was to lose any useful evidence to the auction room.

'Don't worry about that, inspector. It'll take me years to get anything organised. Oh. I found this by the way.' Mrs Johnson stood and retrieved something small from a china bowl on the mantelpiece, handing it to McLean as she returned. He looked at the small, tooled-leather jewellery box, worn rough at the edges. Underneath, in faded gold lettering, was the brief description: Douglas and Footes, Jewellers. Opened, it was lined with dark green ruched velvet, and in the lid was the inscription: 'To Albert Menzies Farquhar, on the reaching of his majority, August 13th 1932'. Stuck into their holes in the velvet were four small shirt studs, topped with sparkling red rubies like little tears of blood. Two further studs had lost their heads. There was a space for the signet ring, but it was empty.

'You found the cufflinks that made up the set.'

'We did, and this nicely confirms what I've suspected all along.' McLean snapped the box shut, handing it back. 'I suppose technically the stolen cufflink belongs to you. Bob, make a note to return both of them to Mrs Johnson when the investigation is finally over.'

'Don't do that, inspector. I don't want the beastly things. I couldn't stand Bertie when he was alive. Frankly it doesn't surprise me at all that he might have killed someone. He ran into that bus stop, after all.'

'Did you know him well?'

'Not enormously, thank God. He was Toby's age, I think, and he was quite fond of my husband, John. But he gave me the creeps, always staring at me with those hooded eyes of his. It made me feel dirty just being in the same room.'

'What about the house in Sighthill? Did you ever visit there?'

'Oh God, Emperor Ming's Folly. That's what we used to call it. I'm sure it was a grand place once. But it just looked so ridiculous in amongst all those council estates. And so close to the prison, too. I don't know why the old man didn't just bulldoze it and have done with it. It's not like he couldn't afford to.'

'I rather think he was trying to keep something hidden.'

McLean reached out for one of the leather-bound photograph albums that Mrs Johnson had laid out on the coffee table. Across from him, Grumpy Bob helped himself to another biscuit and continued flicking through the album he had already begun.

'He knew what his son had done, and tried to cover it up. Even after he died, Farquhar's Bank kept a hold of that empty house. They sold off the rest of the estate, so why keep it? An old established firm like that would have respected the founder's dying wishes, but when they were bought out by Mid-Eastern Finance all bets were off.'

'You found a body in that house?' Mrs Johnson clasped a hand to her throat, her whole body suddenly still.

'I'm sorry. I didn't tell you before. Yes we did. A young girl hidden away in the basement. We think she was killed just after the end of the war.'

'My God. All those times. All those dreadful parties in that place and I never knew. How did she die?'

'Let's just say that she was murdered and leave it at that, Mrs Johnson. I'm more interested in finding out who might have helped Albert Farquhar, and whether anyone involved is still alive.'

'Of course. Well, he had friends, I suppose. I mean Toby and he were . . . You don't think Toby was involved do you?'

'Right now I've an open mind. I know Farquhar was guilty. Your father-in-law died a long time ago, and there's not a lot I can do about the dead. But there's someone out there still alive who's connected to it all, and I'm not giving up until I bring him to justice.'

'Well, look at this.' Grumpy Bob interrupted the conversation with a note of triumph in his voice. He held open the photo album, swinging it round and placing it on top of all the others on the coffee table. McLean leant forward for a better look and was rewarded with a black and white image of five men in white flannel trousers and blazers. They were all young, late teens or early twenties, and sported the sort of hair styles that had been fashionable just before the war. Four of them stood shoulder to shoulder and held a wooden trophy shield. The fifth lay on the ground at their feet, and behind them all, McLean could make out a sleek rowing boat, oars and a river. Beneath the photograph someone had pasted in the caption: 'Edinburgh University Coxed Four. Henley Regatta June 1938', but what interested him more than that were the signatures scrawled on the photograph itself.

Tobias Johnson
Albert Farquhar
Barnaby Smythe
Buchan Stewart
Jonas Carstairs

46

'Do you have a minute, sir?'

McLean stood in the doorway of the largest incident room in the building. It appeared to be a re-run of the Barnaby Smythe investigation, only in place of the banker's photograph now one of Jonas Carstairs was pinned to the wall. Once again Duguid had managed to bully, cajole and order most of the active personnel in the building onto his investigation, and once more it seemed his approach to getting results was to interview everyone over and over again until some clue presented itself. The man himself was standing a few paces away, hands on hips and surveying the general busyness as if activity in itself was a sign that things were going well. Quite probably that was what he truly believed. He'd have made a natural civil servant.

'I thought you were on forced leave until Monday.' The chief inspector didn't look entirely pleased to see him.

'Something came up. I squared it with the chief superintendent.'

'I'll just bet you did.'

McLean ignored the sneer. This was too important. 'I was wondering if you'd got anywhere with the Carstairs investigation?'

'Come to gloat, have you?' A vein ticked in Duguid's temple, his cheeks reddening.

'Not at all, sir. It's just that his name's come up in one of my investigations. The ritual killing?'

'Ah yes. The cold case. Jayne only gave it to you because she didn't think you'd be able to cause much trouble over it. I bet she's regretting that.'

'Actually we've positively identified one of the murderers already.'

'Arrested him, have you?'

'He's dead, actually. Has been for nearly fifty years.'

'So you've achieved bugger all then.'

'Not really, sir.' McLean fought back the urge to punch his superior in the face. It would be fun, but the repercussions would be a pain to live with. 'Actually I've uncovered new evidence that links him to Jonas Carstairs, Barnaby Smythe and your uncle.'

OK, that last jibe might have been unwise, but the man really asked for it. McLean took an involuntary step back as the DCI stiffened, his hands twitching into fists.

'Don't you dare mention that in here.' Duguid's voice was a growl of menace. 'You'll be suggesting he's a suspect next. Bloody ridiculous.'

'Actually, that's exactly what I'm suggesting. Him, Carstairs, Smythe and a couple of others. And I think there's a sixth man involved too. Someone who's still alive and who's doing everything he can to stop us finding him.'

'Including killing his co-conspirators?' Duguid actually laughed, which at least lessened his anger. 'We know who killed Smythe and Buchan Stewart. It's only a matter of time until we catch the sick bastard who did for your lawyer friend too.'

Christ alive. How did you ever get to be a chief inspector? 'So you're close then? You've got a suspect in mind?'

'Actually, I wanted to ask you a few questions about your relationship with Carstairs.'

'Didn't we go over this already? I hardly knew the man.'

'And yet you had dealings with his firm for the past eighteen months.'

McLean fought the urge to sigh. How many times did he have to say this before it sunk into that balding head?

'He was a friend of my gran. His firm had been managing her affairs for years. I just let them get on with it once she'd had her stroke. It seemed easier that way. I never met Carstairs, always dealt with some bloke called Stephenson.'

'And in all those eighteen months you never saw Carstairs? Never talked to this man who was such an old family friend your grandmother had entrusted her not inconsiderable wealth to his care? This man who was so fond of you he left you his entire personal wealth?'

'No. And the first I knew about that was when you told me, the morning after he was killed.' McLean knew he should stop speaking then, just answer the question and no more, but there was something red-rag-to-the-bull about Duguid. He just couldn't help himself. 'I don't know if you remember, sir, but it's often busy being a detective inspector. I was really quite glad there was something in place before my grandmother had her stroke so I didn't have to add managing her affairs to my ever-growing mountain of paperwork. I'd really much rather be out there catching the bad guys.'

'I don't like your tone, McLean.'

'And I don't care, sir. I came here to see if you had any leads on Carstairs' murder, but since it's obvious you haven't got a clue, I'll not keep you any longer.'

McLean started to turn away, not wanting to give Duguid time to react, then thought what the hell? He might as well go for the full house.

'One thing though. You really should re-open the Smythe and

Stewart cases, sir. Go over the forensics with a fresh pair of eyes, double-check the witness statements, that sort of thing.'

'Don't you bloody well tell me how to run my investigation.' Duguid reached for McLean's arm, but he shrugged the grip away.

'They all knew each other, sir. Carstairs, Smythe, your bloody uncle. They were at university together, they were in the army together. I strongly suspect they raped and killed a young woman together. And now they've all died in a remarkably similar way. Don't you think that at least deserves a cursory glance?'

He didn't wait for an answer, left Duguid to stew about it on his own. The chief inspector would either shout at someone to go and look into it or go scuttling off to the chief superintendent to complain. Neither was what was bothering McLean as he hurried down the corridor towards his own incident room. No, what was bothering him was the gut certainty that he was right, about the three men being involved in the ritual murder and about their deaths all being somehow linked. An organ for each of the ritual murderers; an organ ripped from their own bodies and shoved in their mouths. The coincidences had long since stacked too high to be safe. It wouldn't take much to bring the whole lot toppling down.

'What if he's still alive?'

Puzzled faces looked up at McLean as he entered the incident room. Grumpy Bob had at least put his newspaper down for a moment, although his feet were up on the table, so he might have been having a quick forty winks. MacBride was hunched over his laptop, peering at what looked like thumbnail images spread across the screen. When he looked up, McLean was surprised how pale he looked, his eyes rimmed red as if he'd not slept in days. His suit wasn't its normal pressed perfection, and his hair hadn't seen a comb recently either.

'The sixth man. The one who's not there.' McLean pointed at the photograph pinned to the wall and showing the young rowing team. 'What if he's still alive, knows we've uncovered the body and is trying to cover his tracks?'

Grumpy Bob continued to give him the blank stare of the recently roused.

'Look. The body's gone, along with all the organs and jars. The only stuff we've still got are the artefacts they left behind. We know they're clean for prints and DNA traces, so they're not going to be much use. Even if we got a name, we'd have a difficult time pinning anything on them. Just being associated with Bertie Farquhar's not going to be enough. Hell, my grandmother knew at least three of these people, and I don't think she had anything to do with it. But until a month ago, three of those five men were still alive.'

MacBride was the first to pick up the thread. 'But we know Jonathan Okolo killed Barnaby Smythe. And Buchan Stewart was killed by a jealous lover.'

'Are you sure of that, constable? 'Cause I'm not. I think that investigation was wrapped up quickly to save a chief inspector from being embarrassed. Just like Smythe's murder was never investigated once we had Okolo. And Duguid's not got a clue who killed Jonas Carstairs. Now we know that they were all linked to the ritual murder, and someone's been cutting out their organs. Three murders, all too similar to be coincidence.'

'Um, actually, there was something might explain that, sir.' MacBride swivelled his laptop around to reveal the screen. 'I was trying to find a leak. You know, to explain how a copy-cat could know so much about Smythe's murder when we've not told the press anything. Well, it occurred to me that SOC photographs are all digital now. It's easy to make electronic copies. You can fit thousands of photos on a card the size of a stamp. But I couldn't exactly walk into the SOC offices and ask them, and I couldn't think what anyone would want with copies if they weren't going to sell them to the papers.'

'They'd get good money for them in Brazil.'

'What?'

'It's a part of the culture over there, death. They have newspapers that specialise in publishing pictures of fatal accidents. Sometimes the photographers are there before the police and ambulances. You can buy the papers from street vendors. Images like this would be very popular.'

MacBride shuddered. 'How do you know this stuff, sir?'

'Benefits of an expensive education. I know a little bit about a lot of things. That and the Discovery Channel, of course. Anyway, you were telling me about Smythe and his pictures.'

'Was I? Oh, aye. Well, I figured if they were selling them, they'd be doing it online. So I went looking for dodgy photos.'

'On a station computer? That was brave.'

'It's all right, sir. Mike gave me this laptop. It's outside the main tech monitoring loop. Otherwise I'd have had to ask Dagwood to sign a waiver form, and you know what he's like.'

'The pictures, constable.' McLean pointed back at the screen.

'Yes, sir. Well, I found lots. Crime-scene photos, car accidents. I guess some of that Brazilian stuff you were mentioning, though I couldn't understand the language. It was like Spanish only different.'

'That's because they speak Portuguese in Brazil.'

'Portuguese. Right. Anyway, eventually I found this newsgroup tucked away behind some serious security. And there was all this stuff there. Smythe's crime scene, Buchan Stewart, Jonas Carstairs. Even those two suicides. There's loads of other stuff up there too, but the pictures I recognised were all posted by someone calling themselves MB.'

McLean clicked the thumbnail page. Scrolling down, he counted over a hundred pictures, and there were dozens more pages like it.

'Whoever's doing this must have access to every photo we've ever taken,' he said. 'How many SOC photographers are there?'

'About a dozen specialise in it, but they're all trained to use the cameras. And I guess the technicians and support staff might have access, too. But it could be a police officer just as easily, sir. We all have access to these photos.'

'Can we track this MB person back from this site?'

'I doubt it, sir. Mike's going to have a look at it tomorrow, but it's all anonymous servers and routing through overseas accounts. Way over my head. But it does explain how someone might know the details of Smythe's murder. And I guess if you get your kicks from looking at this kind of thing, it's only a matter of time before you escalate.'

Damn. He'd been so sure. Was still sure. But this was too much to ignore. 'That's good work, Stuart. Get a report typed up as soon as and I'll make sure the chief superintendent knows who did all the work. Meantime I still want to work on the theory we've got our sixth man still out there and he's doing everything he can to make sure we don't find him.'

'Did I hear someone mention my name?'

McLean looked around to see the chief superintendent standing in the doorway. MacBride leapt to his feet as if someone had just zapped him with a tazer. Grumpy Bob nodded and took his feet off the desk.

'I asked Constable MacBride to look into the crime-scene leak. I rather think he's found it.' McLean gave McIntyre a quick run-down of what he'd just himself learnt. She fidgeted throughout his short presentation, like a young girl needing to be excused but not knowing how to ask.

'That's top work, constable,' she said when they were finished. 'And Christ only knows, we could do with some good news.'

And now McLean could see what was coming. It was written all over her face.

'Do you want me to . . . ?' He motioned towards the door.

'No. It's OK, Tony. This is my job. And I thought it only fair I tell you myself. Tell all of you.' McIntyre straightened her uniform jacket, momentarily unsure how to go on. 'It's Constable Kydd. She took a turn for the worse. The doctors did their best, but she was too badly injured. She died about an hour ago.'

47

There weren't many places he could go when the shit really hit the fan. There was Phil, of course, except that Phil's normal cure for any ills came on tap or in a bottle, and McLean really didn't feel like getting drunk. Grumpy Bob could usually be relied on to keep him from getting too morose, but the old sergeant seemed to have taken an avuncular liking to Constable Kydd, and took the news of her death with uncharacteristic tears. McIntyre had told him to take the rest of the day off, told them all in that school-matron manner of hers that she didn't want to see any of them for twenty-four hours. She had enough shit of her own to deal with, so he couldn't really burden her with his own guilt. In the past there had been his grandmother; even when she was lying comatose in the hospital she'd been a good listener, but now even she had left him. Which was why, less than an hour after hearing the news, and still slightly numb, McLean found himself in the mortuary. So much for a wide and vibrant social circle.

'We have a phrase for it, Tony. It's called survivor's guilt.' Angus Cadwallader was still wearing his scrubs from the last post-mortem of the day.

'I know, Angus. Psychology. University. Got a First, remember. It's just, knowing doesn't seem to help. She pushed me out of the way. She gave up her own life so I could live. How is that fair?'

'Fairness is something we tell children exists to keep them in line.'

'Hmmm. Not sure that exactly helps.'

'I try my best.' Cadwallader stripped off his long rubber gloves and dumped them in the sterile bin. McLean looked over the mortuary, realising for the first time that there was no sign of any forensic examination going on.

'SOC didn't spend long in here,' he said. 'Normally they like to take days searching for tiny clues.'

'Well, I'm glad they didn't. It was bad enough losing a day's work. People don't stop dying, you know. I've a backlog that's going to take weeks to sort out thanks to your helpful thief.'

'Who's that then?' McLean nodded towards the covered body as Cadwallader guddled around in nearby drawers looking for something.

'That's your suicide victim. The Waverley Station woman. Still haven't got a name for her, poor thing. We examined her this morning. Tracy's still got to finish cleaning her up and then she'll have to wait until she's identified. Strange thing, though. You remember her hands and hair were covered in blood. Couldn't see where it had all come from?'

McLean nodded, although truth was, so much had happened since he'd been called to her suicide he'd forgotten all about it.

'Well that's because it wasn't hers.'

Emma Baird almost walked into him as he was leaving the mortuary. She was fighting with a large insulated box, the contents of which McLean was happy not to know, and had backed through the doorway just as he was opening it. In any other circumstance, the site of her tumbling backwards into his arms would have been amusing.

'Watch yourself there.'

'Bloody stupid . . . what the fuck –' Emma struggled, turned, realised who it was. 'Oh God, Tony. Um, inspector. Sir.'

McLean helped her to her feet, trying to stifle the chuckle that wanted to burst from his throat. She looked so angry and flustered and full of life. He knew if he started laughing he probably wouldn't be able to stop.

'Sorry, Em. I didn't see you coming through the door. And Tony's fine, really. Can't be doing with this sir and inspector nonsense at the best of times.' He didn't need to say that these weren't.

'Yeah. I heard the news. I'm so sorry. She was a nice kid.'

A nice kid. Not much of an epitaph, really. And she was just a kid. Not that long out of training college, keen to make detective as soon as possible. Bright, enthusiastic, friendly, dead.

'You on your way in, or out?' Emma's questioned filled the uncomfortable silence.

'What? Oh. Out.' McLean looked at his watch. Long past knocking-off time, even if the chief superintendent hadn't sent his team home already. He nodded at the box. 'What about yourself? Delivering or collecting?'

'This? Oh I was just dropping it off. Dr Sharp loaned us it last week when we were one short. It was on my way home so I said I'd drop it off.'

'Here, let me give you a hand then.' McLean reached for the box.

'No, you're OK.' Emma hugged it to her side as if it were a cherished keepsake. 'But I wouldn't mind the company.'

It didn't take long to hand over the box and get back to the door. McLean didn't even have to say anything; Emma was quite capable of talking for two.

'That you off for the evening then?' She asked as he held the door open for her.

'Should probably head back to the station. There's a stack of paperwork with my name on it and a duty sergeant who gets more creative with his threats every day.' Even as he said it, the thought filled him with a weary resignation. He'd creep in the back way to avoid being seen, sit there and work his way through the pile until either it was done or he was. And even if he finished it, there would be another one to replace it soon enough. Times like these, he wondered why he did the bloody job. Might as well go work for Gavin Spenser and live in a big house with a swimming pool.

'Say it like that, I could even be tempted to do some paperwork myself. Find some just special.'

'Well, if you're offering . . .'

'Tell you what. Come and have a drink first. Then see how keen you are.' Emma set off up the Cowgate in the direction of the Grassmarket before he could answer. McLean had to hop and skip to catch up, grabbing her by the shoulder.

'Emma.'

'Honestly, inspector. Did anyone ever tell you you're no fun.'

'Not recently, no. It's just that I'm guessing you don't know Edinburgh all that well, aye?' He pointed across the road in the opposite direction. 'The only decent pub round here's that way.'

One beer turned into two, then a quick tour of the better city-centre pubs, a curry. It was almost enough of a distraction that he could forget Alison Kydd was dead. Almost, but not quite. McLean avoided the usual police haunts, knowing they'd be full of coppers raising a few to their fallen comrade. He couldn't cope with their sympathy, and didn't want to have to deal with the inevitable few who'd blame him rather than the hit-and-run driver. Emma had sensed it too, he could tell. She chatted constantly, but mostly about her own work and the delights of moving from Aberdeen down to Edinburgh. They parted with a simple, 'This was fun, we should do it again.' The lightest of touches on his arm and she turned away, disappeared down the dark street to the place of his nightmares. He shook them away, shoved his hands in his pockets, head down for the walk home.

The city never really slept, especially during the Festival. The usual crowd of late-shift workers and rough-sleepers was augmented by drunken students and wannabe actors, dustbin men and road sweepers. The streets were quiet in comparison with the day, but it was early yet, and a steady stream of cars still fought their single-occupant ways to destinations unknown. Vans meandered from drop-off point to drop-off point like fat, smelly bees. McLean tried to push away his guilt as he walked, looked for the rhythm of his feet on the pavement to bring some answers to all the questions milling around his head. There was something he was missing, something that didn't add up. No, there were many things he was missing, many things that didn't add up. Not the least of which was the grisly similarity between the deaths of three elderly men, all friends of old, all connected to one horrible, violent crime. A fanciful man would say that they were being visited by an unholy vengeance. Opus Diaboli. They had dabbled in the devil's work and now he had come to claim them. But the reality was far more mundane. Barnaby Smythe had been gutted by an illegal immigrant with a grudge; Buchan Stewart had fallen victim to a jealous lover; and Jonas Carstairs? Well, no doubt Duguid would find someone to pin that one on.

Click, clack, click, clack, his feet drummed out a steady beat along the flagstones, the slow tempo marking time with his thoughts. He knew that Okolo had killed Smythe, that much was true. He'd bet his job that Timothy Garner hadn't killed Buchan Stewart though, which meant there was a killer still out there. Had someone found DC MacBride's Brazilian photo archive and gone on a spree? Would they be looking for someone else? And if so, how were they choosing their victims? Was it possible that someone else knew about the ritual killing, and had managed to track down the murderers?

Or was it the sixth man covering his tracks, killing his old partners in crime, stealing the body that was the only real piece of evidence, paying someone to run down the policeman investigating? That scenario fitted better than the alternatives, but it wasn't exactly reassuring. McLean stopped suddenly, realising he was alone in the street. He shivered, looking around, expecting to see a white van gunning its engine, heading straight for him. His feet had brought him, perhaps inevitably, to the Pleasance. A big blue 'police notice' sign on the pavement accused him with its own demands. An accident occurred here . . . Did you see . . . Contact us . . . He was standing on the spot where Alison had been hit. Where she'd sacrificed herself so that he could live. Christ, what a waste of a life. He clenched his fists and swore that he'd track down the man responsible. It didn't make him feel any better.

It wasn't far to his flat, which was just as well. Guilt and anger battling each other made it hard to pick up the threads of his earlier thoughts. The door was propped open with a couple of stones again; bloody students losing their keys and too tight to pay for a new set. At least at this hour Mrs McCutcheon should be tucked up asleep. He could be spared the joy of smiling as she voiced her concern for the long hours he worked. He trudged up the stairs feeling the weariness seep in around his eyes. Bed beckoned and he was more than ready for it.

Only there was someone at the top of the stairs.

48

She huddled against the door to his flat, curled up with her knees to her chest, her thin coat pulled around her to ward off the night-time chill. He thought she must have been sleeping, but as he approached she looked up and he recognised her face.

'Jenny? What are you doing here?'

Jenny Spiers stared through puffy eyes, red with crying. Her face was pale, her hair hanging down limply on either side, framing her misery. The tip of her nose shone bright as if she had been suffering with a cold for days.

'It's Chloe,' she said. 'She's gone.' And burst into tears.

McLean took the last couple of steps in one bound. He crouched down and took Jenny's hands.

'Hey, it's all right. We'll find her.' Then he realised he didn't know who was missing. 'Who's Chloe?'

It was probably the wrong thing to say. Jenny burst into even greater floods of tears.

'Look, come on Jen. Get up.' He pulled her to her feet, then unlocked the door and pushed it open, guiding her through into the kitchen and sinking her into a chair. All thoughts of bed and sleep gone, he filled the kettle and set it to boil, fetching out a couple of mugs and a jar of instant coffee.

'Tell me what's happened. Why did you come here?' He handed Jenny a roll of kitchen paper to replace the sodden handkerchief she had scrunched up into her fist.

'Chloe's gone. She should've been home by eleven. She's never late. Even if she's going to be on time she phones.'

'Back a bit, Jen. You'll have to remind me. Who's Chloe?'

Jenny looked up at him with incredulous eyes. 'My daughter. You know, you met her at the shop.'

McLean did a mental somersault. He remembered her, dressed as a 1920s flapper girl, complete with bobbed hair. Working the till whilst Jenny was out the back.

'I'm sorry, I didn't realise. We weren't introduced. To be honest, I didn't even know you were married.'

'I'm not. Chloe was . . . well, let's just say her father was a bit of a mistake. He had his way and that's the last we ever saw of him. But Chloe's a good girl, Tony. She wouldn't stay out late and if she was stuck somewhere she'd phone.'

McLean tried to take the new information in his stride. Concentrate on the problem. 'What time did she go out?'

'About half eight. She had tickets to see Bill Bailey at the Assembly Rooms. They're like gold dust, you know. She was so excited.'

'And you say she should've been back at eleven.'

'That's right. I gave her taxi money. Didn't want her walking the streets at that time of night.'

'Did she go to the show alone?'

'No, she went with a couple of school friends. But they live on the other side of town.'

'And they're home, I take it.'

'I phoned and checked. They both got in at quarter to midnight.'

'How old is Chloe?' McLean tried to imagine the girl in the shop, but her exotic costume made it hard to put an age on her.

'Almost sixteen.' Old enough to be out on her own. Old enough to be pushing the barriers of what she could and couldn't do.

'You've contacted the police?'

Jenny nodded. 'They came round the house, filled in forms. I gave them a photo. They even searched the shop in case she was in there hiding.'

'That's good. It means they're following procedure.' McLean poured boiling water into the mugs, added milk. 'But you have to understand that this could be no more than teenage rebellion. She might just be staying out late for the hell of it.'

'But she never does.' Jenny's face flushed. She clenched her fists. 'She'd never do anything like that.'

'I believe you. I'll give the station a phone and see if anything's come up. You should be at home, Jen. Not here. What if she's come back and you're not there?'

A momentary flicker of doubt passed across Jenny's eyes, a haunted look. 'I left a note. On the kitchen table. But she hadn't come home by one. I had to do something.'

McLean realised that he didn't even know where Jenny Spiers lived. He hadn't known about her daughter; only really knew that she had a sister who was engaged to his best friend. If he was being honest, he didn't know all that much about Rachel either. He'd long since given up trying to remember all of his ex-flatmate's students. Only that she was the one who'd finally got the prize so many before her had failed to win. Quite why Jenny had chosen to come to him he had no idea.

'Do you live above the shop?'

Jenny nodded again, then sniffed and wiped her nose. McLean went through to the hall and dialled the station. It rang for a long time before the duty sergeant finally picked up.

'DI McLean here. You've had a report of a missing girl. Chloe Spiers?'

'Aye, I reckon so. Hang on a minute.' McLean could hear the

rustling of paper in the background as the duty sergeant shuffled through the night logs. 'What's it to you?'

'Her mother's in my kitchen drinking coffee.'

'Lucky you, inspector. She's quite a looker if I remember right. Ah, here we are. Reported at eleven fifty-eight. Nearest patrol attended the scene at twelve-o-nine. Description's been sent out to all stations, details are on the computer. We'll be checking with the hospitals if she's not turned up by morning.'

'Well do me a favour will you, Tom? Put the call out again. And if you've got time to, call the hospitals now.'

'OK, sir. It's a quiet night at the moment. I'll see what I can do.'

'Thanks, Tom. I owe you one.'

'Dinner, is it sir?'

McLean froze. 'You what?'

'I believe that's the going rate for a favour, isn't it? Or was Miss Baird a special case?'

'I . . . Who told you . . . ?' McLean spluttered down the phone as the duty sergeant burst out laughing. 'How many people in the station know?'

'I'd say about all of them, sir. You did meet her at the front door, after all. And taking her to the Red Dragon? Bound to be one or two off-duty coppers in there most evenings, even if they're only picking up a carry-oot.'

McLean fumed as he hung up. Bloody policemen, they could give fishwives a run for their money when it came to gossip. Still, probably wouldn't do his reputation any harm.

'Have they found her?' Jenny's concerned voice brought his mind back to more pressing problems.

'No. I'm sorry. But the full procedure is under way.' McLean told her what the duty sergeant had promised to do. At the mention of hospitals she went very white.

302

'Could she really be?'

'I don't think so, Jen. They'd have contacted you by now if she was in any trouble. It's far more likely she hooked up with some other friends and went out on a bender. She'll be home in the morning feeling like shit and you can tear a strip off her then.'

But in his mind he knew he was only saying that to comfort her.

49

He doesn't know how long he's been standing in this garden, staring up at the silent house. It was dark for a while, and now it is getting light maybe. How many days has he been like this? His mind stopped working properly a long time ago, and now all he can do is obey. The voices don't so much speak to him as direct his actions. He has no more control over his body than a puppet. But he can feel the pain all the more for being helpless to do anything about it.

The prey is in there, he knows. He can smell it, even if he's not sure what it is he can smell. There's leaf mould and warm dry earth; distant fumes of cars and the sweeter malty odour of the brewery. His stomach is a vat of acid, leaching through into his guts in waves of agony, but he stands and waits and watches.

Something rustles in the bushes, pushing through with growling malevolence. He looks down to see a dog, a doberman with its ears cut into sharp points. It bares its teeth at him and utters a menacing snarl. The voices pull his lips apart and issue a hiss from the back of his throat. Startled, the dog yelps, its stubby tail tucked between its back legs. A splatter on the ground beneath it and the warm tang of piss fills the air.

One more sharp hiss and the dog breaks, crashing back into the bushes from where it has come, not even yelping any more as it struggles to get away. He was always terrified of dogs, but the voices are made of sterner stuff.

His head pounds as if all the migraines in the world have come to live in it. His whole body feels swollen and distended, like those starved African children he used to see on the telly. Every joint in his body is red hot; cartilage ripped out and replaced with sandpaper. Still he stands, and watches.

More noise now. A bigger bulk pushing its way into the gloom of his hiding place. He turns slowly to greet the man; screaming inside at the pain of every small movement. The voices keep him silent.

'What're you doing here?' the man asks, but his words are a million miles away. The voices are shouting attack, and he must obey them.

He springs up, but his body is weak with starvation and a thousand terrible ailments. There is a knife in his hand; he cannot remember how he got it, neither a time when it wasn't clasped in his grip. It doesn't matter. Only attacking matters. And pain.

Something snaps, and he realises it is his arm. The man is big, far bigger than him, and built like those men he used to try not to stare at when he went to the gym. But the voices say he must attack him, and so that is what he does, reaching for eyes, clawing at skin.

'You wee shite. I'll fucking kill you.' The man is angry now, and the voices scream their joy. He strikes again, landing a blow that spurts blood from the man's nose. He feels a small moment of triumph through the agony of his wasted body.

And then it is his face being pounded. A hand like a giant claw has him round the throat, squeezing the life out of him. He is lifted off his feet, thrown. He hits the ground with a wet slap and everything goes black. The pain is everywhere, rushing in to claim him. Warm wet, with a taste of bubbling iron that fills his throat and mouth. He can't breathe any more, can't see, can't feel. He can only hear the triumphant cackle of the voices as they leave him to die.

50

Mandy Cowie looked like the sort of girl who didn't agree with mornings. McLean had little experience of teenagers, at least not the kind who didn't hang out in bus shelters drinking Buckfast and hurling abuse at anyone who came near. Mandy was cleaner than the foul-mouthed queenies who bred in the tower blocks in Trinity and Craigmillar, but she was just as sullen as she sat across the kitchen table from him, staring at a bowl of soggy cornflakes.

'You're not in any trouble, Mandy. Quite the opposite.' He guessed she was working on some genetically programmed inability to be helpful to the police. 'I'm not even here as a policeman. I'm here as a friend of Chloe's mum. She's worried sick that Chloe didn't come home last night. Have you any idea where she might have gone?'

Mandy shifted nervously in her seat. Had she been in an interview room, McLean would have read that as meaning she knew something but didn't want to say. Here, he could only guess.

'Did she have a boyfriend? Maybe they'd arranged to meet up.' He left the suggestion hanging in the silent air. Much to his irritation, Mandy's mum jumped into the gap.

'It's OK, hen. You can talk to the inspector. He's no goin' tae lock youse up.'

'Mrs Cowie, would it be possible to speak to your daughter alone for a minute?'

She looked at him as if he were daft. Then grabbed her mug of coffee, slopping brown liquid onto the kitchen table.

'Only a minute, mind. She's got work tae do.' And she shuffled out in her pink bunny slippers. McLean waited for a few moments after the door had closed, hearing a creak on the stairs. Mandy's eyes darted up to the ceiling, then back down to her uneaten cereal.

'Look, Mandy. I'll be straight with you. If there's anything you know that might help us find Chloe you can tell me. I won't say a word of it to your parents, I promise. This isn't about you, it's about Chloe. We need to find her. And the longer she stays missing, the less chance we have.'

The silence hung heavy in the air, spoiled only by the clumping noise upstairs as Mrs Cowie thumped around the bathroom. McLean tried to catch Mandy's eye, but she was fascinated by her cereal bowl. He was about to give up altogether when she finally spoke.

'You'll no' tell Mam?'

'No, Mandy. You have my word. And I won't tell Chloe's mum either.'

'There was this guy, right. She met him on the internet.'

Oh Christ, here we go.

'He seemed . . . I dunno. OK. He was into the whole comedy thing, dead excited when Chloe told him about the tickets to see Bill Bailey. Said he was going to be at the show too. Only he never turned up, did he.'

'How were they supposed to meet?' McLean dredged his memory for the other girl's name. He'd be interviewing her next. 'Did he know you and Karen would be there too?'

'I don't know what Chloe told him. I don't think she gave him her phone number; she's no' that stupid you know. But she gets them wild outfits from her mam's shop an' she was wearing one last night. Maybe she told him tae look out for the 1920s chick. She'd no've bin hard tae spot.'

And easy to pick out on the street after the show. Walking home because it's not far, really, and the taxi money could go on something much more interesting.

'Did this boy have a name?'

'Yeah, he called himself Fergie. Don't know if that was his real name, though.'

'How long had he been . . . how long had Chloe been talking to him?' McLean didn't understand the way internet chat rooms worked.

'No' long. Couple days, maybe a week.'

Such a short time to trust a stranger. Had he been so foolish when he was that age? McLean had to admit that he probably had been. But before the internet, when it was all about screwing up your courage to go and talk to a girl you fancied, things had been a lot more innocent. Kids today were more sophisticated, it was true, but they were just as naive as they had ever been. And Fergie. The name instantly brought to mind McReadie, though there must have been thousands of Ferguses and Fergusons across the city. He needed to think straight, not jump to conclusions based on wild speculation.

'I need to know exactly what time you and Chloe split up last night, Mandy.' Only now did McLean pull out his notebook. 'Retrace your steps from the moment the show ended.'

*

Karen Beckwith told the same story, only it didn't take so much effort to get it out of her. McLean compared the two statements as he stood outside the Assembly Rooms on George Street, looking around at the daytime traffic and trying to imagine what it would have been like at eleven the night before. Around about then he and Emma had been sitting in the Guildford Arms, not five minutes walk away. Karen and Mandy had taken a cab home, walking with Chloe to the taxi rank in Castle Street. He followed their short route, looking up at the sides of the buildings and noting the positions of the security cameras. You couldn't do anything in the city centre without it being filmed by someone.

From the taxi rank, there was only one sensible way to walk back to the shop: along Princes Street, over North and South Bridges and on up Clerk Street. It shouldn't have taken more than half an hour, and there were cameras for a good deal of the way. He knew what time Chloe had last been seen. He knew what she had been wearing. Now it was just a matter of reviewing the CCTV footage, and judging by the number of cameras, that was going to take a while.

'Something here, sir. Want to have a look?'

McLean turned away from the flickering screens filled with blurred people jumping erratically along orange-tinted streets. DC MacBride sat at a nearby console, embarrassingly confident with the technology.

'What've you got?' He rolled his chair across the carpet tiles until he could see the other screen. MacBride twisted the control knob counter-clockwise, speeding the recording back to eleven-fifteen.

'This is the taxi rank in Castle Street, sir.' He put the machine into normal-speed play and pointed at the screen. Summertime and the Festival in full swing meant that the city-centre streets were if anything busier than during the day. 'I think that's our three girls there.' He hit pause and pointed at three figures walking arm in arm. The one in the middle wore a straight-cut plaid skirt, sleeveless top and cloche hat. A familiar feather boa was draped around her neck. Beside her, Karen and Mandy looked rather trashy in their tight jeans and T-shirts.

'That's her,' McLean said. 'Can we see where she goes?'

MacBride flicked the tape forward and they watched as the girls joined the queue at the taxi rank. Chloe waited until the other two had left, then set off down the hill towards Princes Street.

'We have to switch cameras here.' MacBride did something with the confusing array of buttons on the console and the picture changed to a different angle. Chloe walked along the street, alone and confident in her stride. They followed her through two more cameras, and then she stopped as a black car slid along the street beside her.

If he hadn't known better, he would have said it was a classic case of kerb-crawling. Chloe bent down to the car window, obviously talking to whoever was driving. Her body language showed no sign of alarm, and after a couple of moments, she opened the door and got in. The car drove off in the direction of the North British Hotel.

'Can we enhance that picture? Get a number for that car?' McLean asked.

'Only in the movies. These aren't high-resolution cameras and the lighting's atrocious. There should be a better angle from another camera, but it fused last night, apparently.'

'We might be able to track it. Black or dark blue BMW 3 Series. Does it turn up on any of the other cameras?'

MacBride clicked buttons, watching the car turn off Princes Street onto the Mound. It appeared briefly in one more camera shot, then nothing. 'Coverage isn't so good away from the main city hotspots. We can try a sweep of the other cameras, extrapolating the time. See if it shows up.'

'How long will that take?'

'I don't know, sir. We could get lucky, or it could take all day.'

'OK. Make a start. See if you can't get a number from that

image. Even a partial would help. Send it to Emma, she's good with photos –'

McLean froze as he spoke the words. She was good with photos. She'd sorted out the crime-scene images from the house in Sighthill, revealing the strange patterns he'd seen on the floor. And before that, there'd been something else on her computer monitor. Thumbnails of photos. Had she just been processing them for archiving, or was there something more sinister going on? MB. Em B. Emma Baird.

'You all right, sir? You look like someone's walked on your grave.' DC MacBride's pale, round face looked up at him in the semi-darkness of the video viewing room.

'I think I know who might have been posting those crime-scene images to the net.'

But he hoped to Christ he was wrong.

51

'Phone still not working, I take it?'

The duty sergeant, Pete Murray greeted him with a grin as he hurried into the station on the Monday morning. McLean patted his pockets until he found the device, but couldn't remember whether he'd even bothered trying to charge it the night before. He'd been distracted, so the chances weren't good. True enough the phone was dead when he tried pressing any of its buttons.

'What do you do to the poor things? Curse them?' Pete shoved a thick pile of papers in his direction, nodding to the far side of the reception area as he did. 'Here's a stack of messages need dealing with, and that bloke over there's been asking for you by name. Says he's from Hoggett Scotia Asset Management. Looks like a banker to me.'

Puzzled, McLean looked around, trying to remember where he'd heard the name before. Seeing Mr Masters sitting on one of the plain plastic benches didn't help. He looked like any of a thousand faceless suited businessmen: early forties, greying hair; slight paunch that two games of squash a week were no longer enough to burn off; expensive leather briefcase full of electronic gadgets; wife and kids in the suburbs; mistress in an Old Town tenement.

'Inspector McLean? Thank you for seeing me. Jonathan Masters, Hoggett Scotia.' Masters leapt to his feet before McLean was even halfway across the floor. Only then did the pieces of memory begin to slot into place.

'Mr Masters. You were one of the witnesses to Peter Andrews' suicide.'

Jonathan Masters winced at the mention of his former colleague's name. 'It's been a hard week at Hoggett Scotia, inspector. Peter was one of our top analysts. He'll be sorely missed.'

A top analyst. Not 'a great guy', or 'the life and soul of the party'. Not a friend.

'I spoke to his father, Mr Masters. It seemed like he was a man with everything to live for until he discovered he had terminal cancer.'

'That was a complete surprise. He never told any of us. Maybe if he had . . .' Mr Masters trailed off.

'But I'm guessing you didn't come here to tell me about Peter Andrews, sir.'

'Yes, of course. I'm sorry, inspector. It's been a hard week. But we seem to have lost a secretary. Sally Dent.'

'Dent. Wasn't she a witness too?'

'Yes, she was on reception. We gave her the rest of the day off. Well, it was the least we could do. We overlooked her not coming in the next day, and then it was the weekend. But she's not in this morning, not been back since the . . . well, since Peter . . . you know.'

'You've tried to get in contact, I take it.' McLean felt a horrible sense of déjà vu crawling up from the back of his mind, like the shadow of a spider.

'Of course. We phoned her home, but her mother thought she'd gone on a foreign trip. It's stupid really, she was meant to be going to Tokyo with one of our fund managers, but the whole thing was cancelled after . . .'

'So you thought she was at home, and her mother thought she was abroad, and between the two of you no one knows where she's been since the day Peter Andrews killed himself.'

313

'That's pretty much it, inspector.'

Tell me about Sally Dent, Mr Masters,' McLean said. 'What does she look like?'

'Oh, I can do better than that. Here.' Masters put his briefcase down on the plastic bench, flicking open the twin latches. McLean saw a tiny laptop, a tablet, a GPS navigator and a slim mobile phone nestling in the soft leather interior before Masters pulled out an A4 sheet and closed the case back down again. 'Her personnel file.'

McLean took the sheet, holding it up to the light so that he could get a better look at the printed photograph that stared out at him. What surprised him most when he saw the photograph was not that he recognised the woman, but that he had been expecting to see her face there. It was a prettier face in the picture, smiling and full of hope for the future. The last time he had seen her she had been laid out on a stainless-steel examination table in Angus Cadwallader's mortuary; the first time, broken and twisted, hair matted with blood, on the rubbish-strewn oil and gravel of the rail-bed in Waverley Station.

'You really can't keep away, Tony, can you? You know, you could retrain as a pathologist's assistant and then we could give up all this pretence.'

Angus Cadwallader grinned from his office chair as McLean knocked on the open door. He'd left Masters in the public reception area fretting and looking at his watch. The quicker they got this done, the better.

'It's tempting, Angus, but I know you've only got eyes for Tracy.'

The grin wavered ever so slightly — and did the pathologist stiffen slightly? Interesting.

'Yes, well. What can I do for you?'

'The woman who jumped off Waverley Bridge last week. I think she might be a Sally Dent. Can we prep her for ID? I've got her boss upstairs.'

'No problem. I'll get her wheeled out and give you a shout when she's ready.' The pathologist bustled out into the theatre and towards the bank of storage drawers, grabbing a stainless-steel gurney as he went. McLean followed.

'Did you send in the report on her yet?'

'What? Oh, yes. I think so. Tracy usually emails them across as soon as they're done. Why?'

'I haven't seen it, that's all.'

'Ah, then you won't know about the plaques that were eating holes in her brain.'

'The . . . what?' A cold shiver grew in the pit of McLean's stomach. Complications. There were always complications.

'Creutzfeldt–Jakob's. Quite advanced. I suspect she'd been having fairly vivid hallucinations before she jumped. That was probably why she did it.' Cadwallader opened the drawer, revealing the pale, cleaned body of Sally Dent, the cuts on her face neatly sewn up, but still horribly disfiguring. He slid her across onto the gurney and covered her with a long white sheet. Together, they wheeled her to the identification room, where an anxious-looking Jonathan Masters leapt to his feet as if someone had shouted at him.

'Sorry to keep you waiting, Mr Masters. I should warn you she was quite badly injured before she died.'

Masters went a green shade of white, nodding silently as he looked at the shrouded figure. Cadwallader turned back the sheet to reveal just the face. The banker looked down, and McLean could see the horror of recognition on his face. It was a look he'd seen all too many times before.

'What happened to her?' Masters' voice was both high-pitched and croaking, but he hadn't collapsed like some men did. McLean had to give him that much.

'She jumped off North Bridge.'

'The suicide? I heard about that. But Sally . . . No . . . Sally wouldn't . . .'

'She was suffering from a damaging neurological condition.' Cadwallader covered the battered face up again. 'The chances are she didn't even know what she was doing.'

'What about her mother?' Masters looked at McLean with pleading in his eyes. 'Who's going to explain this to her?'

'It's all right, Mr Masters. I'll speak with Mrs Dent.' McLean took the businessman's arm, steered him out of the room. 'Are you going to be OK? Would you like me to arrange for someone to take you back to the office?'

Masters seemed to recover his composure away from the dead body. He straightened his shoulders and looked at his watch again. 'No, I'm fine inspector, thank you. I'd better be getting back to the office. Oh God. Sally.' He shook his head.

'This might seem like an insensitive question, Mr Masters, but was there anything going on between Miss Dent and Mr Andrews?'

Masters looked at McLean with an expression that quite plainly said he thought the inspector insane. 'What do you mean?'

'I just wondered if they had a relationship that went beyond the professional, sir. The two suicides in such quick succession.'

'Peter Andrews was gay, inspector. Didn't you know that?'

By the time McLean had escorted Jonathan Masters from the building and returned to the main examination theatre, Cadwallader had put the dead woman away in her cold cell and returned to his office. McLean looked in, realising for the first time that the ever-cheerful assistant was nowhere to be seen.

'What've you done with Tracy?' he asked.

'You keep your hands off my assistant, Tony.'

McLean held his hands up as if surrendering. 'She's not my type, Angus.'

'No, I heard you preferred SOC officers. Still, nobody's perfect.' Cadwallader laughed. 'Tracy's taken some samples to the lab. I let her out every once in a while. When you're not busy filling up my mortuary with bodies.'

'Sorry about that.' McLean shrugged an apology. 'Tell me more about Sally Dent. There was something about her blood, I seem to remember.'

'Not her blood. She was covered in someone else's.'

'Did you find out whose?'

Cadwallader shook his head. 'We've typed it, but it's fairly common. O rhesus D positive. I've sent a sample off for DNA analysis, but unless you know of someone who's lost a lot recently it could take us a while to find a match.'

Someone who's lost a lot recently. A horrible, impossible thought crossed McLean's mind. 'What about Jonas Carstairs?'

'You what? You think that slight woman in there . . .' Cadwallader pointed towards the rows of cold storage. 'You think she restrained and cut open a strong, healthy man like Carstairs?'

'He was an old man, he couldn't have been that strong.' As he spoke, McLean realised he hadn't seen the report into Carstairs's death either.

'He was as fit as a fiddle. Must have been into all that yoga and muesli that's so fashionable these days.' The pathologist turned back to his computer, tapped at a few keys to bring up the relevant report and scanned down the page. 'Here we are. Analysis of the blood found on Sally Dent's hair and hands.' He clicked again, bringing up another window. 'Blood sample from Jonas Carstairs . . . Good God.'

McLean looked over Cadwallader's shoulder at the report, not really taking in what it said. The pathologist swivelled his chair round slowly. 'They're the same.'

'The same type?'

'No, the same blood. Near as dammit. I'll run the DNA profile to be sure, but all the markers are the same.'

'Do it anyway, please.' McLean leant back against the counter trying to work out where all the conflicting pieces of information were taking him. Opus Diaboli. The devil's work. It wasn't to a very comfortable place.

'Have you still got Peter Andrews in here?' he asked.

Cadwallader nodded. 'Bloody nuisance. He was meant to be shipped down to London last week, but that break-in buggered up all the schedules. I'm still waiting for them to come and get him.'

'What about blood on him?'

'He cut his throat, Tony. He was covered in the stuff.'

'Yes, but was it all his?'

'I'd say so. We cleaned him up. Well, Tracy cleaned him up. She didn't say anything about layers. Where are you going with this, Tony?'

'I'm not sure. At least, I don't think I want to be sure. Look, Angus, could you do me a huge favour?'

'That depends on what it is. If you want me to stand in for you at another of the chief constable's little soirées, then I'm afraid not.'

'No, nothing like that. I was wondering if you could have another look at Peter Andrews.'

'I examined him pretty thoroughly.' The pathologist looked slightly hurt, but McLean knew he was putting it on.

'I know, Angus, but you were looking at a suicide. I want you to go over him like you would if he were a murder victim.'

52

Chief Inspector Duguid was waiting in the tiny incident room, sitting on Grumpy Bob's chair and perusing the photos pinned to the wall. McLean almost ducked back through the door, but some boils you just have to lance straight away.

'Can I help you with anything, sir?'

'Thought you were meant to be having some time off.'

'And I thought my time would be better spent catching criminals, sir. You remember catching criminals, don't you?'

'I don't like your tone, McLean.'

'Not too happy about people trying to kill me, but we all have our crosses to bear. Now what did you want to see me about?'

Duguid levered himself out of the chair, his face darkening. 'I didn't even know you were in the station. I was looking for that young constable of yours, Mac-something. He said you'd got a lead on our leak. Something about some internet site?'

'What about it, sir?'

'Well what is it, McLean? How do you expect me to investigate Carstairs' murder if you don't pull your end? Tracing that leak is a major string of our enquiry.'

The only string, if you're down here bullying my team for answers, thought McLean. He didn't have the nerve to tell the man that the murderer was lying dead in the mortuary. Let Cadwallader run the DNA tests first, make certain and pass those results on himself. He wanted no credit for the discovery if it meant Duguid would be even more antagonistic towards him. He'd made the mistake of solving the chief inspector's cases for him before.

'Detective Constable MacBride found a secure site on the internet where people display and trade gruesome images, including forensic crime-scene photographs, sir. It seems there's quite a collection of ghouls out there in cyberspace. I recognised pictures from Barnaby Smythe's study posted there.'

'So whoever killed Carstairs might be a regular viewer. And what? They've decided to start acting out their sick fantasies? Christ, that's all we need.' Duguid massaged his forehead with his fingers. 'So who is it? Who's posting these pictures and feeding this sicko ideas?'

'I don't know, sir.'

'But you've got an idea, haven't you, McLean. I know the way your mind works.'

'I need to make a few checks first, sir. Before —'

'Bollocks, inspector. You've got a suspicion, then share it. We can't waste time pussyfooting about here. There's a killer out there probably sizing up their next victim.'

No there isn't. They're all dead now. He's cleared up his dirty little secret, though Christ alone knows how he did it. The site's just a red herring.

'I don't think there's a need to rush at all, sir.' McLean tried to choose his words carefully. If he was right, and Emma really had been responsible for posting those photographs, he wanted to be the one to catch her. What he did once his suspicions were confirmed, he just didn't know.

'You're protecting them, aren't you inspector. Hoping to get all the glory of the collar to yourself?' Duguid levered himself out of Grumpy Bob's chair and pushed past, heading out of the incident room. 'Or is it something else entirely?'

321

McLean watched Duguid go, then picked up the phone and tried to dial out. It was dead. He fished his mobile out of his pocket, shook it and pressed the 'on' button. Nothing. Damn. If Cadwallader knew about his dinner with Emma, it was a sure thing that Dagwood did too, and it wouldn't take the chief inspector that long to put two and two together; he was a detective after all, even if it was sometimes hard to believe. He looked at the phone again. Should he really be warning her that she was under suspicion? Yes, he should. If she was guilty, they'd try to pin an accessory to murder charge on her. Even if they couldn't make it stick, they'd drag her name through the media. And if he was being really honest, he didn't want to be blackened by association just as much as he didn't want to see that done to a friend.

Cursing, he stomped out of the room in search of a phone, almost crashing into DC MacBride running down the corridor outside.

'Bloody hell. What's got into you?'

'They've found it, sir.' MacBride's face was flushed with excitement.

'Found what?'

'The van, sir. The one that killed Alison.'

The winds of change had swept through Edinburgh over recent years, clearing out the tired old tenements, the bonded warehouses, goods yards and sink estates; replacing them with new developments, leisure centres, luxury apartments and malls. But there were some places that resisted gentrification with all the grace of a raised middle finger. Newhaven still hung out against the forces of improvement, holding on where Leith and Trinity had succumbed. The windswept south shore of the Firth of Forth was just too bleak to welcome incomers, its reclaimed land too blighted by industry.

McLean watched from the passenger seat of the car as DC MacBride drove in through the jimmied-open wire gates to an abandoned compound. Two squad cars were already in attendance. They parked alongside the SOC van, and McLean felt a sudden surge of hope that Emma would be there. If he could just get a moment to talk to her away from everyone else, he could find out the truth behind the photographs; warn her if necessary. It surprised him that he was also hoping she would be there for purely personal reasons. He couldn't remember the last time he'd felt that way about anyone.

The warehouse had probably stored something valuable once, but now its roof was gone, its cast-iron girders home to pigeons and rust. Even in the summer, after days of dry heat, the concrete floor was puddled with filthy water. In the winter when the east wind blew in sleet from the North Sea, it must have been a really welcoming place. A foul stench filled the area; rotting carcasses and smoke mixed with bird shit and the salt tang of the sea. In the centre, surrounded by SOC officers like ants around a dead bird, stood a blackened Transit van.

They all looked the same, McLean said to himself as he walked closer. But something about this van made him certain it was the one that he'd last seen screeching around the corner at the bottom of the Pleasance, heading towards Holyrood. The plates were missing, but they had been before. Chances were the chassis numbers had been ground off too. There was one identifying mark though; a long, fresh dent in the burnt metalwork of the bonnet, exactly where a promising young life had been cut short.

He walked around the van, keeping well back to avoid contaminating the scene. A white-suited SOC officer crouched close, picking at the blistered and bubbled paint with a pair of tweezers. A flash blinked behind him and he turned, expecting to see

Emma. Another technician was behind the lens this time. Malky, McLean remembered, the photographer from the Farquhar House murder scene. The chap who smelled of soap and reckoned negative thoughts could leach the power from mobile phone batteries. Well, it made a kind of perverse sense. As much sense as this.

'Emma Baird not here?'

'She's on another case.' The accent was Glaswegian, but more cultured than Fergus McReadie's.

'You must be Malky,' McLean said. No sooner were the words out than he realised it was a mistake. The man's features hardened in a mask of distaste that made DCI Duguid seem easy-going.

'It's Malcolm, actually. Malcolm Buchanan Watt.'

'I'm sorry, Malcolm. I was just –'

'I know what the other SOC officers call me, inspector. They show the same carelessness with detail in other aspects of their work. You'd do well to remember that the next time you're working with the likes of Ms Baird.'

'Come off it, Malcolm. Emma's a professional just the same as you.'

The photographer didn't bother responding to this, choosing instead to hide behind his camera and take more photographs. McLean shook his head. Why did people have to be so touchy? He was about to head around to the other side of the van, where the sliding door was wide open to face the sea, but a familiar voice hailed him.

'Thank Christ for that. A detective inspector at last.' Big Andy Houseman grinned. 'Glad they gave it to you, sir. We all want a good result on this one.'

'Actually, I'm not here, Andy. You never saw me, OK?'

'What? Don't tell me they're going to give this to Dagwood.'

'I'm one of the victims, Andy. Can't be involved.' McLean held his hands out in supplication, even though he shared the sergeant's frustration. 'What's the story here?'

'Chap walking his dog down on the shore saw it, thought he'd phone it in. I've a couple of constables asking questions in the units over the road, but my guess is nobody saw anything. Even if they saw something.'

'What about the van. Got an ID on it yet?'

'We're working on it, sir. But from what we can see here it's been professionally cleaned. No plates, no VIN stamp.'

'How d'you know it's the van that hit Alison?'

'We don't. Not for sure. But it's likely. The front end's smashed in like it hit something. You're probably the best witness, but we know it was a Transit. SOC are working on it, but I'd bet my holiday pay it's the same one.'

'Any chance we can get prints? Find out who was driving it?'

'We can do better than that. We've got a body. This way.' Big Andy led McLean around to the other side of the van. A familiar figure hunched over something black and burned inside, the obvious epicentre of the blaze. Angus Cadwallader stood up, his back creaking as he stretched.

'If we keep meeting like this, Tony, I'm going to have to introduce you to my mother.'

'You already did, Angus. That party at Holyrood, remember? What've you got here?'

Cadwallader turned back to the subject of his investigation, pointing with a gloved finger at the pale flecks in what looked like a half-burned roll of carpet. The white latex was smeared with greasy ash. He didn't need to say anything at that point; McLean's nose had already told him what was really there.

'Not so much a what,' the pathologist said, 'as a who.'

53

Cadwallader had promised he would do an initial examination of the body as soon as he got it back to the mortuary. That and the warning that DCI Duguid was on his way to the crime scene meant that McLean had no choice but to leave. He let DC MacBride drive again, watching the city slip past as they fought through the traffic back towards the station.

'Do you believe in ghosts, constable?' he asked as they sat at traffic lights.

'Like that wifey off the telly? Running around with the weird camera that makes everything look green? No. Not really. My uncle swears he saw a ghost once, mind.'

'What about demons? The devil?'

'Nah. That's just stuff made up by the priests to stop you misbehaving. Why? You think there might be something in it, sir?'

'Christ no. Life's hard enough dealing with normal criminals. I don't want to think about having to arrest the infernal hosts. But Bertie Farquhar and his friends believed in something enough to kill that girl. What makes a man so sure, and why do that anyway? What could they possibly get from it?'

'Wealth? Immortality? Isn't that what people usually want?'

'Didn't work out so well for them, then.' Only it had, up to a point. They'd all been fabulously wealthy and successful, and none of them had died of natural causes. What had Angus said about Smythe? Lungs that wouldn't have shamed a teenager? And hadn't he mentioned that Carstairs was fit as a fiddle too? How far could you push the placebo effect before it started to look like other forces were at work?

The car inched forwards, past road works for the trams that would never come. Across the street, the seedy buildings of this poor end of town drifted past in their mottled, dirty colours. Grimy windows looking on to pawn shops, a chippie you'd likely get food poisoning from if you hadn't been raised in the area, immunised against it. His eyes fell on a familiar flaked-paint door, a sign outside: 'palms read, tarots, fortunes told'.

'Pull over, constable. Find somewhere to park.'

MacBride did as he was told, much to the annoyance of the cars behind.

'Where are we going?' he asked as they climbed out. McLean pointed across the road.

'I feel the need to have my fortune told.'

Madame Rose had just finished with a punter; a bewildered-looking middle-aged woman with her hair in a headscarf, recently lightened handbag clutched tightly under one arm. McLean raised an eyebrow but said nothing as they were led through to the study at the back of the building.

'Mrs Brown's been coming to see me ever since her husband died. Must be what, three years now? Every couple of months.' Madame Rose cleared cats from two chairs, pointed for them to sit before taking her own seat. 'I can't do anything for her. Talking to the dead's not really my thing, and I get the feeling her Donald doesn't want to speak to her, anyway, but I can't stop her giving me her money, aye?'

McLean smiled to himself as much as anyone. 'And here's me thought it was all smoke and mirrors.'

'Oh no.' Madame Rose clasped a large bejewelled hand to her substantial but false bosom. 'I'd have thought you of all people would have understood, inspector. What with your past.'

The smile disappeared as quickly as it had come. 'I can't imagine what you mean.'

'And yet here you are. Come to me for advice on demons. Again.'

Maybe this wasn't such a good idea after all. McLean knew it was all mumbo-jumbo, but even he had to admit that Madame Rose's act was very well done. Then again, his past was a matter of public record for all he wished it wasn't. It was all part of the act, to know one's subject just well enough to make them uncomfortable. It took their mind off all the other stuff you were doing. Made it harder to keep to your own script.

'You make it sound like you were expecting us.'

'Expecting you, inspector.' Madame Rose tilted her head towards him. 'I will admit I didn't see your young friend here when last I read the cards.'

And it would probably have been easier to ask what he wanted without MacBride there to listen. McLean almost had to suppress the urge to squirm like a schoolboy needing to be excused but not daring to ask teacher for permission.

'You want to know if they truly exist. Demons, that is.' Madame Rose asked his question before he could speak, answered it just as quickly. 'Come. Let me show you something.'

She stood up, sparking curious glances from the cats. McLean followed, but when MacBride stirred from his seat, Madame Rose waved him back.

'Not you, dear. This is for the inspector's eyes only. Stay here and keep an eye on my babies.'

As if it had been ordered, the nearest cat leapt onto the DC's lap. He put out a hand to ward it off, but it just butted him with its head, purring loudly.

'Better stay here, constable. I don't suppose this will take long.' McLean followed Madame Rose out of the study by a different door to the one they had entered. It led to a storeroom filled with books, shelves lining the walls and marching across the floor, leaving only narrow aisles barely big enough for the clairvoyant, let alone him as well. They were pressed uncomfortably close together and the air had that dry smell of old paper and leather, putting him on edge. Antiquarian bookshops were not his favourite places, and this room was a pure distillation of the essence.

'You're ill at ease with the knowledge, Inspector McLean.' Madame Rose dropped the mystical tones she affected for her customers, the gruff edge of the transvestite coming through. 'But you've been touched by demons yourself.'

'I didn't come here to have my palm read, Madame Rose or Stan or whatever your name is.' McLean wanted to get out of the room, but the tall stacks of books trapped him. Madame Rose stood so close he could see the pores in her skin. His skin, dammit. This was a man, winding him up. What the fuck was he doing here?

'No. You came here to learn about demons. And I brought you in here because I can see you don't want to voice your concerns in front of the young constable back there.'

'Demons don't exist.'

'Oh, I think you and I both know that's not true. And they come in many forms.' Madame Rose pulled a heavy book down from a high shelf, cradling it in her arms like a baby as she flipped through crackly pages. 'Not all demons are evil monsters, inspector, and some only live in your mind. But there are other, rarer creatures that move among us, influence us, and yes, exhort us to

329

do terrible things. That's not to say we can't do terrible things without their help. Here.' She twisted the book around so that he could see the page. He had been expecting an old tome, hand-written Latin script, elegantly illuminated. What he got was something that looked a bit like a high school yearbook, only on closer inspection it appeared to be for middle-aged men. One face in particular stood out, even though it was younger than the man he knew. Just the sight was enough to send a shiver through his whole body. He snapped the book shut, shoved it back at Madame Rose and turned to leave. A heavy hand on his arm stopped him.

'I know what happened to you, inspector. We're not a large community, the clairvoyants and mediums here in the city, but we all know your story.'

'It was a long time ago.' McLean pulled away, but Madame Rose's grip was strong.

'You were touched by a demon then.'

'Donald Anderson isn't a demon. He's a sick bastard who deserves to rot in jail for the rest of his life.'

'He was a man, inspector. He was like me in many ways. More interested in old books than anything else. But he came into con-tact with a demon, and he changed.'

'Donald Anderson was a raping, murdering bastard and that's the end of it.' McLean shook his arm free, turned to face Madame Rose as his anger began to flare. Bad enough he had to deal with the likes of Dagwood on a daily basis, but he wasn't going to put up with this. This wasn't what he'd come here for. What exactly had he come here for?

'Perhaps. But with demons you can never tell.'

'Enough. I didn't come here to talk about Donald bloody Anderson, and I really don't care if demons exist or not. I need to know what these men thought they were getting. What could they possibly gain from ritually murdering a young girl?'

'A young girl?' Madame Rose raised an eyebrow. 'A virgin, I've no doubt. What could they not gain? I would guess they were limited only by their imaginations.'

'So immortality, wealth, the usual sort of thing.' McLean recalled MacBride's earlier suggestion.

'That does seem to be the way of it. Like I said, only limited by their imaginations.'

'And how does it all go wrong? Usually?'

'There is no usual, inspector. We're talking about demons here.' Madame Rose corrected herself. 'Or at least people who earnestly believe they are consorting with demons. Classically, the person invoking the demon stands inside the circle to protect themselves from it while they make their demands. Once they've banished it back to whichever hell it came from, they can leave the circle and go out into the world. That usually goes wrong when some other idiot raises the same demon sometime later. They have long memories, inspector, and they don't like being bossed around.'

'The body was inside the circle,' McLean said.

'In which case they tried to tie the demon to the girl. Which is fine as long as the circle remains closed.'

McLean pictured the scene. A wall broken down by workmen. Rubble strewn across the floor. 'And if it was broken?'

'Well, then you've got a demon that's not just pissed off at being summoned, but which you've had trapped for years, maybe decades. How do you think you'd feel about that?'

331

54

The mortuary was always quiet; no chatter amongst the dead lying in their individual chill coffins. But the afternoon shift was different somehow, as if all the sound had been sucked out of the place. Even his footsteps on the hard linoleum floor echoed distantly as McLean approached Cadwallader's office. Or maybe it was just the after-effect of spending time with Madame Rose. The doctor was nowhere to be seen, but his assistant was busy typing away, headphones over her ears.

''lo, Tracy.' McLean rapped perhaps a little too hard on the open doorframe, not wanting to spook the young woman. She started slightly.

'Inspector. What a surprise.'

McLean smiled at the sarcasm in her voice. 'Is the doctor in?'

'He's taking a shower right now.' Something about the way Tracy said the words made McLean think she wanted to be taking it with him. It was a strange thought; Cadwallader was old enough to be the pathology assistant's father. He pushed the image of the two of them away.

'Long day at the office?'

'Nasty PM. Burnt bodies are never fun.'

'He's finished, then?' McLean felt a surge of relief that he wouldn't have to watch.

'Yup. Hence the shower. I'm just typing up the notes now. Not a nice case at all.'

'How so?'

'He burned to death, I can't imagine it would have been much fun. Third-degree on eighty per cent of his body; scarring in the lungs where he'd inhaled fire. At least he was probably drunk enough not to feel a lot of the pain. Or I hope so, anyway.'

'Drunk?'

'Blood alcohol level was point one eight per cent. Well on the way to being unconscious.'

'Time of death?'

'Difficult to be completely accurate yet, but days not hours.'

McLean cast his mind back to when he'd seen the van. It was within the timescale. 'What about identifying features? Are we anywhere near an identification?'

'Oh ye of little faith.' Tracy pushed herself off her chair and went to the counter that ran along the far wall of the office. A stainless-steel tray was heaped with a number of items, all wrapped in plastic bags, all blackened with the fire. She brought it over. 'We found his wallet in his inside pocket. It's quite charred on the outside, but good-old-fashioned leather takes a lot of burning. Driving licence and credit cards are in the name of a Donald R. Murdo.'

'Mr McAllister's in a meeting, inspector. You can't go in there.'

McLean was in no mood for waiting around. He pushed past the secretary and slammed open the door to McAllister's office. The man himself was on the far side of the desk, deep in conversation with a grey-suited businessman who looked as out of place as a nun in a brothel. They both stared up at him as he entered; the businessman with the haunted eyes of a guilty schoolboy caught smoking behind the bike shed, McAllister with a flash of fury swiftly doused.

'Inspector McLean. This is a surprise.'

'Mr McAllister, I'm sorry. I tried to stop him —'

'Calm yourself, Janette. My door's always open for Lothian and Borders' finest.' McAllister turned back to the businessman, who looked even more alarmed as the words sunk in. 'Mr Roberts, I think everything's in order now, don't you?'

Roberts nodded, seemingly unwilling to speak, and gathered up his papers from the desk, hurriedly putting them into a leather satchel. Every so often he would glance up at McLean, never quite meeting his eye. After what seemed like minutes but was likely no more than a few seconds, he stuffed his still-open case under his arm, nodded swiftly at McAllister and scurried out.

'And what do I owe this pleasant surprise to, inspector? Have you come to tell me I can start work on the house in Sighthill again? Only it's too late. I've just sold it to Mr Roberts there. Or at least the company he represents. Made a bit of a profit on the sale, too.'

'Even with it being the site of a brutal murder?'

'Oh, I suspect because of that, inspector. The buyer was anxious to know all the details I could give him.'

McLean knew that McAllister was trying to goad him into asking who the buyer was. Then the developer would be able to pretend that was confidential information and refuse to divulge it. Petty, really, especially since he'd seen a logo on the top of several sheets of paper that Roberts had shoved into his case. It shouldn't be too hard to reproduce and pass around until someone recognised it.

'We've found something of yours,' he said instead.

'Oh aye?' McAllister settled back in his chair. He hadn't offered McLean the vacated seat.

'A white Transit van. Well, it was white once. It's mostly black now.'

'A Transit? I don't use them, inspector. My brother runs the Fiat franchise across town, does me a nice line in Ducatos. I wasn't aware that I was missing one.'

'This van was in a hit-and-run incident. It mounted the pavement on the Pleasance and ran down a police constable. She died two days later. Do you remember Constable Kydd, Mr McAllister?'

'Let me guess. The bonny lass who was here with you last time? Oh, that is a shame, inspector.' McAllister's insincerity would have made a politician blush. Then his face hardened. 'Are you accusing me of having something to do with that, inspector?'

'Where's Murdo?' McLean asked.

'Donnie? I've no idea. He's not worked for me since you were last here. We had a bit of an argument over the house in Sighthill. I fired him.'

McLean felt the wind knocked out of his sails. He'd been so sure, and now he had the horrible feeling he'd made a complete twat of himself.

'You fired him? Why?'

'If you must know, he was using illegal immigrants as cheap labour. Cash in hand, no questions asked.' McAllister's eyes flashed dangerously, his earlier anger stoked once again. 'I don't run my business that way. Never have and never will. My reputation's all I've got. If you'd asked around you'd know that. I've had nothing but hassle from the police since I reported that body, and now you barge in here with your groundless allegations. Do you have any proof? No of course you don't. Otherwise you'd be arresting me. You haven't got shite but your half-arsed theories and you dare to come in here, blackening my name with them. I'll be sure to make my complaint at your behaviour official. Now if you don't mind, I've got work to do.'

55

The station was quiet when McLean pushed his way in through the back door, which suited his black mood. Nothing worse than being shown up for an idiot to make you angry at everything and anyone. One of the admin staff scurried away in terror after she'd told him that Duguid had called a meeting. Apparently there was some new evidence that could dramatically change the direction of the investigation, or something. Impressed at how quickly Cadwallader, or more likely Tracy, had come up with confirmation on the blood, he headed down to the small incident room the back way so as to avoid being seen. It didn't do him any good. Chief Superintendent McIntyre was waiting for him.

'How is it I knew you'd come here rather than go home?'

'Ma'am?'

'Don't you ma'am me, Tony. I've just been on the phone with a very irate gentleman by the name of McAllister. It seems one of my officers barged into his office and verbally harassed him.'

'I –'

'Just what part of "Keep out of this investigation" do you not understand?'

McLean tried to head off the superintendent before she completely lost her temper. Might as well grab a tiger by the tail. 'Ma'am, I –'

'I'm not finished yet. What the hell were you doing at McAllister's anyway? What's he got to do with your missing teenager?'

'He –'

'Nothing. That's what. Nothing whatsoever. Bad enough that you went to see him. What the hell were you doing snooping around a burnt-out van in Newhaven? Pestering Angus Cadwallader for ID on the driver?'

'I'm sorry, ma'am. It was the van that ran down Constable Kydd. I had to see it.'

'You're a victim of this crime, Tony. You can't be anywhere near the investigation. You know what a half-decent defence lawyer will do to our case if they find out. Jesus wept, it was bad enough you going after McReadie.'

McIntyre slumped against the table, sighed heavily as she pressed the heel of her hand into her eye. She looked tired, and McLean had a sudden insight into what life must be like for her. He moaned about having to juggle the overtime rosters for his small team; she had to deal with the whole station. She'd lost a constable, someone was posting crime-scene photographs on the internet, she was co-ordinating God alone knew how many other investigations, and here he was making life even more difficult for her.

'I'm sorry. I never meant to give you a hard time.'

'With power comes responsibility, Tony. I recommended you for inspector because I thought you were responsible enough for the job. Please don't make me think I made a mistake.'

'I won't. And I'll apologise personally to Tommy McAllister. That was my bad judgement. I let my emotions get the better of me.'

'Leave it a couple of days, eh? Go home.'

'What about Chloe?' McLean wished the words back as he said them, but by then it was too late. McIntyre looked up at him with a mixture of disbelief and desperation.

'You're not the only person on the force looking for her, you know. We're shaking down the usual suspects and working on the CCTV footage to try and identify that car. We'll find her. And it's Grumpy Bob's case anyway. Let him get on with it.'

'I just feel so useless.'

'Well go and speak to her mother then. She's your friend. Maybe you can convince her we're doing all we can.'

Late afternoon in the middle of the Festival season, but the shop was closed. McLean peered in through the window, trying to see if there was anyone about, but the place was empty. Alongside the shop, a door led to the tenements above, and one of the buzzers bore the name 'Spiers'. He pressed the button and was rewarded after a few moments with the tinny sound of a voice.

'Hello?'

'Jenny? It's Tony McLean. Can I come up?'

The door clicked open and McLean pushed his way in. Unlike his own tenement block just around the corner, this hallway didn't smell of cat piss. The floor was swept, and someone had put houseplants on the window sills looking out from the stairwell into a neat drying green and garden at the back.

Jenny stood in the open doorway to her flat, her face a picture of apprehension. She was wearing a dressing gown over a long nightdress, her feet bare. Her hair was a mess, her eyes red-rimmed and sunken.

'Have you found her?' It was a whisper laden with both hope and fear.

'Not yet, no. Can I come in?'

Jenny stood aside, letting McLean into the tiny hallway. He looked around, noting the disarray. How soon chaos descended on the disrupted household. Turning back, he saw Jenny still staring out the front door at the stairwell, as if willing her daughter to come flouncing up the steps.

'We'll find her, Jenny.'

'Will you? Will you really? Or are you just saying that to try and comfort me?' Jenny's voice hardened, the anger beginning to show through. She closed the door and pushed past. McLean followed her into the tiny galley kitchen.

'We picked her up on CCTV cameras walking along Princes Street after the show,' McLean said. Jenny had started to make coffee, but she stopped, turning to face him.

'She was meant to get a taxi.'

'She's a teenager. I bet she's been saving her taxi fares for years now.'

'What happened? Where did she go?'

'A car slowed down. She spoke to the person driving, then got in. We think she might have been in contact with him before. On the internet.'

Jenny's hands went to her face, her fingers pressing deep into her cheeks, leaving white marks on the skin. 'Oh my god. She's been abducted by a paedophile. My little girl.'

McLean stepped forward, taking Jenny's arms and pulling them away from her face. 'It's not all bad, Jenny. We've got a partial number plate and a make and model of car. We're tracking it down right now.'

'But my little girl . . . She's . . . He's . . .'

'Listen to what I'm saying, Jenny. I know it's bad. I won't lie to you about that. But we've got a lot of information to work with. And this was pre-planned, not some random thing. That's good news.'

'Good? How can you see any good in this?'

McLean cursed himself for being so insensitive. There was

339

nothing good about the whole situation, only bits that were less bad.

'It means that whoever did this wants Chloe alive.' For now, at least.

The phone rang as he was pushing the keys into the lock of his front door. McLean thought about letting the answering machine take it; an hour trying to calm down Jenny Spiers had left him drained. Then he remembered that the tape was still in his desk drawer. Rushing through, he managed to grab the handset before it rang off.

'McLean.'

'Ah, sir. Glad I caught you in. It's DC MacBride here.'

'What can I do for you, constable?'

'It's Dag – er, DCI Duguid, sir.' McLean guessed that Mac-Bride must have been in the company of senior officers.

'What's he done this time?'

'He's gone to the SOC offices with a search warrant, sir. Taken all our computer tech boys with him. He's going to arrest Emma Baird.'

56

He arrived just too late to do anything but get in the way. Duguid had gone to town, no doubt hoping to show his superiors in Force HQ that he was thorough in his work. It had probably never occurred to him that the men would be better used searching for Chloe Spiers.

The entrance to the SOC lab was blocked by uniformed constables, and as McLean approached, Duguid pushed through and back out into the car park, closely followed by a pair of sergeants flanking the handcuffed Emma Baird. She looked terrified, her eyes darting this way and that, trying to find a friendly face.

'What the blazes are you doing here, McLean?' Duguid found him first.

'I'm trying to stop you making a big mistake, sir. She's not the one you're looking for.'

'Tony, what's going on?' Emma asked. Duguid turned as he heard her voice, directed his orders at the two sergeants.

'Take her back to the station. Get her processed as quickly as possible.'

'Are you sure that's a good idea, chief inspector?' McLean emphasised the 'chief'.

'Ah, the gallant knight, riding in to save his girlfriend. Don't tell me how to run my investigation, McLean.'

'She's one of us, sir. You're treating her like she's some kind of crack-head junkie.'

Duguid rounded on McLean, prodding him in the chest as he spoke. 'She's an accessory to the murder of Jonas Carstairs. She knows who killed him, I'm sure of it, and I intend to get that information out of her before anyone else dies.'

Crap. The blood results hadn't come through after all. Once again Duguid was barking up the wrong tree.

'She's not accessory to anything, sir. And Sally Dent killed Jonas Carstairs.'

'What are you blabbering about, McLean? It was you who fingered her in the first place. Don't try and weasel your way out of it now.'

'Is that true?' Emma stared straight at him. Her bewilderment was still there, but it was only a step away from fury.

'Why is this woman still here?' Duguid asked. Before McLean could say anything, the two sergeants had dragged her off to a waiting squad car.

'You should have let me handle this, sir.' McLean had to speak through gritted teeth. As he stood out in the car park, technicians began filing out of the SOC building with computers, loading them into a waiting van.

'What, and let you warn your squeeze so she could cover up her tracks? I don't think so, McLean.'

'She's not my "squeeze", sir. She's my friend. And if you'd left it to me I could have used that to find out what was going on without any need for this.' McLean pointed at the mêlée of policemen and bemused-looking SOC officers. 'Right now you've closed down our entire SOC operation, as well as lost any good will we might ever have had with the staff who do the bulk of our crime-scene investigation work. That's fine policing, sir. Well done.'

He stalked off, leaving Duguid open-mouthed behind him.

And only then did he see Emma, staring out of the open window of the squad car, well within earshot. Their eyes met too briefly for him to read her expression, and then she pointedly turned away.

McLean wanted nothing more than to go home and sleep, or failing that climb outside a bottle of whisky. Everything had gone to shit, his head was full of demons, Chloe Spiers had been missing almost twenty-four hours and he couldn't actually remember the last time he'd seen his bed. Emma being arrested was just the icing on the cake, Duguid's most spectacular cock-up to date. He couldn't think straight, but there was one more thing he needed to know. So instead of flagging down a taxi to take him home, he hitched a ride in a squad car back to the station. Despite the late hour, down in the basement, the place was frenetic with activity as a dozen computers from the SOC photographic lab were logged in, stripped down and searched. Mike Simpson looked up from a dog's breakfast of wires and scowled at him as he stepped into the room.

'What do you want?' His tone was angry, accusing. McLean held up his hands in a gesture of surrender.

'Whoa, steady on, Mike. What've I done to deserve this?'

'How about grassing up Em? Or landing us with all this shit.' Mike looked around at his fellow technicians, all peering bleary-eyed at flickering monitors or doing strange things with crocodile clips to the innards of computers.

'I didn't grass up Emma. I was trying to protect her.'

'That's not what Dagwood says.'

'And you believe him over me? I thought you were smarter than that.'

Mike's scowl softened a little. 'I s'pose. But you did suspect her.'

343

'I'm a detective, Mike. It's what I do. Someone with access to all the crime-scene photos, who uses the initials MB to identify themselves? Of course I was going to investigate. I just figured it would be easier to ask her myself, quietly. Would have avoided all this for certain.'

Mike shrugged. 'We've still got a heap of shit to wade through because of it.'

'Well, if it's my fault, I'm sorry. I'll buy you a beer to make up for it.'

That seemed to cheer Mike up remarkably. It was quite probable no one had ever offered such generosity to him before.

'You're on, sir. Now if you don't mind, I've got to get this stripped down and checked before midnight. We're trying to get SOC back up and running for tomorrow morning.'

'There was one thing . . .'

The technician slumped his shoulders with amateur theatricality. 'What?'

'Fergus McReadie. You still got his PC?'

'It's a Power Mac, but yes, we've still got it. Why?'

'We know about Penstemmin Security, but how many other back entrances has he got? Who else did he do security work for?'

'How far do you want to go back?' The technician looked weary and hard-pressed. 'He's been in the security game for over a decade.'

'I don't know. Just the last year maybe. Who was he working for when we caught him? What about his emails?'

Mike pushed himself out of his chair and wandered over to another computer tucked away in the far corner of the room. McLean followed him and watched as the technician pulled up screen after screen of information. Finally a list appeared, sorted alphabetically.

'Here we go, sir. Emails sent and received in the week before we seized Mr McReadie's computer. Looks like he may have had quite a few clients.'

But only one caught McLean's eye. At least two dozen messages sent back and forth between Fergus McReadie and a man by the name of Christopher Roberts of Carstairs Weddell Solicitors.

57

Interview Room 4 was a dark little space, its tiny, high window obscured by the later addition of ductwork to the outside of the building. The air-conditioning unit clonked and burbled, but didn't seem to be conditioning any of the air it dribbled into the room. At least it wasn't too warm yet, the full heat of the sun some hours away.

Christopher Roberts looked as if he hadn't slept a wink since McLean had seen him at McAllister's the day before. He was wearing the same suit, and his face was frizzed with a dark shadow of stubble. He'd been picked up by a patrol car at the Bridge Motel in Queensferry, which was an odd place to stay for a man who lived in Cramond. The number plate on his shiny red BMW matched the partial DC MacBride had managed to lift from the CCTV footage of the car that had picked up Chloe Spiers. It might have been a coincidence; plenty of dark-coloured BMWs with that year number and first two letters. But lately McLean had been seeing rather too much coincidence to believe in it any more.

'Why didn't you go home last night, Mr Roberts?' McLean asked after the formalities of the interview had been dispensed with. Roberts didn't answer, instead studied his hands and picked at his fingernails.

'OK then,' McLean said. 'Let's start things simple. Who are you working for?'

'I work for Carstairs Weddell, the solicitors. I'm a partner in their conveyancing department.'

'That much I know already. Tell me why you were in Tommy McAllister's office yesterday. You were arranging the sale of Farquhar House in Sighthill. Who was the buyer?'

Roberts's face went pale and beads of sweat started to swell on his forehead. 'I can't. Client confidentiality.'

McLean grimaced. This wasn't going to be easy. 'OK, then. Tell me this. Where did you take Chloe Spiers after you picked her up on Princes Street at eleven-thirty the night before last?'

'I . . . I don't know what you're talking about.'

'Mr Roberts, we have CCTV footage of Miss Spiers getting into your car. Even now our forensic experts are taking it apart. It's only a matter of time before they find evidence that she was in it. Now where did you take her?' This was a lie. The car was in the police garage, it was true, but how long it would take to persuade the forensic experts to get to work on it was anyone's guess.

'I can't say.'

'But you did take her somewhere.'

'Please, don't make me say anything. They'll kill me if I say anything. They'll kill my wife.'

McLean turned to Grumpy Bob, who was leaning against the wall behind him. 'Get a patrol car around to Mr Roberts' house and take his wife into protective custody.'

The sergeant nodded and left the room. McLean turned his attention back to Roberts.

'If someone's been threatening you, Mr Roberts, then it's best you tell us who they are. We can protect you and your wife. But if you keep silent and Chloe Spiers is hurt, then I'll make sure you go to prison for a very long time.' He let the words hang in the air,

347

falling silent for the long minutes it took for Grumpy Bob to return. Roberts didn't say a word.

'Tell me how you persuaded Chloe to get in,' McLean said after a while. 'She's a smart kid, so I'm told. She wouldn't just jump into a car with any old stranger.'

Roberts kept his mouth shut, his eyes wide with fear.

'It wasn't a chance meeting, you were looking for her weren't you.'

'I . . . It shouldn't have been me. They made me do it. They said they'd hurt Irene.'

'Who should it have been, Mr Roberts? Should it have been Fergie? Did they make you pretend to be him?'

Roberts said nothing, but his head nodded imperceptibly, as if he wasn't even aware of it.

'So who's Fergie? And why couldn't he do it himself?'

Roberts clamped his mouth shut, twisting his hands together in his lap like a man with a guilty conscience. The fear was like a fever on him; God alone knew what had been used to scare him so. McLean knew it was no good; he wouldn't say anything, at least until he knew his wife was safe. Maybe not even then. But he also reckoned he knew why Fergie had failed to turn up for his appointment with Chloe Spiers. Now all he had to do was prove it.

HMP Saughton was not a place you would want to visit often. McLean hated it, and not just for the inmates he'd put inside its lifeless walls. There was something about the prison that sucked the joy out you, drained your will to live. He'd visited plenty of other jails in his career, and they all had it to some extent, but Saughton was worst.

He and Bob were shown into a small room with a single, high

window and no air conditioning. Even though it was still morning, the heat was enough to be uncomfortable. McReadie's lawyer was already there, waiting. His gaunt face, hooked nose and long mane of silver hair made him look like a vulture; no doubt why he had chosen his profession in the first place.

'You understand that this constitutes harassment of my client, inspector.' No handshake, no nod of greeting or casual hello.

'Your client is a suspect in a child abduction. If that becomes a murder investigation, then I'll show you the meaning of harassment.' McLean stared at the lawyer, who sat impassively and did not respond. Grumpy Bob lurked in the corner, leaning against the wall. After a few minutes, a guard arrived, pushing Fergus McReadie ahead of him. He shoved the prisoner into a seat, jerked his thumb at the door, presumably to indicate that he would be outside if needed, then retreated. The lock clacked shut, just the four of them alone.

McReadie looked tired, as if he hadn't slept well since he'd been placed here on remand. It was a far cry from his usual haunt, the penthouse apartment, neighbour to the stars. He bent towards his solicitor, who whispered something in his ear, then straightened up again, shaking his head and scowling.

'Prison suits you, Fergus,' McLean said, leaning back in his chair.

'That's a pity. I wasn't planning on staying here long.' McReadie sat uncomfortably, his hands cuffed together, his prison clothes ill-fitting for a man used to designer wear.

'You must think you're on easy street, Fergus. White-collar crime, a little bit of hacking, a bit of light burglary. Your record's pretty clean, so the judge'll go easy, even if I ask the chief constable to put in a word. You never know, a good lawyer and you might get away with five years. Knock that back to eighteen months for good behaviour. An open prison, since you're not a violent man. Not much, really, for robbing the dead.'

McReadie said nothing, just stared insolently. McLean smiled at him, leaning forward. 'But if word got out in here that you'd been grooming a fifteen-year-old girl for sex. Well, prisoners are an odd lot. They have this strangely warped moral code. And they like to make the punishment fit the crime, if you see what I mean.'

Silence fell on the room, but McLean could see that his words had got through. The look of insolence disappeared, replaced by a worried stare. McReadie's eyes darted to the door, to his brief, then back to McLean, who leant back in his chair and let the silence grow.

'You've got nothing on me. It's not true.' McReadie broke first.

'Mr McReadie, I'd advise you not to say anything,' the solicitor said. McReadie stared at him, an angry scowl on his face. McLean read the animosity and decided to play it.

'We've got your emails, and Chloe's too. Oh, I think we've got plenty on you, Fergie. Was that wise, using your own name?'

'It . . . It wasn't like that.'

'What was it like, then? Love?'

'I cannae tell youse. He'll kill me.'

'Mr McReadie, as your solicitor I must insist –'

'Who'd kill you?'

McReadie didn't answer. McLean could see the fear in his eyes; it would be hard to break that. Roberts he could understand, but McReadie was a hard man. What had they done to get to him so badly?

'We've picked up Christopher Roberts, Fergus. He had quite a lot to say about you. How you groomed young Chloe. What was it about her that attracted you? She's almost of age. I thought you lot liked them a bit younger.'

350

'What d'you mean, you lot? I'm no' a kiddie fiddler.' Anger blazed in McReadie's eyes. McLean had hit a nerve.

'So you just like to hang around teenage girls' internet chat-rooms, that it?'

'I didnae choose her. They gave me her name. I was just doin' my job.'

'Who gave you her name? What job?'

McReadie said nothing, but McLean could see he was scared of something, worried he might have said too much already. He decided to change tack.

'Why did you try to set me up, Fergus? Was it just petty revenge because I'd caught you?'

McReadie laughed, a nervous little wheeze. 'And waste all that money? You're joking. It was my stupid mistake you caught me. I don't hate you for that.'

'All part of the game, eh. So why'd you do it then? You saying someone set you up to it? They give you the drugs too?'

McReadie's face was a picture as competing emotions fought across it. He was scared, true. Someone had put the wind up him good and proper. But he was also a chancer desperate to play his way out of this hole. 'What's in it for me, eh? Get me out of this shite-hole. Get me on a witness protection scheme an' maybe I'll tell youse.'

'I think I'd like to talk to my client alone for a moment,' the solicitor said. His vulture face looked like he'd been sucking lemons, his eyes popping wider and wider as McReadie had incriminated himself.

McLean nodded. 'That's probably not a bad idea. Try and talk some sense into him. If the girl's hurt, then all deals are off.'

He stood up. Grumpy Bob knocked to have the door unlocked. Outside in the corridor, they were accosted by another prison guard.

'Inspector McLean?'

'Yes?'

'Phone call for you, sir.'

McLean followed him out, along the corridor to an office, where a telephone handset lay on the desk. He picked it up. 'McLean.'

'MacBride here, sir. I think you might want to come over. They've found a body. It's just round the corner from your grand-mother's house.'

He remembered playing in this dark little cul-de-sac as a child. Back then it had been a regular haunt of walkers, the road giving way to a leafy track that angled down the steep side of a narrow glen to the river. Without adequate street lighting, it had fallen out of favour in recent years and was now so overgrown as to be almost impassable. Discarded Coke cans, chip pokes and used condoms showed the use it was being put to nowadays.

Squad cars blocked the road completely, forcing them to park some distance away. McLean and Grumpy Bob walked down the uneven pavement in the shade of huge mature sycamores towards the knot of uniforms clustered at the end

'Over here, sir.' DC MacBride waved them towards the dense bushes and a couple of paper-overalled figures kneeling down.

'Who found it?' McLean asked.

'Old lady walking her dog, sir. It wouldn't come when she called it, so she came down to see what was so interesting.'

'Where is she now?'

'They've taken her off to hospital. She had quite the shock.'

At the sound of the detective constable's voice, the white-clad figure with his back to them stood up and turned. 'You do bring me the most interesting bodies, Tony,' Angus Cadwallader said.

352

'This one seems to have been beaten heavily with fists. I've seen similar bruising on men injured in bare-knuckle boxing fights. Only there doesn't seem to be enough damage to have killed him.'

McLean stepped forward to view the body. He had been a short, stout man, though perhaps bloating had made his stomach stretch at his pale blue shirt a bit more than it would have done in life. He lay sprawled in the leaf mould, arms thrown out as if he had just rolled onto his back to have a snooze. His head was tilted over to one side, his face bruised, nose broken. His clothes were tattered and dirty, a tiny red 'Virgin Rail' insignia on his dark blue jacket.

'Have we got an ID?'

DC MacBride handed over a slim leather wallet. 'He was carrying this, sir. Face fits the photo in his driver's licence.'

'David Brown, South Queensferry. Why does that name ring a bell?'

Grumpy Bob came forward, knelt down and looked at the dead man.

'I know who this is,' he said quietly. 'I interviewed him just a few days ago. He was driving the train that hit Sally Dent. What in God's name is he doing here?'

58

The post-mortem on David Brown was scheduled for later that afternoon. McLean filled the time by wading through the mountain of paperwork on his desk. It didn't matter that he had been told to take a week's leave, the overtime sheets, requisition orders and a thousand and one other useless bits and pieces had still continued to mount up. What would happen if he disappeared for a whole month? Would the office eventually choke up with paper? Or would someone else finally roll up their sleeves and get on with it?

A knock at the door distracted him. Looking up, he saw DC MacBride staring wide-eyed at the chaos.

'Come in, constable. If you can find some room.'

'It's all right, sir. I just thought you ought to know. They're going to charge Emma this afternoon.'

'What with?' McLean clenched his fists in embarrassment and anger. In all the rushing about with Brown, she'd slipped his mind.

'Dagwood wants to go the whole hog with accessory to murder, but I think the super's persuaded him to go with perverting the course.'

'Shit. Do you think she did it, Stuart?'

'Do you, sir?'

'No. But if they're charging her, then they must have some evidence.'

'You've been into the SOC lab, sir. You know they all share their computers and passwords. Security's a joke.'

McLean had a thought. 'That site where you found the pictures. Is it still up?'

MacBride nodded. 'It's hosted on an overseas server. Could take us months to get it pulled.'

'And the crime scenes aren't identified, are they. There's just the pictures.'

'And dates, sir. But no location descriptions. Just stuff like "crushed torso" and "cut throat".'

'Lovely. Have we been able to identify the other scenes posted by MB, whoever she, or he, is?'

'I don't think anyone's tried, sir. The photos from Smythe's and Stewart's crime scenes were enough. Emma was SOC photographer at both.'

'But everyone had access to her computer. And we spread those photos around our incident rooms like it was Christmas. Do me a favour, Stuart. Emma was based in Aberdeen before she came down here. Get a sample of the earlier photos and send them up to Queen Street. See if anyone recognises them as coming from their patch. And find out who else has transferred into our SOC team recently. Do the same for their old areas.'

'I'm on it, sir.' MacBride's eyes filled with enthusiasm as he hurried off to complete his task. McLean wished he could borrow some of it; he'd hardly made any progress on the paperwork. He reached forward for the next folder full of meaningless numbers, knocking the whole pile to the floor by mistake.

'Bollocks!' He squeezed out from behind the desk and bent down to pick up the papers. There were a few case files in with them, and one had fallen open. The dead face of Jonathan Okolo stared up at him with accusing eyes. He picked it up, and was about to put it back in the folder when he noticed the case file for Peter Andrews' suicide lying close by. He flicked it open, seeing another dead face. That same reproachful stare, as if they were criticising him for not caring enough. But what had the two of them got in common, apart from being dead?

'Well, they both slit their throats in a public place.' McLean barely recognised the voice as his own. It was a wild thought, but easily enough checked. And far more interesting than wading through the monthly crime-report statistics. He grabbed both photographs, shoved them in his jacket pocket and headed out the door.

The Feasting Fox was quiet in the afternoon; just a few late lunch-time drinkers cooling their throats before braving the shops once more. A chip-fat fug hung in the air, almost but not quite over-powering the smell of coffee from an underused espresso machine behind the bar. Fewer than half the tables were occu-pied, and the barman looked bored as he polished glasses, his eyes focused on something far away.

'Pint of Deuchars,' McLean said, noticing the hand pump.

'Deuchars's off.' The barman twisted the clip-on label around the handle so it faced away from the punters.

'Never mind then.' McLean reached into his pocket and drew out the two photographs. He put the first one down on the bar, Peter Andrews. 'This man ever come in here?'

'Who's asking?'

McLean sighed, reaching for his warrant card. 'I am. And it's a murder investigation, so being helpful would be your best course of action right now.'

The barman peered at the photo for all of two seconds, then said: 'Yeah, he drinks here most evenings. Works round the block somewhere. Not seen him recently, mind.'

'Did you ever see him talking to this man?' McLean put down

the photograph of Jonathan Okolo. The barman's eyes widened.

'That's the man . . . You know.'

'Yes, I do know,' McLean said. 'But did you ever see him talking to Peter Andrews here?'

'I don't think so. Can't say as I ever saw him before the night he came in here.'

'And exactly what did you see then?'

'Well, like I told the other officers. I was here at the bar. It was crazy busy, know what it's like, with the Fringe and all. But I noticed when this guy comes in, right, coz he's filthy, acting a bit strange, but he heads straight for the gents' before I can get to him. I went after him; we don't want his type in here. But he was bleeding all over the floor. Christ it was a mess.'

'Was there anyone else in the toilets when he killed himself?'

'I dunno. I don't think so.' The barman scratched at his stubble. 'No, hang on. I tell a lie. There was someone came out of there just before I went in. Could've been this man, now you shown me his picture.' He pointed at Peter Andrews.

'I don't suppose you've got CCTV.'

'In the bogs? Nah, that'd be disgusting.'

'What about the rest of the bar?'

'Yeah, there's a couple of cameras, one on the front door, one on the back.'

'How long do you keep the tapes?'

'A week, maybe ten days. Depends.'

'So do you have the tape for the night these two were in here?' McLean pointed to the photographs.

'Nah, sorry. You lot took that one away. Ain't brought it back yet.'

'Back it up a bit. That's right. There.'

The quality was worse than the CCTV on Princes Street, one frame every two seconds making the people jump and disappear like insane wizards. Grainy colour and dim lighting didn't help, either, but at least the camera covering the back door to the pub also covered the entrance to the gents' toilet.

It hadn't been easy getting the tape from Duguid. McLean knew he could expect no good will from the man; he was an arse, after all. But he wished once in a while that the chief inspector wouldn't be quite so obstructive. Still, he had it now, and in the darkened confines of the video-viewing room, otherwise known as Interview Room 4 with the blinds drawn, they could watch the drinkers in the Feasting Fox as they clustered tightly together almost two weeks ago.

'Health and Safety'd love to see this tape,' MacBride said as a pile of drinkers cluttered up the narrow passageway past the gents' towards the back door. From the other camera angle it was easy to see why; the main area of the bar was sardine-packed, standing room only. Then the door opened and Jonathan Okolo came in.

He was filthy; you could see that even on the poor-quality picture. As he made his way past the camera area in a series of small jumps, the crowd seemed to part around him, like the Red Sea in front of Moses. McLean had read the witness statement taken at the time, and wondered how it was that no one had been able to remember seeing much of the man. He must have stunk to high heaven to get them to move like that. But then they were all drinking like booze was going to be banned, and who wanted to talk to the police these days?

A few seconds after disappearing off the first camera, Okolo reappeared on the second one. The crowd in the passageway shifted away from him as he pushed into the gents'. There was a pause for a few seconds, and then the door opened again.

'Freeze that,' McLean said. MacBride hit the pause button. It was a strange angle, looking down from the ceiling. And the fish-eye lens distorted features. But for some reason, the man coming out of the gents' had looked up as he left, as if he had known that this was his moment in the limelight.

And he was unmistakably Peter Andrews.

59

'You're late, Tony. That's not like you.'

'Sorry, Angus. Something came up. Did you start without me?' McLean stepped into the post-mortem examination room without much of a jaunt. This wasn't his favourite place to be, and lately he'd been spending rather too much time here.

'We did indeed,' Cadwallader said. He was hunched over the naked corpse, examining one of its hands. 'Did you X-ray these, Tracy?' he asked.

'Yes, doctor. They're up on the viewer.'

Cadwallader walked over to the wall, where a bank of lights shone through posted X-rays. McLean followed him, grateful not to have to look at the body any more.

'See these?' The doctor pointed at various light and dark shades on the X-rays. 'Multiple fractures to the finger bones. To get that normally you'd expect the hands to be a bloody pulp. Run over by a steam roller or something like that. But he's only got bruises. OK, they're nasty bruises, but not life-threatening. Then there's this.' He pulled down the first lot of X-rays and put up some fresh ones. 'Both his femurs are cracked in several places. His tibia and fibula too. And here.' Another set of prints. 'Ribs are a mess, I think I counted one that hasn't got a fracture in it.'

McLean winced, feeling the pain. 'So he was in a fight?'

'No, not a fight. That would imply some degree of fairness. He was attacked, but he wouldn't have been in any position to fight back. Advanced osteoporosis. His bones are like porcelain. They shatter at the lightest touch. It wouldn't have taken much to kill him. I'm guessing a rib shard punctured his lungs and he drowned in his own blood.'

McLean looked back at the dead man lying on the table. 'But he was a train driver. How could he do a job like that with his bones in that condition?'

'I suspect very carefully,' Cadwallader said. 'Though I doubt he'd have been able to keep it secret for much longer.'

The pathologist returned to his subject, and McLean took up his least favourite position as he watched the post-mortem being undertaken. Tracy succeeded in lifting some partial fingerprints from the bruising around the man's neck, and then together they opened him up.

'Ah, as I suspected,' Cadwallader said after too many long minutes of unpleasant squelching noises. 'The fourth rib, oh and the fifth too. Both on the right, straight into the lung. And on the left, just the fifth. His heart's not in very good shape either. It might well have given out before he had time to drown.'

Once it was all over, and Tracy was busy sewing David Brown back together again, McLean followed Cadwallader back to his little office.

'So what's the verdict, Angus?'

'He was beaten up, probably by someone large; those prints suggest fat fingers. Normally you'd expect a man of his age and weight to survive, but with his weak bones and heart, well he could have just collapsed at any time. And he was a train driver, you say?'

McLean nodded.

'Then I think we've had a lucky break.'

'But not lucky for him.'

'No.' Cadwallader fell silent for a moment, then seemed to remember something. 'Oh, you were right, by the way.'

'I was? What about?'

'That suicide case, Andrews. I went over the body again, and found minute traces of blood and skin under his fingernails. He'd scrubbed them pretty thoroughly, rubbed the skin raw in places, but his father told me he was always fastidious about his cleanliness. Which makes it rather odd that he should choose such a messy way to commit suicide.'

'Any idea whose blood and skin it was?'

'There was scarcely enough for a basic analysis, but I'm pretty sure it wasn't his own. I can send it off to the labs for a DNA test if you want. I assume you think you already know whose it is.'

McLean nodded, but he didn't much like the idea of being right.

Evening was falling fast by the time he made it back to the station. Another day gone in a flurry of confusing events. Another day and no closer to finding Chloe, or Alison's killer. Or the mysterious sixth man. At least McReadie was locked up and going nowhere; that was something

'Ah, inspector. The chief super wants a word.' Bill, the duty sergeant, buzzed him through to the back of the station.

'Did she say what it was about?'

'No, just that it was urgent.'

McLean hurried along the winding corridors, wondering what was up. He knocked on the door frame of the superintendent's office with a slightly anxious feeling. McIntyre looked up from whatever it was she was doing and beckoned him in.

'I've just had Detective Chief Superintendent Jamieson from Glasgow Central and West Division on the phone, Tony. It seems your young protégé DC MacBride sent him some pretty pictures to look at, and he was rather anxious to know where they'd come from.'

Glasgow, not Aberdeen. McLean heaved a sigh of relief. 'I take it he recognised them, ma'am.'

'Yes, he did. They were from a number of cases spread back over the past three years. You might remember reading about the latest round of ice cream wars.'

McLean did, only it wasn't ice cream that the hard men of Glasgow were killing each other over. 'How many different crime scenes were there?'

'He didn't say, but I think we can safely assume that whoever posted those pictures to the internet had access to the Glasgow SOC offices during that period. And since a certain Emma Baird was in training in Aberdeen then, Chief Inspector Duguid has been forced to release her, with a grovelling apology.'

Oh shit. He'd done it again. Trampling over another detective's case and solving it for them.

'He's only partly mollified by the fact that the real culprit is now sitting in the cell Miss Baird so recently vacated.'

'I'm sorry, ma'am. I owed it to her to investigate the matter thoroughly.'

'Even after taking her out to dinner?' McIntyre raised an eyebrow. 'Don't get me wrong, Tony. I think you're a very good detective, but if you keep on treading on people's toes, then you'll stay an inspector for the rest of your career.'

There were worse things that could happen. He wasn't one for scrabbling up the greasy pole over the backs and heads of others. All he really wanted was to catch the bad guys.

'I'll bear that in mind, ma'am.'

'You do that, Tony. And keep out of Charles Duguid's way for a day or two, eh? He's hopping mad.'

McLean hurried through the station to his office, hoping to avoid anyone who would distract him. He needed to get the latest information out of his head and down onto some paper before it all seeped out and was lost. There was a line of connection running between Okolo, Andrews, Dent and Brown. Each one had witnessed the previous one's death. He didn't want to think about how that tied in with what Madame Rose had said. There had to be a rational explanation, but the best he could come up with was that someone had manipulated these people, first to kill and then to kill themselves. Was that even possible? And if so, who had killed Brown and dumped him in the cul-de-sac, and where were they now? And who had Brown killed?

A letter waited for him, placed atop the latest pile of paperwork on his desk. He picked it up, noticing the handwritten address, the logo and name of Carstairs Weddell, Solicitors and Notaries Public. It contained a single sheet of paper, thick and covered with spidery writing, hasty and difficult to read. Turning it over, he saw a signature, and below it, the printed name Jonas Carstairs QC. He squeezed in behind his desk and turned on the lamp the better to read.

My Dear Anthony,

If you are reading this letter, then I am dead, and the sins of my youth have finally caught up with me. I cannot excuse what I did; it was an execrable crime for which I will no doubt burn in hell. But I can try to explain, and perhaps do something to try and make amends.

I knew Barny Smythe well. We were at school together and both went up to Edinburgh at the same time. That is where I met Buchan Stewart, Bertie Farquhar and Toby Johnson. Then when the war started we all signed up together, and ended up being posted out to West Africa. We were an intelligence outfit, tasked with preventing Hitler from gaining information that would be useful to him, and we were quite successful in that. But war changes a man, and we saw things in Africa that no one should ever have to witness.

I am making excuses for myself, but there can be no excusing what we did when we returned home in forty-five. That poor young girl took so long to die; I still hear her screams at night. And now her remains have been discovered, poor Barny is murdered and Buchan too. The beast will come for me next. I can feel it drawing ever closer. Once I am gone, there will only be one of us left, the one who started it all.

I cannot name him; that would betray an oath that binds far more than my honour. But you know him, Tony. And he knows you, the man we all looked up to, who saved our lives more than once during the war and who seduced us all into carrying out our folly. He will gather younger fools around him and try his mad ritual again. It is the only way he can protect himself. I fear another innocent soul will be lost in the process. But if he fails, then that which we trapped will be free to roam, free to kill. It lives in violence, that is all it knows.

There were a number of messages your grandmother asked me to pass on to you. Things she didn't want you to know whilst she was still alive. Things she found deeply embarrassing, hurtful, even shaming, although in truth she was never to blame. This letter is not the place for them; I will speak to you of them face to face, or they will go with me to my grave. They seemed important once, but in truth they are of small consequence. You are plainly not the man she feared you might become, so it may be best if I leave it at that.

Today I have changed my will, leaving all my personal wealth to you. Please understand this is not an attempt to salve my conscience. I am damned and I know it. But you can undo what myself, Barny and the others did and this is the only thing I can do from beyond the grave to help.

Yours in repentance,
Jonas Carstairs

McLean stared at the sprawling handwriting for long minutes, occasionally turning the sheet over as if the information he needed might be on the other side. But Carstairs had not said what he really needed to know, had not named their commander. And what was that paragraph about his grandmother supposed to mean? How like a lawyer never to actually commit. Everything was hedged. It was almost more frustrating than if the letter hadn't existed at all. Here there was nothing more than vague hints, and the threat of another brutal murder.

And then something clicked in his brain. Another murder. Doing the ritual again. A young girl just on the cusp of reaching womanhood. He knew why they had abducted Chloe Spiers. It was so obvious he could only kick himself for not seeing it before. Reaching for the phone, he was about to dial out when it rang in his hand.

'McLean.' He barked the word impatiently, wanting to get the conversation over and done with. Time was running out. He needed answers and no vulture-faced lawyer was going to get in his way this time.

'DC MacBride here, sir. I've just had a call from Saughton.'

'Oh aye? I was just about to call them. We need to speak to McReadie urgently, Stuart. He knows who's taken Chloe Spiers, and I know what they're going to do to her.'

'Ah. That might be difficult, sir.'

McLean's breath caught in his throat. 'Why?'

'McReadie hanged himself in his cell this evening. He's dead.'

60

McLean sat in the darkened video-surveillance centre at Saughton prison, watched the video as a huge man entered the visitors' room and sat down at the lone table. He was dressed casually: dark leather jacket and faded jeans, a T-shirt with some indecipherable logo on it. Out of context, McLean couldn't place him, but there was something very familiar about him.

'I know that man. What's his name?'

The prison officer who had escorted him through the building consulted a sheet of paper attached to a clipboard.

'Signed in as Callum, J. Address in Joppa.'

'Has anyone checked it out?' Alarm bells were going off in McLean's head, but the shrug he received by way of an answer was clear enough. He made a note of the name and address, then turned back to the screen in time to see McReadie ushered into the room. The burglar's reaction on seeing the big man was guarded, but not the terror McLean might have expected.

'D'you get any audio with this?' he asked.

The guard shook his head. 'Nah. There was a big stooshie about human rights a few years back. I'm surprised we're still allowed to lock them up.'

McLean shook his head in agreement at the madness of it all, then returned to watching the screen. The two men talked for a few minutes, McReadie's body language getting increasingly agitated. Then all of a sudden he stopped still, dropped his hands calmly to his sides and stared at his visitor with an almost hypnotised gaze. After about thirty seconds, the big man got up and left. A guard came over and led a very pliant McReadie away, then the tape ended.

'About half an hour after that we were doing the usual round of cell checks and found him dead. He'd ripped his shirt into strips and used it to strangle himself.'

'Strange. He didn't seem the suicidal type.'

'No. We didn't have him on special monitoring or anything.' The guard looked anxious. Perhaps worried he might get into trouble. As far as McLean was concerned, McReadie had done the world a huge favour. But it would have been better if he'd spoken to them about Chloe's whereabouts and his mysterious employer beforehand. That left only one other person to talk to.

'I know what they're going to do to her, Mr Roberts. Do you?'

Another hour had passed, another sixty minutes ticking down the time until it would be too late. If it wasn't already. McLean was back in the station, trying to sweat some answers out of a plainly terrified Christopher Roberts.

'They're going to nail her hands and feet to the floor. They're going to rape her. Then they're going to take a knife and cut open her belly. Whilst she's still alive, they'll start removing her internal organs, one by one. There'll be six of them, and each one will get an organ for himself. Were you meant to be one of the six, Mr Roberts? Was Fergus McReadie? Only both of you are going to miss out on your chance at immortality, or whatever it was you sick bastards thought you could get out of it. You're in here with me, and Fergus is dead.'

Roberts let out a small squeak of alarm at this news, but said nothing more.

'Forensic results have come in. We know Chloe was in your car,' McLean lied. SOC and forensics were still working slow, even though Emma had been cleared. It would be a while before Dagwood could be persuaded to apologise, especially given that there really had been a leak. Longer still before someone got around to checking over Roberts' BMW. 'Where did you take her? Who did you take her to? Was it Callum?'

That elicited some small response. Roberts' eye ticked nervously. 'How did he die?' he asked in a small, shaky voice.

'What?'

'Fergus. How did he die?'

McLean leant on the table, his face close to Roberts'. 'He tore his shirt into strips, tied them round his neck in a noose, tied the other end to the top of the bunk in his cell and then used his own bodyweight to choke himself to death.'

A light knock on the door interrupted them. McLean pushed himself away from the table. 'Come in.'

DC MacBride poked his head through the open doorway. 'Some test results just in that I thought you might be interested in, sir.'

'What is it, Stuart?'

'Fingerprints from David Brown's neck, sir. They've got a fairly good match with your man Callum. Seems he's got form. Used to run with a gang of street thugs out of Trinity. But he dropped off the radar about ten years back. Nobody's seen him since.'

'Well, he's back now. Thanks, constable.' McLean turned back to Roberts. It was time to try a different tack.

'Look, Mr Roberts. We know you did this under duress. You're a lawyer, not a murderer. We can protect you, and we're already protecting your wife. But you've got to help us. If we don't find Chloe soon it'll be too late.'

Roberts sat in his uncomfortable plastic chair and stared at the wall opposite. He wouldn't meet McLean's gaze and his face had turned a deathly white.

'They got to Fergus. They must have done. I can't say anything. They'll know, and they'll kill me.'

And Christopher Roberts would say no more.

'Get an All Ports out on Callum.'

McLean sat in the tiny incident room with DC MacBride and Grumpy Bob, trying not to let his frustration at Roberts get the better of him. It bothered him that he couldn't place the big man, either. The name was familiar, but the prison CCTV footage didn't give a good enough view of his face. 'See if we can't get a decent photo of him too, eh?'

It occurred to him that he was not meant to be part of the ongoing investigation into Chloe's disappearance. It was Grumpy Bob's case. But the old sergeant seemed quite happy to defer to him. Beside him, DC MacBride picked up his airwave set and started making calls, his soft voice filling the silence as McLean stared at the photographs pinned to the wall. The missing dead body and her preserved organs. Why would somebody steal those? What could they possibly want them for?

'Christ I'm stupid.' McLean shot to his feet.

'What?' Grumpy Bob looked up and DC MacBride ended his call.

'It's so bloody obvious. I should have thought of it days ago.'

'Thought of what?'

'Where they've taken the dead body.' McLean pointed at the photos on the wall. 'Where they're going to kill Chloe.'

61

The evening sky burned an angry red as they sped through the gates to Farquhar House. Tommy McAllister had wasted no time in removing his machinery from the site, but the house itself was still boarded up, broken blue and white police tape fluttering in the breeze. The lower windows looked like they'd not been touched since the last time he had been there, and the door was securely fixed with a large hasp and padlock.

'Crowbar, I think. Can't hang around waiting for the keys.' McLean sent DC MacBride off to the car in search of a suitable jimmy whilst he and Bob looked around for clues that anything was amiss. The ground was so churned up with the mess of a building site it was impossible to tell.

The constable returned with a long tyre iron, and after a few moments of frantic levering, the hasp peeled away from the wooden door with a satisfying rip. Inside, the building smelled musty and unused, completely silent and dark as a grave. McLean switched on his torch and crossed the empty, cavernous hallway to the stairs leading down to the basement. The door had been closed and locked. He gave it a hearty kick and the woodworm-infested frame buckled in. Dust billowed up all around, making them cough, but he pressed on, down the stairs, moved by a terrible sense of urgency.

The lights had gone from the basement, but the dark hole in the wall was still there. McLean shone his torch through it, and for an instant his heart stopped. A body lay spread-eagled in the centre of the hidden room, her hands and feet nailed to the wooden floor with shiny new nails. Her head was tilted back in an endless scream of agony and her stomach had been cut open, ribs glistening white in the torchlight. He flicked the beam up to the walls, and there were the six alcoves, their precious organs tucked away in preserving jars.

Then a muffled sob reached his ears. He looked around, bringing the torch to bear on a second figure, huddled against the wall, chains around her ankles and wrists, twisting up to a shiny new hook in the plaster. She was still wearing her 1920s flapper-girl outfit, though somewhere along the line she had lost her cloche hat. Tears had run rivers of dark mascara down her cheeks and her wrists were red raw with struggling against her restraints. But she was alive. Chloe Spiers was alive.

McLean clambered into the hidden room, feeling the temperature drop like it was a fridge. He shone the torch at his own face, letting her see who he was, then bent down to remove the duct tape that had been gagging her.

'It's all right, Chloe. I'm a policeman. We're going to take you home.' She hugged her knees close to her chest, not saying anything as he undid her bonds. Every so often her eyes would sweep the dark room and the ill-defined hump in the middle. How long had she been locked up in here with that body? How much of it had she seen before they'd turned the lights off and left her alone with it?

'Come on. Here.' He pulled her up, half carrying her out of the room to where the others were waiting.

'He was going to cut me open. Like he did to her all those years ago. She told me. In the dark.' Chloe's voice was a pale simulacrum of her mother's, quietly trembling as she clung to him.

'It's all right, Chloe. No one's going to hurt you now. You're safe.' McLean tried to think of soothing things to say as her words began to sink in. 'Who was going to hurt you, Chloe?'

'The scarred man. He killed her. He wants to kill me.'

And so it all began to make sense. If insanity could ever make sense.

62

Back-up had arrived by the time they emerged from the house, McLean carrying Chloe, who clung to him as if her very life depended on it. It took some time to convince her to go with the paramedics; she only relented when he told her he was going to get the scarred man. They left Grumpy Bob behind to do the clear-up and take the credit when the superintendent arrived, since it was his investigation after all. DC MacBride drove, and it took long minutes to negotiate their way out of the narrow drive-way as more and more police cars arrived.

'Where're we going, sir?' he asked as they finally made it onto the Dalry Road. McLean told him the address of the house not far from where his grandmother had lived. Where he'd been taken in a car chauffeured by a suited Jethro Callum. Not far from where the dead body of David Brown had been found. Did the property not even back onto that forgotten lane?

'Head towards Grange. Better put the blue lights on.' He gave MacBride the directions then slumped back in the passenger seat and watched the evening traffic getting out of the way.

'How did you guess, sir? That she'd be there?'

'I had a letter from Jonas Carstairs. He confessed to the mur-der and named all the others we suspected. And he said there was a sixth man, just as we thought. He didn't name him though, which wasn't very helpful. But he did say that he was back in

Edinburgh and would be trying to perform the ritual again. Where else would he do it?'

'That's a bit of a leap, isn't it, sir?'

'Not really. I should've seen it earlier. As soon as we ID'd Roberts as the man who picked Chloe up. He was acting for someone wanting to buy the old house. Someone prepared to pay over the odds for it. I just didn't know who. I concentrated on that, when I should have been asking why.'

'And you know who now?'

'The scarred man, Chloe said. I met a scarred man a few days ago. An old friend of my gran's. Said he was in town to sort out some unfinished business. Christ I can be thick at times. Gavin Spenser. Jethro Callum is his chauffeur; more than that, I'd guess. And Roberts was acting for Spenser Industries. I saw their logo on his papers at McAllister's. Just didn't recognise it until now.'

They drove the rest of the way in tense silence. Closer to the house, MacBride turned off the flashing lights to avoid raising the alarm. McLean directed him towards the address down streets he had known all his life, past houses that had always been familiar to him, but which were now alien and menacing.

'Pull over here.' He pointed to an open gateway. Light spilled out from several downstairs windows over the shiny Bentley parked by the porch. Approaching the house, McLean felt an uncharacteristic shudder of fear run through him, and then he saw that the front door was wide open. He stepped into the house, wanting to hurry, all his years of training urging him to be careful. The hall was dominated by a dark oak staircase that rose up towards the back of the house. Ornate panelled doors led off to either side, all closed except one.

'Shouldn't we –' MacBride started to say. McLean stopped him

375

with a raised hand, then pointed towards the back of the house, indicating for him to look there first. He stepped quietly across the hall towards the open door, imagined he could hear the faintest of noises from the room beyond. Wet, unpleasant noises. Taking a deep breath, he pushed the door wide and stepped in.

The private study was filled with surprisingly modern office furniture. A small desk near the door would have been where a secretary worked, but its typist's chair was empty. Beyond it there was an open space with a couple of functional couches, a low table between them, and beyond that a large desk. Behind which sat Gavin Spenser.

He was naked from the waist up, his clothes neatly folded and placed over a low filing cabinet to one side. Lazy flies crawled over pale flesh and buzzed around the thick blood that hung from his fingertips, dry and dull. His scarred face was white, blind eyes staring in a final expression of terror. He'd been dead a while, his chest ripped open. If he had to guess, McLean would have said someone had removed his heart.

A shadow of movement, and instinct kicked in. He ducked, twisting around as a huge man lunged at him. Jethro Callum held a hunting knife in one hand, and moved with a fluid grace quite at odds with his bulk. Never assume a big man will be slow. That was what they'd taught him in self-defence. McLean dodged the blade, moving in to parry the expected thrust. But instead of trying to fight, Callum stepped back, reaching up with the knife to his own neck.

'Oh no you don't!' McLean leapt forward, knocked the knife out of Callum's hand. Together they crashed to the floor. McLean had the advantage of being on top, but his attacker was a good foot taller and probably half as heavy again. The muscles beneath his leather jacket were like rock, taut and straining. He didn't so much push McLean off as fling him bodily away before rolling over and reaching out for the knife.

McLean pulled a pair of handcuffs out of his pocket, twisting them open as he sprung forward. He slipped on something squelchy on the carpet, losing his balance and pitching onto Callum's back. They both crashed to the floor again, but this time McLean managed to get one cuff on. Callum reached out for the knife, fat fingers scraping at the bloody carpet in desperation. Using the cuff as leverage, McLean twisted the restrained hand up hard into the point between Callum's shoulder blades, kneeling on his neck and grinding his face into the carpet. And still the big man stretched for the knife, thrashing his legs and torso to try and dislodge the heavy weight of detective inspector on his back.

There was no way that he could get control of Callum's other arm, and neither could he get to the knife before him. McLean looked around for something else to use as a weapon, eyes lighting on a china vase sitting on a small oak occasional table just in reach. He grabbed it, feeling an instant's regret as he recognised it as a very valuable Clarice Cliff, and brought it smashing down on Callum's head. The big man grunted, then relaxed onto the floor, unconscious. Footsteps clattered across the hall outside and McLean looked around to see DC MacBride appear in the doorway.

'Thanks for the help,' he said.

63

'Spenser recruited him from a street gang over ten years ago, took him on as a personal bodyguard. He's been working for the old man in America all that time, which is how he dropped off our radar. And you'll never guess who one of his known associates was, back in the day.'

'Donnie Murdo?'

'In one. My guess is Murdo was working for Spenser when he ran down Alison. Probably trying to take the heat off the search for Chloe until he'd finished with her. Christ, what a stupid, petty reason to kill someone.' Grumpy Bob kicked out at an innocent wastepaper basket, sending it and its contents flying in different directions.

'Any reason why he'd suddenly decide to murder his boss?' McLean nodded towards the hulking form of Jethro Callum. They were watching him through the one-way mirror that looked into the interview room. He had a good idea why, but it wasn't a happy place to go.

'I guess we'd better ask him.'

'OK, Bob. Let's get this over with.' McLean grimaced out of the chair; he'd managed to crack three ribs and had picked up a bruise the size and shape of Poland in the fight. He began to have some inkling of just how David Brown might have felt before he died.

Callum didn't move when they pushed open the door, neither did he register their presence when McLean settled himself down gingerly into the chair opposite. GrumpyBob unwrapped two tapes and slipped them into the machine, setting it to record their interview, and still the burly chauffeur said nothing. McLean went through the formalities, then finally leant forward, resting his elbows on the table between him and the murderer.

'Why did you kill Gavin Spenser, Mr Callum?'

Slowly, the bodyguard lifted his head. He seemed to have difficulty focusing his eyes, and his expression was one of shock, as if he had only just noticed where he was.

'Who're you?' he asked.

'We've been through all that, Mr Callum. I'm Detective Inspector McLean, and this is my colleague, Detective Sergeant Laird.'

'Where am I?' Callum pulled at his cuffs. 'Why am I here?'

'Are you seriously expecting me to believe you don't know, Mr Callum?' McLean studied the bodyguard's face. It was something only a mother could love, scarred from numerous fights, nose flat and squint, eyes just slightly too close together to have any hope of conveying intelligence. But there was something in there, lurking behind the bewilderment. He could sense it, and in that instant, McLean knew that it sensed him too. Callum stopped straining against his handcuffs, instead slumping forward as his whole body relaxed.

'I know you. I've smelled you before. You drew the circle around yourself but it won't protect you from me. We're destined to be together, you and I. It's in your blood. His blood.' Where Callum's earlier words had been slurred and hesitant, now he spoke clearly, clipped. It was a voice of control and power, used to being obeyed. Another person entirely.

'Why did you kill Gavin Spenser?' McLean repeated his earlier question.

'He was their leader. The last one. I killed him to be free.'

379

'The last one? You've killed others?'

'You know who I've killed, inspector. And you know they all deserved to die.'

'No, I don't. Who did you kill? What were their names? Why did they deserve to die?'

Callum stared straight at him, face set like stone. And then his features softened again, as if he were remembering something highly emotive. His eyes went wide and his mouth dropped open. He looked left and right, around the small interview room with panicked twists of the head. He pulled at his restraints once, twice, then realising it was hopeless, slumped forwards. Tears filled his eyes, rolling over the scars on his cheeks as he started to mumble in a frightened, childlike voice.

'OhGodOhGodOhGodOhGodOhGod.'

McLean looked at the big man, rocking gently in his chair. Had his hands not been in cuffs, he was sure Callum would have curled up in a ball in the corner of the room. There had been something there, briefly, but now whatever mad instinct had driven the man to commit such a brutal murder was gone, and he was left alone with the memory of what he had done.

'Interview suspended at twenty-one fifty-two.' McLean stood up, gasping as his ribs protested, and clicked off the tape recorder. 'Have him escorted back to the cells. We'll try again in the morning.'

Bob opened the interview room door and called in a couple of uniformed constables. They flanked Callum before one of them reached down and began to undo the cuffs.

It happened in an instant. The bodyguard roared a great scream of rage, exploded out of his chair and lashed out with his fists. The two constables went flying, crashing into the walls. Behind him, McLean could hear Grumpy Bob move to block the doorway, but far from making a break for it, Callum turned to the large mirror that hung on the wall, behind which was the viewing room. He lurched towards it, pulling his head back as he did, and butted it with all his might. Cracks speared up from the point of impact, but it didn't smash. Enraged, Callum pulled his head back again and hammered it once more into the fractured glass. This time the mirror gave, breaking into long shards of lethally sharp glass. One poked up from the bottom of the frame, fully a foot long and needle-sharp. A glistening bead of Callum's blood balanced on the point of it. The bodyguard turned, facing McLean with that powerful, controlled stare. Not scared, not mad, but knowing. Not the prey here, but the predator.

'You'll understand soon,' he said in that voice that wasn't his. Then turned, pulled his head up, arching his back ready to smash forwards and plunge the glass shard deep into his brain. But the two constables were on him, grabbing his arms and wrestling them behind him. Suddenly the room was full of bodies, swarming over Callum like ants. The big man writhed and screamed, but was slowly pushed to the ground, his hands cuffed tightly behind him. When they finally pulled him to his feet and turned him back around, McLean could see ugly cuts in his forehead and nose. A glass splinter had pierced his left eye, leaking aqueous humour down his cheek in a parody of tears.

'Jesus Christ,' he swore. 'Get him to hospital, quick. And keep him restrained. I don't want him having another chance to do that.'

Out in the corridor, McLean leant against the wall and tried to suppress the shaking that had taken hold of him. Grumpy Bob stood by his side, silent for a while.

'He wasn't trying to escape, was he,' the sergeant said finally.

'No. He was trying to kill himself. Like all the others.'

'Others? What do you mean?'

McLean looked up at his old friend. 'Forget it, Bob. I think I need a drink.'

'I second that. It's hours past the end of my shift, and we've at least one success to celebrate.'

'Where's MacBride?' McLean asked. 'He could do with one too.'

'Probably down in the incident room feverishly typing up reports. You know what he's like. Keen as mustard.'

'Don't knock it, Bob.'

'Far from it, sir.' The old sergeant grinned, throwing off some of the shock of recent events. 'If he wants to do the work of two detectives, that's just fine by me. I'm quite happy to be the other one.'

They set off into the bowels of the station, finally arriving at their destination after fending off many congratulations. News of Chloe's safe discovery had spread quickly, unlike the more recent events. The door to the tiny incident room was propped open with a metal chair to let the heat out. Low voices murmured in conversation from within. McLean stepped inside and saw DC MacBride sitting behind his table, the laptop in front of him. Another figure stood talking to him, and she turned as she saw his eyes flick up to meet the inspector's. Emma Baird took two steps towards McLean and then slapped him hard across the face.

'That's for even thinking I could do something so perverse as post crime-scene photos on the internet.'

He lifted his hand to his face, accepting that he probably deserved it. But before he could reach his stinging cheek, she had grabbed him, pulled him towards her and planted a long, wet kiss on his lips.

'And that's for finding a way to prove me innocent,' she added once she had broken away. McLean felt his ears turning bright red. He looked to DC MacBride, but the constable was suddenly very interested in his report. Grumpy Bob was staring off down the corridor in a purposeful manner.

'Ah, sod it, Stuart. You can write that tomorrow,' McLean said. 'Let's go to the pub.'

64

The tinny little buzzing of his alarm clock broke through the pain in his head, reminding him with far too much enthusiasm that it was six o'clock and time to get up. McLean groaned and rolled over to hit the snooze button. Perhaps his hangover would go away in the next ten minutes. It was worth a try. He bumped into something solid beside him and couldn't for the life of him work out what it was. Then it grunted and moved and he was suddenly very wide awake.

Sitting up in bed and rubbing the sleep out of his eyes, he looked down on the prone form of Emma Baird and felt a curious mixture of anger and fear. He'd slept in this bed alone for so long, always keeping his relationships professional, always keeping people at arm's length. A therapist might have said he was afraid to commit, and they'd be right. After Kirsty, the thought of getting close to anyone else was just too painful. And now, after a couple of dinners and a night spent drinking with half of the station, she was asleep alongside him.

He tried to remember the night before. They'd both celebrated having found Chloe safe, but that was another part of his barricade; he never let himself get so drunk he lost control. Never so drunk he couldn't remember what he'd done.

She'd been angry with him, Emma. She'd heard all the things he'd said to Duguid outside the SOC offices at Force HQ. About how he had planned to use his friendship to investigate the leaked

384

photographs. It didn't matter how much he explained, how much he tried to persuade her that what he had meant was different to what she had assumed. From her point of view he had been playing her. She'd only really relented when he'd apologised and begged her forgiveness. But that was women for you, wasn't it?

Then they'd been thrown out of the pub by the cleaners. God only knew what time it was in the morning, and there'd be a fair few sore heads in the station come shift change. Had he suggested whisky at his place, or had it been Grumpy Bob? That memory was a little hazy, but he did recall thinking that company of any sort would be better than returning to the cold, empty, silent flat alone. So a gang of them had come back, and most likely finished off his entire supply of malt. That, at least, would explain the pounding in his head.

Trying not to groan, McLean rolled over and out of bed. He was still wearing his boxer shorts, which was something. His suit was folded over the back of the chair, his shirt and socks in the laundry basket. These were automatic things; he didn't have to think about the routine. But equally, he wouldn't have been so conscientious had he been half cut the night before, or gripped in a fever of unlikely passion. And the more he thought about it, the more he remembered going to bed alone. Grumpy Bob had stayed the course, but MacBride had passed out on the floor, and Emma? Yes, Emma had fallen asleep in the armchair. He'd dug a blanket out of the closet and draped it over her before putting himself to bed. She must have woken up in the night and crawled in under his duvet. Well, that said something pretty loud and clear.

The shower managed to shift some of the grey fog from his mind, but he was still slow when he stepped out and dried himself down. His cracked ribs protested, the bruise around his torso turning yellow at the edges. Towel round his middle, he filled the

385

kettle and set it to boil. Then, taking a deep breath, he went back into his bedroom. Emma was still asleep, but she had rolled over, throwing the duvet askance. Her short black hair covered her face, but pretty much everything else was on view. A trail of clothes covered the floor from door to bedside; items of underwear he'd not seen in a good few years. Not this side of a crime scene, anyway. As quietly as he could, he gathered up his suit, fetched a shirt and a clean set of underclothes from the wardrobe, and retreated to his study to dress.

The Dictaphone sat on his desk, accusing him of callous disregard for the memory of the dead. He ignored that part of his mind, knowing it was just self-indulgence, a protective cocoon of guilt. He knew he'd never throw away the tape, just as he knew he would never forget Kirsty. But perhaps after all these years he really should be taking the advice of all his friends and trying to move on. Shit happened in the world, but sometimes things came good. They'd found Chloe Spiers alive, after all.

Dressed, he went through to the kitchen and made coffee. The carton of milk in the fridge hadn't yet given birth, but it would need inducing soon if it wasn't going to explode. Poking his head into the living room and the spare bedroom revealed one sleeping detective constable and one snoring detective sergeant, both of whom would need coffee and bacon butties. He grabbed his keys from the table in the hall and headed out to the corner shop.

By the time he had returned, the bathroom door was firmly closed and the sound of the shower running hissed through it. Grumpy Bob sat at the kitchen table looking like he'd slept in his suit, and as McLean began making bacon butties, DC MacBride stumbled in, looking slightly nervous.

'Morning, constable,' McLean said, noting how MacBride

winced in pain at the sound. Well, fair enough. He'd drunk the most. But his liver was still young. He'd survive.

'What was I drinking last night?' he asked.

'In the pub, or here?' Grumpy Bob scratched at his chin. He'd be needing the electric razor he kept in his locker at the station.

Confusion spread across MacBride's face, but before he could say anything, a light knocking came at the door.

'Take over the butties, Bob. There's brown sauce in the cupboard.' McLean went through to the hall and opened the door. Jenny Spiers stood on the communal landing.

'Tony, I –'

'Jenny. Hi –'

They both spoke at the same time, then both stopped speaking to let the other one go first. McLean moved aside from the door.

'Come on in. I was just making bacon butties.'

Before he could say any more, she had wrapped him in a huge embrace. 'Thank you for finding my baby,' she said. Then burst into hysterical sobs.

Emma chose that moment to come out of the bathroom. She was wearing McLean's old towelling dressing gown, which revealed rather more thigh than perhaps it should have done. Her hair was spiky where she had rubbed it dry, and she smelled strongly of tea tree oil shampoo. The temperature in the hallway plummeted as the two women stared at each other in silence. McLean could feel Jenny tense as she still held onto him.

'Umm. Jenny, this is Emma. Emma, Jenny.' The tension didn't ease. Then a voice shouted, 'Coming through!' and DC MacBride stumbled out of the kitchen, pushing past Emma on his way into the bathroom. The door slammed and behind it they could all hear the noise of the toilet seat being lifted, followed by quiet retching.

'We had a bit of a party last night.' McLean tried to tactfully extract himself from Jenny's embrace, though she seemed reluctant to let him go. 'It looks like young Detective Constable MacBride may have had a little too much cask-strength Bowmore.'

'More likely the tequila slammers he had in the pub,' Emma said, and padded off in the direction of McLean's bedroom.

'How is Chloe, by the way?' He asked, hoping to distract Jenny, who's gaze had followed the other woman with a sort of haunted, disbelieving look. She dragged her attention back to him, fixed a smile onto her face.

'The doctors say she'll be fine, physically. She was badly dehydrated when you found her. Thank God you did. I really don't know how to thank you enough.'

'It's my job, Jenny.' McLean steered her into the kitchen, where Grumpy Bob was standing at the cooker wearing a long apron with an amusing bikini motif printed on it.

'I just don't know how she'll cope mentally. Being chained up like that. With a corpse.'

McLean wondered just how much Jenny knew. 'She told you?' he asked. She nodded, accepting a proffered mug of coffee. 'Then she's taking the right steps towards dealing with it. She's a tough kid. I'm guessing she gets that from her mother.'

Jenny sipped her coffee, sitting at the kitchen table and saying nothing. Grumpy Bob kept his silence, diligently constructing breakfast for an army. Somewhere in the background, the toilet flushed. Then Jenny put her mug down on the table and looked McLean straight in the eye.

'She said they chose her because of you. They wanted to get to you through me. Why would they do that? I hardly know you.'

'You came to my grandmother's funeral.' It was the only thing he could think of. 'Spenser must have been watching me even then. He was behind it all from the start, trying to discredit me, hiring McReadie to set me up, killing Alison to slow us down. He needed to get me off the investigation into the dead girl, and he needed someone to take her place. Chloe was just the right age. I'm sorry, Jenny. If you'd never met me, they'd have found someone else.'

'One of these days, Tony, you're going to have to tell me how you do it.'

McLean stood in the post-mortem theatre for what felt like the millionth time in the past fortnight. He liked Cadwallader, enjoyed the older man's sharp wit and sense of humour, but he'd rather have met him in the pub. Even the opera would have been preferable.

'How I do what?' he asked, shifting on the balls of his feet as the pathologist went through the motions of examining the body of Gavin Spenser.

'Peter Andrews. You knew that there'd be traces of blood and skin under his nails, didn't you.'

'Call it a hunch.'

'Did the hunch tell you whose blood and skin it would be?'

'Buchan Stewart.'

'You see, that's what I mean, Tony.' Cadwallader stood up, staring at the inspector, quite oblivious to the fact that he was holding Spenser's liver in his hand. 'We've got all this expensive technological wizardry here, costing millions of pounds of taxpayers' money, and you already know the answer before you ask the question.'

'Do me a favour, Angus. Keep that nugget of information to yourself.' It was bad enough that Jonathan Okolo and Sally Dent were down in the annals of history as murderers when it was far more likely they'd been unwitting pawns in Spenser's sick game. There was no need to cause Peter Andrews' family any more anguish.

'Gladly.' Cadwallader finally noticed the dripping liver and placed it on a stainless-steel tray to be weighed. 'It would be very embarrassing to have to admit I missed it in the first place.'

He went back to guddling around in the dead man's chest, taking out unidentifiable bits, peering at them, weighing them and placing them in individual containers; as happy as a pig in shit. Pity poor Tracy, who would have to put them all back again and stitch the cadaver up later.

'So would you like to hazard a cause of death?' McLean asked when he felt he could take no more.

'Heart failure due to massive loss of blood would be my best guess. The knife wound to the throat went deep enough to sever the carotid artery and leave marks on the neck vertebrae. We've got the weapon, haven't we?'

Tracy produced a plastic bag with the hunting knife in it. Cadwallader weighed it in his hand, inspecting the blade and holding it to the dead man's neck.

'Yes, that would do it. And it would also explain these marks here on his sternum and ribs. The killer cut him open to remove his heart. It's a tricky organ to get to without either a great deal of skill or being very messy indeed.'

'Can you hazard a time of death?'

'Thirty-six to forty-eight hours. He'd been sitting there quite a while. I'm surprised your man hadn't made a run for the border. Could've been in a different country before you found the body.'

McLean did the maths. Spenser had been killed not long after David Brown. Dead in the bushes on the boundary of Spenser's garden. Killed by Jethro Callum in a violent fury.

'He was waiting for us, in the room where we found him.' McLean nodded at the eviscerated man lying on the table. 'He tried to kill himself. Right in front of me.'

'Ah. I see a pattern emerging.'

So did McLean, but before he could say anything more, his jacket pocket started to buzz and vibrate furiously. It was such an unusual sensation, it took him a long time to realise that his mobile phone was ringing. He flipped it open, noticing an almost full battery read-out.

'Do carry on without me,' he said to Cadwallader, then stalked out of the room. Past the doors, he answered the call. 'McLean.'

'MacBride here, sir. There's been an incident at the hospital. It's Callum. He's collapsed.'

Violence is all it knows. McLean recalled the words of Jonas Carstairs' letter. And then names: Peter Andrews, watching Jonathan Okolo die violently in a city centre pub; Sally Dent, witnessing Peter Andrews taking his own life; David Brown, watching Sally's body plunge through the glass ceiling of Waverley Station, smashing into the windscreen of the train he was driving; Jethro Callum breaking David's bones, throttling the life out of him; Callum smashing his head into the glass window, trying to kill himself. What had he said? 'You'll understand soon.' That voice so different and strange.

Despite the summer heat, a shiver ran through his whole body. Maybe he did understand. And maybe he knew what had to be done. If he was wrong, he was going to have a hard time explaining himself, but if he was right? Well, that didn't really bear thinking about.

65

The hospital had a sad familiarity for him. McLean had visited his grandmother here too many times to count. The nurses all smiled and said hello as he walked the corridors; he knew most of them by name. Walking beside him, DC MacBride blushed at the attention. A junior doctor, looking tired and harassed, walked up to them as they strode down the corridor.

'Inspector McLean?'

McLean nodded. 'What's the story, doc?'

'It's hard to say. I've never seen anything like it before. Mr Callum's a very fit man, young, too. But his organs are packing up one by one. If we can't stop it, or stabilise him, he could die in hours.'

'Hours? But yesterday he was fine. Better than fine.' McLean felt his bruised ribs, remembered the muscled man he'd fought with not twenty-four hours before. Another piece of the puzzle slotting into place, a picture emerging that he really didn't want to see.

'We're working on the hypothesis that it's some form of steroid reaction. He didn't get the size he is just by pumping iron, and whatever he was on might have made him over-sensitive to something we've given him. But I've never seen anything come on so quickly before. I treated him for his damaged eye yesterday evening, and apart from a little hyperventilation, he seemed fine.'

'Did he speak to you?'

'What? Oh, no. He didn't say a word.'

'Didn't struggle, didn't try to kill himself?'

'No. But he was restrained, and there were three constables with him at all times.'

'Where is he now?'

'We've put him in one of the single rooms up by the coma ward.'

'So that if he becomes too violent, no one will be disturbed?'

'Well, yes. But we've got all the intensive care monitoring kit up there as well. Here, I'll show you the way.'

'That's all right. I know where it is. I'm sure you've got a hundred and one things more important to worry about than a murderer who's going nowhere.'

They left the doctor behind, looking slightly puzzled. McLean led the way through the miles of faceless corridors, MacBride trotting at his heels like a faithful hound to keep up.

'What are we doing here, sir?'

'I'm here to interview our only surviving murder suspect before this mysterious illness kills him,' McLean said as they approached the room he had been seeking. A bored-looking PC sat on an uncomfortable plastic chair outside, reading an Ian Rankin novel. 'You're here because Grumpy Bob's developed a talent for hiding when he knows I'm about to do something the chief superintendent won't approve of.'

'Inspector. Sir. No one told me . . .' The constable stood to attention, trying to hide the book behind his back.

'Don't panic, Steve. I just want a word with the prisoner. Why don't you go off and get yourself a cuppa, eh? DC MacBride'll keep an eye on things.'

'What do you want me to do?' MacBride asked as the relieved policeman scurried off to the canteen.

'You stand guard here.' McLean opened the door and stepped through. 'And don't let anyone in.'

The room was small and soulless, a single narrow window opening onto a view of sun-blasted concrete and glass. Two plastic chairs lined up against the wall, and a narrow cabinet had been pressed into service as a bedside table. Jethro Callum lay at the centre of a bewildering array of humming machinery. Tubes pumped noxious-looking fluids to and from his body. He looked nothing at all like the fit bodyguard McLean had wrestled with just the afternoon before. Propped up in a mound of pillows, his face was sunken and pale, his eyes dark hollows. Most of his hair had fallen out, some still lying on his pillow in dead heaps. The skin on his scalp was mottled with vivid red spots. His arms lay on top of the blankets, fat with muscle but all the tone gone. He still had his bulk, but now it hindered his breathing, pinning him down far more effectively than the leather restraint straps that tied him to the bed frame.

'You came. I knew you would.' Callum's voice was barely audible above the hum of the life-support machinery. But it wasn't the voice of the bodyguard. This was the other one, the voice that had threatened and promised. The voice that had a strangely hypnotic power behind it.

McLean picked up one of the chairs, wedging it under the door handle. He took the emergency cord and looped it out of reach. Then he leant down to study the machines for a moment. Wires trailed from an ECG to a slim sensor attached to one of Callum's fingers. McLean slipped it off, pushing it swiftly onto his own. The machine gave a few hurried bleeps then settled back down into a steady rhythm. He inspected the other machines, but only the ECG seemed to be plumbed into the emergency monitoring system. He searched for the switches and turned them off, one by one. Medical science kept the body alive, but Jethro Callum had really perished the moment he had killed David Brown. Whatever it was that had taken hold of his soul then had been slowly devouring his flesh ever since.

'Tell me about the girl.' McLean settled himself into the other chair.

'What girl?'

'You know who I'm talking about. The girl they killed in their sick ceremony.'

'Ah, yes. Her.' Callum sounded oddly distant, like an emphysemic ventriloquist's dummy, but the pleasure in his voice was sickening. 'Little Maggie Donaldson. Pretty little thing. Can't have been much more than sixteen. Pure, of course. That's what attracted me to her. But they soiled her, all of them. One after the other. The old one, he knew what he was doing. He trapped me inside her and then they split her up. Took a part of me each.'

'Why did they do it?'

'Why do your kind ever do anything? They wanted to live for ever.'

'And you? What happens to you?'

'I go on. In you.'

McLean looked at the pathetic figure dying in front of him. This was what it was all about. This was what had caused all the shit that had happened to him since they'd discovered the dead girl in the basement of Farquhar House. This was what had killed innocent people, twisting them to its purpose without a care. This was why Alison Kydd had been run down in the street. He was filled with an urge to strangle the man. It would be so easy to wrap his hands around his throat and squeeze the life out of him. Or better still, to grind something into his blinded eye, and on through to his brain. He had a pen in his pocket, that would be enough of a weapon. You just needed the right entry point, the right leverage. There were so many ways to kill a man. So many . . .

'Oh no you don't.' He shook the alien thoughts from his head. Barnaby Smythe, Buchan Stewart, Jonas Carstairs, Gavin Spenser. They had all sat calmly, unrestrained as they were butchered and killed. And Fergus McReadie, too. He had taken his own life just because of a word. Now McLean knew why. They had been in thrall to that voice, connected to it by an act of savagery to which they had all been party. But he hadn't killed the girl, hadn't planned to murder Chloe. There was no connection between him and this monster.

'Oh but there is, inspector. You made the circle whole. You're as much a part of this as any of them. More so. You have a strength of spirit they all lacked. His blood runs through your veins. You are a fit vessel to contain me.'

This time the persuasion was like a wall of darkness, pushing against him. McLean saw glimpses of gruesome scenes: Smythe's face contorted in pain as the knife bit into his grey-haired chest; Jonas Carstairs' heart still beating beneath his exposed ribs; Gavin Spenser sitting calmly, only his eyes showing his true state of mind as his throat was slowly cut. And with each image came a surge of power, a feeling of unrestrained excitement and joy. He could have this, be this. He could live for ever.

'I don't think so.' McLean pushed himself out of his chair and crossed to the bed. He reached up to the saline drip, twisting the tap around until the flow was cut off. 'I understand now. I didn't want to believe it, but I guess I have to. You need the violence to pass from one host to the next. Without it you're stuck. And when this one goes, so do you. Back to wherever it was they summoned you from with their foul ceremony.'

'What are you doing? I command you to kill this body.' Callum fought against the straps and the sheets that pinned him to the bed, but it was a weak effort, and he fell swiftly to a fit of gurgling coughs.

'You're doing a good enough job of that yourself.' McLean shrugged off another wave of compulsion, weaker this time, more desperate. He sat himself down again, staring at the wasted form in the bed. 'I'm guessing you never meant to stay in poor Jethro this long, but you had to cover your tracks and that took time. He was never strong enough to carry you, was he?'

'Kill me.' The voice was little more than a faltering breath now. 'Set me free.'

'Not this time.' McLean settled himself into the chair. Watched and waited as Callum's last few breaths rattled out of him like escaping insects.

'This time you die of natural causes.'

Epilogue

Christopher Roberts sat at the table with his head drooped low. He smelled of too many nights in the cells, and his once-fine suit was quite ruined. McLean stood with his back to the wall of the interview room and considered him for a moment, trying to dredge up some sympathy for the man. Failing.

'Gavin Spenser is dead, and Jethro Callum too.'

Roberts looked up as the words sank in, a gleam of hope in his eyes. But before he could say anything, McLean spoke again.

'The thing is, Mr Roberts, I'm almost certain that you were coerced into your actions, and we could well have taken that into consideration. Chloe's safe, though I doubt she'll ever forget being locked in a cellar for days with a mutilated corpse. I could almost see my way to persuading her not to press charges against you.'

'You'd do that?' Roberts looked up at him like a beaten puppy. McLean stepped forward, pulled out the seat and dropped himself down into it.

'No. I won't. Not now. You had your chance, Mr Roberts, when we brought your wife in for her protection. You could have helped us then, and we might have been able to catch Callum before he killed Spenser. As it is, all the people I want to charge with abduction and murder are dead. Except you.'

'But . . . but . . . I was forced. They made me . . .'

'No they didn't, Mr Roberts. You made yourself. You had it all and you wanted more. And now you're going to go to jail for a very long time.'

A grey, windswept cemetery overlooking the Forth. Summer had finally broken; now squalls of rain rushed down the far side of the Firth, leaving the little party dry but cold. McLean was pleasantly surprised at the number of people who'd turned out for the burial. DC MacBride and Grumpy Bob were there, as was Emma. Chief Superintendent McIntyre had found time from her busy schedule to come too, though she fretted a bit and kept looking at her watch. Angus Cadwallader had scandalously brought Tracy with him. But perhaps most surprising was that Chloe Spiers had insisted on coming. She clung to her mother at the graveside, looking down at the plain coffin as the dirt was thrown on top. It had taken some detective work, but he had managed to track down the graves of John and Elspeth Donaldson, and now McLean was making sure that their daughter Maggie was buried alongside them. He hoped no one would ever find out he'd paid for the service himself.

'I still don't understand how you were finally able to identify her,' McIntyre said as they all walked away from the grave.

'We managed to trace a Sighthill builder who went missing in forty-five. That gave us a better idea of the time of death. Mis-Per records are a bit patchy from then, so DC MacBride waded through the *Scotsman* archives. He found a small article about a missing girl. Turns out her mother was a housemaid at Farquhar House. We tracked down a living relative in Canada. DNA profiling did the rest.' It was a slight distortion of the truth, but not much. He'd given MacBride what hints he could, told him to look into it. And McLean could hardly admit where he'd really got the dead girl's name from.

'Most detectives would've been content to have found the killers.'

'You know me, ma'am. I don't like leaving a job half done.'

'Do you think it worked? Do you think they really trapped some demon and used its power to prolong their lives?'

'You should listen to yourself, Jayne. Of course it didn't work. They're all dead, aren't they?' McLean shook his head as if that might dislodge the truth. 'There's no such things as demons.'

'But they were all so fit for their age.'

'Well, except Bertie Farquhar and Toby Johnson. They both died young. No, they lived long because they believed they would. Christ, they couldn't do what they did and not believe it. And they were successful men because they were born into money, had the best education.'

'Let's hope you're right, Tony. This city's bad enough as it is without the supernatural making life a misery for us poor coppers.'

'Gavin Spenser died intestate.' It was a snippet of news that McLean had picked up from the news and which had stuck with him for various uncomfortable reasons. 'He never married, had no family. The lawyers are going mad looking for someone to inherit his fortune. Anyone with a half-decent claim stands to inherit billions. It's a mess. But that's how certain he was he would live for ever.'

'Perhaps there are demons after all. But they're just up here.' McIntyre tapped at her temple with a finger, then twirled it round in little circles.

They reached the cemetery gates and the short line of parked cars waiting to take them all back to their various different lives. A uniformed sergeant stood to attention beside the chief superintendent's car, sandwiched between Phil's elderly rust-coloured Volvo estate and Cadwallader's muddy green Jaguar. McLean's bright red Alfa Romeo was parked off to one side. McIntyre watched in horror as he unlocked it and opened the passenger door for Emma to clamber in.

'Good God, Tony. Is that yours?' she asked.

For a moment, McLean wondered whether she meant the car or Emma. Deciding that even McIntyre couldn't be that rude, he shook his head, trying hard to suppress a grin.

'Not mine, no,' he said. 'It's my dad's.'

He stood in his grandmother's bedroom, looking down at the dressing table with its collection of hairbrushes, make-up brushes and photographs. The black bin liner weighed heavy in his hand, already half-filled with rubbish; the disposable detritus of a life long gone. He should have done this months ago, when it was obvious his grandmother was never going to regain conscious-ness, never return to her home. She had no need of lipstick, disposable hankies, a half-finished roll of extra strong mints, and he had no need of the contents of her wardrobe. Or most of the old photographs that dotted the room, and one in particular.

It hung on the wall, close to the door to the bathroom. Black and white, it showed two men and a woman, Bill McLean, Esther Morrison and A. N. Other. When he'd first noticed it, he'd been intrigued at how little he looked like his grandfather yet how much his own father resembled the other man. How much he himself looked like him. Was this the sordid little secret that his grand-mother had kept, not to be revealed until after she died? Something that she felt she could tell her lawyer but not her grandson? What had the letter said? 'You are plainly not the man she feared you might become.' And then there was Jethro Callum: 'His blood flows through your veins.' The words of a madman, or maybe a demon, but somehow impossible to ignore. Well, it wasn't really difficult to work out what was going on. What had gone on.

He took the photograph down from the wall, flicked it over to see if there was anything written on the back of the frame. Only a neat stencilled mark showing the photo studio who had done the work, their address a street long since bulldozed. It was a professional job, the back sealed with heavy tape. He could cut the photograph out, see if anything had been written on the back of that, but he couldn't really be bothered.

Turning the frame back over, he looked closely at the picture. In her twenties, his grandmother had been quite the looker. She sat between the two men, an arm draped around each shoulder, but she clearly had eyes only for William McLean. The other man was smiling, but there was a coldness in his eyes, a longing for something he couldn't have. Something he might be prepared to take by force. Or was that just being fanciful? McLean shrugged the thought away, pulled open the bin bag and dropped the picture in.

Acknowledgements

This book has been a long time in the writing, but it wouldn't have been written at all if it weren't for Stuart MacBride. It was his suggestion that I stop writing fantasy and instead try my hand at crime fiction, so in many ways it's all his fault. Thanks, Stuart.

I am also indebted to Allan Guthrie, who first alerted me to the possibilities of ebooks and self-publishing, and to my agent, Juliet Mushens, a tiny tornado of energy and leopardskin print. Thanks also to the team at Michael Joseph.

Many helpful people have read drafts of this novel, but particular thanks go to Heather Bain, Keir Allen, John Burrell and Lisa McShine. A special mention also to Graham Crompton for pointing out the obvious fact that veins don't pulse, throb or tick.

And last, but by no means least, thanks to my partner, Barbara, who has not only supported me all these years, but who didn't even complain when I stole her surname for my detective inspector.

The Opening Chapter

Natural Causes first saw light as a short story, published by *Spinetingler* magazine in late 2006. I was new to crime fiction at the time, having spent many years writing comic scripts, fantasy and science fiction. The sum total of my knowledge of the genre came from reading The Hardy Boys and The Famous Five as a child, Agatha Christie as a teenager, and later a few Ian Rankin novels nicked from my father when there was nothing else lying about to read. And, of course, Stuart MacBride's Logan McRae novels, all of which I'd seen in early drafts.

I've known Stuart a long time, and it was he who persuaded me to stop writing about dragons and have a go at something more contemporary and realistic. To that end I wrote half a dozen short stories, all featuring a detective inspector I'd created as a support character in a comic script I pitched, unsuccessfully, to *2000 ad* in the early nineties.

Not being well versed in crime fiction, I was unaware of the Crime Writers Association (CWA) and their Debut Dagger competition for unpublished authors, until *Spinetingler*'s founding-editor Sandra Ruttan mentioned it to me. I had begun the process of turning *Natural Causes* from a short story into a full-length novel by then, and it seemed a good idea to enter it for the 2007 Debut Dagger.

The competition is judged on the opening 3,000 words, along with a synopsis. I had begun the novel with the same opening as the short story, but felt there was a need for something a bit more shocking to grab the attention of the judges. Since the story revolves around a ritual killing, I set about writing a description of that killing, some sixty-five years before the main events of the book unfolds. And what better way to shock than to write it from the point of view of the victim?

It obviously worked, in as much as the book was short-listed that year. I have always had rather mixed feelings about the scene, though. On the one hand it is undoubtedly a powerful hook that sets up the background to the story. On the other, it's a 500-word graphic description of a brutal, ritual gang-rape and murder.

Readers have had mixed feelings about the opening chapter, too. A few have been put off the book altogether, whilst many have commented that the tone of the opening chapter is markedly different from the rest of the story. I still like it as a piece of writing, particularly the final sentence, but it would make more sense perhaps in a work of horror.

And so I have reverted to the original opening chapter; the one I wrote when I started the short story, some time in late 2005. I don't think the book loses anything for the omission of those initial five hundred words, but if you want to judge for yourself, or see what all the fuss was about, they're printed below. Be warned though; they are not for the squeamish.

The Original Chapter 1

She screams when the first nail goes in.

Bright pain rips through her hand as she struggles against him, pinned to the floor by the weight of his body. This isn't right. He shouldn't hurt her. He's a good man, a handsome man. A kind man. He helped her family through the war.

'Please. Don't.' She tries to scream but a hand clasps over her mouth, forcing it closed. Figures move in the shadowy edges of her vision, pawing at her, holding her down, breathing in the heavy darkness. Someone grabs her wrist, pulls her arm wide. Her fingers crack against the floor. Hammer hits nail, ripping skin and cartilage, forcing another scream out through her nose. She kicks out, struggling against the weight on top of her and the cold steel pins that gouge through her flesh. Crucified, her hands slide slippery against the metal as she scrabbles to break free, foiled by the jagged and bent heads, the shafts sunk deep into the wooden floor.

His weight lifts off her, and she catches a glimpse of his face in the darkness. His eyes gleam, his features blurred by her tears, distorted as if something is trying to burst out through his skin. She thrashes against him as he drags up her dress, tears away her panties and her nylon stockings. Something glints in the pale light filtering under the door. She feels a cold, flat pressure on her bare belly, stroking her skin and raising goose-bumps as it traces its way down. A warm wetness trickles between her thighs and the sweet smell of urine fills the air. She is going to die here, violated by this man she has trusted all her life.

Her knees pop as rough hands grab her ankles, stretching her legs wide, pulling the bloody wounds in her palms tight against their cruel bonds. Strong hands push her feet flat to the floor. She can hear bones cracking, the noise of steel on steel as nails are driven home. The agony comes in waves, starring her vision.

He forces himself between her legs, cracking her head against the splintered floorboards with uncaring hands. Rough fingers pull open her mouth, making her retch as they push deep down her throat. She tastes the cold metallic tang of steel, and then a flash of pain as her throat fills with warm, salty liquid. Gagging, she coughs and heaves, vomiting into the face of her attacker. He pulls back, wiping his cheeks to reveal pale grinning teeth. Little drops of her own blood rain down on her face and spatter the dirty floorboards.

One by one they take her, roughly forcing themselves into her, shattering the last of her dreams. The pain is everywhere: in the bright points of the nails; in the burning mess of her tongue; in her bruised flesh and cracked bones. She cannot escape them, she is truly helpless. And all the while, he cuts her, the man who was her friend. Small slices opening up wounds that cover her pale skin with slick red blood.

Death takes a long time to claim her, and even then she isn't at peace.

Read on for a taste of the next in the series of
the Detective Inspector McLean novels,

The Book of Souls,

To be published in summer 2013

1

The streets are empty. An unnatural quiet spreads over the north end of the city as if all the sound has been sucked out of it by the festivities on Princes Street. Only the occasional taxi breaks the calm as he follows his feet who knows where. Away from the crowds, away from the excitement, away from the joy.

He has been wandering for hours now, searching, though in his heart he knows he is too late. Has he been here before? There is a terrible familiarity about it all: the clock-tower arms reaching towards midnight and the opening of a new millennium; the cobbled streets glistening with slippery rain; the orange glow against warm sandstone painting everything with a demonic light. His feet take him downwards, through the nine circles, despair growing with each muffled footfall.

What is it that stops him on the bridge? An impossible sound, perhaps. The echo of a scream uttered years ago. Or maybe it's the sudden hush of the city holding its breath, counting down those last seconds to a new dawn. He can't share their enthusiasm, can't find it in himself to care. If he could stop time, turn it backwards, he would do things so differently. But this is just a moment, and it will be followed by another. Another after that. Onwards to infinity.

He leans on the cold stone parapet, looks down on the dark rushing water below. Something has brought him here, away from the world of celebrations and festive cheer.

A loud explosion marks the end of the old and the start of the new. Fireworks come in quick succession, rising over the tall buildings and lighting the sky. A million new stars fill the heavens, chasing away the shadows, reflecting in the black water, revealing its dread secret.

Flash, and the water sparkles with strange shapes, fading away like afterglow on the back of the eye.

Flash, and startled fish dart from the floating fingers they have been nibbling away.

Flash, and long black hair tugs glossily in the flow, like seaweed on the tide.

Flash, and the pent-up force of a week's rain pushes past the latest obstacle, moving it slowly down towards the sea, rolling it over and over as it goes.

Flash, and a ghostly white face stares up at him with pleading, dead eyes.

Flash . . .

2

'Argh! Jesus! Is that a rat?'

'Keep it down, constable.'

'But sarge, it crawled over my foot. Must've been the size of a bloody badger.'

'I don't care if it was as big as my shiny arse. Keep it quiet until we get the signal.'

A grumbling silence fell over the dark street as the small group of police officers crouched among uncollected rubbish sacks outside a lifeless tenement. The constant quiet roar of the city around them underlined the stillness, the insufficient glow of the one functional street light casting everything in twilight shadow. Early morning and you could rely on the natives of this part of town to be asleep, or stoned out of sensibility.

Two clicks on an airwave set, then a tinny voice through an earpiece. 'All clear round the back. You're good to go.'

The bodies shuffled around, hemmed in by the rubbish on either side. 'OK people. On my mark. Three . . . Two . . . One . . .'

A crash of splintering wood split the air, followed closely by a scream.

'Argh! Bastard wasn't even locked.' Then, 'Jesus Christ! There's shit all over the floor.'

Detective Inspector Anthony McLean sighed and switched on his torch. In front of him he could just make out the black-clad figure of PC Jones struggling to extricate himself from a pile of rubbish sacks inside the tenement hallway.

'Did they not teach you in Tulliallan to check that first?'

He pushed past the struggling constable and into the dank building, sniffing the air and trying not to gag. Rotting garbage mixed with stale piss and mould, the favoured aroma of the Edinburgh slum. It wasn't usually this ripe though, and that didn't bode well for why he was here.

'Bob, you take the ground floor. Jones, help him.' McLean turned to the final member of their party, a baby-faced young detective constable who'd been unlucky enough to be in the canteen at the station an hour earlier looking like he had nothing better to do. That's what you got for being keen. 'Come on then, MacBride. Let's see if there's anything here worth breaking down an unlocked door for.'

There were three storeys to the tenement, two tiny flats on each floor. None of the doors were locked, and the graffiti liberally scrawled over every available surface was at least two generations of squatter out of date. McLean stepped carefully from room to room, the beam of his torchlight playing over broken furniture, ripped-out electrical fittings and the occasional dead rat. DC MacBride never left his side, hovering like an obedient Labrador, almost too close for comfort. Or maybe it was just that he didn't want to brush up against anything. Couldn't blame him, really. The smell of the place would take weeks to wash out.

'Looks like yet another complete bloody waste of time,' McLean said as they left the last flat and stood on the landing at the top of the stairs. All the glass had long since gone from the window looking out over the gardens behind. At least that meant a cold wind could blow away the worst of the smell.

'Um. Why did we come here, sir?' The question choked in

MacBride's throat, as if he had tried to stop himself asking it at the last minute.

'That's a very good question, constable.' McLean shone his torch down into the empty stairwell, then up at the ceiling with its high-angled roofline and reinforced glass light well. That was out of reach of the vandals, and tough enough to withstand thrown missiles, but even so a couple of panes were crazed and sagging. 'An informant. A snitch. What is it they like to call them these days? A Covert Human Intelligence Source?' He made little bunny-ear inverted commas with his fingers, bouncing the light from his torch up and down as he did. 'Bugger that. Mine's a stoner called Izzy and he's a useless tosser. Spun me a load of old crap just to get me out of his hair, I've no doubt. Told me this place was used as a distribution hub. My own fault for believing him, I guess.'

More lights flickering in the darkness downstairs were Detective Sergeant Bob Laird and Police Constable Taffy Jones stumbling through the rubbish sacks in the entrance hall. If they'd found anything they'd have shouted, so it looked like the whole episode was a complete waste of time. Just like every other bloody raid. Wonderful. Dagwood was going to be so pleased.

'Come on then. It's probably best if we don't make Grumpy Bob climb all the way up here. Let's get back to the nice warm canteen.' McLean set off down the stairs, only realising he wasn't being followed when he was halfway to the next floor. He looked back and saw MacBride's torch pointed at a space above the fan-light over one of the flat doors. A small hatch gave entry to the building's loft space. It looked almost completely unremarkable, except for the shiny new padlock hasp screwed into it.

'D'you think there might be something up there, sir?' Mac-Bride asked as McLean rejoined him on the landing.

415

'Only one way to find out. Give us a leg-up.'

McLean shoved his torch in his mouth, then trod gently in the cup made by the constable's interlocked fingers. There was nothing to hold onto except a small lip below the hatch, and he had to stretch his other leg out to the wobbly banister before he could reach up with one hand and unclip the hasp. It gleamed where until recently a padlock had swung.

'Hold steady.' McLean pushed against the hatch. It resisted slightly, then swung in on well-used hinges. Beyond was a different darkness, and a sweet musk quite at odds with the rank odour wafting up from below. He swung his head around until his torch pointed in through the hatchway, seeing aluminium foil over the rafters, low wooden benches, fluorescent lighting.

'I can't hold on much longer, sir.' MacBride's voice shook with the effort of holding twelve stone of detective inspector. Well, maybe thirteen. McLean transferred as much of his weight as he dared to the banister, then swung around and dropped back down to the stone landing. The constable looked at him with a worried expression, as if expecting to be shouted at for his weakness. McLean just smiled.

'Get on your airwave set,' he said. 'I think we're going to need a SOC team here as soon as possible.'

Removing the rubbish bags had helped clear the air, but the flagstone floor they had covered was sticky and slippery with fluids best not thought about too deeply. McLean watched the stream of white-suited SOC officers as they trooped from their van, along the corridor and up the stairs, lugging battered aluminium cases of expensive equipment.

'Pity the poor bastard who's going to have to go through all that.' Grumpy Bob nodded at the pile of rubbish bags each now

416

sporting a 'Police Evidence' tag and waiting in the middle of the road for a truck to come and take them away.

'That would be me, as it happens. Who's the officer in charge here?' A white-suited figure stopped mid-corridor, pulling off a hood to reveal an unruly mop of spiky black hair. Emma Baird either was or wasn't going out with McLean, depending on which station gossip you spoke to. He'd not seen her in a couple of weeks; something about a training course up north. As she scowled in the half-light, he wished their reunion could have been in better circumstances. He looked at Grumpy Bob, who shrugged back at him an eloquent refusal to take any responsibility.

'Hi, Em.' McLean stepped out of the shadows so he could be seen. 'I thought you were still up in Aberdeen.'

'I'm beginning to wish I'd stayed there.' She looked at the growing pile of rubbish. 'You know that attic's not been disturbed in months, right?'

'Shite.' Another dead end. And it had all been looking so promising.

'Exactly, shite. Twenty-three stinking black bin bags of it, to be precise. And I'm going to have to go through every last one of them knowing there's going to be bugger all in there of any use to your investigation. Unless you decide it's unnecessary. . .' She trailed off, looked at the two of them, eyes flicking between them as if unsure who she should be addressing.

'If I could, I would, Em.' McLean tried a smile, knowing it would just look like a grimace. 'But you know Dagwood.'

'Oh crap. He's no' in charge, is he?' Emma scrunched her hood in her gloved hands, shoved it in a pocket of her overalls, turned and shouted to the assembled SOC crowd. 'Come on you lot. Quicker we get started, quicker we can hit the shower.' And she stalked off without another word.